D1452531

◆**ALTERNATIVES** is a new series under the general editorship of Eric S. Rabkin, Martin H. Greenberg, and Joseph D. Olander which has been established to serve the growing critical audience of science fiction, fantastic fiction, and speculative fiction.

The Science Fiction of

Mark Clifton

Edited by
Barry N. Malzberg
and
Martin H. Greenberg

A Memoir and Appreciation
By **Judith Merril**
Afterword
By **Barry N. Malzberg**

Southern Illinois University Press
Carbondale and Edwardsville

Feffer & Simons, Inc.
London and Amsterdam

Library of Congress Cataloging in Publication Data

Clifton, Mark.
    The science fiction of Mark Clifton.

    (Alternatives)
    Bibliography: p.
    CONTENTS: What have I done?—Star, bright.—Crazy
Joey.—What thin partitions.   [etc.]
    1. Science fiction, American.   I. Malzberg,
Barry N.   II. Greenberg, Martin Harry.   III. Title.
PS3553.L46S3   813'.54   80-20977
ISBN 0-8093-0985-8

Contents

A Memoir and Appreciation

by
Judith Merril

The phrase *meaningful relationship* was not yet current when Mark Clifton and I plunged into our long-distance mutual exploration. Done-to-death as it is now, still it is the phrase that fits.

A vividly meaning-full relationship of personal, literary, intellectual and ideological valences exploded to fill some 700 pages of typed single-spaced letters—nearly 500 of them in the first three years.

June 10, 1952
Red Bank, New Jersey

Dear Mark Clifton:

If anybody had asked, and I don't see why they should, I'd have said up till today that I'm far too professional, blasé, and sophisticated, to write a fan letter to anybody.

But nobody hereabouts seems to know anything about you, so I can't just let it off in talk. And I couldn't raise a response when I tried to ESP you yesterday, after I read Star Bright. So here I am, reduced to the simple direct system of writing to tell you how much I liked your story.

And to ask, of course, who are you anyway? It's not often that a new name hits science-fiction with two stories like this one and What Have I Done?. Even less often that a writer, new or old, happens to hit so close to my own current preoccupations with two stories in a row.

I don't know . . . maybe you're a true Bright, and worked this stuff out for yourself, all alone. Seems more reasonable (or at least more comfortable) to believe you are part of what impresses me increasingly as a really wide-spread trend of thought, coming up from all rooms at once, and beginning to achieve some sort of direction that points to the possibility of a new synthesis of social *sciences*.

Obviously, from the two stories, you have some familiarity with what the book "Gestalt Therapy" calls "experiments in self-awareness." Does yours come from the same source, or some other derivation? And the psychosomatic approach to psychology is not often as thoroughly integrated into thinking as it appears to be in yours . . . not to mention the application of the self-awareness "techniques" to ESP . . .

I send this, I might mention, with some hesitancy. Maybe you just got a couple of ideas for a couple of damn good stories, and the philosophic-scientific background that hit me so hard was pure invention; but it doesn't seem that way in the reading. Seems much more like a significantly successful effort at exposition of some very difficult subject matter. Anyhow, I risk being Intense, which as we all know, is the Great American Crime. He who laughs first gets laughed at least.

In any case, maybe I'll get to find out who you are, and whether you meant what you were writing?

Sincerely, and most
curiously,

June 15 '52

Dear Mark Clifton, hello again . . .

After I wrote that one, I decided to hold on to it; was going into NY that evening, and figured Horace Gold might have your address. I could have sent it through Ackerman of course.

HLG not only knew your address, but so much more about you too that I'd had most of my questions answered. However, he added that you are a fluent and fascinating correspondent, and that you brag incessantly about how fast you can type, so that you will write to anyone at the drop of a postage stamp. This I want to see.

Dead serious: Horace satisfied my first curiosities and piqued some new ones. He seems to think well of you; so do a goodly number of folks who've read the two stories. I was particularly startled to learn that you're a new writer, not just a writer new to stef. Still find it hard to believe. You have a smooth and expert touch in the difficult job of interweaving the emotional and informational . . . was propaganda writing part of personnel work?

Hope to hear from you . . .
                    soon? . . .

[A scribbled postscript to this letter expressed dismay and puzzlement about the problem of writing with a ballpoint pen on corrasable paper in warm weather.]

                    Redondo Beach, Calif.
                    June 19, 1952

Dear Judy Merril: At the drop of a postage stamp—

So Horace has disillusioned you. My friend! Still, perhaps it is just as well. I'm accused of enough oddities without allowing any illusions to stand. You see, hesitant pause, I too am intense. I bridle a bit at his accusation that I brag incessantly about my typing skill. I did a little personal favor for him once, and to remove any sense of obligation he might have, I tactfully pointed out that since I was a rapid typist it really was no chore. If this be bragging—but then it is the sad lot of man to be perpetually misunderstood. Heavens, how would we ever hang on to the shreds of our superiority without it? Understand a man and you have dealt him mortal insult. So Horace, as usual, does the most gracious thing after all.

I was delighted with your letter. Never, never get too blasé. Think how much pleasure you would have denied me had you not written and sent it!

Your fourth paragraph on the widespread evolvement of some new form of awareness. Again our thought parallels. I quote from a letter I wrote recently to a chap who was being pretty bitter about it all:

"I have the feeling that things are not as black as they seem. I have the feeling that we are, right now, stumbling around at the door of our next evolutionary level, that if disaster can only be staved off a little while longer, man can take such a step. I have the premonition that only the thinnest door separates us from the landing above ours, from homo superior. I think there is an astonishing number of people ready to take such a step—perhaps a critical mass which can explode into homo superior, if we can find a way of passing through that door."

Not to him, but to you who have progressed farther. I am convinced that the door is composed of editorial fear. Something is happening to our editors and publishers. The fear of getting a few objecting letters, of losing an advertising account, of being hauled up before a congressional committee, has pulled all the teeth, and the literature served up is no more than premasticated pap. I suspect this is the reason why people flock in great droves from one damn fool ism to another. It is as if our food came from wornout soil. It looks good on the surface. The volume is certainly there. But the trace minerals and vitamins are gone. It does not sustain us.

There is enough food to be found by searching in literature for a youth to get his growth. But beyond that point, when he gets into current literature, he finds carefully predigested volume, carefully packaged and wrapped in cotton wool so that no one might feel the impact—and no substance. However much he may absorb of the volume, if there is no value in it, he will start looking to other sources. I do not need to cite examples of such crazes, or why a good Amurican man will be caught up in the fallacies of Communism. He hungers for food substances which we fear to provide him. A man, hungry enough, will do desperate and foolish things. And if he still hungers, he dies.

I wonder what our nation would have been had that small but critical mass of patriots responsible for our nation been fearful of the criticism of a few stupids, or the raised eyebrows of England's social set.

I hadn't realized this until lately, for I am new to the writing game. You complimented my work, but I know I have a long way to go before I can make my written word match my skill in the spoken word. I do not react in pique when an editor tells me that a story is thin, fuzzy, or unconvincing. But when a whole series of editors write, in essence, "Gad Clifton, this is wonderful stuff. I wish I dared print it but I don't." I am filled with foreboding and concern for the future.

I am accustomed to hearing editors and publishers talk about the low mass level of intelligence, and how the writing must be slanted to that level; saying nothing because it will either be misunderstood or not understood at all. I am accustomed to hearing this, but I do not believe it. For more than twenty years I have been intensively interviewing people. Very early I learned the skill of shearing away all the froth and getting down to the real body of the brew within a few sentences.

I mention, not as horn blowing but as fundamental, that it was the custom for a number of years for psyc professors, students, and others to come into my office in pretense of applying for work, so that they might study my interviewing techniques. An amusing sidelight was that within a few sentences they not only confessed their identity, but also confessed they had not intended to reveal it—but that since this had turned into a man to man discussion and was entirely off the record they now felt free to do so. It never occurred to them that that *was* the technique—that all my interviews were man to man and off the record, and therefore each person felt he could talk freely—without fear.

I have had over 200,000 such interviews, almost all of them off the record and man to man. During all this time I looked for this stupid mass level. I never found it. With only a small percentage as exception, I found each man was open for thought, hungry for thought. True, the educational, social and emotional levels varied greatly. I have interviewed everyone from Mexican peons to bank and college presidents, but I was seldom able to find anyone who was not receptive to thought or a new idea—if it was given in his language.

The practical application? During all those years, either as a labor relations director or as a consultant, I never had a strike. Most of my companies were strong union, most of them had been hot spots, for when I had my health and energy I liked hot spots, the challenge; but I never had even ominous labor trouble because I had never been able to find that stupid mass level, and therefore could not treat the people as such.

Invariably, when I was called into a hot labor dispute, I found it existed because management persisted in giving the workmen what it thought was good for them, instead of finding out what the workmen really wanted. And in the majority of cases it would have cost management far less in dollars. For the problem was, perhaps surprisingly, not one of wages—that was merely a symbol, a ''get even'' mechanism for subtle frustrations which would sound foolish if expressed to unsympathetic ears.

This God complex of feeding the people what the publishers think is good for them in literature is a parallel.

People are far more willing to think than we give them credit; and the younger generation—we'd better start giving them something solid, something they can get their teeth into, instead of the frayed old hokum, or we're really going to have a mess on our hands.

With me it is not idle speculation, or science fiction extrapolation, or amusing sophistry—I *know* the evolvement is there, that it is springing up on all sides, the force of new life behind it. What is this terrible fear we have that our egg will crack and a chicken emerge? Why are we clamping steel bands of fear of growth around the egg to prevent the natural growth? Either the steel bands themselves will shatter and destroy us with flying shrapnel, or we will succeed again, as has happened so many times in past civilizations, in killing the chicken still in the egg.

Intense? Perhaps. But when a civilization arrives at a point where the only acceptable reaction is to titter scornfully, that civilization dies. England arrived at that point. "Look here, old boy, there's some things one doesn't say, don't y'know," —and England died. In Japan it was bushido—the one correct reaction to every given circumstance—and Japan died. And in our culture? It may be quite the thing for the flower of our culture to raise a delicate eyebrow, shrug a white shoulder, and die gracefully on the vine; but I believe the plant is still powerful and strong, and if we concern ourselves too much with the flowers and not enough with the roots, there soon won't be any flowers.

To me, it is basic tragedy that our literature of today does no more than titter scornfully. There are tremendously powerful things to be said, and there are the writers to say them, and they may not be pleasant to the delicate shell formed ear of the flowers of our culture; but as long as this door of "I wish I dared print it, but I don't" is closed—

Well, Judy, I touched on one point only of your letter—and somehow it just lengthens out and out. But you can't say Horace didn't warn you. At the drop of a postage stamp—

Drop another, will you?

Cordially,
[Mark]
Mark Clifton

"In order for a ball point pen to write, the ball within the point must rotate, thus bringing the ink from the barrel to the paper. On a warm day the surface of corrasable paper softens, becomes slippery, and does not allow enough friction to develop to turn the ball within the point," he said with profundity, and hoped no one would realize he had made it up on the spur of the moment and didn't really know what he was talking about.

"My, you seem to know everything," she said with a vast admiration.

"Of course," he answered simply, and didn't know she was laughing at him.

Mark and I met, in person, on only one occasion: the 13th World Science Fiction Convention, in Cleveland, in the summer of 1955 (where he and Frank Riley took the Hugo award for the novel, *They'd Rather Be Right*). The meeting was cordial—at times delightful—but some curious inverse chemistry sent each of us away with a sorely wounded sense of rejection by the other. The feeling was strong enough that neither of us found a way to articulate it until several years later. In fact, the correspondence lapsed entirely for a while, and when it resumed (for another five years) was both less obsessive and more intimate—rather like the letters of old, fond, but spent, lovers.

We were, of course, never lovers in the usual explicit sense. Indeed, the symbol of rejection on each side in Cleveland was our failure even to embrace upon meeting. And it may well have been that this wounding abstention was necessary: that the sort of sounding-board function we served for each other, through most of a decade of critical experience for both of us, *could* only work between people whose actual physical lives were in no way interconnected: that we were instinctively, however painfully, protecting the very meaning-fullness of the relationship.

In any case, most of my thinking and awareness, during that dramatic fourth decade of my life, was filtered, or refracted, through Mark's extraordinary perceptions, and modified by his philosophies.

Of course, I was not alone in this. Everyone who read his prolific output (in the days when other writers irritably referred to *Astounding* as the "Clifton House Organ") shared the experience to some extent. Because the important thing to understand about Clifton is just—

He meant every word of it.

When he was not writing simply out of his personal history, he was writing with excruciating honesty out of his personal beliefs and ideals. Among these, of course, were his years of study of "extrasensory" or "paranormal" phenomena—and his years of *prac-*

tice of one particular ability—a sort of hyper-empathy which he called "somming" (from *somatic*), because it required the physical presence of the other person, and consisted of *experiencing* the other's somatic awareness:

> My difficulty lay not in the reluctance to accept esper phenomena, but in the realization that all didn't have them developed to a high degree. Much of the pain of my childhood and youth lay in my belief that everybody knew these things and were simply hypocritical in not conducting themselves accordingly. I was quite grown up before I began to realize that what I thought was hypocrisy was simply blindness. It still requires conscious effort on my part to make allowances. . . .
>
> And yet, everyone is. That was what bothered me in childhood. I sommed that each person *could* esper—it was the fact they didn't, and would not, act according to their esperance which gave me my difficulties. It was like the hysterical blindness so often found in case histories of psychological trauma. Nothing wrong with the eyes, the nerves, or the brain mechanism—the patient simply refuses to see light and therefore is blind. Now if that trauma was a widespread thing, a majority-of-the-people thing, we'd have a good analogy of the esper factor. Perhaps it has its roots in the eons of savagery, when the witch-doctor saw to it that he had no competition—and the racial fear became fixed. A real fear then—the possessor of the quality would find himself eliminated. It wouldn't be the first folk trauma to persist down through "civilization."

Mark was a very private person, almost a recluse: but this was primarily for reasons of (ill) health. He began writing, in fact, after suffering a general physical breakdown which led him to retire from a long and successful career in personal and industrial relations. This also coincided, roughly, with the breakup of his marriage. He seldom referred to his physical problems in any detail (a reference once to some problem with his heart, once to a disturbance in his white cell count) his own diagnosis was that he suffered from essentially psychogenic ailments—that he had, in effect, OD'd on *people*. He shared a small house with a close friend who functioned to some extent in the capacity of nurse and made sure that he kept himself to himself sufficiently to avoid serious setbacks.

He was reticent, then, about personal affairs but even more concerned about the privacy of his statements concerning his interests and beliefs.

With rare exceptions, he exposed his experiences and convictions fully only through science fiction. There were reasons.

The first was simply deeply-ingrained wariness. Mark was the classical Amurican Success Story: poor orphan boy in the Arkansas hills to manicured executive in forty pain-packed years. Some of his stories of Christian Charity in Arkansas are bloodchilling. This one was rather mindchilling—for him:

> When I was thirteen years old I got a job teaching school in the swamp country of Arkansas, a little one room country school, sixteen miles south of Little Rock. (I might mention that I, myself, had never been to school; but I could read and write which was something of an accomplishment in that community.) I was fired for teaching that the world was round—you see this was 30 years ago. There was a sort of schoolboard made up of farmers, the justice of the peace, the preacher-moonshiner. The J. P. (know how the southern country folk love sonorous oratory?) handed down the decision in these words:
>
>> "Solomon plainly says that the earth is flat, has four corners, and is the center of the universe; that the sun and stars revolve around the earth for the glory and the benefit of man." Then with an avenging look of stern reproval, "Who are you to set yourself up as being wiser than Solomon?"
>
> Individually those men might possibly have admitted privately that there might be something to this round world business, but collectively—
>
> I have traveled over most of the world. I have been lucky in knowing some of its great people. I have mingled with scientists, philosophers, the rich, the poor, the educated, the ignorant, and the Great Majority. I have never met a group, as such, who were, in any respect, different from that swamp country schoolboard. Oh, they may admit that the world is round; but their minds are collectively just as tightly closed against other equally obvious facts—particularly when it comes to looking at man, himself.

There was little to ease that wariness in the ambience of the time in which we were writing these letters. In the We/They atmosphere of the Eisenhower-McCarthy years, Clifton's rejection of either/or politics, if it were not actually treachery, could be understood only as idiocy. The idea that "Amuricanism" and Communism could *both* be at fault, or that Labor and Management did not represent automatic polarities, was largely incomprehensible, and almost entirely unpublishable, outside of SF. And in the drab self-defined "realism" of the times, the spectacle of a presumably rational intelligent adult giving credence to the existence of modes of communication and awareness unaccounted-for by existing scientific bookkeeping often called forth something like anathema.

Even among "open-minded" science fiction people, there was a fine-but-hard line drawn between speculation and acceptance. Mark explained what had seemed to me to be a certain coyness in his letters:

> Have been overly timid, but perhaps it was because of a recent experience . . . I mentioned a bit of my ESP to Horace in a letter. He blasted back with expletives of disgust which shocked me into realization that I had broken one of the strict rules which has governed me all through adulthood: that I, never under any circumstances, reveal myself. Painful as all hell even to tell you this much.
>
> (August 4, 1952)

Horace Gold was his first SF editor. He was more cautious with John Campbell:

> You and I have gone far enough now that I don't feel the need to stick to your matrix; but others not so. John Campbell and I, for example, are trading letters back and forth with speed. Last one from him was 10 single spaced pages. But, my God, Judy, I can't see myself stepping very far out of his matrix. The man has such a long, LONG way to go before he would consider some of the things you and I say as being more than drivel. And seeing some unconsidered words could harm him greatly. I think I've already led him farther away from his matrix than he ever went before; but there's a limit. It isn't just a matter of keeping a sales avenue open (I scorn money when there's something interesting in the wind), but he *does* have a good mind—he *is* going through the self awareness exercises I used in my teens; he *may* learn to som! He's trying, but you have to remember the steel strong strands of cocoon which formal education spun around him to protect him from ever thinking again. Thinking is painful, searing and blasting, and he could easily retreat back into his cocoon,

never to emerge again. How many ever outgrow college? No, it is disasterous to show an individual a thought trend before he's ready for it. All we can do is tease a little, coax them out a little farther and a little farther until they find to their surprise that they've grown so much they can't fit back into it again.

(August 20, 1952)

And of course he *had* to keep his science fiction lines open, because he was convinced that the only audience he really cared about reaching was to be found there—Star Bright and her compeers, if you like—the "emergees." His letters are studded with references to the emergees, speculations on what new abilities they might have, and how they might use them, and the urgency of his own need to communicate with them—to tell them all he himself had learned and guessed—little as he felt it was.

That is why I started writing science fiction; because the emergees read it. It is the only place they are able to find thoughts to match their own. . . . We must not join the ranks of those who cannot bear to see something superior than they, and join in pulling it down to our own level. Who is to say that man cannot reach the stature of gods? I would not be one to deny that to the emergees simply because I could not achieve it. I wouldn't want to be *that* human. And neither do you; of that I'm confident.

(June 24, 1952)

I think perhaps we should all be comparing notes, building up this picture of the emergee pattern.

How do I know whether I am an emergee or not? We have built up no pattern of what one is. We throw the concept around too loosely . . . I don't know. The emergee *may* not be one individual at all. The complete emergee *may* be a somgroup . . .

(September 9, 1952)

I suspect that we can build that framework, that synthesis—but not from our own brilliantly warped minds. We want to build up a structure for the emergees? Then let's ask the emergees what they want! Startling, revolutionary! But anyway, ask 'em. And listen. You won't like what they say. I won't like what they say. I know it. But ask them. And listen. They'll tell us. Even if it logical, let's grit our teeth and listen anyway.

(June 24, 1952)

Two years later, in a period of comparative good health, he rallied his resources to attend his first science fiction convention, and wrote with unprecedented excitement:

Who are these fen? I'm just positive they are, or conceal among them, the emergees; but how do you get to know them? They stand for hours just looking at you, and maybe the bolder ones will catch your eye, gulp, blush, and then ask you a carefully-prepared-well-thought-out-significant-question. But it is all in a sort of daze, and you're not really getting through.

You know, Judy, and I'm completely serious, I wonder if they're not the ones really worth exploring—more than we who are on exhibition—but how do you break through? And would it destroy something for them if you did? Hell, I don't know. I saw some awfully interesting faces among the fen, but I botched it every time. . . .

I'd have given any six conversations I had with other writers to have had one real conversation with one of these lads—but no luck. And, Judy, I don't have trouble getting through to people I really want to see. But I had trouble here. It was like trying to pick up mercury with the fingers.

(September 8, 1954)

Yes, I have that feeling now, trying to bring Mark Clifton alive in a few pages of memoirs.

When I was first asked to write something for this book, I accepted with delight. That was many—many—months ago. Successive deadlines have come, and gone; the long-suffering editors have extended their patience again, and yet again. And I meanwhile have constructed marvellous montages of minutiae from the letters, erected elegant edifices of explications around them—and torn them down again.

There is much more I wanted—would still like—to say. I wanted to talk about our quarrels and criticisms of each other's work—about the sunny domesticity of his Redondo Beach existence—about how he made his living (for a while at least) by playing the horses—about the gentle comfort he offered me in times of personal trouble—about his love for his estranged family—but the more I said, the more there was that needed to be said.

So perhaps all that is *another* book.

For this collection, three things I think remain that must be said: two griefs and one satisfaction.

It is appalling to me that I still do not know just when Mark died, or how. The last letters between us were in 1961. I am not even sure who, finally, failed to reply to whom. He died in 1963. I heard of it on the science fiction grapevine some time later. (How much later? I don't know. I don't know the date.) It was a *wrong* time for him to die. A few more years, and he would have seen the beginning of the emergence of the young people he was waiting for: the people who have begun to turn the world around.

He missed the free university movement and the landing on the moon. He missed the ventures into biofeedback and acupuncture. He missed the antiwar movement and the ecology movement.

How much did he have to do with seeding them?

I think he got through to his emergees more than he knew.

The Science Fiction of Mark Clifton

What Have I Done?

From *Astounding Science Fiction*

Clifton's first published story is stunningly bleak (perhaps he masked his vision thereafter; he was never so bleak again) but in its calm, level understatement holds back until the very end—and perhaps beyond—the full implications of his vision.

John W. Campbell, Jr., who bought it, introduced it as follows: "When you've finished this bitter little piece, you might decide for yourself whether Clifton's point is valid. But you won't like it!" And the bitterness was there, a cynicism and resignation that would characterize most of his work in the field. What is so troubling is that Mark Clifton was not your stereotypical lonely writer (although his may well have been a lonely life) who shunned contact with people and spent his life behind a desk.

He had verbal contact with several *hundred thousand* people during his twenty-five-year career as a personnel specialist in industry. He knew a great deal about these people, he knew their backgrounds, and to some extent he knew their motives. And he still wrote this story.

It had to be I. It would be stupid to say that the burden should have fallen to a great statesman, a world leader, a renowned scientist. With all modesty, I think I am one of the few who could have caught the problem early enough to avert disaster. I have a peculiar skill. The whole thing hinged on that. I have learned to know human beings.

The first time I saw the fellow, I was at the drugstore counter buying cigarettes. He was standing at the magazine rack. One might have thought from the expression on his face that he had never seen magazines before. Still, quite a number of people get that rapt and vacant look when they can't make up their minds to a choice.

1

The thing which bothered me in that casual glance was that I couldn't recognize him.

There are others who can match my record in taking case histories. I happened to be the one who came in contact with this fellow. For thirty years I have been listening to, talking with, counseling people—over two hundred thousand of them. They have not been routine interviews. I have brought intelligence, sensitivity and concern to each of them.

Mine has been a driving, burning desire to know people. Not from the western scientific point of view of devising tools and rules to measure animated robots and ignoring the man beneath. Nor from the eastern metaphysical approach to painting a picture of the soul by blowing one's breath upon a fog to be blurred and dispersed by the next breath.

Mine was the aim to know the man by making use of both. And there was some success.

A competent geographer can look at a crude sketch of a map and instantly orient himself to it anywhere in the world—the bend of a river, the angle of a lake, the twist of a mountain range. And he can mystify by telling in finest detail what is to be found there.

After about fifty thousand studies where I could predict and then observe and check, with me it became the lift of a brow, the curve of a mouth, the gesture of a hand, the slope of a shoulder. One of the universities became interested, and over a long controlled period they rated me 92 percent accurate. That was fifteen years ago. I may have improved some since.

Yet standing there at the cigarette counter and glancing at the young fellow at the magazine rack, I could read nothing. Nothing at all.

If this had been an ordinary face, I would have catalogued it and forgotten it automatically. I see them by the thousands. But this face would not be catalogued nor forgotten, because there was nothing in it.

I started to write that it wasn't even a face, but of course it was. Every human being has a face—of one sort or another.

In build he was short, muscular, rather well proportioned. The hair was crew cut and blond, the eyes were blue, the skin fair. All nice and standard Teutonic—only it wasn't.

I finished paying for my cigarettes and gave him one more glance, hoping to surprise an expression which had some meaning. There was none. I left him standing there and walked out on the street and around the corner. The street, the store fronts, the traffic cop on the corner, the warm sunshine were all so familiar I didn't see them. I climbed the stairs to my office in the building over the drugstore. My employment agency waiting room was empty. I don't cater to much of a crowd because it cuts down my opportunity to talk with people and further my study.

Margie, my receptionist, was busy making out some kind of a report and merely nodded as I passed her desk to my own office. She is a good conscientious girl who can't understand why I spend so much time working with bums and drunks and other psychos who obviously won't bring fees into the sometimes too small bank account.

I sat down at my desk and said aloud to myself, "The guy is a fake! As obvious as a high school boy's drafting of a dollar bill."

I heard myself say that and wondered if I was going nuts, myself. What did I mean by fake? I shrugged. So I happened to see a bird I couldn't read, that was all.

Then it struck me. But that would be unique. I hadn't had that experience for twenty years. Imagine the delight, after all these years, of exploring an unreadable!

I rushed out of my office and back down the stairs to the street. Hallahan, the traffic cop, saw me running up the street and looked at me curiously. I signaled to him with a wave of a hand that everything was all right. He lifted his cap and scratched his head. He shook his head slowly and settled his cap back down. He blew a whistle at a woman driver and went back to directing traffic.

I ran into the drugstore. Of course the guy wasn't there. I looked all around, hoping he was hiding behind the pots and pans counter, or something. No guy.

I walked quickly back out on the street and down to the next corner. I looked up and down the side streets. No guy.

I dragged my feet reluctantly back toward the office. I called up the face again to study it. It did no good. The first mental glimpse of it told me there was nothing to find. Logic told me there was nothing to find. If there had been, I wouldn't be in such a stew. The face was empty—completely void of human feelings or character.

No, those weren't the right words. Completely void of human—being!

I walked on past the drugstore again and looked in curiously, hoping I would see him. Hallahan was facing my direction again, and he grinned crookedly at me. I expect around the neighborhood I am known as a character. I ask the queerest questions of people, from a layman's point of view. Still, applicants sometimes tell me that when they asked a cop where was an employment agent they could trust they were sent to me.

I climbed the stairs again, and walked into my waiting room. Margie looked at me curiously, but she only said, "There's an applicant. I had him wait in your office." She looked like she wanted to say more, and then shrugged. Or maybe she shivered. I knew there was something wrong with the bird, or she would have kept him in the waiting room.

I opened the door to my office, and experienced an overwhelming sense of relief, fulfillment. It was he. Still, it was logical that he should be there. I run an employment agency. People come to me to get help in finding work. If others, why not he?

My skill includes the control of my outward reactions. That fellow could have no idea of the delight I felt at the opportunity to get a full history. If I had found him on the street, the best I might have done was a stock question about what time is it, or have you got a match, or where is the city hall. Here I could question him to my heart's content.

I took his history without comment, and stuck to routine questions. It was all exactly right.

He was ex-G.I., just completed college, major in astronomy, no experience, no skills, no faintest idea of what he wanted to do, nothing to offer an employer—all perfectly normal for a young grad.

No feeling or expression either. Not so normal. Usually they're petulantly resentful that business doesn't swoon at the chance of hiring them. I resigned myself to the old one-two of attempting to steer him toward something practical.

"Astronomy?" I asked. "That means you're heavy in math. Frequently we can place a strong math skill in statistical work." I was hopeful I could get a spark of something.

It turned out he wasn't very good at math. "I haven't yet reconciled my math to—" he stopped. For the first time he showed a reaction—hesitancy. Prior to that he had been a statue from Greece—the rounded expressionless eyes, the too perfect features undisturbed by thought.

He caught his remark and finished, "I'm just not very good at math, that's all."

I sighed to myself. I'm used to that, too. They give degrees nowadays to get rid of the guys, I suppose. Sometimes I'll go for days without uncovering any usable knowledge. So in a way, that was normal.

The only abnormal part of it was he seemed to think it didn't sound right. Usually the lads don't even realize they should know something. He seemed to think he'd pulled a boner by admitting that a man can take a degree in astronomy without learning math. Well, I wouldn't be surprised to see them take their degree without knowing how many planets there are.

He began to fidget a bit. That was strange, also. I thought I knew every possible combination of muscular contractions and expansions. This fidget had all the reality of a puppet activated by an amateur. And the eyes—still completely blank.

I led him up one mental street and down the next. And of all the false-fronted stores and cardboard houses and paper lawns, I never saw the like. I get something of that once in a while from a fellow who has spent a long term in prison and comes in with a manufactured past—but never anything as phony as this one was.

Interesting aspect to it. Most guys, when they realize you've spotted them for a phony, get out as soon as they can. He didn't. It was almost as though he were—well, testing; to see if his answers would stand up.

I tried talking astronomy, of which I thought I knew a little. I found I didn't know anything, or he didn't. This bird's astronomy and mine had no point of reconciliation.

And then he had a slip of the tongue—yes he did. He was talking, and said, "The ten planets—"

He caught himself, "Oh that's right. There's only nine."

Could be ignorance, but I didn't think so. Could be he knew of the existence of a planet we hadn't yet discovered.

I smiled. I opened a desk drawer and pulled out a couple science-fiction magazines. "Ever read any of these?" I asked.

"I looked through several of them at the newsstand a while ago," he answered.

"They've enlarged my vision," I said. "Even to the point where I could believe that some other star system might hold intelligence." I lit a cigarette and waited. If I was wrong, he would merely think I was talking at random.

His blank eyes changed. They were no longer Greek statue eyes. They were no longer blue. They were black, deep bottomless black, as deep and cold as space itself.

"Where did I fail in my test?" he asked. His lips formed a smile which was not a smile—a carefully painted-on-canvas sort of smile.

Well, I'd had my answer. I'd explored something unique, all right. Sitting there before me, I had no way of determining whether he was benign or evil. No way of knowing his motive. No way of judging—

anything. When it takes a lifetime of learning how to judge even our own kind, what standards have we for judging an entity from another star system?

At that moment I would like to have been one of those space-opera heroes who, in similar circumstances, laugh casually and say, "What ho! So you're from Arcturus. Well, well. It's a small universe after all, isn't it?" And then with linked arms they head for the nearest bar, bosom pals.

I had the almost hysterical thought, but carefully suppressed, that I didn't know if this fellow would like beer or not. I will not go through the intermuscular and visceral reactions I experienced. I kept my seat and maintained a polite expression. Even with humans, I know when to walk carefully.

"I couldn't feel anything about you," I answered his question. "I couldn't feel anything but blankness."

He looked blank. His eyes were nice blue marble again. I liked them better that way.

There should be a million questions to be asked, but I must have been bothered by the feeling that I held a loaded bomb in my hands. And not knowing what might set it off, or how, or when. I could think of only the most trivial.

"How long have you been on Earth?" I asked. Sort of a when did you get back in town, Joe, kind of triviality.

"For several of your weeks," he was answering. "But this is my first time out among humans."

"Where have you been in the meantime?" I asked.

"Training." His answers were getting short and his muscles began to fidget again.

"And where do you train?" I kept boring in.

As an answer he stood up and held out his hand, all quite correctly. "I must go now," he said. "Naturally you can cancel my application for employment. Obviously we have more to learn."

I raised an eyebrow. "And I'm supposed to just pass over the whole thing? A thing like this?"

He smiled again. The contrived smile which was a symbol to indicate courtesy. "I believe your custom on this planet is to turn your problems over to your police. You might try that." I could not tell whether it was irony or logic.

At that moment I could think of nothing else to say. He walked out of my door while I stood beside my desk and watched him go.

Well, what was I supposed to do? Follow him?

I followed him.

Now I'm no private eye, but I've read my share of mystery stories. I knew enough to keep out of sight. I followed him about a dozen blocks into a quiet residential section of small homes. I was standing behind a palm tree, lighting a cigarette, when he went up the walk of one of these small houses. I saw him twiddle with the door, open it, and walk in. The door closed.

I hung around a while and then went up to the door. I punched the doorbell. A motherly gray-haired woman came to the door, drying her hands on her apron. As she opened the door she said, "I'm not buying anything today."

Just the same, her eyes looked curious as to what I might have.

I grinned my best grin for elderly ladies. "I'm not selling anything, either," I answered. I handed her my agency card. She looked at it curiously and then looked a question at me.

"I'd like to see Joseph Hoffman," I said politely.

She looked puzzled. "I'm afraid you've got the wrong address, sir," she answered.

I got prepared to stick my foot in the door, but it wasn't necessary. "He was in my office just a few minutes ago," I said. "He gave that name and this address. A job came in right after he left the office, and since I was going to be in this neighborhood anyway, I thought I'd drop by and tell him in person. It's sort of rush," I finished. It had happened many times before, but this time it sounded lame.

"Nobody lives here but me and my husband," she insisted. "He's retired."

I didn't care if he hung by his toes from trees. I wanted a young fellow.

"But I saw the young fellow come in here," I argued. "I was just coming around the corner, trying to catch him. I saw him."

She looked at me suspiciously. "I don't know what your racket is," she said through thin lips, "but I'm not buying anything. I'm not signing anything. I don't even want to talk to you." She was stubborn about it.

I apologized and mumbled something about maybe making a mistake.

"I should say you have," she rapped out tartly and shut the door in righteous indignation. Sincere, too. I could tell.

An employment agent who gets the reputation of being a right guy makes all kinds of friends. That poor old lady must have thought a plague of locusts had swept in on her for the next few days.

First the telephone repair man had to investigate an alleged complaint. Then a gas service man had to check the plumbing. An electrician complained there was a power short in the block and he had to trace their house wiring. We kept our fingers crossed hoping the old geezer had never been a construction man. There was a mistake in the last census, and a guy asked her a million questions.

That house was gone over rafter by rafter and sill by sill, attic and basement. It was precisely as she said. She and her husband lived there; nobody else.

In frustration, I waited three months. I wore out the sidewalks haunting the neighborhood. Nothing.

Then one day my office door opened and Margie ushered a young man in. Behind his back she was radiating heart throbs and fluttering her eyes.

He was the traditionally tall, dark and handsome young fellow, with a ready grin and sparkling dark eyes. His personality hit me like a sledge hammer. A guy like that never needs to go to an employment agency. Any employer will hire him at the drop of a hat, and wonder later why he did it.

His name was Einar Johnson. Extraction, Norwegian. The dark Norse strain, I judged. I took a chance on him thinking he had walked into a booby hatch.

"The last time I talked with you," I said, "your name was Joseph Hoffman. You were Teutonic then. Not Norse."

The sparkle went out of his eyes. His face showed exasperation and there was plenty of it. It looked real, too, not painted on.

"All right. Where did I flunk this time?" he asked impatiently.

"It would take me too long to tell you," I answered. "Suppose you start talking." Strangely, I was at ease. I knew that underneath he was the same incomprehensible entity, but his surface was so good that I was lulled.

He looked at me levelly for a long moment. Then he said, "I didn't think there was a chance in a million of being recognized. I'll admit that other character we created was crude. We've learned considerable since then, and we've concentrated everything on this personality I'm wearing."

He paused and flashed his teeth at me. I felt like hiring him myself. "I've been all over Southern California in this one," he said. "I've had a short job as a salesman. I've been to dances and parties. I've got drunk and sober again. Nobody, I say nobody, has shown even the slightest suspicion."

"Not very observing, were they?" I taunted.

"But you are," he answered. "That's why I came back here for the final test. I'd like to know where I failed." He was firm.

"We get quite a few phonies," I answered. "The guy drawing unemployment and stalling until it is run out. The geezik whose wife drives him out and threatens to quit her job if he doesn't go to work. The plainclothes detail smelling around to see if maybe we aren't a cover for a bookie joint or something. Dozens of phonies."

He looked curious. I said in disgust, "We know in the first two minutes they're phony. You were phony also, but not of any class I've seen before. And," I finished dryly, "I've been waiting for you."

"Why was I phony?" he persisted.

"Too much personality force," I answered. "Human beings just don't have that much force. I felt like I'd been knocked flat on my . . . well . . . back."

He sighed. "I've been afraid you would recognize me one way or another. I communicated with home. I was advised that if you spotted me, I was to instruct you to assist us."

I lifted a brow. I wasn't sure just how much authority they had to instruct me to do anything.

"I was to instruct you to take over the supervision of our final training, so that no one could ever spot us. If we are going to carry out our original plan that is necessary. If not, then we will have to use the alternate." He was almost didactic in his manner, but his charm of personality still radiated like an infrared lamp.

"You're going to have to tell me a great deal more than that," I said.

He glanced at my closed door.

"We won't be interrupted," I said. "A personnel history is private."

"I come from one of the planets of Arcturus," he said.

I must have allowed a smile of amusement to show on my face, for he asked, "You find that amusing?"

"No," I answered soberly, and my pulses leaped because the question confirmed my conclusion that he could not read my thoughts. Apparently we were as alien to him as he to us. "I was amused," I explained, "because the first time I saw you I said to myself that as far as recognizing you, you might have come from Arcturus. Now it turns out that accidentally I was correct. I'm better than I thought."

He gave a fleeting polite smile in acknowledgment. "My home planet," he went on, "is similar to yours. Except that we have grown overpopulated."

I felt a twinge of fear.

"We have made a study of this planet and have decided to colonize it." It was a flat statement, without any doubt behind it.

I flashed him a look of incredulity. "And you expect me to help you with that?"

He gave me a worldly wise look—almost an ancient look. "Why not?" he asked.

"There is the matter of loyalty to my own kind, for one thing," I said. "Not too many generations away and we'll be overpopulated also. There would hardly be room for both your people and ours on Earth."

"Oh that's all right," he answered easily. "There'll be plenty of room for us for quite some time. We multiply slowly."

"We don't," I said shortly. I felt this conversation should be taking place between him and some great statesman—not me.

"You don't seem to understand," he said patiently. "Your race won't be here. We have found no reason why your race should be preserved. You will die away as we absorb."

"Now just a moment," I interrupted. "I don't want our race to die off." The way he looked at me I felt like a spoiled brat who didn't want to go beddie time.

"Why not?" he asked.

I was stumped. That's a good question when it is put logically. Just try to think of a logical reason why the human race should survive. I gave him at least something.

"Mankind," I said, "has had a hard struggle. We've paid a tremendous price in pain and death for our growth. Not to have a future to look forward to, would be like paying for something and never getting the use of it."

It was the best I could think of, honest. To base argument on humanity and right and justice and mercy would leave me wide open. Because it is obvious that man doesn't practice any of these. There is no assurance he ever will.

But he was ready for me, even with that one. "But if we are never suspected, and if we absorb and replace gradually, who is to know there is no future for humans?"

And as abruptly as the last time, he stood up suddenly. "Of course," he said coldly, "we could use our alternative plan: Destroy the human race without further negotiation. It is not our way to cause needless pain to any life form. But we can.

"If you do not assist us, then it is obvious that we will eventually be discovered. You are aware of the difficulty of even blending from one country on Earth to another. How much more difficult it is where there is no point of contact at all. And if we are discovered, destruction would be the only step left."

He smiled and all the force of his charm hit me again. "I know you will want to think it over for a time. I'll return."

He walked to the door, then smiled back at me. "And don't bother to trouble that poor little woman in that house again. Her doorway is only one of many entrances we have opened. She doesn't see us at all, and merely wonders why her latch doesn't work sometimes. And we can open another, anywhere, anytime. Like this—"

He was gone.

I walked over and opened the door. Margie was all prettied up and looking expectant and radiant. When she didn't see him come out she got up and peeked into my office. "But where did he go?" she asked with wide eyes.

"Get hold of yourself, girl," I answered. "You're so dazed you didn't even see him walk right by you."

"There's something fishy going on here," she said.

"Well, I had a problem. A first rate, genuine, dyed in the wool dilemma.

What was I to do? I could have gone to the local authorities and got locked up for being a psycho. I could have gone to the college professors and got locked up for being a psycho. I could have gone to maybe the FBI and got locked up for being a psycho. That line of thinking began to get monotonous.

I did the one thing which I thought might bring help. I wrote up the happenings and sent it to my favorite science-fiction magazine. I asked for help and sage counsel from the one place I felt awareness and comprehension might be reached.

The manuscript bounced back so fast it might have had rubber bands attached to it, stretched from California to New York. I looked the little rejection slip all over, front and back, and I did not find upon it those sage words of counsel I needed. There wasn't even a printed invitation to try again some time.

And for the first time in my life I knew what it was to be alone— genuinely and irrevocably alone.

Still, I could not blame the editor. I could see him cast the manuscript from him in disgust, saying, "Bah! So another evil race comes to conquer Earth. If I gave the fans one more of those, I'd be run out of my office." And like the deacon who saw the naughty words written on the fence, saying, "And misspelled, too."

The fable of the boy who cried "Wolf! Wolf!" once too often came home to me now. I was alone with my problem. The dilemma was my own. On one hand was immediate extermination. I did not doubt it. A race which can open doors from one star system to another, without even visible means of mechanism, would also know how to—disinfect.

On the other hand was extinction, gradual, but equally certain, and none the less effective in that it would not be perceived. If I refused to assist, then acting as one lone judge of all the race, I condemned it. If I did assist, I would be arch traitor, with an equal final result.

For days I sweltered in my miasma of indecision. Like many a man before me, uncertain of what to do, I temporized. I decided to play for time. To play the role of traitor in the hopes I might learn a way of defeating them.

Once I had made up my mind, my thoughts raced wildly through the possibilities. If I were to be their instructor on how to walk unsuspected among men, then I would have them wholly in my grasp. If I could build traits into them, common ordinary traits which they could see in men all about them, yet which would make men turn and destroy them, then I would have my solution.

And I knew human beings. Perhaps it was right, after all, that it became my problem. Mine alone.

I shuddered now to think what might have happened had this being fallen into less skilled hands and told his story. Perhaps by now there would be no man left upon Earth.

Yes, the old and worn-out plot of the one little unknown guy who saved Earth from outer evil might yet run its course in reality.

I was ready for the Arcturan when he returned. And he did return.

Einar Johnson and I walked out of my office after I had sent a tearful Margie on a long vacation with fancy pay. Einar had plenty of money, and was liberal with it. When a fellow can open some sort of fourth-dimensional door into a bank vault and help himself, money is no problem.

I had visions of the poor bank clerks trying to explain things to the examiners, but that wasn't my worry right now.

We walked out of the office and I snapped the lock shut behind me. Always conscious of the cares of people looking for work, I hung a sign on the door saying I was ill and didn't know when I would be back.

We walked down the stairs and into the parking lot. We got into my car, my own car, please note, and I found myself sitting in a sheltered patio in Beverly Hills. Just like that. No awful wrenching and turning my insides out. No worrisome nausea and emptiness of space. Nothing to dramatize it at all. Car—patio, like that.

I would like to be able to describe the Arcturans as having long snaky appendages and evil slobbering maws, and stuff like that. But I can't describe the Arcturans, because I didn't see any.

I saw a gathering of people, rougly about thirty of them, wandering around the patio, swimming in the pool, going in and out of the side doors of the house. It was a perfect spot. No one bothers the big Beverly Hills home without invitation.

The natives wouldn't be caught dead looking toward a star's house. The tourists see the winding drive, the trees and grass, and perhaps a glimpse of a gabled roof. If they can get any thrill out of that then bless their little spending money hearts, they're welcome to it.

Yet if it should become known that a crowd of strange acting people are wandering around in the grounds, no one would think a thing about it. They don't come any more zany than the Hollywood crowd.

Only these were. These people could have made a fortune as life-size puppets. I could see now why it was judged that the lifeless Teutonic I had first interviewed was thought adequate to mingle with human beings. By comparison with these, he was a snappy song and dance man.

But that is all I saw. Vacant bodies wandering around, going through human motions, without human emotions. The job looked bigger than I had thought. And yet, if this was their idea of how to win friends and influence people, I might be successful after all.

There are dozens of questions the curious might want answered—such as how did they get hold of the house and how did they get their human bodies and where did they learn to speak English, and stuff. I wasn't too curious. I had important things to think about. I supposed they were able to do it, because here it was.

I'll cut the following weeks short. I cannot conceive of what life and civilization on their planet might be like. Yardsticks of scientific psychology are used to measure a man, and yet they give no indication at all of the inner spirit of him, likewise, the descriptive measurements of their civilization are empty and meaningless. Knowing about a man, and knowing a man are two entirely different things.

For example, all those thalamic urges and urgencies which we call emotion were completely unknown to them, except as they saw them in antics on TV. The ideals of man were also unknown—truth, honor, justice, perfection—all unknown. They had not even a division of sexes, and the emotion we call love was beyond their understanding. The TV stories they saw must have been like watching a parade of ants.

What purpose can be gained by describing such a civilization to man? Man cannot conceive accomplishment without first having the dream. Yet it was obvious that they accomplished, for they were here.

When I finally realized there was no point of contact between man and these, I knew relief and joy once more. My job was easy. I knew how to destroy them. And I suspected they could not avoid my trap.

They could not avoid my trap because they had human bodies. Perhaps they conceived them out of thin air, but the veins bled, the flesh felt pain and heat and pressure, the glands secreted.

Ah yes, the glands secreted. They would learn what emotion could be. And I was a master at wielding emotion. The dream of man has been to strive toward the great and immortal ideals. His literature is filled with admonishments to that end. In comparison with the volume of work which tells us what we should be, there is very little which reveals us as we are.

As part of my training course, I chose the world's great literature, and painting, and sculpture, and music—those mediums which best portray man lifting to the stars. I gave them first of all, the dream.

And with the dream, and with the pressure of the glands as kicker, they began to know emotion. I had respect for the superb acting of Einar when I realized that he, also, had still known no emotion.

They moved from the puppet to the newborn babe—a newborn babe in training, with an adult body, and its matured glandular equation.

I saw emotions, all right. Emotions without restraint, emotions unfettered by taboos, emotions uncontrolled by ideals. Sometimes I became frightened and all my skill in manipulating emotions was needed. At other times they became perhaps a little too Hollywood, even for Hollywood. I trained them into more ideal patterns.

I will say this for the Arcturans. They learned—fast. The crowd of puppets to the newborn babes, to the boisterous boys and girls to the moody and unpredictable youths, to the matured and balanced men and women. I watched the metamorphosis take place over the period of weeks.

I did more.

All that human beings had ever hoped to be, the brilliant, the idealistic, the great in heart, I made of these. My little 145 I.Q. became a moron's level. The dreams of the greatness of man which I had known became the vaguest wisps of fog before the reality which these achieved.

My plan was working.

Full formed, they were almost like gods. And training these things into them, I trained their own traits out. One point I found we had in common. They were activated by logic, logic carried to heights of which I had never dreamed. Yet my poor and halting logic found point of contact.

They realized at last that if they let their own life force and motivation remain active they would carry the aura of strangeness to defeat their purpose. I worried, when they accepted this. I felt perhaps they were laying a trap for me, as I did for them. Then I realized that I had not taught them deceit.

And it was logical, to them, that they follow my training completely. Reversing the position, placing myself upon their planet, trying to become like them, I must of necessity follow my instructor without question. What else could they do?

At first they saw no strangeness that I should assist them to destroy my race. In their logic the Arcturan was most fit to survive, therefore he should survive. The human was less fit, therefore he should perish.

I taught them the emotion of compassion. And when they began to mature their human thought and emotion, and their intellect was blended and shaded by such emotion, at last they understood my dilemma.

There was irony in that. From my own kind I could expect no understanding. From the invaders I received sympathy and compassion. They understand at last my traitorous action to buy a few more years for Man.

Yet their Arcturan logic still prevailed. They wept with me, but there could be no change of plan. The plan was fixed, they were merely instruments by which it was to be carried out.

Yet, through their compassion, I did get the plan modified.

This was the conversation which revealed that modification. Einar Johnson, who as the most fully developed had been my constant companion, said to me one day, "To all intents and purposes we have become human beings." He looked at me and smiled with fondness, "You have said it is so, and it must be so. For we begin to realize what a great and glorious thing a human is."

The light of nobility shone from him like an aura as he told me this, "Without human bodies, and without the emotion-intelligence equation which you call soul, our home planet cannot begin to grasp the growth we have achieved. We know now that we will never return to our own form, for by doing that we would lose what we have gained.

"Our people are logical, and they must of necessity accept our recommendation, as long as it does not abandon the plan entirely. We have reported what we have learned, and it is conceived that both our races can inhabit the Universe side by side.

"There will be no more migration from our planet to yours. We will remain, and we will multiply, and we will live in honor, such as you have taught us, among you. In time perhaps we may achieve the greatness which all humans now have.

"And we will assist the human kind to find their destiny among the stars as we have done."

I bowed my head and wept. For I knew that I had won.

Four months had gone. I returned to my own neighborhood. On the corner Hallahan left the traffic to shift for itself while he came over to me with the question, "Where have you been?"

"I've been sick," I said.

"You look it," he said frankly. "Take care of yourself, man. Hey—Lookit that fool messing up traffic." He was gone, blowing his whistle in a temper.

I climbed the stairs. They still needed repainting as much as ever. From time to time I had been able to mail money to Margie, and she had kept the rent and telephone paid. The sign was still on my door. My key opened the lock.

The waiting room had that musty, they've-gone-away look about it. The janitor had kept the windows tightly closed and there was no freshness in the air. I half hoped to see Margie stting at her desk, but I knew there was no purpose to it. When a girl is being paid for her time and has nothing to do, the beach is a nice place to spend it.

There was dust on my chair, and I sank down into it without bothering about the seat of my pants. I buried my head in my arms and I looked into the human soul.

Now the whole thing hinged on that skill. I know human beings. I know them as well as anyone in the world, and far better than most.

I looked into the past and I saw a review of the great and fine and noble and divine torn and burned and crucified by man.

Yet my only hope of saving my race was to build these qualities, the fine, the noble, the splendid, into these thirty beings. To create the illusion that all men were likewise great. No less power could have gained the boom of equality for man with them.

I look into the future. I see them, one by one, destroyed. I gave them no defense. They are totally unprepared to meet man as he genuinely is—and they are incapable of understanding.

For these things which man purports to admire the most—the noble, the brilliant, the splendid—these are the very things he cannot tolerate when he finds them.

Defenseless, because they cannot comprehend, these thirty will go down beneath the ravening fury of rending and destroying man always displays whenever he meets his ideal face to face.

I bury my head in my hands.

What have I done?

5/52

Star, Bright

From *Galaxy Science Fiction*

"Star, Bright" was Mark Clifton's first appearance in Horace Gold's *Galaxy;* he was to appear only twice more ("We're Civilized" 8/53 and "A Woman's Place" 2/55) and his private correspondence indicated that Gold—not uncharacteristically—editorially savaged the story, which appeared in truncated or severely altered form. Moving (although not unreminiscent of Kuttner/Moore's "Mimsy Were the Borogroves" published in *Astounding* seven years earlier), it obviously possessed some personal significance.

Friday, June 11

At three years of age, a little girl shouldn't have enough functioning intelligence to cut out and paste together a Moebius Strip.

Or, if she did it by accident, she surely shouldn't have enough reasoning ability to pick up one of her crayons and carefully trace the continuous line to prove it has only one surface.

And if by some strange coincidence she did, and it was still just an accident, how can I account for this generally active daughter of mine—and I do mean *active*—sitting for a solid half hour with her chin cupped in her hand, staring off into space, thinking with such concentration that it was almost painful to watch?

I was in my reading chair, going over some work. Star was sitting on the floor, in the circle of my light, with her bluntnosed scissors and her scraps of paper.

Her long silence made me glance down at her as she was taping the two ends of the paper together. At that point I thought it was an accident that she had given a half twist to the paper strip before joining the circle. I smiled to myself as she picked it up in her chubby fingers.

"A little child forms the enigma of the ages," I mused.

But instead of throwing the strip aside, or tearing it apart as any other child would do, she carefully turned it over and around—studying it from all sides.

Then she picked up one of her crayons and began tracing the line. She did it as though she were substantiating a conclusion already reached!

It was a bitter confirmation for me. I had been refusing to face it for a long time, but I could ignore it no longer.

Star was a High I.Q.

For half an hour I watched her while she sat on the floor, one knee bent under her, her chin in her hand, unmoving. Her eyes were wide with wonderment, looking into the potentialities of the phenomenon she had found.

It had been a tough struggle, taking care of her since my wife's death. Now this added problem. If only she could have been normally dull, like other children!

I made up my mind while I watched her. If a child is afflicted, then let's face it, she's afflicted. A parent must teach her to compensate. At least she could be prepared for the bitterness I'd known. She could learn early to take it in stride.

I could use the measurements available, get the degree of intelligence, and in that way grasp the extent of my problem. A twenty-point jump in I.Q. creates an entirely different set of problems. The 140 child lives in a world nothing at all like that of the 100 child, and a world which the 120 child can but vaguely sense. The problems which vex and challenge the 160 pass over the 140 as a bird flies over a field mouse. I must not make the mistake of posing the problems of one if she is the other. I must know. In the meantime, I must treat it casually.

"That's called the Moebius Strip, Star," I interrupted her thoughts.

She came out of her reveries with a start. I didn't like the quick way her eyes sought mine—almost furtively, as though she had been caught doing something bad.

"Somebody already make it?" she disappointedly asked.

She knew what she had discovered! Something inside me spilled over with grief, and something else caught at me with dread.

I kept my voice casual. "A man by the name of Moebius. A long time ago. I'll tell you about him sometime when you're older."

"Now. While I'm little," she commanded, with a frown. "And don't tell. Read me."

What did she mean by that? Oh, she must be simply paraphrasing me at those times in the past when I've wanted the facts and not garbled generalizations. It could only be that!

"Okay, young lady." I lifted an eyebrow and glared at her in mock ferociousness, which usually sent her into gales of laughter. "I'll slow you down!"

She remained completely sober.

I turned to the subject in a physics book. It's not in simple language, by any means, and I read it as rapidly as I could speak. My thought was to make her admit she didn't understand it, so I could translate it into basic language.

Her reaction?

"You read too slow, Daddy," she complained. She was childishly irritable about it. "You say a word. Then I think a long time. Then you say another word."

I knew what she meant. I remember, when I was a child, my thoughts used to dart in and out among the slowly droning words of any adult. Whole patterns of universes would appear and disappear in those brief moments.

"So?" I asked.

"So," she mocked me impishly. "You teach me to read. Then I can think quick as I want."

"Quickly," I corrected in a weak voice. "The word is 'quickly,' an adverb."

She looked at me impatiently, as if she saw through this allegedly adult device to show up a youngster's ignorance. I felt like the dope!

September 1

A great deal has happened the past few months. I have tried a number of times to bring the conversation around to discuss Star's affliction with her. But she is amazingly adroit at heading me off, as though she already knows what I am trying to say and isn't concerned. Perhaps, in spite of her brilliance, she's too young to realize the hostility of the world toward intelligence.

Some of the visiting neighbors have been amused to see her sit on the floor with an encyclopedia as big as she is, rapidly turning the pages. Only Star and I know she is reading the pages as rapidly as she can turn them. I've brushed away the neighbors' comments with: "She likes to look at the pictures."

They talk to her in baby talk—and she answers in baby talk! How does she know enough to do that?

I have spent the months making an exhaustive record of her I.Q. measurements, aptitude speeds, reaction, tables, all the recommended paraphernalia for measuring something we know nothing about.

The tables are screwy, or Star is beyond all measurement.

All right, Pete Holmes, how are you going to pose those problems and combat them for her, when you have no conception of what they might be? But I must have a conception. I've got to be able to comprehend at least a little of what she may face. I simply couldn't stand by and do nothing.

Easy, though. Nobody knows better than you the futility of trying to compete out of your class. How many students, workers, and employers have tried to compete with you? You've watched them and pitied them, comparing them to a donkey trying to run the Kentucky Derby.

How does it feel to be in the place of the donkey, for a change? You've always blamed them for not realizing they shouldn't try to compete.

But this is my own daughter! I *must* understand.

October 1

Star is now four years old, and according to State Law her mind has now developed enough so that she may attend nursery school. Again I tried to prepare her for what she might face. She listened through about two sentences and changed the subject. I can't tell about Star. Does she already know the answers? Or does she not even realize there is a problem?

I was in a sweat of worry when I took her to her first day at school yesterday morning. Last night I was sitting in my chair, reading. After she had put her dolls away, she went to the bookshelves and brought down a book of fairy tales.

That is another peculiarity of hers. She has an unmeasurably quick perception, yet she has all the normal reactions of a little girl. She likes her dolls, fairy stories, playing grownup. No, she's not a monster.

She brought the book of fairy tales over to me.

"Daddy, read me a story," she asked quite seriously.

I looked at her in amazement. "Since when? Go read your own story."

She lifted an eyebrow in imitation of my own characteristic gesture.

"Children of my age do not read," she instructed pedantically. "I can't learn to read until I am in the first grade. It is very hard to do and I am much too little."

She had found the answer to her affliction—conformity! She had already learned to conceal her intelligence. So many of us break our hearts before we learn that.

But you don't have to conceal it from me, Star! Not from me!

Oh, well, I could go along with the gag, if that was what she wanted.

"Did you like nursery school?" I asked the standard question.

"Oh, yes," she exclaimed enthusiastically. "It was fun."

"And what did you learn today, little girl?"

She played it straight back to me. "Not much. I tried to cut out paper dolls, but the scissors kept slipping." Was there an elfin deviltry back of her sober expression?

"Now, look," I cautioned, "don't overdo it. That's as bad as being too quick. The idea is that everybody has to be just about standard average. That's the only thing we will tolerate. It is expected that a little girl of four should know how to cut out paper dolls properly."

"Oh?" she questioned, and looked thoughtful. "I guess that's the hard part, isn't it, Daddy—to know how much you ought to know?"

"Yes, that's the hard part," I agreed fervently.

"But it's all right," she reassured me. "One of the Stupids showed me how to cut them out, so now that little girl likes me. She just took charge of me then and told the other kids they should like me too. So of course they did because she's leader. I think I did right, after all."

"Oh, no!" I breathed to myself. She knew how to manipulate other people already. Then my thought whirled around another concept. It was the first time she had verbally classified normal people as "Stupids," but it had slipped out so easily that I knew she'd been thinking to herself for a long time. Then my whirling thoughts hit a third implication.

"Yes, maybe it was the right thing," I conceded. "Where the little girl was concerned, that is. But don't forget you were being observed by a grownup teacher in the room. And she's smarter."

"You mean she's older, Daddy," Star corrected me.

"Smarter, too, maybe. You can't tell."

"I can," she sighed. "She's just older."

I think it was growing fear which made me defensive.

"That's good," I said emphatically. "That's very good. You can

learn a lot from her then. It takes an awful lot of study to learn how
to be stupid.''

My own troublesome business life came to mind and I thought to
myself, ''I sometimes think I'll never learn it.''

I swear I didn't say it aloud. But Star patted me consolingly and
answered as thought I'd spoken.

''That's because you're only fairly bright, Daddy. You're a
Tween, and that's harder than being really bright.''

''A Tween? What's a Tween?'' I was bumbling to hide my confusion.

''That's what I mean, Daddy,'' she answered in exasperation.
''You don't grasp quickly. An In Between, of course. The other
people are Stupids, I'm a Bright, and you're a Tween. I made those
names up when I was little.''

Good God! Besides being unmeasurably bright, she's a telepath!

All right, Pete, there you are. On reasoning processes you might
stand a chance—but not telepathy!

''Star,'' I said on impulse, ''can you read people's minds?''

''Of course, Daddy,'' she answered, as if I'd asked a foolishly
obvious question.

''Can you teach me?''

She looked at me impishly. ''You're already learning it a little. But
you's so slow! You see, you didn't even know you were learning.''

Her voice took on a wistful note, a tone of loneliness.

''I wish—'' she said, and paused.

''What do you wish?''

''You see what I mean, Daddy? You try, but you're slow.''

All the same, I knew. I knew she was already longing for a companion whose mind could match her own.

A father is prepared to lose his daughter eventually, Star, but not
so soon.

Not so soon . . .

June again

Some new people have moved in next door. Star says their name
is Howell. Bill and Ruth Howell. They have a son, Robert, who
looks maybe a year older than Star, who will soon be five.

Star seems to have taken up with Robert right away. He is a
well-mannered boy and good company for Star.

I'm worried, though. Star had something to do with their moving
in next door. I'm convinced of that. I'm also convinced, even from

the little I've seen of him, that Robert is a Bright and a telepath.

Could it be that, failing to find quick accord with my mind, Star has reached out and out until she made contact with a telepath companion?

No, that's too fantastic. Even if it were so, how could she shape circumstances so she could bring Robert to live next door to her? The Howells came from another city. It just happened that the people who lived next door moved out and the house was put up for sale.

Just happened? How frequently do we find such abnormal Brights? What are the chances of one *just happening* to move in next door to another?

I know he is a telepath because, as I write this, I sense him reading it.

I even catch his thought: "Oh, pardon me, Mr. Holmes. I didn't intend to peek. Really I didn't."

Did I imagine that? Or is Star building a skill in my mind?

"It isn't nice to look into another person's mind unless you're asked, Robert," I thought back, rather severely. It was purely an experiment.

"I know it, Mr. Holmes. I apologize." He is in his bed in his house, across the driveway.

"No, Daddy, he really didn't mean to." And Star is in her bed in this house.

It is impossible to write how I feel. There comes a time when words are empty husks. But mixed with my expectant dread is a threat of gratitude for having been taught to be even stumblingly telepathic.

Saturday, August 11

I've thought of a gag. I haven't seen Jim Pietre in a month of Sundays, not since he was awarded that research fellowship with the museum. It will be good to pull him out of his hole, and this little piece of advertising junk Star dropped should be just the thing.

Strange about the gadget. The Awful Secret Talisman of the Mystic Junior G-Men, no doubt. Still, it doesn't have anything about crackles and pops printed on it. Merely an odd-looking coin, not even true round, bronze by the look of it. Crude. They must stamp them out by the million without ever changing a die.

But it is just the thing to send to Jim to get a rise out of him. He could always appreciate a good practical joke. Wonder how he'd feel to know he was only a Tween.

Monday, August 13

Sitting here at my study desk, I've been staring into space for an hour. I don't know what to think.

It was about noon today when Jim Pietre called the office on the phone.

"Now, look, Pete," he started out, "what kind of gag are you pulling?"

I chortled to myself and pulled the dead pan on him.

"What do you mean, boy?" I asked back into the phone. "Gag? What kind of gag? What are you talking about?"

"A coin. A coin." He was impatient. "You remember you sent me a coin in the mail?"

"Oh, yeah, that." I pretended to remember. "Look, you're an important research analyst on metals—too damned important to keep in touch with your old friends—so I thought I'd make a bid for your attention thataway."

"All right, give," he said in a low voice. "Where did you get it?" He was serious.

"Come off it, Jim. Are you practicing to be a stuffed shirt? I admit it's a rib. Something Star dropped the other day. A manufacturer's idea of kid advertising, no doubt."

"I'm in dead earnest, Peter," he answered. "It's no advertising gadget."

"It means something?"

In college Jim could take a practical joke and make six out of it.

"I don't know what it means. Where did Star get it?" He was being pretty crisp about it.

"Oh, I don't know," I said. I was getting a little fed up; the joke wasn't going according to plan. "Never asked her. You know how kids clutter up the place with their things. No father even tries to keep track of all the junk that can be bought with three boxtops and a dime."

"This was not bought with three boxtops and a dime," he spaced his words evenly. "This was not bought anywhere, for any price. In fact, if you want to be logical about it, this coin doesn't exist at all."

I laughed out loud. This was more like the old Jim.

"Okay, so you've turned the gag back on me. Let's call it quits. How about coming over to supper some night soon?"

"I'm coming over, my friend." He remained grim as he said it. "And I'm coming over tonight. As soon as you will be home. It's no gag I'm pulling. Can you get that through your stubborn head? You say you got it from Star, and of course I believe you. But it's no toy. It's the real thing." Then, as if in profound puzzlement, "Only it isn't."

A feeling of dread was settling upon me. Once you cried "Uncle" to Jim, he always let up.

"Suppose you tell me what you mean," I answered soberly.

"That's more like it, Pete. Here's what we know about the coin so far. It is apparently pre-Egyptian. It's hand-cast. It's made out of one of the lost bronzes. We fix it at around four thousand years old."

"That ought to be easy to solve," I argued. "Probably some coin collector is screaming all over the place for it. No doubt lost it and Star found it. Must be lots of old coins like that in museums and in private collections."

I was rationalizing more for my own benefit than for Jim. He would know all those things without my mentioning them. He waited until I had finished.

"Step two," he went on. "We've got one of the top coin men in the world here at the museum. As soon as I saw what the metal was, I took it to him. Now hold onto your chair, Pete. He says there is no coin like it in the world, either museum or private collection."

"You museum boys get beside yourselves at times. Come down to earth. Sometime, somewhere, some collector picked it up in some exotic place and kept it quiet. I don't have to tell you how some collectors are—sitting in a dark room, gloating over some worthless bauble, not telling a soul about it—"

"All right, wise guy," he interrupted. "Step three. That coin is at least four thousand years old *and it's also brand-new!* Let's hear you explain that away."

"New?" I asked weakly. "I don't get it."

"Old coins show wear. The edges get rounded with handling. The surface oxidizes. The molecular structure changes, crystalizes. This coin shows no wear, no oxidation, no molecular change. This coin might have been struck yesterday. *Where did Star get it?*"

"Hold it a minute," I pleaded.

I began to think back. Saturday morning. Star and Robert had been playing a game. Come to think of it, that was a peculiar game. Mighty peculiar.

Star would run into the house and stand in front of the encyclopedia shelf. I could hear Robert counting loudly at the base tree outside in the backyard. She would stare at the encyclopedia for a moment.

Once I heard her mumble: "That's a good place."

Or maybe she merely thought it and I caught the thought. I'm doing that quite a bit of late.

Then she would run outside again. A moment later, Robert would run in and stand in front of the same shelf. Then he also would run outside again. There would be silence for several minutes. The silence would rupture with a burst of laughing and shouting. Soon, Star would come in again.

"How does he find me?" I heard her think once. "I can't reason it, and I can't ESP it out of him."

It was during one of their silences when Ruth called over to me.

"Hey, Pete! Do you know where the kids are! Time for their milk and cookies."

The Howells are awfully good to Star, bless 'em. I got up and went over to the window.

"I don't know, Ruth," I called back. "They were in and out only a few minutes ago."

"Well, I'm not worried," she said. She came through the kitchen door and stood on the back steps. "They know better than to cross the street by themselves. They're too little for that. So I guess they're over at Marily's. When they come back, tell 'em to come and get it."

"Okay, Ruth," I answered.

She opened the screen door again and went back into her kitchen. I left the window and returned to my work.

A little later, both the kids came running into the house. I managed to capture them long enough to tell them about the cookies and milk.

"Beat you there!" Robert shouted to Star.

There was a scuffle and they ran out the front door. I noticed then that Star had dropped the coin and I picked it up and sent it to Jim Pietre.

"Hello, Jim," I said into the phone. "Are you still there?"

"Yep, still waiting for an answer," he said.

"Jim, I think you'd better come over to the house right away. I'll leave my office now and meet you there. Can you get away?"

"Can I get away?" he exclaimed. "Boss says to trace this coin down and do nothing else. See you in fifteen minutes."

He hung up. Thoughtfully I replaced the receiver and went out to my car. I was pulling into my block from one arterial when I saw Jim's car pulling in from a block away. I stopped at the curb and waited for him. I didn't see the kids anywhere out front.

Jim climbed out of his car, and I never saw such an eager look of anticipation on a man's face before. I didn't realize I was showing my dread, but when he saw my face, he became serious.

"What is it, Pete? What on Earth is it?" he almost whispered.

"I don't know. At least I'm not sure. Come on inside the house."

We let ourselves in the front, and I took Jim into the study. It has a large window opening on the back garden, and the scene was very clear.

At first it was an innocent scene—so innocent and peaceful. Just three little children in the backyard playing hide and seek. Marily, a neighbor's child, was stepping up to the base tree.

"Now look, you kids," she was saying. "You hide where I can find you or I won't play."

"But where can we go, Marily?" Robert was arguing loudly. Like all little boys, he seems to carry on his conversations at the top of his lungs. "There's the garage, and there's those trees and bushes. You have to look everywhere, Marily."

"And there's going to be other buildings and trees and bushes there afterward," Star called out with glee. "You gotta look behind them too."

"Yeah!" Robert took up the teasing refrain. "And there's been lots and lots of buildings and trees there before—especially trees. You gotta look behind them too."

Marily tossed her head petulantly. "I don't know what you're talking about, and I don't care. Just hide where I can find you, that's all."

She hid her face at the tree and started counting. If I had been alone, I would have been sure my eyesight had failed me, or that I was the victim of hallucinations. But Jim was standing there and saw it too.

Marily started counting, yet the other two didn't run away. Star reached out and took Robert's hand and they merely stood there. For an instance they seemed to shimmer and—*they disappeared without moving a step!*

Marily finished her counting and ran around to the few possible hiding places in the yard. When she couldn't find them, she started to blubber and pushed through the hedge to Ruth's back door.

"They runned away from me again," she whined through the screen at Ruth.

Jim and I stood staring out the window. I glanced at him. His face was set and pale, but probably no worse than my own.

We saw the instant shimmer again. Star, and then immediately Robert, materialized from the air and ran up to the tree, shouting, "Safe! Safe!"

Marily let out a bawl and ran home to her mother.

I called Star and Robert into the house. They came, still holding hands, a little shamefaced, a little defiant.

How to begin? What in hell could I say?

"It's not exactly fair," I told them. "Marily can't follow you there." I was shooting in the dark, but I had at least a glimmering to go by.

Star turned pale enough for the freckles on her little nose to stand out under her tan. Robert blushed and turned to her fiercely.

"I told you so, Star. I *told* you so! I said it wasn't sporting," he accused. He turned to me. "Marily can't play good hide-and-seek anyway. She's only a Stupid."

"Let's forget that for a minute, Robert." I turned to her. "Star, just where did you go?"

"Oh, it's nothing, Daddy." She spoke defensively, belittling the whole thing. "We just go a little ways when we play with her. She ought to be able to find us a little ways."

"That's evading the issue. *Where* do you go—and *how* do you go?"

Jim stepped forward and showed her the bronze coin I'd sent him.

"You see, Star," he said quietly, "we've found this."

"I shouldn't have to tell you my game." She was almost in tears. "You're both just Tweens. You couldn't understand." Then, struck with contrition, she turned to me. "Daddy, I've tried and tried to ESP you. Truly I did. But you don't ESP worth anything." She slipped her hand through Robert's arm. "Robert does it very nicely," she said primly, as though she were complimenting him on using his fork the right way. "He must be better than I am, because I don't know how he finds me."

"I'll tell you how I do it, Star," Robert exclaimed eagerly. It was as if he were trying to make amends now that grownups had caught on. "You don't use any imagination. I never saw anybody with so little imagination!"

"I do too have imagination," she countered loudly. "I thought up the game, didn't I? I told you how to do it, didn't I?"

"Yeah, yeah!" he shouted back. "But you always have to look at a book to ESP what's in it, so you leave an ESP smudge. I just go the encyclopedia and ESP where you did—and I go to that place—and there you are. It's simple."

Star's mouth dropped open in consternation.

"I never thought of that," she said.

Jim and I stood there, letting the meaning of what they were saying penetrate slowly into our incredulous minds.

"Anyway," Robert was saying, "you haven't any imagination." He sank down cross-legged on the floor. "You can't teleport yourself to any place that's never been."

She went over to squat down beside him. "I can too! What about the Moon People? They haven't been yet."

He looked at her with childish disgust.

"Oh, Star, they have so been. You know that." He spread his hands out as though he were a baseball referee. "That time hasn't been yet for your daddy here, for instance, but it's already been for somebody like—well, say, like those things from Arcturus."

"Well, neither have you teleported yourself to some place that never was," Star was arguing back. "So there."

Waving Jim to one chair, I sank down into another. At least the arms of the chair felt solid beneath my hands.

"Now look, kids," I interrupted their evasive tactics, "let's start at the beginning. I gather you've figured a way to travel to places in the past or future."

"Well, of course, Daddy." Star shrugged the statement aside nonchalantly. "We just TP ourselves by ESP anywhere we want to go. It doesn't do any harm."

And these were the children who were too little to cross the street!

I have been through times of shock before. This was the same— somehow, the mind becomes too stunned to react beyond a point. One simply plows through the rest, the best he can, almost normally.

"Okay, okay," I said, and was surprised to hear the same tone I would have used over an argument about the biggest piece of cake. "I don't know whether it's harmful or not. I'll have to think it over. Right now, just tell me how you do it."

"It would be so much easier if I could ESP it to you," Star said doubtfully.

"Well, pretend I'm a Stupid and tell me in words."

"You remember the Moebius Strip?" she asked very slowly and carefully, starting with the first and most basic point in almost the way one explains to an ordinary child.

Yes, I remembered it. And I remembered how long ago it was that she had discovered it. Over a year, and her busy, brilliant mind had been exploring its possibilities ever since. And I thought she had forgotten it!

"That's where you join the ends of a strip of paper together with a half twist to make one surface," she went on, as though jogging my undependable, slow memory.

"Yes," I answered. "We all know the Moebius Strip."

Jim looked startled. I had never told him about the incident.

"Next you take a sheet and you give it a half twist and join the edge to itself all over to make a funny kind of holder."

"Klein's Bottle," Jim supplied.

She looked at him in relief.

"Oh, you know about that," she said. "That makes it easier. Well, then, the next step. You take a cube—" Her faced clouded with doubt again, and she explained, "You can't do this with your hands. You've gotta ESP it done, because it's an imaginary cube anyway."

She looked at us questioningly. I nodded for her to continue.

"And you ESP the twisted cube all together the same way you did Klein's Bottle. Now if you do that big enough, all around you, so you're sort of half twisted in the middle, then you can TP yourself anywhere you want to go. And that's all there is to it," she finished hurriedly.

"Where have you gone?" I asked her quietly.

The technique of doing it would take some thinking. I knew enough physics to know that was the way the dimensions were built up. The line, the plane, the cube—Euclidian physics. The Moebius Strip, the Klein Bottle, the unnamed twisted cube—Einsteinian physics. Yes, it was possible.

"Oh, we've gone all over," Star answered vaguely. "The Romans and the Egyptians—places like that."

"You picked up a coin in one of those places?" Jim asked.

He was doing a good job of keeping his voice casual. I knew the excitement he must be feeling, the vision of the wealth of knowledge which must be opening before his eyes.

"I found it, Daddy," Star answered Jim's question. She was about to cry. "I found it in the dirt, and Robert was about to catch me. I forgot I had it when I went away from there so fast." She looked at me pleadingly. "I didn't mean to steal it, Daddy. I never stole anything, anywhere. And I was going to take it back and put it right where I found it. Truly I was. But I dropped it again,and then I ESP'd that you had it. I guess I was awful naughty."

I brushed my hand across my forehead.

"Let's skip the question of good and bad for a minute," I said, my head throbbing. "What about this business of going into the future?"

Robert spoke up, his eyes shining. "There isn't any future, Mr. Holmes. That's what I keep telling Star, but she can't reason—she's just a girl. It'll all pass. Everything is always past."

Jim stared at him, as though thunderstruck, and opened his mouth to protest, I shook my head warningly.

"Suppose you tell me about that, Robert," I said.

"Well," he began on a rising note, frowning, "It's kinda hard to explain at that. Star's a Bright and even she doesn't understand it exactly. But, you see, I'm older." He looked at her with superiority. Then, with a change of mood, he defended her. "But when she gets as old as I am, she'll understand it okay."

He patted her shoulder consolingly. He was all of six years old.

"You go back into the past. Back past Egypt and Atlantis. That's recent," he said with scorn. "And on back, and on back, and all of a sudden it's future."

"That isn't the way I did it." Star tossed her head contrarily. "I *reasoned* the future. I reasoned what would come next, and I went there, and then I reasoned again. And on and on. I can too reason."

"It's the same future," Robert told us dogmatically. "It has to be, because that's all that ever happened." He turned to Star. "The reason you never could find any Garden of Eden is because there wasn't any Adam and Eve." Then to me, "And man didn't come from the apes, either. Man started himself."

Jim almost strangled as he leaned forward, his face red and his eyes bulging.

"How?" he choked out.

Robert sent his gaze into the far distance.

"Well," he said, "a long time from now—you know what I mean, as a Stupid would think of Time-From-Now—men got into a mess. Quite a mess—

"There were some people in that time who figured out the same kind of traveling Star and I do. So when the world was about to blow up and form a new star, a lot of them teleported themselves back to when the Earth was young, and they started over again."

Jim just stared at Robert, unable to speak.

"I don't get it," I said.

"Not everybody could do it," Robert explained patiently. "Just a few Brights. But they enclosed a lot of other people and took them along." He became a little vague at this point. "I guess later on the Brights lost interest in the Stupids or something. Anyway, the Stupids sank down lower and lower and became like animals." He held his nose briefly. "They smelled worse. They worshiped the Brights as gods."

Robert looked at me and shrugged.

"I don't know all that happened. I've only been there a few times.

It's not every interesting. Anyway," he finished, "the Brights finally disappeared."

"I'd sure like to know where they went." Star sighed. It was a lonely sigh. I helplessly took her hand and gave my attention back to Robert.

"I still don't quite understand," I said.

He grabbed up some scissors, a piece of cellophane tape, a sheet of paper. Quickly he cut a strip, gave it a half twist, and taped it together. Then rapidly, on the Moebius Strip, he wrote: "Cave men, This men, That men, Mu Men, Atlantis Men, Egyptians, History Men, Us Now Men, Atom Men, Moon Men, Planet Men, Star Men—"

"There," he said. "That's all the room there is on the strip. I've written clear around it. Right after Star Men comes Cave Men. It's all one thing, joined together. It isn't future, and is isn't past, either. It just plan *is*. Don't you see?"

"I'd sure like to know how the Brights got off the strip," Star said wistfully.

I had all I could take.

"Look, kids," I pleaded, "I don't know whether this game's dangerous or not. Maybe you'll wind up in a lion's mouth, or something."

"Oh, no, Daddy!" Star shrilled in glee. "We'd just TP ourselves right out of there."

"But fast," Robert chortled in agreement.

"Anyway, I've got to think it over," I said stubbornly. "I'm only a Tween, but, Star, I'm your daddy and you're just a little girl, so you have to mind me."

"I always mind you," she said virtuously.

"You do, eh?" I asked. "What about going off the block? Visiting the Greeks and Star Men isn't my idea of staying on the block."

"But you didn't say that, Daddy. You said not to cross the street. And I never did cross the street. Did we, Robert? Did we?"

"We didn't cross a single street, Mr. Holmes," he insisted.

"My God!" said Jim, and he went on trying to light a cigarette.

"All right, all *right!* No more leaving this time, then," I warned.

"Wait!" It was a cry of anguish from Jim. He broke the cigarette in sudden frustration and threw it in an ashtray. "The museum, Pete," he pleaded. "Think what it would mean. Pictures, specimens, voice recordings. And not only from historical places, but Star men, Pete. *Star men!* Wouldn't it be all right for them to go places they know are safe? I wouldn't ask them to take risks, but—"

"No, Jim," I said regretfully. "It's your museum, but this is my daughter."

"Sure," he breathed. "I guess I'd feel the same way."

I turned back to the youngsters.

"Star, Robert," I said to them both, "I want your promise that you will not leave this time, until I let you. Now I couldn't punish you if you broke your promise, because I couldn't follow you. But I want your promise on your word of honor you won't leave this time."

"We promise." They each held up a hand, as if swearing in court. "No more leaving this time."

I let the kids go back outside into the yard. Jim and I looked at one another for a long while, breathing hard enough to have been running.

"I'm sorry," I said at last.

"I know," he answered. "So am I. But I don't blame you. I simply forgot, for a moment, how much a daughter could mean to a man." He was silent, and then added, with the humorous quirk back at the corner of his lips, "I can just see myself reporting this interview to the museum."

"You don't intend to, do you?" I asked, alarmed.

"And get myself canned or laughed at? I'm not that stupid."

September 10

Am I actually getting it? I had a flash for an instant. I was concentrating on Caesar's triumphant march into Rome. For the briefest of instants, *there is was!* I was standing on the roadway, watching. But, most peculiar, it was still a picture; I was the only thing moving. And then, just as abruptly, I lost it.

Was it only a hallucination? Something brought about by intense concentration and wishful thinking?

Now let's see. You visualize a cube. Then you ESP it a half twist and seal the edges together— No, when it has the half twist there's only one surface. You seal that surface all around you. . . .

Sometimes I think I have it. Sometimes I despair. If only I were a Bright instead of a Tween!

October 23

I don't see how I managed to make so much work of teleporting myself. It's the simplest thing in the world, no effort at all. Why, a child could do it! That sounds like a gag, considering that it was two children who showed me how, but I mean the whole thing is easy enough for even almost any kid to learn. The problem is understanding the steps . . . no, not understanding, because I can't say I do, but working out the steps in the process.

There's no danger, either. No wonder it felt like a still picture at first, for the speeding up is incredible. That bullet I got in the way of, for instance—I was able to go and meet it and walk along beside it while it traveled through the air. To the men who were dueling, I must have been no more than an instantaneous streak of movement.

That's why the youngsters laughed at the suggestion of danger. Even if they materialized right in the middle of an atomic blast, it is so slow by comparison that they could TP right out again before they got hurt. The blast can't travel any faster than the speed of light, you see, while there is no limit to the speed of thought.

But I still haven't given them permission to teleport themselves out of this time yet. I want to go over the ages pretty carefully before I do; I'm not taking any chances, even though I don't see how they could wind up in any trouble. Still, Robert claimed the Brights went from the future back into the beginning, which means they could be going through time and overtake any of the three of us, and one of them might be hostile . . .

I feel like a louse, not taking Jim's cameras, specimen boxes, and recorders along. But there's time for that. Plenty of time, once I get the feel of history without being encumbered by all that stuff to carry.

Speaking of time and history—what a rotten job historians have done! For instance:

George III of England was neither crazy nor a moron. He wasn't a particularly nice guy, I'll admit—I don't see how anybody could be with the amount of flattery I saw—but he was the victim of empire expansion and the ferment of the Industrial Revolution. So where all the other European rulers at the time, though. He certainly did better than Louis of France. At least George kept his job and his head.

On the other hand, John Wilkes Booth was definitely psychotic. He could have been cured if they'd had our methods of psychotherapy then, and Lincoln, of course, wouldn't have been assassinated. It was almost a compulsion to prevent the killing, but I didn't dare. . . . God knows what effect it would have had on history. Strange thing, Lincoln looked less surprised than anybody else when he was shot, sad, yes, and hurt emotionally at least as much as physically, yet you'd swear he was expecting it.

Cheops was *plenty* worried about the number of slaves who died while the pyramid was being built. They weren't easy to replace. He gave them four hours off in the hottest part of the day, and I don't think any slaves in the country were fed or housed better.

I never found any signs of Atlantis or Lemuria, just tales of lands far off—a few hundred miles was a big distance then, remember—that had sunk beneath the sea. With the Ancients' exaggerated notion of geography, a big island was the same as a continent. Some islands did disappear, naturally, drowning a few thousand villagers and herdsmen. That must have been the source of the legends.

Columbus was a stubborn cuss. He was thinking of turning back when the sailors mutinied, which made him obstinate. I still can't see what was eating Genghis Khan and Alexander the Great—it would have been a big help to know the languages, because their big campaigns started off more like vacation or exploration trips. Helen of Troy was attractive enough, considering, but she was just an excuse to fight.

There were several attempts to federate the Indian tribes before the white man and the Five Nations, but going after wives and slaves ruined the movement every time. I think they could have kept America if they had been united and, it goes without saying, knew the deal they were going to get. At any rate, they might have traded for weapons and tools and industrialized the country somewhat in the way the Japanese did. I admit that's only speculation, but this would certainly have been a different world if they'd succeeded!

One day I'll put it all in a comprehensive and *corrected* history of mankind, *complete with photographs,* and then let the "experts" argue themselves into nervous breakdowns over it.

I didn't get very far into the future. Nowhere near the Star Men, or, for that matter, back to the beginning that Robert told us about. It's a matter of reasoning out the path and I'm not a Bright. I'll take Robert and Star along as guides, when and if.

What I did see of the future wasn't so good, but it wasn't so bad, either. The real mess obviously doesn't happen until the Star Men show up very far ahead in history, if Robert is right, and I think he is. I can't guess what the trouble will be, but it must be something ghastly if they won't be able to get out of it even with the enormously advanced technology they'll have. Or maybe that's the answer. It's almost true of us now.

November, Friday 14

The Howells have gone for a weekend trip and left Robert in my care. He's a good kid and no trouble. He and Star have kept their promise, but they're up to something else. I can sense it and that feeling of expectant dread is back with me.

They've been secretive of late. I catch them concentrating intensely, sighing with vexation, and then breaking out into unexplained giggles.

"Remember your promise," I warned Star while Robert was in the room.

"We're not going to break it, Daddy," she answered seriously.

They both chorused, "No more leaving this time."

But they both broke into giggles!

I'll have to watch them. What good it would do, I don't know. They're up to something, yet how can I stop them? Shut them in their rooms? Tan their hides?

I wonder what someone else would recommend.

The kids are gone!

I've been waiting an hour for them. I know they wouldn't stay away so long if they could get back. There must be something they've run into. Bright as they are, they're still only children.

I have some clues. They promised me they wouldn't go out of this present time. With all her mischievousness, Star has never broken a promise to me—as her typically feminine mind interprets it, that is. So I know they are in our own time.

On several occasions Star has brought it up, wondering where the Old Ones, the Bright Ones, have gone—how they got off the Moebius Strip.

That's the clue. How can I get off the Moebius Strip and remain in the present?

A cube won't do it. There we have a mere journey along the single surface. We have a line, we have a plane, we have a cube. And then we have a supercube—a tesseract. That is the logical progression of mathematics. The Bright Ones must have pursued that line of reasoning.

Now I've got to do the same, but without the advantage of being a Bright. Still, it's not the same as expecting a normally intelligent person to produce a work of genius. (Genius by our standards, of course, which I suppose Robert and Star would classify as Tween.) Anyone with a pretty fair I.Q. and proper education and training can follow a genius' logic, provided the steps are there and especially if it has a practical application. What he can't do is initiate and complete that structure of logic. I don't have to, either—that was done for me by a pair of Brights and I "simply" have to apply their findings.

Now let's see if I can.

By reducing the present-past-future of man to a Moebius Strip, we have sheared away a dimension. It is a two-dimensional strip, because it has no depth. (Naturally it would be impossible for a Moebius Strip to have depth; it has only one surface.)

Reducing it to two dimensions makes it possible to travel anywhere you want to go on it via the third dimension. And you're in the third dimension when you enfold yourself in the twisted cube.

Let's go a step higher, into one more dimension. In short, the tesseract. To get the equivalent of a Moebius Strip with depth, you have to go into the fourth dimension, which, it seems to me, is the only way the Bright Ones could get off this closed cycle of past-present-future-past. They must have reasoned that one more notch up the dimensions was all they needed. It is equally obvious that Star and Robert have followed the same line of reasoning; they wouldn't break their promise not to leave the present—and getting off the Moebius Strip into *another* present would, in a sort of devious way, be keeping that promise.

I'm putting all this speculation down for you, Jim Pietre, knowing first that you're a Tween like myself, and second that you're sure to have been doing a lot of thinking about what happened after I sent you the coin Star dropped. I'm hoping you can explain all this to Bill and Ruth Howell—or enough, in any case, to let them understand the truth about their son Robert and my daughter Star, and where the children may have gone.

I'm leaving these notes where you will find them, when you and Bill and Ruth search the house and grounds for us. If you read this, it will be because I have failed in my search for the youngsters. There is also the possibility that I'll find them and that we won't be able to get back onto this Moebius Strip. Perhaps time has a different value there, or doesn't exist at all. What it's like off the Strip is anybody's guess.

Bill and Ruth: I wish I might give you hope that I will bring Robert back to you. But all I can do is wish. It may be no more than wishing upon a star—my Star.

I'm trying now to take six cubes and fold them in on one another so that every angle is a right angle.

It's not easy, but I can do it, using every bit of concentration I've learned from the kids. All right, I have the six cubes and I have every angle a right angle.

Now if, in the folding, I ESP the tesseract a half twist around myself and—

Crazy Joey

with Alex Apostolides

From *Astounding Science Fiction*

This story was the seed of the subsequent novel, *They'd Rather Be Right,* and was rewritten to be scattered through the early chapters; in its emphasis upon psionic (magical) powers induced technologically it is not uncharacteristic of *Astounding* stories of that era, but Clifton was not writing paranoid fantasy as some of Campbell's other contributors in this genre were accused of having done.

Joey pulled the covers up over his head, trying to shut out the whispers which filled the room. But even with the pillow over his head, their shrill buzz entered up through the roof of his mouth, tasting acrid and bitter, spinning around in his brain. Fingers in his ears simply made the words emerge from a sensation of cutting little lights into words.

"It worries me, Madge, more and more, the way that boy carries on. I was hoping he'd outgrow it, but he don't."

His father's voice was deep and petulant, sounding from the pillow on his side of the bed there in the other room. "Hanging back, all the time. Not playing with the other kids, staying out of school, claiming the teachers don't like him. It ain't natural, Madge. I don't like it."

"Now you're working yourself up again, Bob." His mother's patient voice from her side of the bed cut across the deeper tones. "What good is it going to do you?"

"Did some good when I thrashed him." His father spoke sharply, and a little louder. Joey could hear the buzz of the voice itself coming through the walls. "Stopped him talking about whispers. I tell you I ain't gonna have a kid of mine acting crazy. I passed a bunch of the little brats on the way home tonight. 'There goes Crazy Joey's father,' I heard one of them say. I won't stand for it. Either Joey learns to stand up and be a real boy, or—''

"Or what, Bob?" His mother's voice had both defiance and fear in it.

"Or . . . oh, I don't know what—" His father's voice trailed off in disgust. "Let's go to sleep, Madge. I'm tired."

Joey felt his mother's lift of hope. Perhaps she could keep awake a little longer, waiting for his deep breathing to assure her he was asleep, so she could move from her extreme edge of the bed and be more comfortable—without touching him.

The deep, rasping sensation of his father's weary hopelessness; desire, but not for her. Drab and uninteresting. He was still young enough, still a man; tied down tight to this drab.

The lighter, more delicate thought of his mother. She was still young enough, still hungered for romance. The vision of a green slope of hill, starred with white daisies, the wind blowing through her flowing hair, a young man striding on firm brown legs up the hill toward her, his sloping shoulders swinging with his stride. Tied to this coarse hulk beside her, instead.

The heavier rasp of thought demanded attention. Those girls flouncing down the hallway of the school; looking out of the corners of their eyes at the boys; conscious only of the returning speculative stares; unconscious of the old janitor who was carrying baskets of wastepaper down the hall behind them.

Joey buried his head deeper into the bed beneath his pillow. The visions were worse than the whispers. He did not fully understand them, but was overwhelmed by them, by a deep sense of shame that he had participated in them.

He tried to will his mind to leave the visions, and there leaped, with startling clarity, the vision of his father holding him down on the bed, a terrible rage in his face, shouting at him.

"How come you know how I looked at those two girls in the hall at school? You spying little sneak!" The blows. The horror. The utter confusion.

And the imaginings were worse than the visions. So clear, so intricately clear, they became memories. Memories as sharp and clear as any other reality. Eight-year-old Joey could not yet know the reasoned verbalization: an imaginary experience can have as profound an effect upon personality development as a real one. He knew only that it was so.

But he must never tell about this beating, must never tell anyone.

Others wouldn't have any such memory and they would say he was crazy. He must store it away, with all the other things he had stored away. It was hard to keep remembering which were the ones others could remember, and which were his alone. Each was as real as the other, and that was the only distinction.

Sometimes he forgot, and talked about the wrong things. Then they called him a little liar. To keep away from that he always had to go into their minds first, and that was sometimes a terrible and frightening thing; their memories were not the same as his, and often hard to recognize.

Then it was morning. The whispers were all about him again. In half-awake reverie, he shuddered over the imagined beating he had received. He twisted and turned under the covers, trying to escape the also twisting threads of thought between his father and mother in the kitchen. The threads became ropes; gray-green and alive; affection turned resentment coiling and threatening; held back from striking only by hopelessness. He stared into the gray morning light seeping in around the shade at his window. He tried to trace the designs on the wallpaper, but they, too, became twisting worms of despair. And transferred again into the memory of the beating. Involuntarily, a sob escaped his throat, aloud.

"Madge!" This was no whsiper, but his father shouting at his mother. "That kid is in there sniveling again. I'll give him something to bawl about." The sudden terrible rage was a dead black smothering blanket.

"Bob!" The sharp fear in his mother's voice stopped the tread of feet across the kitchen floor, changing the rage back to hopelessness.

He felt his father go away from his door, back to his place at the table. He felt the sudden surge of resolution in his father.

"Madge, I'm going to talk to Dr. Ames this morning. He gets in early. He's the head of the psychology department. I'm going to talk to him about Joey."

Joey could feel the shame of his father at such a revelation. The shame of saying, "Dr. Ames, do you think my son is crazy?"

"What good will that do?" His mother's voice was resentful, fearful; afraid of what the doctor might say.

"I'll tell him all about Joey. He gives loony tests, and I'm going to find out about—"

"Bob! Saying such a thing about your own son. It's—it's sinful!" His mother's voice was high, and her chair creaked as she started to move from her side of the table.

"Take it easy, Madge," his father warned her. "I'm not saying he's crazy, mind you. I just want to get to the bottom of it. I want to know. I want a normal boy." Then, desperately: "Madge, I just want a boy!" The frustration, the disappointment welled over Joey as if it were his own.

"I'll talk to the doctor," his father was continuing, reasoning with her. "I'll try to get him to see Joey. I'm janitor of his building, and he shouldn't charge me anything. Maybe he'll see you and Joey this afternoon. I'll call you on the phone if he will. You be ready to take Joey up there if I should call." The voice was stern, unbending.

"Yes, Bob." His mother recognized the inflexibility of the decision.

"Where's my lunch pail, then?" his father asked. "I'll get to work early, so I can have a talk with Dr. Ames before class time."

"On the sink, Bob. Where it always is," his mother answered patiently.

The sudden rage again. Always is. Always is. That's the trouble, Madge. Everything always is. Just like yesterday, and the day before. That's why it's all so hopeless. But the bitterness switched suddenly to pity.

"Don't worry so, Madge." There was a tone of near affection in his father's voice. Belated consideration. Joey felt his father move around the table, pat his mother awkwardly on the shoulder. But still the little yellow petals of affection were torn and consumed by the gray-green worms of resentment.

"Bob—" His mother spoke to the closing door. The footsteps, heavy, went on down the back steps of their house, each a soundless impact upon Joey's chest.

Joey felt his mother start toward his room. Hastily he took the pillow from over his head, pulled the blanket up under his chin, dropped his chin and jaw, let his mouth open in the relaxation of deep sleep, and breathed slowly. He hoped he could will away the welts of the belt blows before she would see them. With all his might he willed the welts away, and the angry blue bruises of his imagination. All the signs of the terrible consequences of what might have been.

He felt her warm tenderness as she opened his door. Now the lights were warm and shining, clear and beautiful, unmuddied by any resentments. He felt the tenderness flow outward from her, and wrapped it around him to clear away the bruises. He willed back the tears of relief, and lay in apparent deep sleep. He felt her kneel down by his bed, and heard the whispers in her mind.

"My poor little different boy. You're all I've got. I don't care what they say, Joey. I don't care what they say." Joey felt the throb of grief arise in her throat, choked back, the tremendous effort to smile at him, to make her voice light and carefree.

"Wake up, Joey," she called, and shook his shoulder lightly. "It's morning, darling." There was bright play in her voice, the gladness of morning itself. "Time all little fellows were up and doing."

He opened his eyes, and her face was sweet and tender. No one but a Joey could have read the apprehension and dread which lay behind it.

"I sure slept sound," he said boisterously. "I didn't even dream."

"Then you weren't crying a while ago?" she asked in hesitant puzzlement.

"Me, Mom? Me?" he shouted indignantly. "What could there be to cry about?"

The campus of Steiffel University was familiar to Joey from the outside. He knew the winding paths, the stretches of lawn, the green trees, the white benches nestled in shaded nooks. The other kids loved to hide in the bushes at night and listen to the young men and women talking. They snickered about it on the school playground all the time. Joey had tried it once, but had refused to go back again. These were thoughts he did not want to see—tender, urgent thoughts so precious that they belonged to no one else except the people feeling them.

But now walking up the path, leading to the psychology building with his mother, he could feel only her stream of thought.

"Oh I pray, dear God, I pray that the doctor won't find anything wrong with Joey. Dear God . . . dear God . . . don't let them find anything wrong with Joey. They might want to take him away, shut him up somewhere. I couldn't bear it. I couldn't live. Dear God . . . oh dear God—"

Joey's thought darted down another bypath of what might be, opened by his mother's prayer. He willed away the constriction in his throat.

"This is interesting, Mom," he exclaimed happily. "Pop is always talking about it. But I've never been inside the building of a college before. Have you?"

"No, son," she said absently. Thank heaven he doesn't know. "Joey—" she said suddenly, and faltered.

He could read the thought in her mind. Don't let them find anything wrong with you. Try not to talk about whispers, or imagination, or—

"What, Mom?" It was urgent to get her away from her fear again.

"Joey . . . er . . . are you afraid?"

"No, Mom," he answered scornfully. "Course not. It's just another school, that's all. A school for big kids."

He could feel his father watching them through a basement window, waiting for them to start up the steps of the building. Waiting to meet them in the front hall, to take them up to Dr. Ames's study. He could feel the efforts his father was making to be casual and normal about it all; Bob Carter, perhaps only a janitor, but a solid citizen, independently proud. Didn't everyone call him "Mr. Carter?" Recognize his dignity?

Joey's father, with his dignity upon him, met them at the doorway of the building; looked furtively and quickly at the rusty black clothing of his wife, inadvertently comparing the textiles of her old suit to the rich materials the coeds wore with such careless style.

"You look right nice, Madge," he said heavily, to reassure her, and took her arm gallantly. When they had reached the second floor, up the broad stairs, he turned to Joey.

"I've been telling the professors how bright you are, Joey. They want to talk to you." He chuckled agreeably.

Pop, don't laught like that. I know you're ashamed. But don't lie to me, Pop. I know.

"Just answer all their questions, Joey," his father was saying. "Be truthful." He emphasized the word again, "Truthful, I said."

"Sure, Pop," Joey answered dutifully; knowing his father hoped he wouldn't be truthful—and that his mother might die if he were. He wondered if he might hear the whisperings from the professors' minds. What if he couldn't hear! How would he know how to answer them, if he couldn't hear the whispers! Maybe he couldn't hear, wouldn't know how to answer, and then his mother would die!

His face turned pale, and he felt as if he were numb; in a dull dead trance as they walked down the hall and into a study off one of the big classrooms.

"This here is my wife and my son, Dr. Martin," his father was saying. Then to Joey's mother: "Dr. Martin is Dr. Ames's assistant."

The boy is very frightened. The thought came clearly and distinctly to Joey from the doctor's mind.

"Not any more," Joey said, and didn't realize until it was done that he had exclaimed it aloud in his relief. He could hear!

"I beg your pardon, Joey?" Dr. Martin turned from greeting his mother and looked with quick penetration into Joey's eyes. His own sharp blue eyes had exclamation points in them, accented by his raised blond brows in a round face.

"But of course he is Dr. Ames's assistant," his father corrected him heartily, with an edge behind the words. You little fool, you're starting in to demonstrate already.

That isn't what the boy meant. Dr. Martin was racing the thought through his mind. I had the thought that the boy was frightened, and he immediately said he wasn't. All the pathological symptoms of fright disappeared instantly, too. Yes. Put into the matrix of the telepath, all the things Carter told us this morning about him would fit. I hadn't considered that. And I know that old fool Ames would never consider it.

If there ever was a closed mind against ESP, he's got it. Orthodox psychology!

"We will teach nothing here but orthodox psychology, Dr. Martin," Ames had said. "It is the duty of some of us to insist a theory be proved through time and tradition. We will not rush down every side path, accepting theories as unsubstantial as the tobacco smoke which subsidizes them."

So much for ESP. Well, even Rhine says that the vast body of psychology, in spite of all the evidence, still will not accept the fact of ESP.

But if this kid were a telepath—a true telepath. If by any chance he were . . . If his remark and the disappearance of the fear symptoms were not just coincidence!

But another Ames's admonition dampened his elation. "Our founder, Jacob Steiffel, was a wise man. He believed in progress, Martin, as do I. But progress through conservative proof. Let others play the fool, our job is to preserve the bastions of scientific solidity!"

"Dr. Ames has not arrived yet," he said suddenly to Joey's parents. "He's been called to the office of the university president, But, in the meantime, leave the boy with me. There's preliminary work to do, and I'm competent to do that." He realized the implications of bitterness in his remark, and reassured himself that these people were not so subtle as to catch it.

"I got work to do anyhow," Joey's father said. His relief was apparent, that he would not be required to stand by, and he was using it to play the part of the ever faithful servant.

"Here's a room where you may wait, Mrs. Carter," Dr. Martin said to Joey's mother. He opened a door and showed her in to a small waiting room. "There are magazines. Make yourself quite comfortable. This may take an hour or so."

"Thank you, Doctor." It was the first time she had spoken, and her voice contained the awe and respect she felt. A thread of resentment, too. It wasn't fair; some had so many advantages to get educated. Others—But the resentment was drowned out in the awe and respect. These were not just ordinary doctors. They *taught* doctors!

She sat tentatively on the edge of a wooden chair, the hardest one in the room. The worn red feather in her hat drooped, but her back remained straight.

Joey felt the doctor thinking, "Relax, woman! We're not going to skin him alive!" But he merely closed the door. Joey could still see her sitting there, through the closed door; not relaxing, not reaching for a magazine. Her lips were pulled tight against her teeth to keep her prayer from showing. "Dear God, oh, dear God—"

Dr. Martin came back over from closing the door, and led Joey to a chair near the bookcase.

"Now, you just sit down there and relax, Joey. We're not going to hurt you. We're just going to visit a little, and ask you some questions." But his mind was darting in and out around his desires. I'd better start in on routine IQ tests, leave the Rorschach for Ames. Now that it's standard, he'll use it. Leave word association for him, too. That's his speed. Maybe I should give the multiphasic; no, better leave that for Ames. He'll discredit it, but it'll make him feel very modern and up-to-date to use it. I mustn't forget I'm just the errand boy around here. I wish I could run the Rhine ESP deck on the boy, but if Ames came in and caught me at it—"

The office phone rang, and Martin picked it up hurriedly. It was the president's office calling.

"Dr. Ames asked me to tell you he will be tied up for almost an hour," the operator said disinterestedly. "The patient will just have to wait."

"Thank you," Martin said slowly. Joey felt his lift of spirit. I can run a few samples of the Rhine cards. I just have to know. I wish I could get away from this place, into a school where there's some latitude for research. I wish Marion weren't so tied down here with her family and that little social group she lords it over. "My husband is assistant to the dean of psychology!" That's much more important to her than any feeling I've got of frustration. If I quit here, and got into a place where I could work, really work, it would mean leaving this town. Marion wouldn't go. She's a big frog in a little puddle here. And still tied to her parents—and I'm tied to Marion. If anybody needs psych help, I do. I wish I had the courage—"

Joey, as frequently with adults, could not comprehend all the words and sentences, but the somatic indecision and despair washed over him, making him gasp for breath.

Martin went over to a desk, with sudden resolution, and from far back in a drawer he pulled out a thin deck of cards.

"We're going to play a little game first, Joey," he said heartily, as he sat down at his desk and pulled a sheet of paper toward him. "There are twenty-five cards here. Five of them have a circle, five a star, a wavy line, a cross, a rectangle. Do you know what a rectangle is, Joey?"

Joey didn't, but the vision of a square leaped into his mind.

"Yes, sir," Joey said. "It's a sort of square."

"That's right," Martin said approvingly, making a mental note that the boy shouldn't have known the word, and did. "Now I'm going to look at a card, one at a time, and then you guess what kind of an image there is on it. I'll write down what the card really shows, and what you say it is, and then we'll see how many you get right."

Too short a time! Too short a time! But maybe long enough to be significant. If I should just get a trace. All right, suppose you do? The question was ironic in his mind. He picked up the first card and looked at it, holding it carefully so that Joey would have no chance to see the face of it.

A circle leaped with startling clarity into Joey's mind. And the circle contained the image of Joey's mother, sitting on the edge of her chair in the other room, praying over and over, "Don't let them find anything wrong with him. Don't let them find—"

"Square," Joey said promptly. He felt the tinge of disappointment in Martin's mind as he recorded the true and the false. Not a perfect telepath, anyway.

"All right, Joey," Martin responded verbally. "Next card."

"Did I get that one right?" Joey asked brightly.

"I'm not supposed to tell you," Martin answered." "Not until the end of the game." Well, the boy showed normal curiosity. Didn't seem to show too much anxiety, which sometimes damped down the ESP factor. He picked up the next card. Joey saw it contained a cross.

"Star," he said positively.

"Next card," Martin said.

It was in the nineteenth card that Joey sensed a new thought in Martin's mind. There was a rising excitement. Not one of them had been correct. Rhine says a negative result can be as revealing as a positive one. He should get every fifth card correctly. Five out of the twenty-five to hit the law of averages, Martin picked up the twentieth card and looked at it. It was a wavy line.

"Wavy line," Joey answered. He felt the disappointment again in Martin's mind, this time because he had broken the long run of incorrectness.

The twenty-first card was a star.

"Star," Joey said.

And the next three were equally correct. Joey had called five out of the twenty-five correctly, as the law of averages required. The pattern was a bit strange. What would the laws of chance say to a pattern such as this? Try it again.

"Let's try it again," he suggested.

"You were supposed to tell me how I did at the end of the game," Joey prompted.

"You were correct on five of them, Joey," Martin said, noncommittally.

"Is that pretty good?" Joey asked anxiously.

"Average," Martin said, and threw him a quick look. Wasn't that eagerness to please just a bit overdone? "Just average. Let's try it again."

This time Joey did not make the mistake of waiting until the end of the deck before he called correct cards. The doctor had said every fifth card should be called correctly. Joey did not understand statistical language. Dutifully, he called every fifth card correctly. Four wrong, one right. And again, the rising excitement near the twentieth card. Again, what are the laws of chance that the boy would call four wrong, one right, again and again, in perfect order?

Joey promptly called two of them right together. And felt Martin's disappointment. The pattern had been broken again. And then a rise of excitement, carefully suppressed.

"Let's run them again," Martin said. And he whispered strongly to himself. "This time he must call every other one of them right, in order to pass as just an average boy."

Joey was bewildered. There seemed to be a double thought in Martin's mind, a tenseness he could not understand. He wavered, and then doubtfully, doubting he was doing the right thing, he began to call every other card correctly.

Halfway through the deck Martin laid the cards down. Joey caught the flash of undisguised elation in his mind, and sank back into his own chair in despair. He had done it wrong.

"O.K., Joey," Martin said quietly. There was a smile of tender bitterness around his lips. "I don't know what the idea is. You've got your reasons, and they must be pretty terrible ones. Do you think you could talk to me? Tell me about it?"

"I don't know what you mean, Dr. Martin," Joey lied. Perhaps if he didn't admit anything—

"In trying to avoid a pattern, Joey, you made one. Just as soon as I realized you were setting up an unusual pattern, you immediately changed it. Every time. But that, too, is a pattern." And then he asked, quite dryly, "Or am I talking over your head?"

"Yes, sir," Joey said. "I guess you are." But he had learned. The whole concept of patterned response as against random response leaped from Martin's mind into his. "Maybe if I tried it again?" he asked hopefully. At all costs he must get the idea out of Martin's mind that there was anything exceptional about him. This time, and forever afterwards, he knew he could avoid any kind of a pattern. Just one more chance.

"I don't blame you, Joey," Martin answered sadly. "If you've looked into my mind, well, I don't blame you. Here we are. You're a telepath and afraid to reveal it. I'm a psychologist, supposed to be, and I'm afraid to investigate it. A couple of fellows who caught the tiger by the tail, aren't we, Joey? Looks as if we'd better kind of protect one another, doesn't it?"

"Yes, sir," Joey answered and tried to hold back the tears of relief. "You won't even tell my mother? What about my father?" He already knew that Martin didn't dare tell Ames.

"I won't tell anybody, Joey," Martin answered sadly. "I've got to hang onto my job. And in this wise and mighty institution we believe only in orthodox psychology. What you have, Joey, simply doesn't exist. Dr. Ames says so, and Dr. Ames is always right. No, Joey," he sighed, "I'm not likely to tell anybody."

"Maybe he'll trick me like you did," Joey said doubtfully, but without resentment. "Maybe with that ink-blot thing, or that 'yes' and 'no' pile of little cards."

Martin glanced at him quickly.

"You're quite perfect at it, aren't you?" He framed it a question and made it a statement. "You go beyond the words to the actual thought image itself. No, Joey, in that case I don't think he will. I think you can keep ahead of him."

"I don't know," Joey said doubtfully. "It's all so new. So many new things to think about all at once."

"I'll try to be in the room with you and him," Martin promised. "Ill think of the normal answer each time. He won't look very deep. He never does. He already knows all the answers."

"Thank you, sir." Joey said, and then, "I won't tell on you, either."

"O.K., Joey. We'd better be finishing the IQ test when he comes in. He's about due now. I suppose you'd better grade around a hundred. And you'd better miss random questions, so as not to show any definite pattern, for him to grab onto. All right, here goes. Tell me what is wrong with this statement—"

The tests were over. Joey sat quietly in his chair watching Dr. Martin grade papers at his desk, watching him trying not to think about Joey, He watched his mother in the waiting room, still sitting on the edge of her chair, where she had been for the last two hours, without moving, her eyes closed, her lips still drawn tight. He watched Dr. Ames, sitting in his own office, absently shuffling papers around, comparing the values of the notes he had taken on Joey's reaction.

But the nearer turmoil in Dr. Martin's mind all but drowned out the fear of his mother, the growing disgust of Dr. Ames.

"It's a choice between Joey and holding my job. No matter how secretly I worked, Ames would find out. Once you're fired from a school, it's almost impossible to get a comparable job. All this subversive business, this fear of investigating anything outside the physical sciences that isn't strictly orthodox. No matter what explanation was given out, they'd suspect me of subversion. Oh Marion, Marion! Why can't I count on you to stand beside me? Or am I just using you as an excuse? Would I have the courage even if there were no Marion?"

He rubbed his hand across his eyes, as if to shut out the vision of a world where there was no Marion. He replaced it with a world where constant fear of becoming grist for some politician's publicity ground all research to a halt. He had quite forgotten that Joey was sitting across the room, and could follow at least the somatics of his thought.

Consciously he shoved the problem into the background, and made himself concentrate on the words of the student's paper before him. The words leaped into startling clarity, for they were a reflection of his own train of thought.

". . . it becomes apparent then that just as physical science varies it techniques from one material to the next to gain maximum result, psychology must obtain an equal willingness to become flexible. I suggest that objective physical science methodology will never permit us to know *a man; that such methodology limits us merely to knowing* about *a man. I suggest that an entirely new science, perhaps through somatics and methodology derived therefrom, must be our approach."*

Dr. Martin shoved the paper away from him. Must warn that student. His entire train of thought was a violation of orthodox psychology. Ames would crucify the boy if he ever saw this paper. Did he dare warn the boy? Students show so little caution or ethics. He could hear him now down at the milkshake hangout.

"Martin told me to soft-pedal my thinking if I wanted to get a grade."

And the answering chorus from all around the room, the Tannenbaum chant:

"Oh, Steiffel U will stifle you,
We all must think as granddads do!"

Best just to give the student a failing grade on the paper, and let him draw his own conclusion. Got to be orthodox.

With his thumb and fingers he pulled the flesh of his forehead into a heavy crease, grinding it between his fingers, taking pleasure that the pain of the flesh lessened the pain of his spirit. If only the kid had never shown up here!

His thought stream was interrupted in Joey's mind by the scene now taking place in the waiting room. Dr. Ames had taken a chair beside Joey's mother.

"Oh no, no, no, no, Mrs. Carter," he was saying consolingly. "Don't be so frightened. There's absolutely nothing wrong with your boy. Nothing at all—yet. I've never tested a more average boy."

Characteristically, he had overlooked the most vital point, a point also forgotten by Martin when he was thinking of the proper answers for Joey to give—that no boy can possibly be as average as Joey had graded. It never occurred to him that mean average is a statistical concept in psychology, never to be found in one individual.

"Notice I said "yet,' Mrs. Carter," Ames said heavily. "He's an only child, isn't he?"

"Yes," Joey's mother barely breathed the word. Her fear had not abated. She knew that doctors sometimes did not tell all the truth. In the soap operas they always started out comfortingly, and only gradually let you know the terrible truth.

"I thought so," Ames said with finality. "And as with many one-child families, you've spoiled him. Spoiled him so dreadfully that now you must take stern measures."

"He's all I've got, Doctor," she said hesitantly.

"All the more reason why you want him to grow up into a strong, solid man. A man such as your husband, for example. A child is a peculiar little entity, Mrs. Carter. The more attention you give him, the more he wants."

He continued the development of his theme inexorably.

"Their bodies can be little, but their egos can be enormous. They learn little tricks for getting attention. And then they add to these with others. They're insatiable little monsters. They never get enough. Once they get you under their thumb, they'll ride you to death. They'll try anything, anything at all to get special attention, constant attention. That's what has happened to your Joey."

"I'm not sure I understand, Doctor."

"Well, Mrs. Carter, to put it bluntly, Joey has been pretending, telling lies, deliberately keeping you worried and fearful so that you will give him more attention. He hasn't been able to fool his father so well, so in line with Oedipus complex, he set about to win you away from his father, to come between you. Your husband is a fine man, a good worker; but your son wants to make you turn against your husband so he will get all of your attention."

He was enjoying the development of his logic, sparing no impact upon her.

"And it could be bad for the boy. Too much attention is like too much candy. It makes them sick." He pulled an ancient trick upon her, deliberately confusing her to impress her with the gravity, and his knowledge. "If this continues, the boy could easily become a catatonic schizophrenic!"

Joey's mother shrank back, her eyes opening wide. The horror of the unknown was worse than the reality might be.

"What is that, Doctor?"

The doctor, gratified by her reaction, pulled another ancient one.

"Well . . . er . . . without the proper background . . . er . . . well, in layman's language, Mrs. Carter, we might roughly define it as an incurable form of insanity."

"Oh, no, no! Not my Joey!"

The doctor leaned back in his chair. In this changing world of thought anarchy, it was good to see there were some who still retained the proper respect, placed the proper value upon the words of a man of science. These flip kids he got in his classes these days; this younger generation! Without respect, that flip kid he'd had to get expelled.

"Just give us the facts, Doctor, and let us draw our own conclusions. Yours haven't worked so well."

Yes, it was gratifying to see there were still some who recognized a man of position.

"But you can prevent it, Mrs. Carter." He leaned forward again. "Joey is eight, now. No longer a baby. It is time he began to be a little man. He plays hooky from school, says the teachers don't like him. Why, Mrs. Carter, when I was eight, I got up before daylight, did my farm chores without complaint, and walked two miles through the snow for the wonderful privilege of going to school!

"Now here is what you must do. You must regard this just as you would a medical prescription; with full knowledge of the penalty if you do not use the prescription: You must stop mothering him. Stop catering to him. Pay no attention to his tricks. Let his father take over, Mrs. Carter. The boy needs a strong man's hand.

"He must be forced to play with the other boys. A black eye never hurt a boy, now and then, a real boy. Your boy must get in there and scrap it out with the rest of them, gain his place among them, just as he will have to scrap later to gain his place in society."

A sigh, almost a sob, escaped her. A doctor knows. And this doctor *teaches* doctors. Relief from tension, fear of the terrible words the doctor had said; and then a growing anger, anger at herself, anger at Joey. He had tricked her. Her son had lied to her, betrayed her love, pretended all sorts of terrible things just to worry her. She stood up suddenly, her face white with grief-rage.

"Thank you, Doctor. Thank you so much. I'm sorry we took up your time." Her humiliation was complete.

"No thanks needed, Mrs. Carter. Glad to help. We've caught it in time. If it had been allowed to go on a little longer—"

He left the phrase hanging in the air, ominously. He patted her arm in a fatherly fashion, and turned absently away, dismissing her.

Joey saw her open the door into the room where he was sitting. "Come, Joey," she said firmly.

Dr. Martin did not look up from the papers he was now grading with furious speed, furious intensity, slashing angrily with his blue pencil at any thought variant from the orthodox. But even while he checked, circled, questioned, the thought crept into his mind.

"I could write an anonymous letter to Dr. Billings of—yes, that's the thing to do. It's out of my hands then. If Billings chooses to ignore the follow-up, that's his business."

Joey followed his mother out of the room and down the hall. She walked ahead of him, rapidly, her eyes blazing with anger and humiliation, not caring whether he followed her or not.

In one corner of the schoolyard, the boys were playing ball. Joey knew they saw him coming down the sidewalk, alone, but they pointedly paid no attention to him.

He did not try to join them. Even though they were not looking at him, he could hear the hated refrain singing through their minds.

> Crazy Joe
> Such a schmo!
> Hope he falls
> And breaks his toe!

It was simply their resentment because he was different. Their unconscious wish that he stumble and fall now and then, as they did. He realized that he must learn to do this. Then he shrugged. No, if he carried out his plan, it wouldn't matter.

He walked on down past the fence of the play yard. The boys were concentrating on their ball game.

Without a warning a warmth suffused him, singing sympathy, hope, joy. He stopped, looked about him, and saw no one. Yet the somatic feeling had been near—so very near.

Then he saw it. A dirty, lop-eared dog looking at him quizzically from under a shrub near the playground gate. He thought at the dog, and saw its head come up. They stood and looked at one another, each letting the warmth, the tenderness, affection wash over them. So lonely. Each of them had been so lonely.

Joey knelt down and began to whisper.

"My mother is mad at me right now. So I can't take you home." The dog cocked his head to one side and looked at him.

"But I'll get food for you," Joey promised. "You can sleep under our back steps and nobody will know if you just keep out of sight."

The dog licked a pink tongue at his face. Joey nuzzled his face in the dirty hair of the dog's neck.

"I was going to die," he whispered. "I was going to die just as soon as my mother got over being mad at me. I was going to wait until then, because I didn't want her to blame herself later. I can do it, you know. I can stop my blood from moving, or my heart from beating; there's a hundred ways. But maybe I won't need to do it now. I won't need to die until you do. And that will be a long time; a long, long time. You see, if I can stop your heart from beating, I can keep it beating, too."

The dog wagged his stumpy tail; and then stiffened in Joey's arms.

"Yes," Joey thought quickly at the dog. "Yes, I know the kids are watching us now. Pretend like—" the thought hurt him, but he said it anyway. "Pretend you don't like me, that you hate me."

Slowly the dog backed away from Joey.

"Here, doggy, doggy!" Joey called.

The dog gave a wavering wag of his stump tail.

"No, no!" Joey thought desperately. "No, don't let them know. They'll want to hurt you if they find out. They're—People are like that."

The dog backed away another step and lifted his lip in a snarl.

"Yah! Yah! Yah!" the kids called out. "Joey can't even make friends with a dog!"

They were standing in a semicircle about him now. Joey stood up and faced them then for a moment. There was no anger or resentment in his face. There never would be now. One just shouldn't get angry at blind and helpless things.

Without a word he started walking down the street, away from them. The dog crouched far back in the corner under the shrub.

"Yah! Yah! Crazy Joey!" the kids called out again.

Joey did not look back. They couldn't see. They couldn't hear. They couldn't know. He felt a rush of pity.

The kids went back to their play, arguing loudly about who was at bat.

The dog waited until their attention was fully on the game again. Then he crept out from under the bush, and started ambling aimlessly down the street in the direction Joey had gone, trotting awkwardly on the bias as some dogs do.

He did not need to sniff for tracks. He knew.

8/53

What Thin Partitions

with *Alex Apostolides*
From *Astounding Science Fiction*

"What Thin Partitions," "Sense from Thought Divide," "How Allied," and "Remembrance and Reflection," interconnected stories with a common protagonist, were scattered through two magazines over half a decade. (It is a fair presumption that John Campbell rejected the last one and also *Pawn of the Black Fleet,* a novel with Ralph Kennedy as protagonist, which appeared in *Amazing Stories* in early 1962.) These four stories give some indication of Clifton's stylistic range and unobtrusive self-mockery; the psychologist, after all, is wrong and the Swami *right.* "Sense from Thought Divide" might have been the best-known and most controversial magazine story of its year.

Remembrance and reflection, how allied;
What thin partitions sense from thought divide.

POPE

Even after four years, the changing of the shifts at Computer Research, Inc., fascinated me. Perhaps it was because the plant had grown so fast, fed by the steadily increasing government orders. Perhaps it was seeing the long line of windowless buildings across the grassy square suddenly boil at their base as two thousand employees surged in and out at the sound of the shift bell.

Could be, as personnel director, I liked to speculate on which of those intent or laughing faces would suddenly cease to be an abstract problem and become a real one. Or the other way around; could be I liked to get away from the pile of reports on my desk, and just remind myself by looking at all these people that there could be even more problems than there were.

There could be problems I had never faced before. Could be there were things behind those faces streaming past my window of which

I'd never dreamed. I found myself staring even more intently at the faces, trying to catch a glimpse of such possibilities. But, then, how could we recognize something of which we've never even dreamed? "Is your intercom signal out of order, Mr. Kennedy?" my secretary's voice broke in on my reflections. I turned from the window and looked at her with a start. She was standing in the doorway with that half accusing and half understanding look on her face, so characteristic of her.

"I suppose I just didn't hear it, Sara," I answered. "Or didn't want to hear it," I amended, being honest with her. "What is it this time?"

"A termination," she answered. "P–1, Assembler. Annie Malasek."

I sighed and walked over to my desk. I wasn't in much of a mood to go into my act; it was late in the afternoon and I felt I'd done my day's work already. But it was my job to keep any employee who rated P–1, Production Very Top Class, from leaving us if it were possible. There weren't many who ever got that good, and the few who did were too valuable to entrust to the assistants, interviewers and counselors, in the outer offices.

"O.K., Sara," I agreed. "Send her in."

Sara turned away from my door, and I picked up some papers from my desk and began looking at them. I was above making employees stand and wait while I pretended to be busy; that was a little man's trick. But I wasn't above pretending I was glad to interrupt important work just for them. It was a part of my act which worked—sometimes.

It didn't seem to have much effect on Annie, however. She just stood there in my doorway looking hostile.

"All I want is my check," she said with emphasis.

I smiled a little more and indicated the crying chair with my eyes. She didn't obey my unspoken request. So I spoke it. She still hesitated in the doorway, her training to obedience battling with her independence. Independence won, temporarily.

"All I want is my check," she repeated, and then made the expected mistake. "I ain't here to make trouble for nobody."

"Is that the reputation I've got over in the plant, Mrs. Malasek?" I asked softly, putting the right amount of ruefulness in my voice, shrugging my shoulders a little bitterly. "That nobody wants to talk to me because I'll make trouble?"

It caught her off base, of course, as I'd intended. "No sir," she said hastily, "I didn't mean that."

"Then suppose you sit down," I said firmly, "and tell me what the trouble is." This time obedience won, naturally. She sat down on the edge of the chair and leaned forward. She wasn't committing herself completely, not until she'd got her anger off her chest. They never do. They steam themselves up for days or weeks, and you've got to turn the right pet cocks and let the steam escape gradually, or else they'll blow their top.

She started in with a lot of trivialities and I let her run on for a while. They seldom tell you what's really bothering them—it's too close to them, they're afraid you'll think it is silly. That's where most counselors fall down. They take these surface complaints as being the real issues, and waste all their effort striking at shadows.

"What's really bothering you, Annie?" I asked after a time. I gave her that look which says, "These things you've been talking about are all right to tell other people; but you and I, we know—"

It caught her off base again. As usual, she hadn't intended to tell me the real trouble. And now she had to. She sat back a little into the crying chair, an unconscious admission that I'd won. Two large crystal tears began forming to her black eyes and began to run down her leathery cheeks.

Without making a production out of it, I opened my top drawer and took a clean handkerchief from the stack. I shoved it across the desk at her, without appearing to notice what I was doing. Without appearing to notice what she was doing, she picked it up and dabbed at her cheeks.

"It's about Jennie," she said after a moment's hesitation. She wasn't sobbing. It was just that the tears kept welling up and starting to run down her cheeks before she remembered to wipe them away.

"Jennie?" I prompted.

"My kid," she answered. "She don't get along with the other kids in your nursery."

I winced inwardly as she identified the plant nursey as my personal project. It was. And it was a sore spot, maybe a mistake. I hadn't thought it out very far. It seemed like such a good idea to make provision for care of the small children right there at the plant. But it's one thing to handle employees. It's something else entirely to start handling their children—and do it successfully.

"The teachers neither," she said, and this time her hostility flared up, hotter than ever. Unreason took over again. "I want my check, and then I'm going to march straight down to the Industrial Welfare Commission. They'd be very interested in certain things about certain teachers and certain foremen—"

"What did the teachers do?" I interrupted in a casual tone, just as if her threat to call in the IWC weren't a real one. Once those lovely theorists who learned sociology from a book written by a sociologist who learned things from a book written by—

"They lie about my little Jennie," Annie answered hotly. But her eyes showed she wasn't too sure they were lying. Too plainly they showed dread, uncertainty, guilt, fear.

I picked up my pencil and began twirling it in my fingers. I wasn't ready for her to realize I had looked into her eyes. She had to go through her defensive pattern first, get it out of her system. I kept my eyes on the pencil.

"What kind of lies?" I asked.

"They say I got to take Jennie outta the nursery," she said, her eyes glaring anger. "They say my Jennie ain't good enough to be with other kids."

I knew the teachers in the nursery well. I'd picked them. Considering the jobs they had, they were pretty nice gals. Reasonably practical, too, considering they had degrees in education that were exceptional.

"What do they really say, Annie?" I asked quietly.

"They say they can't manage Jennie," she answered truculently. "They say she throws things." We were getting down to bedrock now. A fond mother defending a spoiled brat, a little monster sweet only to mother's eyes.

"And does she?" I asked, and was so far off the beam I wasn't even braced for the answer.

"She can't help it if things just fly through the air when she gets mad," Annie said defensively. "They always gripe over there because fires start around her. I just get burned up, Mr. Kennedy, when I think about it. She can't help it if she starts fires. Anyway, they're only little ones that really don't hurt anyone."

I kept quiet.

"She don't start the fires because she don't have no matches," Annie said with determined logic. "How could she start fires without no matches?"

"Did it ever happen at home?" I asked.

Annie dropped her eyes and began to twist her fingers around one another in her lap.

"Lately," she said almost soundlessly. "That's why I brought her down to the nursery here. She was all alone in the room we rent. I got nobody but her, nobody to look out for her. I got to work hard all the time."

I had a sudden vision of the stark barrenness of this woman's life. Husband gone, or maybe never had one. Neighbors with their nasty little suspicions kept in a roiling turmoil these days by world conditions, delighting in relieving the monotony of their lives by dark looks, remarks they'd know she'd overhear. A small child, locked in a bare room all day, not playing with the other children, a mother coming home at night too tired to more than feed her.

The picture was all too clear, and nagging somewhere at the back of my mind was a series of case histories of children with similar environments.

"Annie," I said suddenly, "let me look into it. Let me talk to the teachers, get their side of the story. And I'd like to talk to Jennie too, if you don't mind."

The tears welled up faster now, flowed in a steady stream. She dabbed at her eyes and blew her nose with a loud honk. A part of my mind registered that Sara would hear the honk and interpret it as the signal to get the next interview ready. This one was over. The problem had been transferred from the employee to me, as usual. Only this time I wasn't sure yet what the problem was, or whether I could handle it.

"Now suppose you go on over to work, Annie," I said, "and forget about this quitting business. There'll be time to do that later, if I can't help you."

She stood up now and walked toward the door "I'll get a demerit for being absent from my bench too long," she said, as she put her hand on the door. "I've got a P–1 rating. I don't want no demerits." There didn't seem to be much distinction in her mind between her big problems and her little ones.

"I'll sign a slip to your foreman," I agreed, and pulled a pad toward me. Of course I knew the foremen saved these excuse slips to flourish as an alibi when their production slumped; but I'd fight that battle out, as usual, at the next management conference.

Annie walked out the door, holding the white slip aloft as if it were a prize of some sort. Sara stood silently in the doorway until the outer door had closed.

"You took nine minutes on that beef," she said. "You're slipping."

"The union prefers we call them grievances," I said loftily.

"Well, there's another beef waiting," she said pointedly. "And this time it's a beef, because it's one of the scientists, Dr. Auerbach, not a union member."

"No, Sara," I said with exaggerated patience, just as if she weren't the best secretary I'd ever had. "That isn't a beef either. With scientists it's nothing less than a conflict problem. We don't have beefs here at Computer Research."

"Some day I'm going to have just a good old-fashioned beef," Sara said dreamily, "just for the novelty of seeing what's it like to be a human being instead of a personnel secretary."

"Well, while you're trying to work yourself into it, get me little Jennie Malasek out of the nursery," I said dryly.

"It's not enough," she answered tartly, "that you should twist us intelligent, mature adults around your little finger. Now you got to start picking on the little kids."

"Or vice versa," I answered with a sigh. "I don't know which, yet. Send in Dr. Auerbach, and have Jennie waiting. I want to go home sometime tonight. I, too, am human."

"I doubt it," she said, and without closing the door, signaled the receptionist to let in Dr. Auerbach.

Dr. Karl Auerbach walked in with the usual attitude of the technical man; a sort of zoo keeper walking into a den of snakes attitude, determined but cautious. I waved him to the crying chair and refrained from reassuring him that it would not clamp down upon him and start measuring his reflexes.

He was tall, thin, probably not past forty, a little gray at the temples, professionally handsome enough to mislead a television audience into thinking he was a medical doctor on a patent nostrum commercial. In his chemically stained fingers he held a plastic cylinder, oh maybe four inches long by two in diameter. He carried it with both care and nonchalance, as if it were nitroglycerine he just happened to have with him.

"I understand a personnel director handles employee problems of vocational adjustment," he stated carefully after he had seated himself.

I gave him a grave nod to indicate the correctness of his assumption.

"I assume it is handled on an ethically confidential basis," he pursued his pattern faithfully.

Again I nodded, and this time slowly closed my eyes to indicate assent.

"I am unacquainted with how much an employee tells you may remain off the record, and how much your position as company representative requires you place on the record." He was scouting the essential area to determine precisely where he stood.

"The company is liberal," I stated in the hesitant, pedantic tones so approved by technical men. "Everything is off the record until we have the problem with its ramifications. Then . . . ah . . . by mutual agreement, we determine what must be placed on the record."

Apparently it won his confidence. Well, there was no difference between the learned and the unlearned. Each approaches an unknown with extreme caution. Each takes about the same length of time under skilled handling to get to the point. Each throws up a lot of false dummies and loses confidence if you concern yourself with them. Learned or illiterate, anger is anger; frustration is frustration. A problem is a problem, with the complexity of it purely a relative thing. To each is given problems slightly beyond his capacity to handle them adequately.

"I find myself frustrated," he stated flatly.

I still had a long way to go, for that's nothing new. Who isn't?

Slowly and carefully, disposing of each point as it arose, we threaded our way into the snakepit. The essential facts were that he had been employed as a research chemist, placed under Dr. Boulton, head of the experimental department. This, I knew. Instead of being permitted to do the research chemistry for which he had been employed, he had been kept on routine problems which any high school boy could do.

This I doubted, but recognized it as the stock complaint of every experimental research man in industry.

Dr. Boulton was approaching the cybernetics problem on a purely mechanical basis which was all wrong. I began to get interested. Dr. Auerbach had discussed with Dr. Boulton the advisability of a chemical approach to cybernetics. I began to get excited. Dr. Boulton had refused to consider it. Apparently he had *not* been excited.

I knew Dr. Boulton pretty well. As heads of our respective departments we sat in on the same management conferences. We were not particularly friendly. He regarded psychology and all applications of it with more than a little distrust. But more important, I had for a long time sensed a peculiar tension in him—that he was determined to keep human thought processes mysterious, determined not to see more than a narrow band of correlation between the human mind and a cybernetic machine.

I had already determined that Dr. Boulton would outlive his usefulness to us.

"And how would you approach the problem chemically?" I asked Dr. Auerbach.

We had more discussion in which I proved to him that I was top security cleared, that my chemistry was sadly lacking and he would have to speak as though to a layman, that indeed he was not going over his superior's head in discussing it with me, that there was a possibility I might assist if I became convinced enough to convince general management a separate department should be set up. And finally he began to answer my question.

"Let us take linseed oil as a crude example," he said, and waved my offer of a cigarette aside. "Linseed oil, crudely, displays much of the same phenomena as the human mind. It learns, it remembers, it forgets, it relearns, it becomes inhibited, it becomes stimulated."

I don't usually sit with my mouth hanging open, and became conscious of it when I tried to draw on my cigarette without closing my lips.

"Place an open vessel of linseed oil in the light," he instructed, and touched the tips of his two index fingers together, "and in about twenty-four hours it will begin to oxidize. It continues oxidization to a given point at an accelerated rate thereafter, as though finally having learned how, it can carry on the process more easily."

I nodded, with reservations on how much of this could fairly be termed "mental," and how much was a purely chemical process. Then, in fairness, I reversed the coin and made the same reservations as to how much of brain activity could be called a chemical response to stimuli, and how much must be classed as pure thought over and beyond a specialized chemistry. I gave up.

"Put it in the dark," he continued, "and it slows and ceases to oxidize. Bring it back into the light, within a short time, and it immediately begins to oxidize again, as if it had remembered how to do it." He moved to his middle finger. "We have there, then, quite faithful replicas of learning and remembering."

I nodded again to show my willingness to speculate, at least, even if I didn't agree.

"But leave it in the dark for twenty-four hours," he moved to his third finger, "then bring it back into the light and it takes it another twenty-four hours to begin oxidizing again. Now we have an equally faithful replica of forgetting and relearning." He tapped each of his four fingers lightly for emphasis.

"The inhibitions and stimulations?" I prompted.

"Well, perhaps we go a little farther afield for that," he said honestly, "in that we introduce foreign substances. We add other chemicals to it to slow down its oxidization rate, or stop it entirely—inhibitions. We add other substances to speed up the rate, as quick driers in paints. Perhaps it's a little far-fetched, but not essentially different from adrenalin being pumped into the bloodstream to make the brain act at a faster rate. The body has quite a few of these glandular secretions which it uses to change the so-called normal mental processes."

"Where do we go from there?" I asked, without committing myself. But he was not through with his instruction.

"I fail to see any essential difference," he looked me squarely in the eyes, "between a stored impulse in a brain cell, a stored impulse in a mercury tube, a stored impulse in an electronic relay, or for that matter a hole punched in an old-fashioned tabulator card."

I pursed my lips and indicated I could go along with his analogy. He was beginning to talk my language now. Working with its results constantly, I, too, was not one to be impressed with how unusually marvelous was the brain. But I murmured something about relative complexity. It was not entirely simple either.

"Sure, complexity," he agreed. He was becoming much more human now. "But we approach any complexity by breaking it down into its basic parts, and each part taken alone is not complex. Complexity is no more than arrangement, not the basic building blocks themselves."

That was how I approached human problems and told him so. We were getting to be two buddies now in a hot thinking session.

"Just so we don't grow too mechanistic about it," I demurred.

"Let's don't get mystical about it, either," he snapped back at me. "Let's get mechanistic about it. What's so wrong with that? Isn't adding two and two in a machine getting pretty mechanistic? Are we so frightened at that performance we will refuse to make one which will multiply three and three?"

"I guess I'm not that frightened," I agreed with a smile. "We're in the computer business."

"We're supposed to be," he amended.

"So you want time and money to work on a chemical which will store impulses," I said with what I thought was my usual brilliant incisiveness. I began to remember that Sara probably had little Jennie Malasek outside by now, and that was an unfinished problem I had to handle tonight.

"No, no," he said impatiently and rocked me back into my chair, "I've already got that. I wouldn't have come in here with nothing more than just an idea. I've been some years analyzing quantitatively and qualitatively the various chemicals of brain cells. I've made some crude syntheses."

He placed the cylinder on the desk. I looked at the long dark object; I looked particularly at the oily shimmering liquid inside the unbreakable plastic case. It caught the light from my window and seemed to look back at me.

"I want," he continued, "to test this synthesis by hooking it up to a cybernetic machine, shooting controlled impulses through it, seeing what it will store on one impulse and give up on another. I simply want to test the results of my work."

"It will take a little doing," I stuck my neck out and prepared to go to bat for him. "The human mind is not as logical or as accurate as a machine. There are certain previous arrangements of impulses stored in certain brains which will cause the mouth to say 'No!' I'll have to do some rearranging of such basic blocks first."

I was grinning boadly now, and he was grinning back at me.

He got up out of his chair and walked toward my door. "I'll leave the cylinder with you," he said. "I read in a salesmanship course that a prospect will buy much easier if you place the article in his hands."

"What were you doing, studying salesmanship?" I asked, still grinning.

"Apparently it was justified," he said cryptically, and walked out the door.

Sara came to the door and looked in. "You took long enough on that one," she accused.

"It takes a little longer," I said with pedantic gravity, "to lead a scientist to the essential point. He's a little more resourceful in figuring out hazards to keep himself from getting where he wants to go."

But I remembered Auerbach's remarks about salesmanship. "However, in this instance," I mused honestly, "I'm not just sure as to who was leading whom."

"You wanted little Jennie Malasek," Sara said. "You may have her."

I wasn't reassured by the phrasing, the emphasis, or the look on her face.

The time I had lost on the last two interviews, I made up on this one. Children are realists and only poorly skilled in hypocrisy. They will go along with the gag if an adult insists on being whimsical, conciliatory or fantastic, but only because adults are that way and there's nothing they can do about it.

Sara brought Jennie in, gave me a cryptic look, and closed the door behind her as she left.

Jennie stood at the door, a dark little thing, showing some evidence that the nursery teachers had made an attempt to clean her up before sending her over. They hadn't quite succeeded. There was no chocolate around her pinched little mouth, so Sara hadn't succeeded in capturing her either. I wondered why they hadn't combed her black hair, and then realized Jennie might have pulled it down in front of her face for something to hide behind. Her black eyes gleamed as she peered at me through the oily strands.

"Sit in this chair, Jennie," I said casually, and went on being busy with things on the top of my desk. My request wasn't quite a command, but took obedience entirely for granted. It didn't work with Jennie.

She still stood at the door, the toe of one slippered foot on the arch of the other, her thin little legs twisted at an odd angle. Her look was neither defiant nor bashful. Nor was it courage covering fear. I was the nearest source of immediate danger. I should be watched. It was simply that, no more.

I felt I should pity her, that I should warm to her desperate isolation. I was willing to feel sympathy because she did not ask for it, Because ordinarily I admired and liked people who did not accentuate their pathos with calculated fraud.

I found, to my surprise, that I did not like her. Oddly, I felt she knew it. And even worse, I felt that, knowing it, she was not hurt. But at least she did call for respect. Whatever she was, she was sincerely—whatever she was. I would not be a fraud either. I went to the point.

"They tell me, Jennie," I said as matter-of-factly as I could, and I'm experienced at it, "that you throw things and set things on fire."

If I expected either a burst of tears or defiance, I was mistaken. I didn't have time to observe reactions at all.

It was as if a sudden hurricane and earthquake had hit the room at the same time. A desk tray full of papers whizzed by my head; my pen stand crashed through the window back of me; I got a shower of paper clips in the chest; my intercom described an arc and crashed broken into a corner. By the time I had wiped the ashes and tobacco from my ashtray out of my eyes and got them to stay open again, Jennie was gone. Sara was standing in the doorway with a look of consternation on her face.

I was on my way home before I remembered that when Sara and I had cleaned up the mess, I had not remembered picking up Auerbach's little cylinder, his chemical impulse storer. I last saw it laying on the corner of my desk where Auerbach had left it.

Probably Sara had picked it up and put it away. Anyway, the office was within security boundaries. The cylinder would be safe there.

I put it out of my mind, and wondered if the library had a card index classification under the heading of "Poltergeist."

I wasn't much better prepared when I came into my office the following morning. Yes, of course, there was plenty of literature on the subject under such writers as Fort, books on oriental philosophy and the like. Orthodox psychologists had left the subject strictly alone, their attitude apparently being better to ignore the phenomenon than to risk precious and precarious reputation.

Poltergeism, then, remained something which one read about as an obscure, far away thing. I found no handy hints to help when one had it to deal with at first hand, no how-to-do-it books on the subject.

Worse, I found myself with a hangover of uncertainty, indecision. My deft incisiveness was gone. I felt a growing doubt that I had always been as smart as I thought I was.

I shook off the mood as I walked through the outer personnel offices toward my own. No matter how unsure, one must be positive and definite for the sake of the people who depend upon him for some certainties.

Sara had not quite come to the same decision. There was a look of puzzlement on her face when I started through her office toward mine. Uncertainty of whether she should pick up the usual banter as though nothing had happened; or was I really in trouble? I decided to set her mind at rest at least.

"When you picked up last night, after that little wildcat had her tantrum," I greeted her, "did you put away a little plastic cylinder?"

"Why no, Mr. Kennedy," she said and followed me into my office. "I didn't see one."

We looked in the corners of the room, under the desk, behind the chairs. We did not find it. I opened the window where the broken pane had been replaced, and looked out on the ground. It might have followed the pen stand out the window. I did have a vague recollection of something dark flashing by my head just before I got my face full of ashes. There was no cylinder on the ground.

When Sara is puzzled, she has a way of tapping her chin with her finger and looking up at the ceiling.

"Is that what you're looking for?" she asked, and pointed to the corner above my head.

I looked up and saw the cylinder embedded in the broken plaster. Apparently the jagged edges had caught it and kept it from falling. We hadn't noticed it before, because who looks at a ceiling in a familiar room? Apparently the janitors don't look at ceilings, either.

"O.K., Sara, thanks," I dismissed her. "Try to hold the hounds at bay, gal. I've got some thinking to do this morning."

"I shouldn't wonder," she grinned. "Anybody who calls himself a personnel psychologist, and then forces little children to have tantrums in spite of themselves—" The door closed, and saved me the trouble of hearing the completion of her sentence.

Yes, Sara was back on familiar ground. I wished I were.

I dragged a spare straight chair over and stood up on it to get the cylinder. It didn't want to move. Plaster fell around me. The jagged pieces holding it now fell away, and still it didn't move. It gave off the impression of pressing upward against the buttonboard.

I took hold of it and tugged. It came away reluctantly, an identical sensation of lifting a heavy object from the ground, in reverse. It remained heavy, invertedly heavy, as I carried it down and over to my desk.

Habit made me lay it on top of my desk and take my hand away. Habit made me grab for it as it shot upward, just as habit makes me grab for a thing which is falling. This time I put it into a drawer, and held my hand over it to keep it down as I closed the drawer.

I sank back into my chair and hooked my toes under the ledge of the desk. It raised into the air, slowly, buoyantly. I took the pressure of my toes away hurriedly. The desk hovered for a moment, tilted in the air. I put my hand on the top and nervously pressed it back to the floor again. I didn't really expect to hear raps on wood or tin bugles blowing, because I knew it was the cylinder in the drawer which was lifting the desk corner.

There was a very logical explanation of why the desk was trying to float upward. The cylinder was pushing it upward, of course. Yes, very logical. I took one of my nice clean handkerchiefs from another drawer and wiped the sweat off my forehead. There was a logical reason for the sweat, too. I was scared.

"Get me Auerbach," I said to Sara in my new intercom. No doubt it was all over the plant by now that I had smashed my old one in a fit of rage. I settled back into my chair again, and pressed my knees against the desk to keep them from shaking. I shouldn't have done it. The desk bobbed away from me and settled slowly again. I left it there and waited. I sat well away from it, and tried to speculate on what survival factor shaking knees could represent.

Auerbach was not long in arriving. His expression, when he came through the door, was a mixed one of hope I had already got some results for him and touchiness that he should have been summoned like an ordinary employee.

"Take hold of that corner of the desk and lift," I suggested. He looked puzzled, but complied. The desk buoyed upward, this time so strongly that my papers and pen stand slid off to the floor.

"Not so hard, man," I shouted.

"But I barely touched it," he said, incredulously.

I waved him to the crying chair and ignored the accusation written all over his face that I was playing tricks on him. I reached into the desk drawer and pulled out the cylinder. I handed it to him and he took it—from beneath, naturally, to hold it up. It shot up out of his hand and crashed against the ceiling. Plaster fell around him. He spit a sliver of it out of his open mouth as he gazed up at the cylinder.

"Must you be so careless and drop it up?" I snapped.

He didn't answer, and I just let it lay there where it had fallen against the ceiling.

"It isn't particular about what it learns, is it?" I asked, as if there were nothing at all abnormal about the situation.

He brought his eyes away from it and tried to answer, but there was a glaze over his eyes. I noticed his hands begin to shake, and that gave me confidence. My knees had stopped now, with only a small tremor now and then. Auerbach reached over and tugged at the desk corner, but the desk now hugged the floor as if it liked it and refused to budge.

"It doesn't care what it learns, does it?" I repeated. This time he did a better job of trying to come to his senses. His face was a study in attempts to rationalize what he had seen with what he thought he knew. Apparently he wasn't having much luck. But at least he didn't deny what he had seen. I took courage from that. He might prove to be more intelligent than learned after all.

"Let us," I began in a dry classroom manner, "assume, for sake of discussion, that your cylinder can store impulses."

He nodded, as if this were a safe enough assumption. It was a hopeful sign that I was getting through to him.

"It wouldn't know, of itself, which was up and which was down," I pursued.

"Gravity is a real world condition," he started answering now. "Not dependent upon knowledge. It works whether we know it or not."

"Well that's a point which has been debated for the last several thousand years to no conclusion," I disagreed. "But let's take an illustration. Let's formulate a hypothesis, a variant world condition where biologists might know only natural air breathing animals."

He nodded again, a little more of the daze gone from his eyes. He was capable of a hypothesis.

"An entirely different structure of theory and expression of natural laws would be built up from that," I reasoned. "One of these would be the basic law that to be classified as alive a thing must breathe natural air." I pushed the point into my desk top with my finger.

He felt he should object as a matter of principle; should, in scientific tradition, discard the main point in favor of arguing semantics and definitions. That was always safe and didn't require one to think. But I didn't let him escape that easily.

"Now suppose, within that framework, a biologist fished a minnow out of a stream, carried it dry to his laboratory and proceeded to analyze it. You and I know the minnow would die in transit. Now he observes that it does not breathe air, and could not have breathed air down in the water, therefore it does not represent a life form at all. That is his real world condition, isn't it?"

"Yes," he agreed hesitantly. "But there would be so many other evidences that it does represent life. He would have to be extremely stupid not to recognize that his basic rules defining life were wrong."

"Let us concede," I said dryly, "that he is very stupid. But let us be kind. Let us say that it is the entire framework of thought in which he finds himself which is stupid. All his life, he has been educated to this framework. Science and society have weighted him down with immutable laws. To question them would represent nothing less than chaos."

"Yes," he urged me now to go on.

"We come along, you and I, and we operate in a different framework of thought. In our world condition, fish obtain oxygen directly from water. *But we could not prove that to him.*"

"I don't see—"

"Look," I said patiently, "since his base law requires life to breathe air, he would demand, as proof of our contention, that we show it breathing air. We couldn't do it. He will not give up the foundation of his science. We can't prove our claim until he does."

"Stalemate," Auerbach agreed. "But where does that leave us?"

"It leaves us with the conception that there may be any number of frameworks, separated from one another by perhaps the thinnest of partitions, each containing its own set of real world conditions, natural laws, consistent within itself, obeying its own logic, having its own peculiar cause-effect sequences."

"And one of these substitutes down for up?" he asked skeptically.

"Some of the most noted thinkers the world has ever produced contend that the mind is the only reality," I said slowly. "Now suppose we have a child of an ignorant parent. The child has been neglected, left to vegetate alone in its room, never associates with other children, never has the opportunity to learn what our framework of thinking calls natural law, real world conditions. Such a child might formulate for itself a real world matrix quite different from ours."

Auerbach was silent, but looked at me fixedly.

"For one example, it might take things very literally," I said. "It might form natural laws out of slang phrases. The child's mother uses the phrase, 'It just burns me up.' Suppose then the child, when it was vexed, just literally 'burned things up.' Ever hear of a poltergeist?"

"Oh come now, Kennedy," he remonstrated, "that fairy tale stuff."

"There are hundreds of carefully documented case histories," I said, without getting heated about it. "Refusal to look at poltergeist phenomena is on the order of the biologist refusing to consider the minnow alive. Things just catch on fire where these poltergeists are. Things just fly through the air where they are. There must be an explanation. We know that."

"We have some statements to that effect," he corrected.

"We have some statements about what is our own basic natural law, too," I countered. "And that's all we have. Just some statements."

"And such statements apply only within the partitions of the framework?" he asked, neither skeptically nor in agreement. He looked up at the cylinder again. "So your explantion for that is a poltergeist phenomenon?" he mused.

"Yes."

"I wish you had some other explanation," he said. "I don't like that one. Almost any other kind of an explanation would be better."

"So do I," I answered in complete agreement, "but that's the only one I've got. You see, I saw a poltergeist activate it. Apparently the force of her mind, acting on it, stored it with impulses from her own framework of reality. It would not be particular what it learns, so long as what it learns is consistent with the process used in learning it."

He sighed deeply. "I wish that biologist hadn't picked up that minnow," he said, wistfully.

After my secretary had made suitable protocol negotiations with the general manager's secretary, I headed for Old Stone Face's office, Mr. Henry Grenoble, that is. On the way out of my office, I had trouble with my feet. I was almost floating as I walked along, carrying the cylinder. I detoured over by Receiving and surreptitiously weighed myself on the scales. They read thirty pounds.

"Obviously out of order," I found myself giggling, and wondered if the mood had anything to do with my sensation of weightlessness. Suddenly from the odd looks of employees, it occurred to me that I was buoyantly tripping down the corridor on my toes and giggling to myself. I blushed and tried to look stern. It wasn't easy to stride purposefully when you weren't sure your feet were touching the floor. I hoped they wouldn't think I was drunk, or worse.

"Morning, Henry," I said to the general manager, and received his noncommittal nod. I wasn't his fair-haired boy, but neither was I a thorn in his side. We got along all right by mutual and tacit agreement to leave one another alone. It was the regret of his life that such inefficient machines as people had to be used in his plant, and he was glad enough to leave their management to my care.

I walked over to a straight chair, put the cylinder down under its seat, and watched the chair float upward toward the ceiling. Old Stone Face watched it, too.

I had the satisfaction of seeing a slight widening of his eyes, a quick breath, and a slight thinning of his lips. Obviously, he thought it cataclysmic. I pulled the chair down by grabbing hold of one of its legs, and retrieved the cylinder.

I stooped down and placed it under one corner of the desk.

"Lift," I said.

He took hold of the desk corner hesitantly, as if he were reaching for a pen to sign a raise authorization. The desk corner tilted upward and slid some papers off on to the floor. I reached under and pulled out the cylinder. I handed it to him, this time taking care that it didn't shoot out of his hands toward the ceiling. He felt how heavy it was, in reverse. Out of habit, he laid it down on the desk top, but I was ready for that. I grabbed it about two feet up in the air. Too many broken up ceilings would really start gossip in the building maintenance crew.

Old Stone Face reached for it again, and headed for his little private bathroom. I followed him to the door, and watched him step on the scales. He came out, and handed me the cylinder.

"And I've been trying to do it by dieting," he commented. He sat down at his desk and picked up the phone.

"Get me the Pentagon," he commanded. "Yes, sure, the one in Washington. I don't suppose anybody's walked away with that in their pocket yet. The last time I was in Washington it was still there." He put the receiver back on the hook. "She wants to know if

I mean the one in Washington," he commented without expression.
"Now look, Henry," I said warily, "aren't you jumping the gun a little? You haven't asked any questions. You don't know what this is. You don't know how it was made. You don't know any of the scientific principles behind it. You don't know if we've got legal rights to it. You don't know how it works or why."

"Details," he said contemptuously. "You've got it, haven't you? A man made it, didn't he? What a man can make once he can make again, can't he? What do I care about the legal details? We got lawyers, haven't we? What do I care about scientific hows and whys? We got experts, haven't we? Why should I ask questions at all? We got antigravity, haven't we? Don't answer. I know the answers."

They weren't precisely the questions I would have asked, but then, each to his own framework. Then it struck me with a twist of my stomach muscles. I hadn't realized. I'd been so busy thinking about poltergeists and frameworks of different natural law. I'd been thinking in terms of cybernetics, ability to store impulses, even wrong ones.

"Could be antigravity," I agreed in an awed tone.

"What else did you think it was?" he asked.

"I'd rather not say," I murmured.

"Who made it?" he asked.

"Auerbach, partly," I answered.

"Who's he?"

"Research chemist. Works under Boulton."

"Why didn't Boulton bring it to me? Don't answer. Boulton wouldn't believe it would work. What do we keep Boulton around here for? Don't answer. I hired him. Well don't just stand there. Tell Auerbach to get busy. Promote him. Tell him to put them into mass production."

"It's not that simple," I said, and wondered how to tell him.

"Don't give me alibis." His face took on an expression which he apparently hoped was conciliatory. "Ralph, don't you start giving me any of this stall about further research, testing, difficulties, all that folderol. Just put it into production."

"It's a custom made job," I said, trying to slow him down. "Only an experimental model."

"Custom made today, production line tomorrow," he shook his head in exasperation. "Well, what's holding you up?"

"Money, for one thing," I clutched at the first excuse I could think of, and wished it were as simple as that.

He grabbed the phone again.

"Get me the controller," he barked, and waited. "Tim! What took you so long? Give Kennedy all the money he wants!" He listened for a moment and then turned to me. "He wants to know if you'll need more than a hundred dollars. He's got systems, or something." He turned back to the phone without waiting for my reply. "Well," he conceded, "I didn't actually mean *all* the money he wants. Let me know if he draws over a million dollars."

He took the receiver away from his ear and looked at it in puzzlement.

"Must have fainted," he commented dryly, and hung up.

"But," I tried to object, thinking how the organization would be split wide open if I went out into the plant and started carrying out his instructions—all the noses out of joint, the toes stepped on. "I'm just the personnel director. I'm not a plant superintendent. I can't go around building buildings, setting up production lines—even if I knew how."

"Get going," he said. "I don't want any more alibis. All I want is a steady stream of antigravity units. That's not too much to ask for, I'm sure!"

"Maybe a million dollars won't do it," I said hopefully, and truthfully, as I reached for the door.

"Well, all right," he almost shouted. "We'll get a billion, then. We'll get a hundred billion. What do you think we got taxpayers for?"

"You've been spending too much time in Washington," I commented, as I went through the door. "You're beginning to talk like them."

Maybe Old Stone Face hadn't heard about things which money can't buy—such as a little girl who looks at you from behind strings of black hair. Maybe he hadn't heard about frameworks where money wasn't a consideration. Maybe he hadn't heard about a matrix where the question, "If you're so smart, why ain't you rich?" was on the order of the question, "If it's alive, why don't it breathe air?" Maybe he hadn't heard about frameworks, period.

I hoped I wouldn't have to be the one to tell him about them.

Annie Malasek was waiting for me in the outer personnel waiting room. She had little Jennie by the hand. Annie looked stern, Jennie looked penitent. Annie stopped me as I started past her.

"I just came over to tell you, Mr. Kennedy," she began, "I found out what Jennie did to your nice office last night. I whipped her good. Tell Mr. Kennedy you're sorry, Jennie." She looked down at Jennie sternly, and squeezed her hand.

"I'm sorry," Jennie mumbled.

"Tell Mr. Kennedy you won't do it again," Annie went on remorselessly.

"I won' do it again," Jennie repeated dutifully.

"Tell Mr. Kennedy you're going to be a good little girl from now on, and not burn things up or throw things," Annie pursued with a determined gleam in her eye.

"Good girl," Jennie murmured, and rubbed the arch of one foot with the toe of the other.

I looked at them both, and for once I didn't have anything to say.

There were more conferences with Auerbach. Yes, he could produce more cylinders. Some of the synthetic protein strings were a bit tricky, but otherwise it wouldn't be difficult to duplicate the cylinder. No, just an ordinary laboratory would do, at least until we went into mass production. That's nice, he'd always wanted to be a department head. The latter was said absently, and I doubted he had even heard me.

"How are you going to activate the cylinders?" he asked curiously. I noticed the particular use of the second person pronoun, because in everything else it was "we." Activating them was not his responsibility.

There were conferences with Boulton, whose nose was out of joint that Auerbach had been taken out from under his jurisdiction without consulting him about it. For the sake of organization I had to mollify him. There were conferences with the plant superintendent, who could throw all sorts of petty hazards in my way if he were pulling against me. There were conferences with the controller, the carpenter boss. In short there were people, and therefore there were personal tensions to be unsnarled.

There was another conference in Old Stone Face's office, this time with a pink cheeked colonel, sent out as an advance scout from the Pentagon. From the look of him it was the most dangerous scouting mission he had ever tried. His pink cheeks grew red as he watched me go through my act with the antigrav cylinder. His pink cheeks grew purple when I evaded his questions with something approaching idiocy. He was certainly not one I wished to introduce to frameworks and partitions. He was a rocket man, himself.

Auerbach was at that conference, and where I had been idiotic, the good doctor was a glib double talker. He sounded so impressive that it didn't occur to anybody he wasn't making sense.

Since the colonel didn't believe what he saw, and didn't understand what he heard, the brass staff, deployed well back of the front lines, would have got a very poor report from their advance scout had we not been Computer Research and had not Old Stone Face been a frequent visitor to the Pentagon. In this case the colonel was afraid to embroider what he saw with too much of his own opinion. We were duly notified of an impending visitation from a full dress parade of brass and braid. Stirred to unusual action, no doubt, by the plaintive and public outcry of a country-boy Congressman, "But what do all of them *do*, over there in that big building?"

During this time my staff, like good boys and girls, took over the burden of my work without complaint. I spent a great deal of my time in Auerbach's new laboratory.

We tried all sorts of attempts to make the antigrav aspect of the first cylinder rub off on others he had made. We let them lay coyly side by side for hours and days. We lashed the first to another and let it zoom up to the now padded ceiling. We tried shocking them, freezing them, heating them. Nothing worked. Either the new cylinders had already learned that down was down—that old tired framework—or more likely hadn't learned anything at all.

We thought at them. We stood there, Auerbach and I, working singly, working in tandem, thinking at them. Apparently our thoughts didn't amount to much; or we had learned too early in life that you can't get any effect on a physical object by just thinking about it. They just lay there, fat, oily, and inert.

Auerbach went back to his test tubes and beakers, trying to see if antigrav wasn't inherent, somehow, in the chemical arrangements. He had accepted the hypothesis of other frameworks as an intellectual exercise, but he still hoped to prove they were not a reality, that the aspect could be accounted for within the framework he knew. He had not accepted the partitions, that his real world condition was circumscribed, confined, limited.

I went back to Jennie.

Obviously, to me, it was the mental force of her fear, hatred, anger, survival potential, whatever it was, acting through whatever framework she had devised for herself, which activated the first cylinder. So I gave up being stubborn, and called for little Jennie Malasek once more.

She came in the door of my office and stood as she had before. This time her hair was pulled back tightly and tied with a ribbon. So she hid behind a glaze over her eyes, instead.

I had about a dozen of the cylinders on the top of my desk, and had a lot of mixed hope and hopelessness within me. I wondered if the admonishments of her mother had had any basic effect upon her. I wondered if the additional attention she was now getting over in the nursery, since the teachers had learned I had taken notice of her, had changed anything in her.

"I didn't tell your mother on you, when you messed up my office that time," I said as an opening sentence.

She didn't answer, just looked at me impassively. But it did seem that she blushed a little. Had she grown ashamed of throwing things and burning things up?

"Just a secret between you and me," I said. "I don't think it is wrong to throw things the way you did. I think it was very clever."

She didn't answer.

"I wish you would do it again. I'd like to see you do it."

"I can't," she whispered in a very small voice. "I'm a good girl now."

Oh no. Character doesn't change that fast. Maybe she thought she was a good girl, but down underneath—

"I don't think you're a good girl," I said with a sneer. "I think you're a very naughty girl, a nasty little girl."

I hoped, how I hoped she would flare up in anger, or protection, and hurl the cylinders at me. I hoped to get a face full of ashes, and office full of broken windows and flying cylinders.

Her face still did not change its expression. She still stood there, impassive. Her only reaction was two large, crystal tears which formed in the corners of her eyes and began to roll slowly down her cheeks.

I flipped my intercom and called Sara.

"Take her back to the nursery, Sara," I said wearily.

Sara came in, saw the tears, and without speaking to me, she took Jennie's hand and led her away.

I sat at my desk and hated myself with contempt and loathing. There were times when I didn't like my job; when I didn't like myself for being skilled enough to do it. There were times when people became a little more than just some material to be shaped and directed into the best use for it.

But my mood did not last. I had a job to do. This was no time to grow soft, sentimental, wavering.

The fact that Jennie was outwardly changing from the strange little creature which excited no sympathy to a bewildered and hurt little girl who very definitely called for compassion changed the facts not at all.

The prime necessity was to activate more of the cylinders. Jennie was the only means at hand by which that could be done. I wasn't sure that even she could do it, but I had to find out. I had to see if down beneath the surface she wasn't still the same wild instrument of an even wilder talent.

Basic character doesn't change that fast, not just because somebody says it ought to change, not unless there is a violent and traumatic shock jolting the individual completely out of his framework and into another.

I had to go ahead and try.

I spent more, quite a bit more, of the funds at my disposal. The controller O.K.'d my vouchers as if the dollars were individual drops of his blood, and read the legends on the vouchers with a firm conviction that I had really lost my mind.

Old Stone Face asked no questions. He was not one to assign a job to a man and then nag him about the details. He wanted results. But there was puzzlement in his face when he saw no building wings being converted, no assembly lines and moving belts being constructed, no supervisors, cost accountants, production control people assigned to the new work.

Instead, I spent money on animated cartoons, three-dimensional cartoons. A director, experimenting in that new medium, had told me the most difficult job was to keep the action behind the screen, give it depth without illusion that it was projecting out into the audience—to give a stage depth effect without getting a poke in the eye effect.

I wanted the oppostite. I wanted my audience, an audience of one, to get the illusion of a poke in the eye. I caused a special nursery to be built, just for Jennie. I had a studio make a short but elaborate sequence which only one person would view.

I placed Auerbach's total supply of new cylinders in various spots around the room, a dozen or so of them. I had the projectors installed in an adjoining room, and a tiny window, lost in some decoration effects, where I could watch through.

I went to the nursery and got Jennie. She was neither glad nor protesting. The nursery teacher objected a little. Jennie was doing such a fine job of adjusting to the other children now. They had had no more trouble. Apparently all that had been wrong was that Jennie had been starved for attention and affection. But now she was becoming a perfectly normal little girl. Didn't I think so too, Mr. Kennedy? And, are you ill, Mr. Kennedy? You don't look well at all! How kind you are, ill and everything, to think of little Jennie!

I led Jennie out of the nursery over to the new room built especially for her. I did not react. I did not react! I did not react! I could not react, I was one solid mass of self-contempt and loathing.

I put Jennie in the room, wordlessly, and she stood near the door, where I left her. I walked into the adjoining projection room, closed the door behind me, and started punching buttons. It was a form of punishment to make myself walk over to my little window and watch when the automatic machinery took over.

Darkness blotted out the room, then an eerie blue light began to glow over the complex meshes of the screen in front and to the sides of Jennie. Trees, vines, bushes took on form, swayed a little, seemed alive. Knots on the trunks of the trees suggested faces, not kind faces. Limbs and twigs stirred and seemed to reach toward Jennie.

I saw her take a small step backward until she had her back to the door. She turned and pulled at the knob, but the door wouldn't open. She turned back then and faced the growing light, the clearer scene all around her. I saw her lips move stiffly, and though I could not hear her, they seemed to form the words, "Good girl now."

Far in the distance in front of her a deep red glow appeared, took form, part animal, part reptile and even more horrible, part man. Slowly it seemed to become aware of her; its very deliberateness, its sureness was its greatest horror.

The room was a pandemonium then. The cylinders flew through the air toward the trees, toward the monster, crashing through the screen, tearing it to shreds, crashing against the padded walls.

On the floor, in a crumpled heap, lay Jennie. She was still and lifeless. I punched a control button to bring the room back to normalcy, and ran into the room to her. Her heart was beating faintly, her pulse a thin string of fluttering.

I shouted into the hall, "Get a doctor!"

I ran back and began to administer first aid for acute shock. It was not until the doctor came from our hospital room and carried Jennie away that I looked around me.

Most of the cylinders lay on the floor, inert, but five of them pushed against the ceiling at the back of the room. The experiment had been a success!

I went to see Jennie in the hospital room. She had come out of her faint and was sobbing brokenly now. As soon as I came into the room, she reached out her hands, grabbed mine.

"I got scared," she said. "You went away and left me. The lights went out. But I didn't do anything, really I didn't. I just got scared."

The suspicion and anger smoothed out of the faces of the nurse and doctor. Her unaccountable reaction of being glad to see me after what I had done to her, her words seeming to carry a completely normal conviction of what might happen to any imaginative little girl who was afraid of the dark, closed off their possibility of searching into what really happened.

But I knew that I would never use Jennie again, no matter what the urgency for antigravity. Some other way would have to be found. I would not do it again. And I doubted now, after this shock—the surface shock of normal fear, the deeper shock of conflict in using the wild talents which made her a bad girl against the affection she was getting for being a good girl—whether she could ever use her framework again, even if I would.

It had been a severe thing, a terrible thing I had done; but no worse than the methods used constantly in mental hospitals to transfer the minds of patients from one framework to another.

I went back to my office, took the cylinder out of my desk, and sat, holding it in my hands, for a long time.

Through the days that passed I became more distrait, overwhelmed by the insolubility of my problem. My staff still handled the bulk of my work, for it was obvious to them that my interest was far from the petty conflicts and situations of normal plant operation. Department heads became cool toward me, for Sara managed to turn them away before they got in to me.

I wandered the corridors searching faces for some hint of a wild talent beneath the too tame eyes. I thought of advertising for poltergeists in the help wanted columns, and then realized what would happen if some alert reporter happened to pick up the item. I thought of contacting various universities and shuddered at the reception I would get. I even found myself visiting the nursery again, hoping for the improbable coincidence of another poltergeist. But all the little children were being good little fairies and elves and brownies.

The announcement that a full complement of high-ranking military men were going to visit us and assist us in our lagging production of the antigrav cylinders did not reassure me. I had dealt with the military mind, singly and in coveys, before.

I hadn't told Old Stone Face the problem, either. His total framework seemed to consist of "Get out production. Give me no alibis." This was hardly conducive to philosophical meandering.

The day came when staff cars carried generals, admirals, colonels and captains from the airport to our plant. Word filtered over the intercom system that they had been closeted in the big conference room with Stone Face for an hour—apparently playing with the five cylinders.

I hoped they wouldn't scratch the varnish of the big conference table against the ceiling of the room. I hoped they wouldn't try to ride around in buoyant chairs. Learning to balance, doing that, was tricky and if they tilted, a big blob of blubber would find the floor hard and unyielding.

Finally they sent for me.

I left my cylinder locked in my desk and walked up to the conference room under normal gravity, hoping the weight would pull me down to a worried, heavy, lugubrious frame of mind so stylish in the real-world framework.

The conference room was an aroma of dignity, an overpowering impressiveness of brass and braid. Thin faces, fat faces, long faces, squeezed up faces, but Pinky was not there. Apparently he was off on some other dangerous mission. The faces did not, could not, live up to the scrambled eggs and fruit salad of their caps and collars and sleeves and chest.

I thought of Emerson's dissertations on compensation and giggled. What they lacked in those faces they tried to make up for in decorations. I knew that I would not discuss frameworks in this room.

They pressed me for explanations. They bored in deeper and deeper. I could not help it. My mood began to lighten, become irresponsible. I hung on to what dignity I could muster for the sake of the apprehension and alarm in Old Stone Face's eyes. He wasn't such a bad guy. At least he didn't depend on uniforms to make him impressive.

"The first cylinder was an accident," I said to the blur of faces down the long table. "Sometimes accidents are hard to duplicate. So many factors, gentlemen."

"But you did duplicate it," the commanding general pointed out. "You activated five more. We have questioned Dr. Auerbach at length. He knows absolutely nothing of the method you use in activating these cylinders. Apparently no one knows but you. It is imperative that we know."

I was in for it now. I had to explain somehow, or something.

"But, gentlemen," I protested hesitantly, and then heard myself saying, "I spoiled my poltergeist in making this half dozen, and I don't have another."

There was a sigh of relief around the table, relaxation, suppressed contempt. I had not realized before how tense they all were.

"I'm certain," the commanding general said placatingly as if he were trying to reason with a small child, "that it can be replaced."

"They're hard to get," I faltered.

"We will get them," he stated pompously, confidently. "Difficult perhaps for you personally, yes, or even Computer Research." He smiled patiently, "But for the military it is another matter entirely." He turned and waved down the table toward another member of the brass trust.

"General Sanfordwaithe is Supply and Matériel. I am sure it is within the power of the combined armed forces to get you all the whatever-it-is you may need."

I looked down the table at General Sanfordwaithe with a question in my eyes. He looked smugly back at me.

"Do you know what a poltergeist is?" I asked.

He looked slightly piqued.

"I am administrative," he reproved gently and patiently, as only a military man can put a civilian in his place. "I do not pretend to be personally familiar with the specifications of every one of the several million items under my jurisdiction." He smiled, and his voice became almost waggish. "But I am certain you will find our poltergeist division sympathetic to your needs."

That did it.

"Oh goodie," I exclaimed. "Then maybe you'd better send me a half dozen to start with."

"And is that all that's been holding you up?" the commanding general asked, softly reproving.

"And this time, make them little boy poltergeists," I urged. "Mine was a little girl poltergeist, and maybe that was what was wrong—just too delicate for the job."

I could see by their faces they assumed I was talking about some gadget similar to a male and female electrical plug, and was being cute in my terminology.

"Mr. Kennedy hasn't been feeling well lately," Old Stone Face put in hurriedly. "He's been working very hard. Much too hard. I would have sent him on a long rest weeks ago had this not been so urgent."

They looked at me with some pity beneath their contempt—a soft civilian.

From there on it was no more than a diplomatic and tactical withdrawal of forces. I withdrew early, to allow Old Stone Face further time for excuses of my behavior.

But they would be back.

The order would go out from General Sanfordwaithe's office to supply me with a half dozen male type poltergeists immediately. It would flow down through the echelons of command, getting sterner and terser. There would be some scrambling around trying to find the poltergeist division, but no one would become alarmed that it had been lost. That was customary.

There would be days, perhaps weeks when the orders would be pigeonholed, on the theory that if you just forget to do anything about it, the need will pass. But General Stanfordwaithe would not let them forget this time. There would be memorandums, each one dredging a little farther down the chain of command before it, in turn, became pigeonholed.

And finally, somewhere down the line, some clerk would know what a poltergeist was. He would first go to the source books and look it up, so that he could have the paragraphs to substantiate him when he tried to tell his commanding officer what was wanted. From there the explanations would flow back up through the echelons of command. Faces would get redder and redder, angrier and angrier.

Yes, they would be back. But until then, I could go back to being a personnel director. I thought, this time with genuine pleasure, of the simple little problems waiting for me back at my office. Nothing more than imminent strikes, lockouts, legal tangles, visits from the Industrial Welfare Commission, and Miss Jones won't let Miss Smith have a fresh pencil until she brings the stub of her old one to supply room.

I walked on down the corridors of the plant and nodded pleasantly to department heads and key personnel who caught my eye. I saw their faces break with relief, and then grow tart with, "Well, it's about time you came off your high horse and noticed us."

I would have a lot of ruffled feathers to smooth down in the next few days.

Much to their surprise, I spoke pleasantly to the members of my staff when I came into the outer rooms of the personnel department, and ruefully saw them start to dig down into stacks of papers for problems they had been hoarding until I got in a good mood again.

I walked on into Sara's office and quipped something at her. She almost fell out of her chair in astonishment, and began to sniffle. Her feelings had been badly bruised.

"There are handkerchiefs in my desk," I said drily. Her sniffles stopped instantly.

"Now," I said. "Take a letter. General Sanfordwaithe, Pentagon. Confirming our conference of this date, production on the imple-

ment in question will not proceed until your Division of Supply and
Matériel furnishes us with one half dozen, six, male-type poltergeists."

"Are you feeling all right?" Sara interrupted me with wide eyes.

"I feel wonderful," I answered. "I have learned something from
our employees. I have shifted the responsibility for my problem onto
other shoulders. I feel swell!"

"But what if they should supply them to you after all?" she asked.

9/53

Sense from Thought Divide

From *Astounding Science Fiction*

"Remembrance and reflection, how allied;
What thin partitions sense from thought di-
vide."

POPE

When I opened the door to my secretary's office, I could see her
looking up from her desk at the Swami's face with an expression of
fascinated skepticism. The Swami's back was toward me, and on it
hung flowing folds of a black cloak. His turban was white, except
where it had rubbed against the back of his neck.

"A tall, dark, and handsome man will soon come into your life,"
he was intoning in that sepulchral voice men habitually use in their
dealings with the absolute.

Sara's green eyes focused beyond him, on me, and began to
twinkle.

"And there he is right now," she commented dryly. "Mr. Kennedy, Personnel Director for Computer Research."

The Swami whirled around, his heavy robe following the movement in a practiced swirl. His liquid black eyes looked me over
shrewdly, and he bowed toward me as he vaguely touched his chest,
lips and forehead. I expected him to murmur, "Effendi," or "Bwana
Sahib," or something, but he must have felt silence was more
impressive.

I acknowledged his greeting by pulling down one corner of my
mouth. Then I looked at his companion.

The young lieutenant was standing very straight, very stiff, and a
flush of pink was starting up from his collar and spreading around his
clenched jaws to leave a semicircle of white in front of his red ears.

"Who are you?" I asked.

"Lieutenant Murphy." He managed to open his teeth a bare quarter of an inch for the words to come out. "Pentagon!" His light gray eyes pierced me to see if I were impressed.

I wasn't.

"Division of Matériel and Supply," he continued in staccato, imitating a machine gun.

I waited. It was obvious he wasn't through yet. He hesitated, and I could see his Adam's apple travel up above the knot of his tie and back down again as he swallowed. The pink flush deepened into brilliant red.

"Poltergeist Section," he said defiantly.

"*What?*" The exclamation was out before I could catch it.

He tried to glare at me, but his eyes were pleading instead.

"General Sanfordwaithe said you'd understand." He intended to make it matter of fact in a sturdy, confident voice, but there was the undertone of a wail. It was time I lent a hand.

"You're West Point, aren't you?" I asked kindly.

He straightened still more. I hadn't believed it possible.

"Yes, sir!" He wanted to keep the gratitude out of his voice, but it was there. And for the first time, he had spoken the habitual term of respect to me.

"Well, what do you have here, Lieutenant Murphy?" I nodded toward the Swami who had been wavering between a proud, free stance and that of a drooping supplicant.

"According to my orders, sir," he said formally, "you have requested the Pentagon furnish you with one half dozen, six, male-type poltergeists. I am delivering the first of them to you, sir."

Sara's mouth, hanging wide open, reminded me to close my own.

So the Pentagon was calling my bluff. Well, maybe they did have something at that. I'd see.

"Float me over that ash tray there on the desk," I said casually to the Swami.

He looked at me as if I'd insulted him, and I could anticipate some reply to the effect that he was not applying for domestic service. But the humble supplicant rather than the proud and fierce hill man won. He started to pick up the ash tray from Sara's desk.

"No, no!" I exclaimed. "I didn't ask you to hand it to me. I want you to TK it over to me. What's the matter? Can't you even TK a simple ash tray?"

The lieutenant's eyes were getting bigger and bigger.

"Didn't your Poltergeist Section test this guy's aptitudes for telekinesis before you brought him from Washington all the way out here to Los Angeles?" I snapped at him.

The lieutenant's lips thinned to a bloodless line.

"I am certain he must have qualified adequately," he said stiffly, and this time left off the "sir."

"Well, I don't know," I answered doubtfully. "If he hasn't even enough telekinetic ability to float me an ash tray across the room—"

The Swami recovered himself first. He put the tips of his long fingers together in the shape of a swaybacked steeple, and rolled his eyes upward.

"I am an instrument of infinite wisdom," he intoned. "Not a parlor magician."

"You mean that with all your infinite wisdom you can't do it," I accused flatly.

"The vibrations are not favorable—" he rolled the words sonorously.

"All right," I agreed. "We'll go somewhere else, where they're better!"

"The vibrations throughout all this crass, materialistic Western world—" he intoned.

"All right," I interrupted, "we'll go to India, then. Sara, call up and book tickets to Calcutta on the first possible plane!" Sara's mouth had been gradually closing, but it unhinged again.

"Perhaps not even India," the Swami murmured, hastily. "Perhaps Tibet."

"Now you know we can't get admission into Tibet while the Communists control it," I argued seriously. "But how about Nepal? That's a fair compromise. The Maharajadhiraja's friendly now. I'll settle for Nepal."

The Swami couldn't keep the triumphant glitter out of his eyes. He had me.

"I'm afraid it would have to be Tibet," he said positively. "Nowhere else in all this troubled world are the vibrations—"

"Oh go on back to Flatbush!" I interrupted disgustedly. "You know as well as I that you've never been outside New York before in your life. Your accent's as phony as the pear-shaped tones of a midwestern garden club president. Can't even TK a simple ash tray!"

I turned to the amazed lieutenant.

"Will you come into my office?" I asked him.

He looked over at the Swami, in doubt.

"He can wait out here," I said. "He won't run away. There isn't any subway, and he wouldn't know what to do. Anyway, if he did get lost, your Army Intelligence could find him. Give G–2 something to work on. Right through this door, lieutenant."

"Yes, sir," he said meekly, and preceded me into my office.

I closed the door behind us and waved him over to the crying chair. He folded at the knees and hips only, as if there were no hinges at all in the ramrod of his back. He sat up straight, on the edge of his chair, ready to spring into instant charge of battle. I went around back to my desk and sat down.

"Now lieutenant," I said soothingly, "tell me all about it."

I could have sworn his square chin quivered at the note of sympathy in my voice. I wondered, irrelevantly, if the lads at West Point all slept with their faces confined in wooden frames to get that characteristically rectangular look.

"You knew I was from West Point," he said, and his voice held a note of awe. "And you knew, right away, that Swami was a phony from Flatbush."

"Come now," I said with a shrug. "Nothing to get mystical about. Patterns. Just patterns. Every environment leaves the stamp of its matrix on the individual shaped in it. It's a personnel man's trade to recognize the make of a person, just as you would recognize the make of a rifle."

"Yes, sir. I see, sir," he answered. But of course he didn't. And there wasn't much use to make him try. Most people cling too desperately to the ego-saving formula: Man cannot know man.

"Look, lieutenant," I said, getting down to business, "Have you been checked out on what this is all about?"

"Well, sir," he answered, as if he were answering a question in class, "I was cleared for top security, and told that a few months ago you and your Dr. Auerbach, here at Computer Research, discovered a way to create antigravity. I was told you claimed you had to have a poltergeist in the process. You told General Sanfordwaithe that you needed six of them, males. That's about all, sir. So the Poltergeist Division discovered the Swami, and I was assigned to bring him out here to you."

"Well then, Lieutenant Murphy, you go back to the Pentagon and tell General Sanfordwaithe that—" I could see by the look on his face that my message would probably not get through verbatim. "Never mind, I'll write it," I amended disgustedly. "And you can carry the message."

I punched Sara's button on my intercom.

"After all the exposure out there to the Swami," I said, "if you're still with us on this crash, materialistic plane, will you bring your book?"

"My astral self has been hovering over you, guarding you, every minute," Sara answered dreamily.

"Can it take shorthand?" I asked dryly.

"Maybe I'd better come in," she replied.

When she came through the door the lieutenant gave her one appreciative glance, then returned to his aloof pedestal of indifference. Obviously his pattern was to stand in majestic splendor and allow the girls to fawn somewhere down near his shoes. These lads with a glamour-boy complex almost always gravitate toward some occupation which will require them to wear a uniform. Sara catalogued him as quickly as I did, and seemed unimpressed. But you never can tell about a woman; the smartest of them will fall for the most transparent poses.

"General Sanfordwaithe, dear sir," I began, as she sat down at one corner of my desk and flipped open her book. "It takes more than a towel wrapped around the head and some mutterings about infinity to get poltergeist effects. So I am returning your phony Swami to you with my compliments—"

"Beg your pardon, sir," the lieutenant interrupted, and there was a certain note of suppressed triumph in his voice. "In case you rejected our applicant for the poltergeist job you have in mind, I was to hand you this." He undid a lovingly polished button of his tunic, slipped his hand beneath the cloth and pulled forth a long, sealed envelope.

I took it from him and noted the three sealing-wax imprints on the flap. From being carried so close to his heart for so long, the envelope was slightly less crisp than when he had received it. I slipped my letter opener in under the side flap, and gently extracted the letter without, in any way, disturbing the wax seals which were to have guaranteed its privacy. There wasn't any point in my doing it, of course, except to demonstrate to the lieutenant that I considered the whole deal as a silly piece of cloak and dagger stuff.

After the general formalities, the letter was brief: "Dear Mr. Kennedy: We already know the Swami is a phony, but our people have been convinced that in spite of this there are some unaccountable effects. We have advised your general manager, Mr. Henry Grenoble, that we are in the act of carrying out our part of the agreement, namely, to provide you with six male-type poltergeists, and to both you and him we are respectfully suggesting that you get on with the business of putting the antigravity units into immediate production."

I folded the letter and tucked it into one side of my desk pad. I looked at Sara.

"Never mind the letter to General Sanfordwaithe," I said. "He has successfully cut off my retreat in that direction." I looked over at the lieutenant. "All right," I said resignedly, "I'll apologize to the Swami, and make a try at using him."

I picked up the letter again and pretended to be reading it. But this was just a stall, because I had suddenly been struck by the thought that my extreme haste in scoring off the Swami and trying to get rid of him was because I didn't want to get involved again with poltergeists. Not any, of any nature.

Old Stone Face, our general manager, claimed to follow the philosophy of building men, not machines. To an extent he did. His favorite phrase was, "Don't ask me how. I hired you to tell me." He hired a man to do a job, and I will say for him, he left that man alone as long as the job got done. But when a man flubbed a job, and kept on flubbing it, then Mr. Henry Grenoble stepped in and carried out his own job—general managing.

He had given me the assignment of putting antigrav units into production. He had given me access to all the money I would need for the purpose. He had given me sufficient time, months of it. And, in spite of all this cooperation, he still saw no production lines which spewed out antigrav units at some such rate as seventeen and five twelfths per second.

Apparently he got his communication from the Pentagon about the time I got mine. Apparently it contained some implication that Computer Research, under his management, was not pursuing the cause of manufacturing antigrav units with diligence and dispatch. Apparently he did not like this.

I had no more than apologized to the Swami, and received his martyred forgiveness, and arranged for a hotel suite for him and the lieutenant, when Old Stone Face sent for me. He began to manage with diligence and dispatch.

"Now you look here, Kennedy," he said forcefully, and his use of my last name, rather than my first, was a warning, "I've given you every chance. When you and Auerbach came up with that antigrav unit last fall, I didn't ask a lot of fool questions. I figured you knew what you were doing. But the whole winter has passed, and here it is spring, and you haven't done anything that I can see. I didn't say anything when you told General Sanfordwaithe that you'd have to have poltergeists to carry on the work, but I looked it up. First I thought you'd flipped your lid, then I thought you were sending us all on a wild goose chase so we'd leave you alone, then I didn't know what to think."

I nodded. He wasn't through.

"Now I think you're just pretending the whole thing doesn't exist because you don't want to fool with it."

I couldn't argue with that.

"For the first time, Kennedy, I'm asking you what happened?" he said firmly, but his tone was more telling than asking. So I was going to have to discuss frameworks with Old Stone Face, after all.

"Henry," I asked slowly, "have you kept up your reading in theoretical physics?"

He blinked at me. I couldn't tell whether it meant yes or no.

"When we went to school, you and I—" I hoped my putting us both in the same age group would tend to mollify him a little, "physics was all snug, secure, safe, definite. A fact was a fact, and that's all there was to it. But there's been some changes made. There's the co-ordinate systems of Einstein, where the relationships of facts can change from framework to framework. There's the application of multivalued logic to physics where a fact becomes not a fact any longer. The astronomers talk about the expanding universe—it's a piker compared to man's expanding concepts about that universe."

He waited for more. His face seemed to indicate that I was beating around the bush.

"That all has a bearing on what happened," I assured him. "You have to understand what was behind the facts before you can understand the facts themselves. First, we weren't trying to make an antigrav unit at all. Dr. Auerbach was playing around with a chemical approach to cybernetics. He made up some goop which he thought would store memory impulses, the way the brain stores them. He brought a plastic cylinder of it over to me, so I could discuss it with you. I laid it on my desk while I went on with my personnel management business at hand."

Old Stone Face opened a humidor and took out a cigar. He lit it slowly and deliberately and looked at me sharply as he blew out the first puff of smoke.

"The nursery over in the plant had been having trouble with a little girl, daughter of one of our production women. She'd been throwing things, setting things on fire. The teachers didn't know how she did it, she just did it. They sent her to me. I asked her about it. She threw a tantrum, and when it was all over, Auerbach's plastic cylinder of goop was trying to fall upward, through the ceiling. That's what happened," I said.

He looked at his cigar, and looked at me. He waited for me to tie the facts to the theory. I hesitated, and then tried to reassure myself. After all, we were in the business of manufacturing computers. The general manager ought to be able to understand something beyond primary arithmetic.

"Jennie Malasek was a peculiar child with a peculiar background," I went on. "Her mother was from the old country, a Slav. There's the inheritance of a lot of peculiar notions. Maybe she had passed them on to her daughter. She kept Jennie locked up in their room. The kid never got out with other children. Children, kept alone, never seeing anybody; get peculiar notions all by themselves. Who knows what kind of a coordinate system she built up, or how it worked? Her mother would come home at night and go about her tasks talking aloud, half to the daughter, half to herself. 'I really burned that foreman up, today," she'd say. Or, 'Oh, boy, was he fired in a hurry!' Or, 'She got herself thrown out of the place,' things like that.''

"So what does that mean, Ralph?" he asked. His switch to my first name was encouraging.

"To a child who never knew anything else," I answered, "one who had never learned to distinguish reality from unreality—as we would define it from our agreed framework—a special coordinate system might be built up where 'Everybody was up in the air at work, today,' might be taken literally. Under the old systems of physics that couldn't happen, of course—it says in the textbooks— but since it has been happening all through history, in thousands of instances, in the new systems of multivalued physics we recognize it. Under the old system, we already had all the major answers, we thought. Now that we've got our smug certainties knocked out of us, we're just fumbling along, trying to get some of the answers we thought we had.

"We couldn't make that cylinder activate others. We tried. We're still trying. In ordinary cybernetics you can have one machine punch a tape and it can be fed into another machine, but that means you first have to know how to code and decode a tape mechanically. We don't know how to code or decode a psi effect. We know the Auerbach cylinder will store a psi impulse, but we don't know how. So we have to keep working with psi gifted people, at least until we've established some of the basic laws governing psi."

I couldn't tell by Henry's face whether I was with him or far far away. He told me he wanted to think about it, and made a little motion with his hand that I should leave the room.

I walked through the suite of executive offices and down a sound-rebuffing hallway. The throbbing clatter of manufacture of metallic parts made a welcome sound as I went through the far doorway into the factory. I saw a blueprint spread on a foreman's desk as I walked past. Good old blueprint. So many millimeters from here to there, made of such and such an alloy, a hole punched here with an allowance of five ten-thousandths plus or minus tolerance. Snug, secure, safe. I wondered if psi could ever be blueprinted. Or suppose you put a hole here, but when you looked away and then looked back it had moved, or wasn't there at all?

Quickly, I got myself into a conversation with a supervisor about the rising rate of employee turnover in his department. That was something also snug, secure, safe. All you had to do was figure out human beings.

I spent the rest of the morning on such pursuits, working with things I understood.

On his first rounds of the afternoon, the interoffice messenger brought me a memorandum from the general manager's office. I opened it with some misgivings.

Mr. Grenoble felt he should work with me more closely on the antigrav project. He understood, from his researches, that the most positive psi effects were experienced during a seance with a medium. Would I kindly arrange for the Swami to hold a seance that evening, after office hours, so that he might analyze the man's methods and procedures to see how they could fit smoothly into Company Operation. This was not to be construed as interference in the workings of my department but in the interest of pursuing the entire matter with diligence and dispatch—

The seance was to be held in my office.

I had had many peculiar conferences in this room—from union leaders stripping off their coats, throwing them on the floor and stomping on them; to uplifters who wanted to ban cosmetics on our women employees so the male employees would not be tempted to think Questionable Thoughts. I could not recall ever having held a seance before.

My desk had been moved out of the way, over into one corner of the large room. A round table was brought over from the salesmen's report writing room (used there more for surreptitious poker playing than for writing reports) and placed in the middle of my office—on the grounds that it had no sharp corners to gouge people in their middles if it got to cavorting about recklessly. In an industrial plant one always has to consider the matter of safety rules and accident insurance rates.

In the middle of the table there rested, with dark fluid gleaming through clear plastic cases, six fresh cylinders which Auerbach had prepared in his laboratory over in the plant.

Auerbach had shown considerable unwillingness to attend the seance; he pleaded being extra busy with experiments just now, but I gave him that look which told him I knew he had just been stalling around the last few months, the same as I had.

If the psi effect had never come out in the first place, there wouldn't have been any mental conflict. He could have gone on with his processes of refining, simplying and increasing the efficiency ratings of his goop. He would have settled gladly for a chemical compound which could have added two and two upon request; but when that compound can learn and demonstrate that there's no such thing as gravity, teaching it simple arithmetic is like ashes in the mouth.

I said as much to him. I stood there in his laboratory, leaned up against a work bench, and risked burning an acid hole in the sleeve of my jacket just to put over an air of unconcern. He was perched on the edge of an opposite work bench, swinging his feet, and hiding the expression in his eyes behind the window's reflection upon his polished glasses. I said even more.

"You know," I said reflectively, "I'm completely unable to understand the attitude of supposedly unbiased men of science. Now you take all that mass of data about psi effects, the odd and unexplainable happenings, the premonitions, the specific predictions, the accurate descriptions of far away simultaneously happening events. You take that whole mountainous mass of data, evidence, phenomena—"

A slight turn of his head gave me a glimpse of his eyes behind the glasses. He looked as if he washed I'd change the subject. In his dry, undemonstrative way, I think he liked me. Or at least he liked me when I wasn't trying to make him think about things outside his safe and secure little framework. But I wasn't going to stop.

"Before Rhine came along, and brought all this down to the level of laboratory experimentation," I pursued, "how were those things to be explained? Say a fellow had some unusual powers, things that happened around him, things he knew without any explanation for knowing them. I'll tell you. There were two courses open to him. He could express it in the semantics of spiritism, or he could admit to witchcraft and sorcery. Take your pick; those were the only two systems of semantics available to him.

"We've got a third one now—parapsychology. If I had asked you to attend an experiment in parapsychology, you'd have agreed at once. But when I ask you to attend a seance, you balk! Man, what difference does it make what we call it? Isn't it up to us to investigate the evidence wherever we find it? No matter what kind of semantic debris it's hiding in?"

Auerbach shoved himself down off the bench, and pulled out a beat-up package of cigarettes.

"All right, Kennedy," he said resignedly, "I'll attend your seance."

The other invited guests were Sara, Lieutenant Murphy, Old Stone Face, myself, and, of course, the Swami. This was probably not typical of the Swami's usual audience composition.

Six chairs were placed at even intervals around the table. I had found soft white lights overhead to be most suitable for my occasional night work, but the Swami insisted that a blue light, a dim one, was most suitable for his night work.

I made no objection to that condition. One of the elementary basics of science is that laboratory conditions may be varied to meet the necessities of the experiment. If a red-lighted darkness is necessary to an operator's successful development of photographic film, then I could hardly object to a blue-lighted darkness for the development of the Swami's effects.

Neither could I object to the Swami's insistance that he sit with his back to the true North. When he came into the room, accompanied by Lieutenant Murphy, his thoughts seemed turned in upon himself, or wafted somewhere out of this world. He stopped in midstride, struck an attitude of listening, or feeling, perhaps, and slowly shifted his body back and forth.

"Ah," he said at last, in a tone of satisfaction, "there is the North!"

It was, but this was not particularly remarkable. There is no confusing maze of hallways leading to the Personnel Department from the outside. Applicants would be unable to find us if there were. If he had got his bearings out on the street, he could have managed to keep them.

He picked up the nearest chair with his own hands and shifted it so that it would be in tune with the magnetic lines of Earth. I couldn't object. The Chinese had insisted upon such placement of household articles, particularly their beds, long before the Earth's magnetism had been discovered by science. The birds had had their directionfinders attuned to it, long before there was man.

Instead of objecting, the lieutenant and I meekly picked up the table and shifted it to the new position. Sara and Auerbach came in as we were setting the table down. Auerbach gave one quick look at the Swami in his black cloak and nearly white turban, and then looked away.

"Remember semantics," I murmured to him, as I pulled out Sara's chair for her. I seated her to the left of the Swami. I seated Auerbach to the right of him. If the lieutnant was, by chance, in cahoots with the Swami, I would foil them to the extent of not letting them sit side by side at least. I sat down at the opposite side of the table from the Swami. The lieutenant sat down between me and Sara.

The general manager came through the door at that instant, and took charge immediately.

"All right now," Old Stone Face said crisply, in his low, rumbling voice, "no fiddle faddling around. Let's get down to business."

The Swami closed his eyes.

"Please be seated," he intoned to Old Stone Face. "And now, let us all join hands in an unbroken circle."

Henry shot him a beetlebrowed look as he sat down between Auerbach and me, but at least he was cooperative to the extent that he placed both his hands on top of the table. If Auerbach and I reached for them, we would be permitted to grasp them.

I leaned back and snapped off the overhead light to darken the room in an eerie, blue glow.

We sat there, holding hands, for a full ten minutes. Nothing happened.

It was not difficult to estimate the pattern of Henry's mind. Six persons, ten minutes, equals one man-hour. One man-hour of idle time to be charged into the cost figure of the antigrav unit. He was staring fixedly at the cylinders which lay in random positions in the center of the table, as if to assess their progress at this processing point. He stirred restlessly in his chair, obviously dissatisfied with the efficiency rating of the manufacturing process.

The Swami seemed to sense the impatience, or it might have been coincidence.

"There is some difficulty," he gasped in a strangulated, high voice. "My guides refuse to come through."

"Harrumph!" exclaimed Old Stone Face. It left no doubt about what *he* would do if *his* guides did not obey orders on the double.

"Someone in this circle is not a True Believer!" the Swami accused in an incredulous voice.

In the dim blue light I was able to catch a glimpse of Sara's face. She was on the verge of breaking apart. I managed to catch her eye and flash her a stern warning. Later she told me she had interpreted my expression as stark fear, but it served the same purpose. She smothered her laughter in a most unladylike sound somewhere between a snort and a squawk.

The Swami seemed to become aware that somehow he was not holding his audience spellbound.

"Wait!" he commanded urgently; then he announced in awe-stricken tones, "I feel a presence!"

There was a tentative, half-hearted rattle of some castanets—which could have been managed by the Swami wiggling one knee, if he happened to have them concealed there. This was followed by the thin squawk of a bugle—which could have been accomplished by sitting over toward one side and squashing the air out of a rubber bulb attached to a ten-cent party horn taped to his thigh.

Then there was nothing. Apparently his guides had made a tentative appearance and were, understandably, completely intimidated by Old Stone Face. We sat for another five minutes.

"Harrumph!" Henry cleared his throat again, this time louder and more commanding.

"That is all," the Swami said in a faint, exhausted voice. "I have returned to you on your material plane."

The handholding broke up in the way bits of metal, suddenly charged positive and negative, would fly apart. I leaned back again and snapped on the white lights. We all sat there a few seconds, blinking in what seemed a sudden glare.

The Swami sat with his chin dropped down to his chest. Then he raised stricken, liquid eyes.

"Oh, now I remember where I am," he said. "What happened? I never know."

Old Stone Face threw him a look of withering scorn. He picked up one of the cylinders and hefted it in the palm of his hand. It did not fly upward to bang against the ceiling. It weighed about what it ought to weigh. He tossed the cylinder, contemptuously, back into the pile, scattering them over the table. He pushed back his chair, got to his feet, and stalked out of the room without looking at any of us.

The Swami made a determined effort to recapture the spotlight.

"I'm afraid I must have help to walk to the car," he whispered. "I am completely exhausted. Ah, this work takes so much out of me. Why do I go on with it? Why? Why? Why?

He drooped in his chair, then made a valiantly brave effort to rise under his own power when he felt the lieutenant's hands lifting him up. He was leaning heavily on the lieutenant as they went out the door.

Sara looked at me dubiously.

"Will there be anything else?" she asked. Her tone suggested that since nothing had been accomplished, perhaps we should get some work out before she left.

"No, Sara," I answered. "Good night. See you in the morning."

She nodded and went out the door.

Apparently none of them had seen what I saw. I wondered if Auerbach had. He was a trained observer. He was standing beside the table looking down at the cylinders. He reached over and poked at one of them with his forefinger. He was pushing it back and forth. It gave him no resistance beyond normal inertia. He pushed it a little farther out of parallel with true North. It did not try to swing back.

So he had seen it. When I'd laid the cylinders down on the table they were in random positions. During the seance there had been no jarring of the table, not even so much as a rap or quiver which could have been caused by the Swami's lifted knee. When we'd shifted the table, after the Swami had changed his chair, the cylinders hadn't been disturbed. When Old Stone Face had been staring at them during the seance—seance?, hah!—they were lying in inert, random positions.

But when the lights came back on, and just before Henry had picked one up and tossed it back to scatter them, every cylinder had been laid in orderly parallel—and with one end pointing to true North!

I stood there beside Auerbach, and we both poked at the cylinders some more. They gave us no resistance, nor showed that they had any ideas about it one way or the other.

"It's like so many things," I said morosely. "If you do just happen to notice anything out of the ordinary at all, it doesn't seem to mean anything."

"Maybe that's because you're judging it outside of its own framework," Auerbach answered. I couldn't tell whether he was being sarcastic or speculative. "What I don't understand," he went on, "is that once the cylinders having been activated by whatever force there was in action—all right, call it psi—well, why didn't they retain it, the way the other cylinders retained the antigrav force?"

I thought for a moment. Something about the conditional setup seemed to give me an idea.

"You take a photographic plate," I reasoned. "Give it a weak exposure to light, then give it a strong blast of overexposure. The first exposure is going to be blanked out by the second. Old Stone Face was feeling pretty strongly toward the whole matter."

Auerbach looked at me, unbelieving.

There isn't any rule about who can have psi talent," I argued. "I'm just wondering if I shouldn't wire General Sanfordwaithe and tell him to cut our order for poltergeists down to five."

I spent a glum, restless night. I knew, with certainty, that Old Stone Face was going to give me trouble. I didn't need any psi talent for that; it was an inevitable part of his pattern. He had made up his mind to take charge of this antigrav operation, and he wouldn't let one bogus seance stop him more than momentarily.

If it weren't so close to direct interference with my department, I'd have been delighted to sit on the side lines and watch him try to command psi effects to happen. That would be like commanding some random copper wire and metallic cores to start generating electricity.

For once I could have overlooked the interference with my department if I didn't know, from past experience, that I'd be blamed for the consequent failure. And there was something else, too; I had the feeling that if I were allowed to go along, carefully and experimentally, I just might discover a few of the laws about psi. There was the tantalizing feeling that I was on the verge of knowing at least something.

The Pentagon people had been right. The Swami was an obvious phony of the baldest fakery, yet he had something. He had something, but how was I to get hold of it? Just what kind of turns with what around what did you make to generate a psi force? It took two thousand years for man to move from the concept that amber was a stone with a soul to the concept of static electricity. Was there any chance I could find some shortcuts in reducing the laws governing psi? The one bright spot of my morning was that Auerbach hadn't denied seeing the evidence of the cylinders pointing North.

It turned out to be the only bright spot. I had no more than got to my office and sorted out the routine urgencies from those which had to be handled immediately, when Sara announced the lieutenant and the Swami. I put everything else off, and told her to send them right in.

The Swami was in an incoherent rage. The lieutenant was contracting his eyebrows in a scowl and clenching his fists in frustration.

In a voice, soaring into the falsetto, the Swami demanded that he be sent back to Brooklyn where he was appreciated. The lieutenant had orders to stay with the Swami, but he didn't have any orders about returning either to Brooklyn or the Pentagon. I managed, at last, to get the lieutenant seated in a straight chair, but the Swami couldn't stay still long enough. He stalked up and down the room, swirling his slightly odorous black cloak on the turns. Gradually the story came out.

Old Stone Face, a strong advocate of Do It Now, hadn't wasted any time. From his home he had called the Swami at his hotel and commanded him to report to the general manager's office at once. They all got there about the same time, and Henry had waded right in.

Apparently Henry, too, had spent a restless night. He accused the Swami of inefficiency, bungling, fraud, deliberate insubordination, and a few other assorted faults for having made a fool out of us all at the seance. He'd as much as commanded the Swami to cut out all the shilly-shallying and get down to the business of activating anti-grav cycliners, or else. He hadn't been specific about what the "or else" would entail.

"Now I'm sure he really didn't mean—" I began to pour oil on the troubled waters. "With your deep insight, Swami—The fate of great martyrs throughout the ages—" Gradually the ego-building phrases calmed him down. He grew willing to listen, if for no more than the anticipation of hearing more of them.

He settled down into the crying chair at last, his valence shifting from outraged anger to a vast and noble forgiveness. This much was not difficult. To get him to cooperate, consciously and enthusiastically, might not be so easy.

Each trade has its own special techniques. The analytical chemist has a series of routines he tries when he wishes to reduce an unknown compound to its constituents. To the chemically uneducated, this may appear to be a fumbling, hit or miss, kind of procedure. The personnel man, too, has his series of techniques, which may appear to be no more than random, pointless conversation.

I first tried the routine process of reasoning. I didn't expect it to work; it seldom does, but it can't be eliminated until it has been tested.

"You must understand," I said slowly, soothingly, "that our intentions are constructive. We are simply trying to apply the scientific method to something which has, heretofore, been wrapped in mysticism."

The shocked freezing of his facial muscles gave me the answer to that.

"Science understands nothing, nothing at all!" he snapped. "Science tries to reduce everything to test tubes and formulae; but I am the instrument of a mystery which man can never know."

"Well, now," I said reasonably. "Let us not be inconsistent. You say this is something man was not meant to know; yet you, yourself, have devoted your life to gaining a greater comprehension of it."

"I seek only to rise above my material self so that I might place myself in harmony with the flowing symphony of Absolute Truth," he lectured me sonorously. The terminology didn't bother me; the jargon of the sciences sometimes grows just as esoteric. Maybe it even meant something.

One thing I was sure it meant. There are two basic approaches to the meaning of life and the universe about us. Man can know: That is the approach of science, its whole meaning. There are mysteries which man was not meant to know: That is the other approach. There is no reconciling of the two on a reasoning basis. I represented the former. I wasn't sure the Swami was a true representative of the latter, but at least he had picked up the valence and the phrases.

I made a mental note that reasoning was an unworkable technique with this compound. Henry, a past master at it, had already tried threats and abuse. That hadn't worked. I next tried one of the oldest forms in the teaching of man, a parable.

I told him of my old Aunt Dimity, who was passionately fond of rummy, but considered all other card games sinful.

"Ah, how well she proves my point," the Swami countered. "There is an inner voice, a wisdom greater than the mortal mind to guide us—"

"Well now," I asked reasonably, "why would the inner voice say that rummy was O.K., but casino wasn't?" But it was obvious he liked the point he had made better than he had liked the one I failed to make.

So I tried the next technique. Often an opponent will come over to your side if you just confess, honestly, that he is a better man than you are, and you need his help. What was the road I must take to achieve the same understanding he had? His eyes glittered at that.

"First there is fasting, and breathing, and contemplating self," he murmured mendaciously. "I would be unable to aid you until you gave me full ascendancy over you, so that I might guide your every thought—"

I decided to try inspiration.

"Do you realize, Swami," I asked, "that the one great drawback throughout the ages to a full acceptance of psi is the lack of permanent evidence? It has always been evanescent, perishable. It always rests solely upon the word of witnesses. But if I could show you a film print, then you could not doubt the existence of photography, could you?''

I opened my lower desk drawer and pulled out a couple of the Auerbach cylinders which we had used the night before. I laid them on top of the desk.

"These cylinders," I said, "act like the photographic film. They will record, in permanent form, the psi effects you command. At last, for all mankind the doubt will be stilled; man will at once know the truth; and you will take your place among the immortals."

I thought it was pretty good. It should have done the trick. But the Swami was staring at the cylinders first in fascination, then fear, then in horror. He jumped to his feet, without bothering to swirl his robe majestically, rushed over to the door, fumbled with the knob as if he were in a burning room, managed to get the door open, and rushed outside. The lieutenant gave me a puzzled look, and went after him.

I drew a deep breath, and exhaled it audibly. My testing procedures hadn't produced the results I'd expected, but the last one had revealed something else—or rather, had confirmed two things we knew already.

One: The Swami believed himself to be a fraud.

Two: He wasn't.

Both cylinders were pointing toward the door. I watched them, at first not quite sure; like the Swami, I'd have preferred not to believe the evidence. But the change in their perspective with the angles of the desk made the motion unmistakable.

Almost as slowly as the minute hand of a watch, they were creeping across the desk toward the door. They, too, were trying to escape from the room.

I nudged them with my fingers. They hustled along a little faster, as if appreciative of the help, even coming from me. I saw they were moving faster, as if they were learning as they tried it. I turned one of them around. Slowly it turned back and headed for the door again. I lifted one of them down to the floor. It had no tendency to float, but it kept heading for the door. The other one fell off the desk while I was fooling with the first one. The jar didn't seem to bother it any. It, too, began to creep across the rug toward the door.

I opened the door for them. Sara looked up. She saw the two cylinders come into view, moving under their own power.

"Here we go again," she said, resignedly.

The two cylinders pushed themselves over the door sill, got clear outside my office. Then they went inert. Both Sara and I tried nudging them, poking them. They just lay there; mission accomplished. I carried them back inside my office and lay them on the floor. Immediately both of them began to head for the door again.

"Simple," Sara said dryly, "they just can't stand to be in the same room with you, that's all."

"You're not just whistling, gal," I answered. "That's the whole point."

"Have I said something clever?" she asked seriously.

I took the cylinders back into my office and put them in a desk drawer. I watched the desk for a while, but it didn't change position. Apparently it was too heavy for the weak force activating the cylinders.

I picked up the phone and called Old Stone Face. I told him about the cylinders.

"There!" he exclaimed with satisfaction. "I knew all that fellow needed was a good old-fashioned talking to. Some day, my boy, you'll realize that you still have a lot to learn about handling men."

"Yes, sir," I answered.

At that, Old Stone Face had a point. If he hadn't got in and riled things up, maybe the Swami would not have been emotionally upset enough to generate the psi force which had activated these new cylinders.

Did that mean that psi was linked with emotional upheaval? Well, maybe. Not necessarily, but Rhine had proved that strength of desire had an effect upon the frequency index of telekinesis.

Was there anything at all we knew about psi, so that we could start cataloguing, sketching in the beginnings of a pattern? Yes, of course there was.

First, it existed. No one could dismiss the mountainous mass of evidence unless he just refused to think about the subject.

Second, we could, in time, know what it was and how it worked. You'd have to give up the entire basis of scientific attitude if you didn't admit that.

Third, it acted like a sense, rather than as something dependent upon the intellectual process of thought. You could, for example—I argued to my imaginary listener—command your nose to smell a rose, and by autosuggestion you might think you were succeeding; that is, until you really did smell a real rose, then you'd know that you'd failed to create it through a thought pattern. The sense would have to be separated from the process of thinking about the sense.

So what was psi? But, at this point, did it matter much? Wasn't the main issue one of learning how to produce it, use it? How long did we work with electricity and get a lot of benefits from it before we formed some theories about what it was? And, for that matter, did we know what it was, even yet? "A flow of electrons" was a pretty meaningless phrase, when you stopped to think about it. I could say psi was a flow of psitrons, and it would mean as much.

I reached over and picked up a cigarette. I started fumbling around in the center drawer of my desk for a matchbook. I didn't find any. Without thinking, I opened the drawer containing the two cylinders. They were pressing up against the side of the desk drawer, still trying to get out of the room. Single purposed little beasts, weren't they?

I closed the drawer, and noticed that I was crushing out my cigarette in the ash tray, just as if I'd smoked it. My nerves weren't all they should be this morning.

Which brought up the fourth point, and also took me right back to where I started.

Nerves. . . .

Emotional upheavals.

Rhine's correlations between interest, belief, and ability to perform. . . .

It seemed very likely that a medium such as the Swami, whose basic belief was There Are Mysteries, would be unable to function in a framework where the obvious intent was to unveil those mysteries!

That brought up a couple more points. I felt pretty sure of them. I felt as if I were really getting somewhere. And I had a situation which was ideal for proving my points.

I flipped the intercom key, and spoke to Sara.

"Will you arrange with her foreman for Annie Malasek to come to my office right now?" I asked. Sara is flippant when things are going along all right, but she knows when to buckle down and do what she's asked. She gave me no personal reactions to this request.

Yes, Annie Malasek would be a good one. If anybody in the plant believed There Are Mysteries, it would be Annie. Further, she was exaggeratedly loyal to me. She believed I was responsible for turning her little Jennie, the little girl who'd started all this poltergeist trouble, into a Good Little Girl. In this instance, I had no qualms about taking advantage of that loyalty.

While I waited for her I called the lieutenant at his hotel. He was in. Yes, the Swami was also in. They'd just returned. Yes, the

Swami was ranting and raving about leaving Los Angeles at once. He had said he absolutely would have nothing more to do with us here at Computer Research. I told Lieutenant Murphy to scare him with tales of the secret, underground working of Army Intelligence, to quiet him down. And I scared the lieutenant a little by pointing out that holding a civilian against his will without the proper writ was tantamount to kidnaping. So if the Army didn't want trouble with the Civil Courts, all brought about because the lieutenant didn't know how to handle his man—

The lieutenant became immediately anxious to cooperate with me. So then I soothed him. I told him that, naturally, the Swami was unhappy. He was used to Swamiing, and out here he had been stifled, frustrated. What he needed was some credulous women to catch their breath at his awe-inspiring insight and gaze with fearful rapture into his eyes. The lieutenant didn't know where he could find any women like that. I told him, dryly, that I would furnish some.

Annie was more than cooperative. Sure, the whole plant was buzzing about that foreign-looking Swami who had been seen coming in and out of my office. Sure, a lot of the Girls believed in seances.

"Why? Don't you, Mr. Kennedy?" she asked curiously.

I said I wasn't sure, and she clucked her tongue in sympathy. It must be terrible not to be sure, so . . . well, it must be just terrible. And I was such a kind man, too . . .

But when I asked her to go to the hotel and persuade the Swami to give her a reading, she was reluctant. I thought my plan was going to be frustrated, but it turned out that her reluctance was only because she did not have a thing to wear, going into a high-toned place like that.

Sara wasn't the right size, but one of the older girls in the outer office would lend Annie some clothes if I would let her go see the Swami, too. It developed that her own teacher was a guest of Los Angeles County for a while, purely on a trumped-up charge, you understand, Mr. Kennedy. Not that she was a cop hater or anything like that. She was perfectly aware of what a fine and splendid job those noble boys in blue did for us all, but—

In my own office! Well, you never knew.

Yet, what was the difference between her and me? We were both trying to get hold of and benefit by psi effects, weren't we?

And the important thing was that we could combine our efforts to our mutual advantage. My interviewer's teacher had quite a large following, and now they were all at loose ends. If the Swami were willing, she could provide a large and ready-made audience for him. She would be glad to talk to him about it.

Annie hurriedly said that she would be glad to talk to him about it, too; that she could get up a large audience, too. So, even before it got started, I had my rival factions at work. I egged them both on, and promised that I'd get Army Intelligence to work with the local boys in blue to hold off making any raids.

Annie told me again what a kind man I was. My interviewer spoke up quickly and said how glad she was to find an opportunity for expressing how grateful she was for the privilege of working right in the same department with such an understanding, really intellectually developed adult. She eyed Annie sidelong, as if to gauge the effects of her attempts to set me up on a pedestal, out of Annie's reach.

I hoped I wouldn't start believing either one of them. I hoped I wasn't as inaccurate in my estimates of people as was my interviewer. I wondered if she were really qualified for the job she held. Then I realized this was a contest between two women and I, a mere male, was simply being used as the pawn. Well, that worked both ways. In a fair bargain both sides receive satisfaction. I felt a little easier about my tactical maneuvers.

But the development of rivalry between factions of the audience gave me an additional idea. Perhaps that's what the Swami really needed, a little rivalry. Perhaps he was being a little too hard to crack because he knew he was the only egg in the basket.

I called Old Stone Face and told him what I planned. He responded that it was up to me. He'd stepped in and got things under way for me, got things going, now it was my job to keep them going. It looked as if he were edging out from under—or maybe he really believed that.

Before I settled into the day's regular routine, I wired General Sanfordwaithe, and told him that if he had any more prospects ready would he please ship me one at once, via air mail, special delivery.

The recital hall, hired for the Swami's Los Angeles debut, was large enough to accommodate all the family friends and relatives of any little Maribel who, having mastered "Daffodils In May," for four fingers, was being given to the World. It had the usual small stage equipped with pull-back curtains to give a dramatic flourish, or to shut off from view the effects of any sudden nervous catastrophe brought about by stage fright.

I got there, purposely a little late, in hopes the house lights would already be dimmed and everything in progress; but about a hundred and fifty people were milling around outside on the walk and in the corridors. Both factions had really been busy.

Most of them were women, but, to my intense relief, there were a few men. Some of these were only husbands, but a few of the men wore a look which said they'd been far away for a long time. Somehow I got the impression that instead of looking into a crystal ball, they would be more inclined to look out of one.

It was a little disconcerting to realize that no one noticed me, or seemed to think I was any different from anybody else. I supposed I should be thankful that I wasn't attracting any attention. I saw my interviewer amid a group of Older Girls. She winked at me roguishly, and patted her heavy handbag significantly. As per instructions, she was carrying a couple of the Auerbach cylinders.

I found myself staring in perplexity for a full minute at another woman, before I realized it was Annie. I had never seen her before, except dressed in factory blue jeans, man's blue shirt, and a bandanna wrapped around her head. Her companion, probably another of the factory assemblers, nudged her and pointed, not too subtly, in my direction. Annie saw me then, and lit up with a big smile. She started toward me, hesitated when I frowned and shook my head, flushed with the thought that I didn't want to speak to her in public; then got a flash of better sense than that. She, too, gave me a conspiratorial wink and patted her handbag.

My confederates were doing nicely.

Almost immediately thereafter a horsefaced, mustached old gal started rounding people up in a honey-sweet, pear-shaped voice; and herded them into the auditorium. I chose one of the wooden folding chairs in the back row.

A heavy jowled old gal came out in front of the closed curtains and gave a little introductory talk about how lucky we all were that the Swami had consented to visit with us. There was the usual warning to anyone who was not of the esoteric that we must not expect too much, that sometimes nothing at all happened, that true believers did not attend just to see effects. She reminded us kittenishly that the guides were capricious, and that we must all help by merging ourselves in the great flowing currents of absolute infinity.

She finally faltered, realized she was probably saying all the thinge the Swami would want to say—in the manner of people who introduce speakers everywhere—and with a girlish little flourish she waved at someone off stage.

The house lights dimmed. The curtains swirled up and back.

The Swami was doing all right for himself. He was seated behind a small table in the center of the stage. A pale violet light diffused through a huge crystal ball on the table, and threw his dark features into sharp relief. It gave an astonishly remote and inscrutable wisdom to his features. In the pale light, and at this distance, his turban looked quite clean.

He began to speak slowly and sonorously. A hush settled over the audience, and gradually I felt myself merging with the mass reaction of the rest. As I listened, I got the feeling that what he was saying was of tremendous importance, that somehow his words contained great and revealing wonders—or would contain them if I were only sufficiently advanced to comprehend their true meanings. The man was good, he knew his trade. All men search for truth at one level or another. I began to realize why such a proportionate few choose the cold and impersonal laboratory. Perhaps if there were a way to put science to music—

The Swami talked on for about twenty minutes, and then I noticed his voice had grown deeper and deeper in tone, and suddenly, without any apparent transition, we all knew it was not really the Swami's voice we were hearing. And then he began to tell members of the audience little intimate things about themselves, things which only they should know.

He was good at this, too. He had mastered the trick of making universals sound like specifics. I could do the same thing. The patterns of people's lives have multiple similarities. To a far greater extent than generally realized the same things happen to everyone. The idea was to take some of the lesser known ones and word them so they seemed to apply to one isolated individual.

For instance, I could tell a fellow about when he was a little boy there was a little girl in a red dress with blond pigtails who used to scrap with him and tattle things about him to her mother. If he were inclined to be credulous, this was second sight I had. But it is a universal. What average boy didn't, at one time or another, know a little girl with blond pigtails? What blond little girl didn't occasionally wear a red dress? What little girl didn't tattle to her mother about the naughty things the boys were doing?

The Swami did that for a while. The audience was leaning forward in a rapture of ecstasy. First the organ tones of his voice soothed and softened. The phrases which should mean something if only you had the comprehension. The universals applied as specifics. He had his audience in the palm of his hand. He didn't need his crystal ball to tell him that.

But he wanted it to be complete. Most of the responses had been from women. He gave them the generalities which didn't sound like generalities. They confirmed with specifics. But most were women. He wanted the men, too. He began to concentrate on the men. He made it easy.

"I have a message," he said. "From . . . now let me get it right . . . from R. S. It is for a man in this audience. Will the man who knew R. S. acknowledge?"

There was a silence. And that was such an easy one, too. I hadn't planned to participate, but, on impulse, since none of the other men were cooperating, I spoke up.

"Robert Smith!" I exclaimed. "Good old Bob!"

Several of the women sitting near me looked at me and beamed their approval. One of the husbands scowled at me.

"I can tell by your tone," the Swami said, and apparently he hadn't recognized my tone, "that you have forgiven him. That is the message. He wants you to know that he is happy. He is much wiser now. He knows now that he was wrong."

One of the women reached over and patted me on the shoulder.

But the Swami had no more messages for men. He was, smart enough to know where to stop. He'd tried one of the simplest come-ons, and there had been too much of a pause. It had almost not come off.

I wondered who good old Bob Smith was? Surely, among the thousands of applicants I'd interviewed, there must have been a number of them. And, being applicants, of course some of them had been wrong.

The Swami's tones, giving one message after another—faster and faster now, not waiting for acknowledgment or confirmation—began to sink into a whisper. His speech became ragged, heavy. The words became indistinguishable. About his head there began to float a pale, luminescent sphere. There was a subdued gasp from the audience and then complete stillness. As though, unbreathing, in the depths of a tomb, they watched the sphere. It bobbed about, over the Swami's head and around him. At times it seemed as if about to float off stage, but it came back. It swirled out over the audience, but not too far, and never at such an angle that the long, flexible dull black wire supporting it would be silhouetted against the glowing crystal ball.

Then it happened. There was a gasp, a smothered scream. And over at one side of the auditorium a dark object began bobbing about in the air up near the ceiling. It swerved and swooped. The Swami's luminescent sphere jerked to a sudden stop. The Swami sat with open mouth and stared at the dark object which he was not controlling.

The dark object was not confined to any dull black wire. It went where it willed. It went too high and brushed against the ceiling.

There was a sudden shower of coins to the floor. A compact hit the floor with a flat spat. A handkerchief floated down more slowly.

"My purse!" a woman gasped. I recognized my interviewer's voice. Her purse contained two Auerbach cylinders, and they were having themselves a ball.

In alarm, I looked quickly at the stage, hoping the Swami wasn't astute enough to catch on. But he was gone. The audience, watching the bobbing purse, hadn't realized it as yet. And they were delayed in realizing it by a diversion from the other side of the auditorium.

"I can't hold it down any longer, Mr. Kennedy!" a woman gasped out. "It's taking me up into the air!"

"Hold on, Annie!" I shouted back. "I'm coming!"

A chastened and subdued Swami sat in my office the following morning, and this time he was inclined to be cooperative. More, he was looking to me for guidance, understanding, and didn't mind acknowledging my ascendancy. And, with the lieutenant left in the outer office, he didn't have any face to preserve.

Later, last night, he'd learned the truth of what happened after he had run away in a panic. I'd left a call at the hotel for the lieutenant. When the lieutenant had got him calmed down and returned my call, I'd instructed him to tell the Swami about the Auerbach cylinders; to tell the Swami he was not a fake after all.

The Swami had obviously spent a sleepless night. It is a terrible thing to have spent years perfecting the art of fakery, and then to realize you needn't have faked at all. More terrible, he had swallowed some of his own medicine, and all through the night he had shivered in fear of some instant and horrible retaliation. For him it was still a case of There Are Mysteries.

And it was of no comfort to his state of mind right now that the four cylinders we had finally captured last night were, at this moment, bobbing about in my office, swooping and swerving around in the upper part of the room, like bats trying to find some opening. I was giving him the full treatment. The first two cylinders, down on the floor, were pressing up against my closed door, like frightened little things trying to escape a room of horror.

The Swami's face was twitching, and his long fingers kept twining themselves into King's X symbols. But he was sitting it out. He was swallowing some of the hair of the dog that bit him. I had to give him A for that.

"I've been trying to build up a concept of the framework wherein psi seems to function," I told him casually, just as if it were all a formularized laboratory procedure, "I had to pull last night's stunt to prove something."

He tore his eyes away from the cylinders which were over exploring one corner of the ceiling, and looked at me.

"Let's go to electricity," I said speculatively. "Not that we know psi and electricity have anything in common, other than some similar analogies, but we don't know they don't. Both of them may be just different manifestations of the same thing. We don't really know why a magnetized core, turning inside a coil of copper wire, generates electricity.

"Oh we've got some phrases," I acknowledged. "We've got a whole structure of phrases, and when you listen to them they sound as if they ought to mean something—like the phrases you were using last night. Everybody assumes they do mean something to the pundits. So, since it is human to want to be a pundit, we repeat these phrases over and over, and call them explanations. Yet we do know what happens, even if we do just theorize about why. We know how to wrap something around something and get electricity.

"Take the induction coil," I said. "We feed a low-voltage current into one end, and we draw off a high-voltage current from the other. But anyone who wants, any time, can disprove the whole principle of the induction coil. All you have to do is wrap your core with a nonconductor, say nylon thread, and presto, nothing comes out. You see, it doesn't work; and anybody who claims it does is a faker and a liar. That's what happens when science tries to investigate psi by the standard methods.

"You surround a psi-gifted individual with nonbelievers, and probably nothing will come out of it. Surround him with true believers; and it all seems to act like an induction coil. Things happen. Yet even when things do happen, it is usually impossible to prove it.

"Take yourself, Swami. And this is significant. First we have the north point effect. Then those two little beggars trying to get out the door. Then the ones which are bobbing around up there. Without the cylinders there would have been no way to know that anything had happened at all.

"Now, about this psi framework. It isn't something you can turn on and off, at will. We don't know enough yet for that. Aside from some believers and those individuals who do seem to attract psi forces, we don't know, yet, what to wrap around what. So, here's what you're to do: You're to keep a supply of these cylinders near you at all times. If any psi effects happen, they'll record it. Fair enough?

"Now," I said with finality. "I have anticipated that you might refuse. But you're not the only person who has psi ability. I've wired General Sanfordwaithe to send me another fellow; one who will cooperate."

The Swami thought it over. Here he was with a suite in a good hotel; with an army lieutenant to look after his earthly needs; on the payroll of a respectable company; with a ready-made flock of believers; and no fear of the bunco squad. He had never had it so good. The side money, for private readings alone, should be substantial.

Further, and he watched me narrowly, I didn't seem to be afraid of the cylinders.

"I'll cooperate," he said.

For three days there was nothing. The Swami called me a couple times a day and reported that the cylinders just lay around his room. I didn't know what to tell him. I recommended he read biographies of famous mediums. I recommended fasting, and breathing, and contemplating self. He seemed dubious, but said he'd try it.

On the morning of the third day, Sara called me on the intercom and told me there was another Army leiutenant in her office, and another . . . gentleman. I opened my door and went out to Sara's office to greet them.

The new lieutenant was no more than the standard output from the same production line as Lieutenant Murphy, but the wizened little old man he had in tow was from a different and much rarer matrix. As fast as I had moved, I was none too soon. The character reached over and tilted up Sara's chin as I was coming through the door.

"Now you're a healthy young wench," he said with a leer. "What are you doing tonight, baby?" The guy was at least eighty years old.

"Hey, you, pop!" I exclaimed in anger. "Be your age!"

He turned around and looked me up and down.

"I'm younger, that way, than you are, right now!" he snapped.

A disturbance in the outer office kept me from thinking up a retort. There were some subdued screams, some scuffling of heavy shoes, the sounds of some running feet as applicants got away. The outer door to Sara's office was flung open.

Framed in the doorway, breast high, floated the Swami!

He was sitting, cross-legged, on a hotel bathmat. From both front corners, where they had been attached by loops of twine, there peeked Auerbach cylinders. Two more rear cylinders were grasped in Lieutenant Murphy's strong hands. He was propelling the Swami along, mid air, in Atlantic City Boardwalk style.

The Swami looked down at us with aloof disdain, then his eyes focused on the old man. His glance wavered; he threw a startled and fearful look at the cylinders holding up his bathmat. They did not fall. A vast relief overspread his face, and he drew himself erect with more disdain than ever. The old man was not so aloof.

"Harry Glotz!" he exclaimed. "Why you . . . you faker! What are you doing in that getup?"

The Swami took a casual turn about the room, leaning to one side on his magic carpet as if banking an airplane.

"Peasant!" He spat the word out and motioned grandly toward the door. Lieutenant Murphy pushed him through.

"Why, that no good bum!" the old man shouted at me. "That no-good from nowhere! I'll fix him! Thinks he's something, does he? I'll show him! Anything he can do I can do better!"

His rage got the better of him. He rushed through the door, shaking both fists above his white head, shouting imprecations, threats, and pleading to be shown how the trick was done, all in the same breath. The new lieutenant cast a stricken-look at us and then sped after his charge.

"Looks as if we're finally in production," I said to Sara.

"That's only the second one," she said mournfully. "When you get all six of them, this joint's sure going to be jumping!"

I looked out of her window at the steel and concrete walls of the factory. They were solid, real, secure; they were a symbol of reality, the old reality a man could understand.

"I hope you don't mean that literally, Sara," I answered dubiously.

3/55

How Allied

From *Astounding Science Fiction*

Remembrance and reflection, how allied,
What thin partitions sense from thought divide.

POPE

Occasionally, in every personnel man's life, there comes a day when there are no pressing problems. Perhaps out of sheer boredom with perpetual squabbling, all the workers and department heads at Computer Research were giving their attention to getting some work done for a change. Even Old Stone Face—Mr. Henry Grenoble, General Manager—hadn't bothered me for a day or so about how much less dependable people were than machines, and why wasn't I doing something about that? The lull gave me a breather.

I was sitting at my desk, experimenting with my little psi machine, when Sara, my secretary, stuck her head through our adjoining door. She looked my little gadget over, looked at me, and stepped all the way into my office.

"Your retrogression to childhood seems to be progressing nicely, Mr. Kennedy," she said in that dry, flip manner she affects, or really feels, with me.

"This is a psi machine," I instructed loftily. "Good for testing psi force. Works better for some than for others. Follows Rhine's card-calling patterns, works better for the first few tries than later in the run—sometimes. Sometimes the other way around, just to keep us confused."

She grinned at me and tossed her shoulder-length bob of red hair in the latest movie queen gesture. But no matter how hard she tried, her face could not assume that expression of vacuous idiocy men are supposed to find irresistible.

"Maybe we could find out how strong your psi force is, Sara," I suggested. "Want to try?"

"I'll stick to tea leaves," she answered. "Or maybe take a course of lessons from that fake Swami you hired last month."

114

"That fake Swami is doing all right," I answered her back. "Or as well as might be expected. Now and then he does activate some Auerbach psi cylinders."

"Just so we don't all go overboard," she murmured, and looked pointedly at my gadget. In spite of her overtones of disdain, I knew she was interested.

"Sometime, in the deep privacy of your apartment, where you don't have to maintain your sophisticated dignity, you might like to try this little gadget," I said seriously. "Take a piece of cardboard, draw a clock face on it, stick a pin up through the center. Cut a small arrow out of ordinary paper and balance it, without piercing, on the pin point. Think of a number on the card, and if your psi force is anything to brag about the arrow will swing around and point to that number. It's very simple, anybody can make one."

"Of course the air currents in the room have nothing whatever to do with swinging the arrow around," she scoffed. Still, she did come closer and perch herself on the arm of the crying chair—the chair that looks comfortable but actually slants a little so the sitter slowly slides outward, a gentle hint that even the most enjoyable grievance or calculated hysterics must come to an end sometime.

"Sure," I agreed. "The point is the arrow goes to the right number too often for random chance."

Sara surprised me, and shouldn't have because I knew she was a bright girl.

"You sit there thinking at that little thing," she said, and gazed out of my window at the long cement wall of factory building number three. "Air currents move it around. It hesitates at the wrong number, so you go on concentrating. Finally it gets around to the right number and wham! You score a hit. How can you lose?"

"You want to go out and find a nice soft tree crotch to sleep in because investigating the idea of a cave is too radical?" I asked sourly.

I shoved the little gadget over to one side of my desk beside another one that had, instead of numbers, the brief answers to questions written on it. Such as "Yes," "No," "Tomorrow," things like that. In a fit of whimsy I'd filled in one space with "Don't do it, Ralph!"

"What did you want, Sara?" I asked with one more glance at the psi machines. "You didn't come in here just to browbeat me."

"There's an applicant by the name of George to see you," she answered.

"George? George Who?" I asked, automatically.

"Just George," she shrugged. "That's all the interviewer told me."

"What's the matter with the interviewers? Why can't they talk to this George? Why should I have to take my attention away from important things—"

Her eyes swiveled over to my psi gadgets, and she couldn't help grinning.

"All right," I agreed. "Maybe not so important, but how are we to know? Anyway, why should I interview raw applicants when we've got a whole staff for that purpose?"

"This George seems to be something special, and you gave orders that you, personally, wanted to see anybody with—anybody like that. Who knows? Maybe you'll turn up another fake Swami, or another little poltergeist girl like Jennie Malasek."

I looked at her, grimaced wryly, and sighed.

"Not again," I said. "That was when the heat was on from the Military. They've cooled down now, and so have I. I've had my fill of screwballs. I—" I sighed again at her patient certainty I'd see the applicant as soon as I'd grumbled enough. "All right," I agreed. "Send him in. If the interviewers can't handle him, well, I'd better do something to keep from asking myself on the way home, 'And what bright hope did you give to the World today, Ralph Kennedy?' Send him in."

"Yes, sir," she said formally, and stood up. She still says "sir" to me now and then. I'm never sure if it is respect, derision, or just an old habit hanging on from young and hopeful days when she dreamed of being secretary to a dynamic tycoon of industry. Was it ever possible she might have thought the Director of Industrial Relations at Computer Research Corporation was a dynamic tycoon? If so, I may have let her down.

While she was out of the office I started to ditch my psi machines into a desk drawer, then decided to let them stay. After all, it was only an applicant I'd be interviewing.

"Is George going to be something special—more trouble?" I asked the answer machine. The arrow pointed to "Yes." This was not so remarkable, since the arrow had been pointing there before I'd asked. I could have made precognition out of that if I wanted to.

I lit a cigarette.

My door opened again to gust the number arrow off its moorings and send the answer arrow swirling around. Five young men came in, single file, through the doorway. Behind them Sara was making signs with her eyes and shoulders that she hadn't known it was to be a convention. She made wide eyes, and closed the door.

At first glance they were easily classified as fresh, young college grads. A couple were big and bulky, a couple were medium and one was a wiry little guy. They were assorted blondes, brunettes and betweens. Each had two eyes, a nose. a mouth, and assorted ears. They didn't exactly have the trademark "Made At Stanford" stamped on their foreheads, but it was pretty apparent they'd all been turned out by the same mass production education machine.

I waved to conference chairs grouped together over in one corner of the office.

"Have seats, fellows," I said.

They all sat down, as close to one another as the chairs permitted, as if to draw reassurance and warmth from one another. Their movement was just enough off beat not to be the precision of a drill team. I sighed silently: Young grads always made such a big thing out of a Job Interview. I hoped I wouldn't be a disappointment to them.

"Before we begin," I said, and put a little of the classroom lecture tone in my voice to make them feel at ease, "I should check you fellows out on something. It's a bad idea to go job hunting in a gang, or even in pairs. When you become adult you're supposed to be able to walk into an office all by yourself, without your gang to hold you up. All right, which one of you is looking for work? Which one is . . . er . . . George?"

They looked at one another with something like a secret smile, then they looked at me. And there was pity for me in their faces. That was normal enough. The young grad naturally assumes that no one, before his time, ever cracked a textbook, or even learned how to read. And at that time I was still secure enough in my mature ascendancy not to realize I might need their pity.

"Sir," Chair Number One said boldly. Then his immaturity got the best of him. He gulped and swallowed. But the sentence wasn't interrupted, because Chair Number Two picked it up without a pause.

"Word has got around that this company hires oddballs!" He used the term with a certain pride, then felt he should define it for me. "People with unusual talents."

I made a wry grimace.

"I hope such word doesn't filter through to Management," I said ruefully. "I've got enough troubles already."

"You should be proud of it," Number Four, the wiry little guy, spoke up. "Unusual achievements require unusual people!" Somehow I could picture a framed motto of those words hanging on his study wall. If so, it would be a cultural step forward from Kipling's "If."

"Let's get down to cases," I said. "What's the pitch? Which one is George?"

"We're all George," Number Three said. Their little secret smile was more apparent now, and had a touch of delight in it.

"Great," I answered dryly. "A valuable asset. Just what industry needs. Your first names are all George."

"Not exactly, sir," Number Five said, as if he wished I weren't quite so slow in comprehension. "None of our names is George. That's just the name we adopted. He's the only one who really counts. You might say he's the sixth one of us, only that wouldn't be quite right."

"Oh," I said, and began to realize why the interviewer had passed these guys on to me. "There's a sixth one, and he's the only one who counts. All you fellows are just here to pave the way for his interview. Must be quite a man to get all you fellows to strew rose petals in his path."

"You're close," Number One said, and his grin grew wider.

"Closer than you know," Number Two agreed.

"Although you couldn't accurately call him a man," Number Three qualified.

Numbers Four and Five nodded approvingly.

"All right, guys," I said. "I know when I'm getting the needle. But this is your job interview, not mine. I've already got a job, such as it is. It's up to you to make the pitch, not me. So trot on out and tell George to come in and speak for himself."

"George is already here," Number Four said.

"He's been here all the time," Two agreed.

"Certainly," One said. "Otherwise this conversation wouldn't make sense."

I felt the first twinge of uncertainty. It wasn't making any sense to me—and it was, to them. They were quite serious, too. I bit down on my lower lip, and glanced over at the psi machine. The arrow was pointing to "Don't do it, Ralph!"

Somehow it failed to satisfy me. Don't get mad? Don't throw 'em out? Don't talk to 'em any more at all? Don't pass up this wonderful opportunity? Nicely ambiguous, it could mean anything.

"Maybe you fellows had better start explaining," I said mildly. I wasn't taking the lead in the interview any longer.

"Sir," Two said, and appeared ready to launch into a prepared speech. "You've no doubt noticed that individualism is being replaced in our times with collective effort, teamwork, group activity?"

I nodded affirmatively that I had noticed it. I'd also observed something else just now. Number Two had started the sentence, but Number Three had finished it. The switch was so smooth that I hadn't quite noticed just which word had been used as the pivot.

"I've got some reservations about group effort," I said, and pretended I hadn't noticed the switch. If it were a gag, I wouldn't give them the satisfaction of being impressed with their drill precision. "I've noticed a group can better develop an old idea, but it still takes an individual to come up with a new one."

They looked at me with pity again. I was in my late thirties, and to them doddering with age. Their faces showed they thought I was ready to turn out to pasture. Suddenly I remembered reading about experiments of free-wheeling idea association groups and the remarkable new ideas that came out of it. Maybe they were right, maybe I was doddering and should be turned out to pasture. But apparently they somehow agreed among themselves to overlook my lapse, which had definitely placed me in a former generation.

"And have you observed," Number Four smoothly picked up at the point where I'd inanely interrupted, but he transferred the rest of the question to One, "that sometimes a group or a crowd seems to take on a definite mass Personality?"

"Theater entertainers talk about—"

"A hot audience or a cold audience. Rabble rousers can make—"

"Some audiences turn handsprings, and fall flat with others. In a mob—"

"Something seems to take possession of the people, causing—"

"Them to do things they wouldn't dream of doing as separate individuals. Or you take a delinquent gang in a no-reason assault. Afterwards, they don't seem to realize what they did, or why they did—"

"It. Some kind of an interplay and mental feedback takes place, transforming the mental current into a palpable power—"

"Something seems to come into being—"

"A mass entity—"

"A thing—"

"A personality—"

"A being—"

"It exists, and the people in the mob or group are just its parts, its extensions, its senses, hands, feet, eyes, ears—pseudopods!"

"Well, sir, our entity is—"

"GEORGE!"

They all sat there, beaming at me, pleased with themselves—or pleased with George. They seemed to realize I needed a moment to absorb what they had told me. And I did. I was trying to figure out what kind of a con game they were trying to pull. It wasn't anything vicious. I was pretty confident of that. I'd seen my share of angel-faced sadists, but these kids were fine lads, I'd bet on it. I found an explanation which seemed rational.

It was what they'd call an interest catcher. Their vocational counselors would have given them the same old line, "Now when you go out to look for that very special niche in life you deserve, you've got to think of something special, something to catch the employer's interest, make him see you as a person instead of just another applicant." It was a good theory, and sometimes it worked. They'd tried. They'd offered something very special, with drilled precision that must have cost many hours of rehearsal.

But this time it had failed, because I didn't see them as individuals at all, just as a group. I didn't even know their names, or care to know them. One, Two, Three, Four and Five was quite good enough. So their con game, innocent and harmless but still a con game, had failed.

Or had it? Was that the whole point? That they didn't want me to see them as individuals, but only as a group? A group called George?

"These ordinary mob entities," Two began the conversation again, but the phrases were tossed from one to another like a basketball. "Are just flash existences. They come into reality for a while, and then they don't exist any longer. After they go they leave their pseudopods, the people involved, bewildered and ashamed if the entity was an evil thing which made them do evil deeds. Or, if it was something good, like a music jam session, or a football rally, or a panty raid, or maybe just a quiet talk about what is life, then the people remember it. They remember it as one of the deep and lasting experiences of their lives, they long for it to happen again; like army buddies who have been under fire together, there's a kinship deeper than blood, they never forget, they get together again and again trying to make the entity come alive once more so they can enjoy, really enjoy, living in the fullest sense."

All of them had contributed to the speech, but I found it easier to follow the thread of their argument if I half closed my eyes and made no effort to keep track of the rapid shunting of the conversational ball from one to the other. Ridiculous though it seemed, it was easier to accept George as the real entity and these lads as merely his parts, than attempt to keep them separate; easier to conclude it was George speaking without any discrimination as to whose mouth he was using.

"We've been together ever since we were kids living in the same block," they said, or George said, and I gave up trying to make that distinction, too. "We grew up together. It got so our parents hardly knew which of us was whose. We've always stayed together, even managed to keep in the same company during our military hitch. We don't remember when George became into being, when we stopped being separate boys and all became a part of George. Other entities, bad and good ones, come and go; but as long as we can stay together, and we will, George stays with us."

"So we think there ought to be some kind of a job in your Company for George—"

"Something that five unconnected guys couldn't do, but George could do—"

"Something unusual—"

"And as long as you hire oddballs anyway—"

"Well, unusual achievements require unusual people!"

I wasn't buying any of this, of course. It was clever, and marvelously executed. I was intrigued in spite of my years of being subjected to the tricks the brighter applicants could dream up. And of course it would all fall to pieces if I switched the conversation onto a subject they couldn't have rehearsed in advance.

Yet I found myself reluctant to do that. I liked these kids, and behind my expression which I hoped was noncommittal, I was applauding them. If anybody ever deserved A for effort— I'd long ago realized that an applicant didn't stand a chance if I really wanted to take him apart, that my years of experience with every kind of a human dodge and gimmick made it like turning a machine gun on a kid with a toy bow and arrow. Unless something vital was at stake, I usually let people get away with their carefully contrived frameworks simply because destroying them would give me no pleasure.

But I was intrigued beyond this point with these kids.

What if there really were a George? Of course there wasn't, but what if there were? They'd made a powerful case for his existence, and the idea of a superentity would explain much in mass psychology heretofore unexplainable. The more we learned of electronics the more we were realizing that through interplay and feedback, impalpable force fields were brought into being which had measurable effects—effects impossible to any one of the machines contributing to the whole. The echo effect in a broadcasting studio was a rudimentary example.

Yes, what if there were a George? Why didn't I feel him, if there were? Because I was not one of the parts? Because, like a spectator standing off from a mob scene who looked with incredulous wonder upon their behavior, I could only see the effects from the outside? I felt a twinge of envy, for like everyone else, I, also, in fleeting instances, had known a sense of "belonging together." The thing the *Gestalt* school was trying to develop.

"What a basketball or hockey team you guys would make," I said. "Imagine a team where every member was completely in tune with every other member, the whole acting as one coordinated entity."

"That's the idea, sir," one of them said. But their faces told me of their disappointment in me. Their idea of something for George to do went far deeper than winning some sports events. George was real, George was earnest, and the gym was not his goal.

"Or a music jam session," I said. "Wow!"

They sat politely and waited.

"Mind you," I said, "I'm not convinced of George, but on the hypothesis that he could exist, there must be dozens, hundreds of things, things we've never been able to do in industry or science because of imperfect communication and coordination."

Their faces brightened. At last the old guy was getting down to something solid.

But I was stopped right there. There must be dozens, hundreds— But at the moment I couldn't think of any. Very well, Kennedy, do what you always do with an applicant. Find out what he is trained for, what he can do, then it is simple to fit him in to what you need done—if he qualifies.

These boys qualified, there was no doubt of it. In spite of their closeness, they hadn't taken the same courses in school. One was a mechanical engineer, one an electronics engineer. Another had specialized in cybernetics, and that fitted neatly because our major line was making computers and mechanical brains for hush-hush missiles and so forth. A fourth one had specialized in production control, and the fifth one in industry procedures, such as accounting, purchasing, supervision, organization, things like that.

They were qualified. Every one of them was an ideal trainee. But it still gave me nothing for George to do! There were a lot of unformed ideas teasing me just back of mental consciousness, and a considerable self-disgust that I couldn't put my finger on anything specific. But, there it was. Given time, I'd no doubt think of something. I didn't want to lose these lads while I thought it over. I'd have hired them like a shot if they'd come in separately, so why let them go on to some competitor while I mulled around trying to dream up something for George—who didn't exist anyway?

I launched into my young-grad—industrial-trainee speech, all about the need for converting knowing about things to doing them, the necessity for taking a beginning place while they learned the ropes. While they were learning, we would be observing them, finding out where they would best fit in our total organization, et cetera, et cetera. The same old line each young grad accepts cynically because there is nothing else he can do.

A little to my astonishment, they accepted enthusiastically. That was the idea. They realized that it was too much to expect something unusual for George right away, that like any other new employee, George would have to prove himself before he could expect anything of importance.

I was further astonished that the menial jobs I described for them didn't insult them. Usually a young grad's idea of starting at the bottom means Assistant to the President.

I called in the interviewer who had shunted the boys on to me, and told him to process the lads for the trainee jobs, the three engineers as draftsmen in their respective fields, a production control man as a stock chaser and expediter, and the business administration lad as a clerk in the purchasing department.

These were the open jobs, and it should be obvious to any interviewer that these were the lads to fill them. The interviewer looked at me with mingled emotions. Part of him was asking "How do you do it?" with admiration, and the other part was sore at me because I had been able to do it, when all he'd got was irrational confusion.

I failed to reveal that I was also somewhat irrationally confused.

I had never run a personnel department on the usual policy of forgetting your promises as soon as you saw the back of the employee. One of the reasons we had so little organization trouble was because they knew that if I failed to keep my promise it wasn't because I hadn't tried.

In the days that followed, I tried to find something for George. I talked to various supervisors whose intelligence I respected. I went to administrative engineers. I threw the problem into the theoretical research lab. Everyone had the same reaction.

"Why sure, there must be dozens, hundreds—"

"Name me one, just one," I'd say. "Name me something that theoretically we know how to do, but can't do, because we can't ever get the perfect coordination and communication to meet unforeseen developments."

Of course they accepted my statement that this was just a hypothetical situation. I wasn't sticking out my neck any farther than that. But it was an intriguing thought, and the more imaginative engineers pounced upon it with delight. Why there must be dozens—

Name one, just one.

And they did name problems by the score. But these always fitted into one of two categories—either science didn't yet know how to solve the problem even with perfect communication and coordination, or it was only a little better performance than five separate guys could do without complete empathy. Never anything that only a George could do, a thing that couldn't be done without a George.

Some of them tried a different approach.

"Tell me what qualities George has, and then it should be easy to think of something that only he could do."

I learned to counter that one, because it led into endless discussions about qualities of mind, and never produced anything specific for George to do anyway.

"Give him any rational qualities you want," I'd say. "Anything that fits into our present framework of science and industry. Let's don't deal in magic, or this time in the usual concepts of psi. Here we've got five guys, who are just ordinary guys without any wild talents. But they've worked out *Gestalt* empathy to the point where they think and act as a unit, as one organism. Now, granted this organism as a whole may equal more than the sum of its parts, still it doesn't have any wild talents. It can't turn the Auerbach cylinder into an antigravity unit, for example. But it *is* greater than the sum of its parts, it *is* more than just five well-trained guys who would bog down in confusion as soon as an unforeseen circumstance arose, who would have to stop whatever they were doing to compare notes and agree on where to go from there. This . . . this George, would react instantly, drawing his decision from the combined minds and talents of the whole group, and all parts of the group would carry out the decision just as if they were parts of one body directed by one brain. Give him any background, any training, any knowledge, any rational qualities you like. What good is he? What could he do that we can't already do?"

They'd grin and mumble something about if I didn't have anything more important than that to occupy my time they certainly did. They'd agree to think about it, because, like myself, just behind the frame of consciousness there was the teasing certainty that there must be dozens, hundreds—

That, in itself, intrigued me. Was man evolving into a kind of group entity, instead of separate individuals? Some philosophers had said so. The whole social structure was trending in that direction. Were we on the verge of a whole new concept of mind and existence? Something we could intuitively feel but not put into words?

It became important to me, far beyond the importance of merely keeping my promise to think of something for George to do, my promise to the five lads. The five boys had settled into their new jobs without a disturbing ripple on the surface of the organization, and a couple of supervisors had gone out of their way to tell me that if there were any more of the same floating around to grab them.

One supervisor said it was astonishing the way his man seemed to grasp total orientation in his job, seemed to know without being told how the work he did fitted into the total structure. He thought this very unusual, because it usually took months or years for the concept to dawn that each job fitted into the pattern of all other jobs, like a big jigsaw puzzle.

I agreed that it was unusual. And felt a chill run down my spine. It wouldn't be unexpected if what was being taught the other four trainees was instantly available to him! Where did empathy leave off and telepathy begin?

I went beyond my usual conversations with the engineers and theoretical scientists. I even thought of taking the problem to Old Stone Face, and then got the practical thought that the general manager would flay me alive for wasting time on a hypothetical problem when there were so many real ones to solve—such as how to make people behave like machines.

I did take up the problem, tentatively, with Colonel Backhead. Along with other private industries working on hush-hush government contracts, we had our contingent of Army-Air Force-Navy personnel, who acted to interpret contracts, pass on plans and specifications, inspect output, needle the security police into ever increasing suspicions of everybody, stamp Top Secret on every piece of paper they saw. An organization within an organization. "A cancerous growth in the body of free enterprise," Old Stone Face would mutter when he was particularly perturbed by some foolish regulation.

Still, I'd got to the point of desperation. I'd even accept an idea from Colonel Backhead, if he had one. He did, and it astonished me. "Good thing such a thing doesn't exist," he said in his clipped, raspy tones. "Rob a bank too easy."

Now what kind of a subconcious mind did *he* have?

Repeated failure and time dulled my enthusiasm for the quest. Other wheels were squeaking louder than my five lads; Company wheels, and Military wheels.

A certain realization also dulled my search, and faced me with defeat. Both industry and science are founded upon the basic premise that there *cannot* be perfect communication and coordination between individuals. The procedures are all set up to compensate for that lack. Deeper still, like any hypothesis founded upon a basic premise that is unquestioned, all theories and questions are shaped by that premise, and all evidence is rationalized to fit it—like the wondrous structure of astronomy built around Ptolemy's basic premise that the Earth was the center of the universe. It takes a complete breakthrough, a destruction of the basic premise, before we can think of the questions, much less arrive at answers.

I would have to be a Copernicus to think of something for George to do—and I wasn't.

I salved my conscience over the broken promise to the five lads by rationalizing that this betrayal was no more than any other young grad could expect. Most of them came in with bright hopes, eager ambitions, wondrous talents, and one by one we ground them down to fit into the total organization machine. They were malleable material. That was evidenced by the fact that their college had been able to pound and pummel them all into the same mental and attitude shape, so that they all could come out of the same production machine. Industry would follow the same process, and in five, ten, twenty years they would be unmistakably business executives. Was that bad?

What a terrible waste of unusual talents! Still, what could I do? If George was so unusual, let him find his own niche! Every other employee had to!

Accepting the rationalization was gall, but what else? And in the meantime, I did have other problems, problems I could solve.

Six months went by. A short time in the span of a lifetime job, a long time to a bright young trainee who took a temporary job only until something better, to make use of his unusual abilities, could be worked out. I forgot about the five guys. No special trouble over them came to my attention, and they became just five out of five thousand employees.

I had never accepted George as more than a hypothetical idea, and my wisdom in this course was apparent. If George did exist, he wasn't making his presence known to anybody. I even rationalized George away. Kids often dream up imaginary companions, talk to them, insist that mother set a place at the table for them, make a place for them in their beds. Such a thing had occurred to these five lads when they were kids—and because of their constant association they'd simply kept the idea alive. But now that they had jobs in separate departments, and were growing up, taking on more adult responsibilities in their jobs, the whole childish idea would soon appear silly to them.

I was glad I'd always kept it purely hypothetical when talking with the engineers and scientists.

With that final rationalization, I dismissed them from my mind completely. In the usual sink-or-swim fashion, they would either climb on up in their jobs through the usual channels, or they wouldn't. Until they became troublesome, they were none of my affair—now.

My little psi machines had likewise been discarded. Association and consequent guilt feelings? Something as childish as the idea of George?

The months slipped away, and almost a year passed. I had forgot the boys.

My phone rang with that long, persistent shrill the switchboard operator uses to tell me that Old Stone Face is on the other end of the wire and chomping impatiently.

"Kennedy here," I said, before I'd got the phone well up to my face.

"What have you been up to this time, Kennedy?" His voice had that patient, measured, grating tone he uses when he is particularly disgusted.

"What is it now, Mr. Grenoble?" I asked with a patience as deadly as his own. Old Stone Face is always saying that he doesn't meddle, and then proceeds to louse up labor relations.

"You must have been up to something," he said. "The Army, the Navy, the Air Force, the Marines, the Coast Guard are crawling all over me. I haven't heard yet from the Girl Scouts," he finished with a plaintive note creeping into his voice.

"What about?" I asked. I was busily running over my many programs in my mind to see which might be interpreted as cardinal sins by the military, but I couldn't think of anything.

"Sometimes I wish the services hadn't combined," the plaintive note was stronger now. "Used to be, when they played dog in the manger toward each other a business man could appeal to reason— or at least prejudice. But now—"

"What's happened?" I asked again.

"Maybe you'd better come up here to my office," he said. Then, as an afterthought, "When it is convenient for you." The latter was a sop to his often repeated but seldom observed lecture that company executives should show mutual respect toward one another.

"It's convenient right now," I said. We both knew it was a fiction, that he meant get there on the double, and I'd better interpret it that way.

I took a short-cut through factory building Number Two, and had to fend off two supervisors who saw me coming and thought it would be a good time to get in some juicy grievances. One of them did get in a few words before I could tell him that Mr. Grenoble was waiting for me.

"I think I oughta be told what's going on in my own department," he complained. "Even the stock room knows more about production schedules than I do. Sometimes they load the bins with raw stock a full day before I get the work orders telling me what to do with it."

"I'll speak to production control," I said hurriedly. "Or you take it up with the works manager. It's his baby, not mine."

His eyes reproached me for passing the buck, but I was already too far away from him to smooth him down.

When I passed through the secretary's office, I raised my eyebrows in a question and nodded toward Old Stone Face's door. She made a sign of holding a shield over her head, or hiding under the covers, to tell me that he wasn't at his most affable today. She picked up her shorthand book and followed me into his office.

"What's the trouble, Mr. Grenoble?" I greeted him, and sat down in a chair, informally. His secretary sat down in another, formally, and poised her pencil.

"The trouble is that the Pentagon is sending investigation teams of their bright bóys to find out how we do it," he grumbled.

"Do what?" I asked.

He glowered at me as if I were stalling.

"Finish up contracts on time," he exploded.

"You mean we actually met a deadline, and the product passed inspection?" I asked, puzzled.

"Not just one," he said. "Four!"

He got up from behind his desk, clasped his hands behind his back and started pacing the floor. I remembered television shots where a head football coach would start pacing up and down in front of the player benches. All the sub coaches would leap to their feet and start pacing, too. I wondered if Old Stone Face felt I should.

"It's unheard of," he whirled around and shouted at me. "They draw up a contract. They put in a deadline for performance. Then everytime somebody in Congress sneezes, or some petty politician in Europe spouts off a lot of nonsense, they scrap everything and start all over. As soon as a contract gets signed, the Pentagon starts throwing rocks at our feet to make us stumble over them. Nobody ever finishes a contract on time, it just isn't possible, and here we've finished four. So there's going to be an investigation. So what have you been up to, Kennedy?"

I felt like saying, "Who, me?" or "Honest, boss, I didn't do it."

"First time I ever got a complaint that the organization was functioning as it should," was what I really said.

He whirled around from the window where he had been gazing disconsolately out at the smog.

"Oh, I'll grant you that if we were let alone, it's no more than I'd expect," he conceded—and he would expect it, too. "But the Military is involved, and they're not used to efficiency. They just don't know how to cope with it."

"But we've got Colonel Backhead and his gang . . . er, staff . . . of bright boys watching every move we make," I argued. "Have they found any fault?"

For the first time his face brightened a little.

"It all sneaked up on them, too. Caught 'em with their contracts down. When they realized it they went all frozen faced on me, gave me the silent treatment. They've been busy as little beavers ever since they realized what was happening. Doing their own investigating before the real investigation begins."

"Maybe I'm naive," I said. "I still don't see what all the fuss is about."

"It isn't normal," he said. "And anything that isn't normal sends them into a gibbering tizzy. I've asked Backhead if he'd mind stepping in here. He minded, but he said he'd do it."

"Backhead and I are not exactly buddies," I said. "You know that, Henry. I refused to allow them to turn this place into a swarm of keyhole peekers and tattlers, and in his mind that's pretty strong evidence that I must be working for the enemy."

"I appreciate it, Ralph," he said in a grudging tone. "Nothing wrecks an organization quicker than to encourage informers. That's why I backed you up."

"So maybe you'll get farther with Backhead if I'm not here."

"Maybe I won't get anywhere at all, with or without you," he mumbled. "But I want you to stay." He grabbed up the phone and barked at the switchboard operator. "Check Backhead's office and see if he is coming."

"It's only been five minutes," his secretary cautioned.

He glowered at her and threw up his hands, as if to say that everyone was fighting against him. The phone tingled, and he grabbed it up.

"His office says he's already on the way," the thin, tinny voice of the operator sounded loud through the receiver.

"Probably stopped to harass some—" A discreet tap at his door stopped his comment.

"Let's be calm," I said, as the secretary got up to open the door and admit the colonel.

I have since thought it was the look of intense irritation Old Stone Face threw me as the colonel came through the door, which melted Backhead down rather easily. He probably thought Grenoble was sore at me, and this would be his chance to cut my throat.

Still he must have come prepared for he had his black brief case with TOP SECRET in big gold letters emobssed on its side, to advertise its contents, or its owner's importance.

We got through amenities, such as they were, pretty hurriedly.

"Must be quite a feather in your cap, colonel," I said brightly. "With repeated contracts under your jurisdiction getting out on time. I suppose the Pentagon wants to study how it's done, so they can install the same procedures elsewhere? Probably put you in charge on a national scale?"

It set him back. It was obvious he hadn't thought of it in that light, before. So intently looking for the evil, he hadn't even considered there might be good. And he wasn't ready to start now.

There was a good deal of humming and hawing, a full fifteen minutes worth, before he was ready for us to get a peek at what he had in his brief case. And when he dragged it out, it was evident that his staff had been busy. They had names, dates, facts, times, and figures.

"On March 7th, at 9:45 a.m., the design drawings on the . . . um . . . a certain mechanism was released to the mechanical drawing department. As according to procedure, a certain mechanical engineer, one James P. Bellows, analyzed these drawings preparatory to breaking them down into job lots for the detailed mechanical drawings which would later become the blueprints for this . . . ah

. . . certain mechanism." He looked at me. "Does the name, James P. Bellows, mean anything to you, Mr. Kennedy?" he asked ominously.

"No—o," I said honestly.

"It would mean more to me," he said heavily, "if your department had released his file to my staff, as they were requested to do."

Good old faithful personnel clerks!

"No such request came to my attention," I said coldly. "And you know procedure requires all such requests must go through the head of a department."

"There are times, in the interests of national security, when—" he left the sentence dangling.

Yes, when the department head was, himself, suspected.

He didn't pursue it. He picked up another sheet from the stack. "That was on March 7th, at 9:45 a.m." he reminded. "On the same date, at 11:20, the Acme Components Company—who patriotically opened all their records to us without question—received a telephone order, from your Purchasing Department, bearing your Purchase Order Number 4B6872K requesting urgent delivery of six gross . . . ah . . . of a certain item which is used only in the assembly of that aforesaid mechanism. This was only one hour and thirty-five minutes from the time the design drawings were released to the mechanical drawing department, and *seven weeks* before all the drawings were released for processing to the various departments.

"A careful check of this one contract alone shows many instances where your Purchasing Department bought materiel, before they could have obtained, through normal channels, the information of what they needed to buy; your Production Control Department issued work orders to your own various production departments to make component parts of this . . . ah . . . mechanism, weeks before they had received the drawings telling them what to make."

"The works manager must have finally got off the dime and started doing his job," Old Stone Face said sourly. There is a bitter feud between the two. Henry hired the works manager under protest. He was recommended by the Military and tied to certain contracts. But he'd been in charge of a civil service project before he came to us, and he'd brought their kind of thinking with him. So there was not exactly a sympathetic harmony between the general manager and the works manager.

"The works manager knows nothing of this," Colonel Backhead said crisply.

"That figures," Henry said.

"He has been most cooperative," Backhead commented. "Without him we couldn't have got anywhere in this preliminary survey, which, I trust, will save much valuable time for the investigating committee."

"Oh I'm sure," I murmured.

"Our survey has not been definitive," Backhead continued. "But we have uncovered an incredible number of incidents, where, under normal procedure things could not have happened in the way they did. In all, five departments seem most involved—Mechanical Engineering, Electronics Engineering, Cybernetics Engineering, Production Control and Purchasing Departments."

"That just about covers the bulk of our production planning departments," I commented.

"And I find that the majority of these items seem to have originated with, or gone through the hands of a single individual in each of those departments. Bellows, whom I've named; a Claude N. Masters, William Huffman, Thomas Meuhl, and one Robert Osborne. The reason I am frank about these names at this time is that I expect the same frankness from you, Mr. Kennedy. There is an obvious out-of-procedure communication about Top Secret material among these men. You have not been too cooperative in the past, but the Pentagon has overlooked it because . . . er . . . your file reveals nothing conclusively discreditable."

"You mean Oliver Cromwell would approve of me?" I asked dryly.

He ignored it.

"So I'm making this last appeal for your wholehearted cooperation. What do you know of these men?"

"Nothing," I said instantly.

He raised his eyebrows and pursed his little mouth.

"Look," I said. "We've got five thousand employees. My department interviews a couple hundred new applications every day, many of them come to my desk for study. I make no attempt whatever to memorize names or case histories; that's why we have records. I have probably seen those names on departmental employee lists many times, but they ring no bells for me."

"But you will instantly make your records available to me," he said confidently.

And now I knew what made him tick. Quite aside from the desire to button this all up before the reps from Pentagon got here and the feather in his cap, he wanted to muckrake all down through our records. We'd had security police like him, men who, on their own time, would stake out all night close to some woman employee's house to see if they could uncover some amorous situation. It was a filthy kind of mind that was permeating our whole social structure. "No," I said flatly. "I'll wait for the accredited Pentagon officials."

He stuffed his papers back into his brief case, snapped its lock, stood up, glared at me, and stalked out of the office.

"I don't know, Ralph," Grenoble said with a worried shake of the head. "He's a mean one. He can hurt."

"I'd rather wash dishes for a living," I said, "than help that kind of a guy along."

"Sometimes I think we'd be better off without government contracts," he said in a tone which suggested it wasn't the first time he'd thought of it. "Profits or no profits."

"They've made the whole security program into a blind for the real purpose of enforcing an Oliver Cromwell kind of morality," I said. "And you can't kick, because that would make you an enemy sympathizer and in favor of unbridled sin."

"You think something is really going on in the plant?" he asked with a worried look.

"Sure," I said. "They'll uncover plenty of dirt. We've probably got a full dozen or so employees who drop into a bar for a glass of beer now and then. And there are probably at least two secretaries out of our couple hundred who aren't married but ought to be. Real hot stuff to make the headlines. By the time they get through with it, these will be highly trusted subversives in key positions who are just begging for some enemy agent to blackmail them into revealing where Grant's Tomb is located."

"I mean is something really going on, Ralph?" he insisted.

"I don't know," I said, and shrugged. Underneath my disgust I was just as worried as he. "I'll look up these guys he named. He was overconfident that he had barreled us over, that we couldn't refuse him, so he did us that much of a favor, anyway. I'll let you know if there is anything to it."

"I made a list of the names for you, Mr. Kennedy," the secretary said, and tore a sheet out of her book. Her quizzical, but approving look made me wonder if she might be one of the secretaries I'd referred to. I wanted to tell her that it was none of my business, or anybody else's, so long as she did her work. I couldn't, of course. She might not be one of those secretaries, she might only wish she were.

I gave her a quick wink that would cover either situation. She gave me a blush that would also fit either case.

On the way back to my office I stopped off at the department of the complaining supervisor and told him never mind reporting to the works manager that stock got to his department ahead of work orders; that this was a part of a larger picture I was investigating, and just to sit tight. He grinned, and shrugged, and implied that he just worked there anyhow. If that's the way we wanted to run a company, he guessed he could put up with it. Only would I please keep that two-bit Napoleon, meaning Colonel Backhead, out of his hair. I suggested patience and fortitude.

In my own department I picked up the five dossiers from the files and started for my own office.

"Trouble again?" Sara asked, as I walked past her desk.

"Nothing unusual," I said. "Just another investigation by the big brass from Pentagon."

"Oh that," she shrugged. "You haven't been fooling around with more poltergeists, have you?"

"Why does everyone assume it is my fault when something goes haywire over in the factory?" I asked plaintively. I went on into my office and spread the dossiers out on my desk.

There was a connection between them. They all lived at the same address. They'd all been hired on the same day. They'd all graduated from Stanford the same year. Obviously, if they were speaking to each other, they could communicate about their work. And they wouldn't have to wait until they got home. We have telephones, and intercoms. So a mechanical engineer picks up a phone and says "Hey Bob, here's an advance flash on some stuff we're going to need that might be hard to get. Why not order it now instead of waiting for the specs?"

Would that be anything to excite the cloak-and-dagger boys?

Yes, each file had a form showing that the employee had been cleared for secret work. So they could talk to each other without overloading Russia's spy ring.

I pulled their progress records. Each of them had climbed remarkably fast. In one year, each of them had made lead man, or group leader, in his department. Not particularly remarkable in engineering, where there's always too few with knowhow, and plenty of opportunity for kids with knowwhat. A little tougher in purchasing and production control, but not if you really grasped how everything tied together.

I flipped back to their original applications. Personnel uses various codes to grade applications and give the interviewer a memory clue so he can call up a mental picture of the individual. But each of these applications had a code word in the top left hand corner I didn't understand.

In quotes, "George!!"

So the interviewer had thought these lads were real George. He'd been right. Their progress records confirmed his opinion that they were good material. But I'd have to caution him against introducing slang codes of his own. A code is worthless unless it communicates the same thing to each of us.

And then it hit me.

I burst out laughing. So George hadn't waited for me to find something for him to do! But while I was still chuckling, I felt the hair on my nape begin to prickle. Maybe the mechanical engineer hadn't *needed* to use a telephone to tell purchasing about the hard-to-buy item! Maybe they hadn't *needed* to send a memo for the expediter to have his stock chasers start delivering matériel to the production machines.

No wonder we'd got contracts out on time. Paperwork is the biggest bottleneck in any large company. It passes from hand to hand, and lays on each desk for hours or days before it is processed and sent along. Weeks can pass between the sender and final receiver. Change orders—and when the military is mixed up in the deal there's a million—sluggishly flow along behind the original. The started work is scrapped and begun again, and again, and again. The orders saying "Do it" are cancelled out by other orders saying "Don't do it."

George had by-passed the red tape. Each of these guys, now in a minor key spot, had flashed all information on to the others, and the busy little pseudopods had just gone ahead and done things, or made the necessary changes days or weeks before the paperwork could catch up.

I knew how auditors worked, and that's what the Pentagon would send—procedure auditors looking for information leaks, finding them by comparing dates and times and work flow, things that showed prior knowledge to the arrival of the authority to know and do. I knew, right then, that the auditors would find dozens, hundreds of discrepancies.

I was tempted, I was sorely tempted, to sit back and do nothing. Let them spend days, weeks, months—or if they'd been civil service trained, *years*—to find out what I already knew.

And then come face to face with the inexplicable.

I think I would have kept my hands off except for those kids. They were just naive enough to think that getting the job done was more important than the paperwork, which showed their service hadn't taught them very much about the Military. I didn't want their F.B.I. files to carry the information that these were dangerous characters to be barred from any sensitive job for the rest of their lives just because they'd tried, in their fashion, to push the job along to get finished by contract deadline date.

Another thought nagged at me. How had they managed to by-pass red tape without fouling everything up for all those people who didn't have a share in George? With all its faults, red tape is a necessity; it is communication telling everybody what has happened or should happen. It can bottleneck, but without it the whole organization falls to pieces.

And ours hadn't!

I supposed they'd kept prior knowledge in their own hands until the rush paperwork had followed through. I dimissed it with that, I shouldn't have. If I'd pursued my thought a little farther, I'd have realized it couldn't have been done that way.

I picked up the phone and put a call through to Old Stone Face.

"I know the answer to that little problem, Henry," I said.

There was a full fifteen seconds of silence.

"So it was something you'd been up to, after all," he answered.

"In a way, I guess it was," I admitted. "I hired the guys. In that sense it was my fault. In that sense, anything that anybody does is my fault."

He wasn't buying any sophistry today.

"So now I'll ask my first question all over again, Ralph! What have you been up to?"

"I'd better come up and talk to you," I said. "But while I'm on my way you can be thinking of the little poltergeist girl, the Swami, and frameworks."

"Oh no!" he said, heavily. "Not another one of those."

"Yes, sir," I affirmed.

Our first act was to send a telegram to General Sandfordwaithe at the Pentagon, the general in charge of Matériel and Supply, and our most frequent Pentagon contact. My first brush with him had been over little Jennie Malasek and the antigrav units. He was a stuffed shirt of the stiffest kind, and it had delighted me to trap him into a promise to furnish us with some poltergeists—male type. But when he found out what they were, instead of exploding, the guy had actually followed through and tried to produce. I suspected that back of the deep encrusted years of military formality there was a human being. The following series of telegrams bore me out.

Our first one said,

CALL OFF YOUR DOGS. WE KNOW WHY CON-
TRACTS FINISHED ON TIME. IT IS OKAY.

HENRY GRENOBLE,
GENERAL MANAGER
CORPORATION

In two hours we got his ubiquitous answer.

YOUR REASSURANCE INSUFFICIENT. COLONEL
BACKHEAD REPORTS YOUR COMPANY RIDDLED
WITH SECRET AGENTS LEAVING TRACKS OF
NEFARIOUS WORK EVERYWHERE AND MANY EM-
PLOYEES MORALLY UNSUITABLE FOR WORK ON
GOVERNMENT CONTRACTS. URGENT WE COME AT
ONCE SINCE YOU WILL NOT COOPERATE IN UN-
MASKING SAME. SUSPECTS KENNEDY IS A LIB-
ERAL.

SANDFORDWAITHE

With Henry's permission, I replied to that dastardly charge personally.

SUGGEST YOU GIVE BACKHEAD DOUBLE BILLED
CAP AND MAGNIFYING GLASS AND SEND HIM TO
ANTARCTICA. UNDERSTAND SECRET AGENTS DIS-
GUISED AS PENGUINS TRYING TO SABOTAGE AN-
NEXATION ATTEMPT DISGUISED AS GEOPHYSICAL
SURVEY. WE ARE TOO BUSY GETTING WORK DONE
TO BOTHER WITH BACKHEAD'S FANCIES AND
ALSO HAVEN'T TIME TO BE COURT-MARTIALED
AGAIN.

RALPH KENNEDY,
DIRECTOR
OF INDUSTRIAL
RELATIONS, CRC.

His reply came within an hour.

IF YOU, KENNEDY, REPEAT YOU IN ITALICS, ARE
DIRECTLY INVOLVED I HAD BETTER COME PER-
SONALLY. WHAT IS THIS NONSENSE ABOUT
COURT-MARTIAL? BILL EMPOWERING PENTAGON
TO COURT-MARTIAL PRIVATE COMPANIES DE-
FEATED IN CONGRESSIONAL COMMITTEE BY MIS-
GUIDED LIBERALS AS YOU SHOULD KNOW. BUT
STAFF AND I WOULD BE PLEASED TO HEAR EX-
PLANATION OF WHY CONTRACTS GET FINISHED
ON TIME. HIGHLY DISTURBING ABNORMALCY.
SANFORDWAITHE

I called young Bellows in the mechanical engineering department
on the interphone. I chose him solely because he was the first name
on my list of five. I sketched in the story and the furor it was
causing.

"Now," I said, "here's the deal. When you boys told me about
George I didn't believe you, and I'm a pushover for believing in
oddballs. You lads are going to have to appear before some top brass
from the Pentagon tomorrow, and if I didn't believe in George, what
do you think *their* reaction will be?"

"We can convince them, sir," Bellows said instantly, and confidently.

"Not by just saying so," I cautioned.

"No, sir. George has learned a lot since he has been employed
here, and we're very grateful to you for giving him the opportunity."

"I don't know," I argued dubiously. "I tried for months to dig up
something that would prove he existed, something that only he could
do."

"Don't worry about it, sir," Bellows said in a comforting voice.

"Anything you want to tell me in advance of the hearing?" I asked
hopefully.

"We'd rather not, sir. You might not give permission, and then we
wouldn't be able to prove."

"Now look," I said warningly. "Oh, never mind. Just don't
jeopardize the company if you can help it."

"Oh no, sir," he said in a shocked voice. "Nothing like that."

"O.K." I replied in a tone that said I washed my hands of the
whole thing. "It's your necks."

I failed to add it was also my neck if they let me down.

The company grapevine told me when the Pentagon Brass arrived and were ushered directly into the big conference room. Old Stone Face accompanied them. It was his idea that he would first explain George to them, then if they wanted to observe us pariahs from the lower strata, we should be assembled in the anteroom awaiting their summons.

I wasn't sure how adequately Henry could explain George, but I had to agree that since the idea of caste was so firmly imbued in the military mind that generals could speak only to generals, they would consider it lese majesty if anyone lower than a general manager attempted to brief them.

I gave them five minutes to get settled, and then called five supervisors to get the pseudopods of George sent down to the anteroom. That done, I cut through factory building Number Two to sit with the boys and be ready for the inquisition.

On the way I was stopped by the production supervisor who had complained about the foul-ups in scheduling.

"I don't know why I squawked about the raw stock getting here before the work orders, Mr. Kennedy," he said. "It's all straightened out now."

"Then you got the work orders through?" I asked.

"Naw," he answered disgustedly. "Didn't need 'em. If I'd just used my head, I'd have known what to do."

I looked over at the storage racks.

"Looks like ordinary bar stock to me," I said dubiously. "I don't see how you could expect to know what should come out of your turret lathes, milling machines and screw machines. Not without work orders and blueprints."

He gave me that disgusted look a production man always keeps in reserve for a white collar.

"If I'd used my head, I'd have known," he repeated. "It's working fine now."

I shrugged, grinned, and left him. I supposed the expediter, one of the five lads, had told him, and he was trying to redeem his position by showing off, by saying that a supervisor just knows these things. The alternative, that he might be speaking the literal truth, that nobody had had to tell him, didn't occur to me.

The short talk delayed me, and when I got to the conference anteroom the boys were all sitting in a cluster of chairs in a corner of the room. I hadn't seen them for a year, and I only vaguely remembered their faces. Yet as a composite group, I remembered them very well. Individually they hadn't changed much, yet, as a composite, I got the impression that this was a much more mature and assured group than it had been during my interview with them. For their sakes, and mine, I hoped so.

I greeted them, all of them returned my greeting in unison. I sat down, a little apart from them. I felt there were many things I should say. I didn't want it on their conscience, or mine, that I had briefed them in attitude or cooked up any phony story. Still, on the way up from my office, I'd felt I'd be remiss if I didn't sketch in for them what was likely to happen in the conference room.

But now that I was in the room with them, there seemed nothing to say, nothing at all. They weren't nervous, and, for a wonder, neither was I. At most it seemed like an unnecessary interruption in our day's work.

We hadn't long to wait. A major, one of Colonel Backhead's men, and the lowest ranking man in the conference room opened the door and nodded in our general direction. He didn't give us the courtesy of meeting our eyes, but his face was a study in curiosity.

We stood up and filed into the conference room. I brought up the rear. The brass and braid were all grouped around the far end of the huge walnut table. The chairs at this end of it were evidently for us to use. When the maintenance department had set up the room for the meeting, I'd checked it and noted that the chairs were all evenly spaced around the table. But a shift had taken place. The Military had pulled their chairs closer together and left a wide gap between themselves and the chairs to be occupied by civilians. Old Stone Face was sitting at this end of the table, apparently to be associated with the culprits. We culprits sat down, three on one side, three on the other.

There were cool nods from the brass and braid, a frosty smile for me from General Sanfordwaithe on the grounds that we had once met before. He was accompanied by a gorgeous Pentagon colonel. To their right sat an admiral and his man, and an equally gorgeous Navy captain. To the left sat a pair of Air Force brass who had mastered that wonderful technique of appearing informally formal. Down toward the middle of the table, and dangerously close to the civilians sat Colonel Backhead and his major. There was no greeting for us from either of these two.

In fact, Backhead appeared to consider our entrance as a distasteful interruption to what he had been saying.

"The most that can be said of your explanation, Mr. Grenoble," he continued, and the way he pronounced mister made it an insult, "disregarding its fantastic incredibility for the moment, is that it is naive." Then in an excess of generosity he excused Old Stone Face. "Of course it wouldn't be expected that an industrialist would be trained in spotting the nefarious and subtle work of master saboteurs. But we are trained. I submit that you may have been taken in by this wildly preposterous explanation, and that from your point of view you have been honest in offering it to us.

"But let me show you how it looks from another point of view."

Beside me, I felt one of the boys stir a little in his chair. I glanced at them sidelong, and saw that flicker of secret delight behind their solemn faces.

"This is how it looks to me," Colonel Backhead said again for emphasis.

Without a change of accusing expression, he stood up, climbed up on his chair, leaned forward in a crouch, crawled over into the middle of the conference table, put his head down on the table, and bracing himself with his hands, he slowly lifted his posterior and feet into the air, until he was standing on his head.

"It looks all upside down," he said sternly.

Then he toppled and fell over sideways.

I glanced at Henry and saw that his mouth was hanging open. A glance down the table showed me that General Sanfordwaithe had clamped his grim jaws tightly while he stared with unbelieving eyes. The faces of the rest of the Military showed only pity and contempt. It was the Navy captain who bore out that expression.

"If that's the best headstand you can do," he said icily, "you're no credit to the services."

He crawled up on the table, and with crisp, sure movements formed a triangle with his head and hands. Then, with fluid precision, he raised his feet, brought his legs together, straightened them out, and pointed his toes ceilingward.

"You have to do this regularly," he said in a didactic voice. "I do it everytime I want to get a new perspective on things. That is why the Navy is pulling so far ahead of the Army, we practice getting a new point of view."

"The Navy is no better than the Air Force," the pair of wings shouted in unison. "We're upside down most of the time!" The pair of them climbed up on the table and stood on their heads also.

They seemed to be enjoying themselves hugely. I felt a little sorry for the admiral. He was trying to crawl up on the table, but age was against him. He looked as if, for the first time, he might have to admit he had to face retirement. Couldn't even stand on his head any more!

Old Stone Face had pushed himself back from the table, and his hands were still upraised, as if it were a holdup. I looked down the table at Sanfordwaithe. His eyes met mine, and the horror in them dissolved into laughter. The explanation had occurred to both of us at the same time. He stood up, he roared with laughter, he gasped, he pounded futilely on his chest, trying to get air back into his lungs. Then a new horror spread over his face, a certainty that he would laugh himself to death. Abruptly, he stopped.

"No," he gasped as soon as he could draw a breath. "Not me, too." He gasped in another breath, and trusted himself to look at the squirming men in the center of the table. They were shoving, pushing one another like little boys in a rough and tumble game in a schoolyard.

"I can stand on my head longer than you can!"

"Can't either!"

"Can, too!"

"My ships can lick your ol' airplanes any day!"

"Can't either!"

"Can, too!"

"Ol' Army's no good for nothin'!" the admiral shouted.

"Yah, yah, yah," agreed the Air Force.

"Is, too!" Backhead's major shouted. "Good for mopping up." He crawled down off the table and started running around the conference room. "Where's the mop?" he whined plaintively.

I caught a glimpse of Backhead's face where he still huddled in the middle of the table, down toward our end. He was no longer caught up in the mob psychology. Like Henry, Sanfordwaithe, and myself, he was an observer. His face was sick with despair.

"Call off *your* dogs, Kennedy," Sanfordwaithe shouted at me about the tumult. "I'm convinced."

I was, too. George was no longer confined to the five lads, not necessarily so. Now I knew why there had been no disruption of our organization when red tape had been bypassed. George had simply taken over.

And what George could take over, he could also let go.

The majestic military crumbled into a heap in the middle of the table, and began to slide off its edges onto the carpeted floor. Back in their own military mind framework again, they scrambled to their feet and stood at disheveled attention. Their faces were masks of horror, for like the participants in a mob, they remembered everything they had done, but with the guiding entity gone from their minds, they could find no excuse for it.

No one shouted "At Ease!" to them, and slowly they remembered that they were big boys now, far enough along in the Military hierarchy so that someone didn't have to tell them every little move to make. Sheepishly, they relaxed and slid back into their chairs. Furtively, they began to straighten their ties, button their tunics, rearrange their medals, preen themselves, recapture the impregnable Military attitude.

I recalled the caption to a cartoon. A dear little old lady was talking to a marine general. "I can understand why you must toughen them up for battle purposes," she said. "But when you're through with them, how do you retenderize them so they'll be fit to mingle with human beings?"

Perhaps these men had now been tenderized to the point where they could think rationally. It would seem so.

"Perhaps, Mr. Kennedy," General Sanfordwaithe said, with a twitch of his lips, "we should run over the explanation of George once more. I think we may have missed some of the fine points."

I turned to the five lads.

"You boys can go on back to your departments now. You won't be needed here any longer."

I looked at General Sanfordwaithe, and his nod of agreement seemed to contain a considerable measure of relief.

"Yes, sir," one of the boys said. They stood up, not quite with the precision of a drill team, a move that I now knew was calculated disorder. They looked at me, as if wanting to be reassured that they had done well. I smiled, and so did they.

For one incredible instant George took control of me, and I shared the wondrous delight of being, belonging, the ecstacy of being something beyond human. Then he released me as the boys filed out the door, and was left grubby, incomplete, ineffectual, bumbling—alone.

I turned around in my chair and faced the brass and braid again. All of them were looking at me, now without accusation, except Backhead and his major. Those two sat slumped in their chairs, with bent heads, staring fixedly at the center of the table.

"It's been coming for a long time," I began. "The whole civilization has been trending in that direction. It had to come. With billions of human beings now inhabiting the world, there is simply no way that individualism can survive. This is just an advance flash of what may be commonplace before long. It is something new, gentlemen. We don't know how these boys are allied to produce a George. More important, perhaps, we don't know what to do with George.

"And we must think of something, for idle hands, gentlemen, you know—"

Remembrance and Reflection

From *The Magazine of Fantasy and Science Fiction*

Remembrance and reflection how allied!
What thin partitions sense from thought divide!

POPE

"You know anything about hypnotism, Sara?" I asked my secretary when she brought in my share of the morning's memos.

She dropped the papers into my IN box and backed away from the desk as if it were a hot fire.

"Now Mr. Kennedy," she began warily. "You're not going to start stirring things up again are you?" She looked as if she wanted to run right back to her own office, and maybe right on out of the plant.

"Isn't it about time?" I wondered.

"Why don't you let sleeping dogs lie, Mr. Kennedy?" she asked plaintively. "It's been so nice these last few months."

"Can't think of anything more useless than a sleeping dog lying around," I grumbled. "That's the trouble. Trouble with everybody. Everybody's massively fed, massively diverted, massively tranquilized—"

"Peace, it's wonderful," she murmured.

"Most dangerous condition this country ever faced," I said. "Want to know something, Sara? Even the usually discontented intellectuals have gone over to this happy-happy kick where anybody who views-with-alarm is a you-know-what. Scares me, Sara, when all the rest of the world—"

"Every time you get like this things happen around Computer Research," Sara complained. "Why can't you be just an ordinary Personnel Director? Why can't you be contented just doing an ordinary job like everybody else?"

"What, for instance, am I neglecting in my ordinary job?"

"There's enough in those memos to keep you busy—"

"I'll tell you what's in those memos even before I look at them," I interrupted. "There'll be one from Safety Engineering complaining that a certain supervisor fishes bits of metal out of the machinery with his hands without shutting down the whole production line first, and that's the way fingers get smashed. There'll be a companion piece from the supervisor asking me to tell Safety Engineering to keep its nose out of his department, and if he wants to smash his fingers they're his fingers. Big challenge to Personnel, Sara."

"You know what accidents do to our insurance rates," she reminded.

"I know what overprotection does to production," I reminded back. "Then there'll be a memo," I went on, "from the Chief of Security Guards complaining that the Maintenance Supervisor refuses to stop for positive identification when he passes through security check points. The companion to that will be from the Maintenance Supervisor complaining that he passes every one of those unprintable security guards twenty times a day and if they don't know who his great grandmother kissed on her first date by now they never will and the whole thing is a bunch of nonsense anyhow—everybody playing Junior G–Man."

"That was yesterday's memos," Sara said loftily.

"All right," I answered. "Idea's the same. For instance I haven't had a complaint for quite a while from Office Supply that the design engineers refuse to turn in old pencil stubs when they want new ones—and you can't tell me they're really doing it."

"I'll keep an eye out for it, and rush it right in to you when it comes," Sara promised, and tossed her long bob of red hair.

"You know what worries me the most of all, Sara?" I asked.

She looked wary again.

"The Pentagon," I said. "More specifically the Poltergeist Division. I haven't heard from the Poltergeist Division of the Pentagon in over a year."

"Well, you know these government bureaus," Sara tried to console me. "They start out going to do big things. Everybody in them rushes around designing forms and reports and statistics to impress people. First thing, they get so snowed under with filling out those forms, making those reports, and compiling those statistics there just isn't any time left to *do* anything. You should try it, Mr. Kennedy. Nothing like big charts and graphs and engineering curves done in colored inks to impress people with how important you are. Cover your desk and your walls with those, and you won't need to do anything at all. Except, maybe, keep them dusted."

I ignored her.

"Even General Sandfordwaithe has stopped hounding me," I said. "Ever since the George incident, he's left me strictly alone."

"You should be glad."

"It worries me, Sara. It worries me a lot. When our own Pentagon gets so massively . . . well massively something that it stops hounding us scientists—"

"You scientists!" she scoffed. Then, lest she had gone too far, "All his hounding didn't help you to produce more antigrav units."

"That's something else," I said. "That fake Swami sits over there in his plush laboratory, holding hands with the female production line workers, and so far he hasn't learned a thing about how to activate antigrav cylinders on any kind of a dependable schedule."

"So what can you do about it?" she asked, not with curiosity but with a tone telling me I should accept the inevitable, like everybody else.

"Maybe hypnotism . . ." I began.

"This is where I came in," she answered. And went out.

I got up and followed her to the connecting door between our offices. She had already sat down back of her own desk, and now couldn't very well escape without making a point of it. I leaned against the door jamb.

"Do you think you'd have time to run over to the UCLA library this morning," I asked, "to see if you can pick up anything on the relationship of hypnosis to psi—if any?"

She looked at her own IN box pointedly. It was stacked up a foot thick, a mute reminder that she tried to take over all the detail work and leave me with only the creative.

Creative! As, for example, I should go over to Design Engineering and say, "Please, fellows, would you mind trying to cooperate a little with Industrial Engineering's ideas and save up your pencil stubs?" I already knew what Industrial Engineering could do with pencil stubs. I didn't need Design Engineering to tell me.

Or maybe go over to Industrial Engineering and say, "Look, fellows, did it ever occur to you that it might not be maximum efficiency to bring Design Engineering minds down to the level of saving up pencil stubs?" I already knew their answer, too, about what the creative geniuses really designed and passed around when they thought nobody was looking, and how it would be raising, not lowering, their mind level to get them considering costs. This was creative personnel?

"Never mind," I said. "I'll find time during the morning to go over to the library. Maybe that would be better, because I know what I want." I stood there for a moment. "I think I know what I want," I amended.

I closed the door and went back to my desk. I picked up the stack of interoffice memos. The top one was from Old Stone Face, Mr. Henry Grenoble, the General Manager. He mentioned, rather gently I thought, that I hadn't been caught trying to wreck the company for quite a while now, and what was I doing? Just sitting around drawing my pay?

I felt better. I had seen the evidence of George taking over more and more of the production functions of Computer Research, and the workers getting more and more like ants who knew exactly what they were supposed to do from some central source that had no corporeal identity. Marvelously efficient, and I was afraid Old Stone Face had let it soothe him into tranquility. Apparently he hadn't. I didn't feel so alone now.

My drive to the UCLA library turned out to be a waste of time. Oh, there had been a few half hearted attempts to rouse psi through hypnotism, with results about as indecisive as other experiments. It looked as if I'd have to do my own experiments. As I leafed through the few references, I wondered how I'd be as a hypnotist.

Of course I might get the Swami to help me, but the habit of faking was so deeply ingrained in his character one couldn't tell when he was being honest because he didn't know, himself.

I managed to snag a couple of profs in the psych department, but my questions on the subject were met with much the same disdain as if I'd asked for the real truth about Unidentified Flying Objects. I should have known. There is a breed who calls himself a scientist but is really concerned only with maintaining a reputation for esoteric knowledge. As soon as the layman picks up the idea, he drops it like a hot coal, for to be identified with it now would associate him with the untouchables. Bridey Murphy and various television programs had vulgarized hypnotism until these men, whose only real concern was their own prestige, wouldn't touch it. They had the same attitude toward psi—and for the same reason.

As I climbed back into my car, I reflected that fortunately there were a few, not many but some, who were more concerned with knowledge than with REPUTATION. Lucky mankind! Otherwise . . .

When I got back to the plant, Sara had a surprise waiting for me in my office. Another colonel from the Pentagon.

"Logart," he identified himself. To his credit he did not add and emphasize, "*Colonel* Logart." He let the eagles on his collar speak for themselves. He did add, "Poltergeist Division, Pentagon," but his face broke into a broad grin when he said it.

Out of his uniform he would have been more or less nondescript, displaying none of that rugged, masculine handsomeness of the fair-haired career men in the services and denoting a possible latent something-or-other in high places. I nodded, shook hands perfunctorily, and waved him to the crying chair in front of my desk.

"Know anything about mass hypnotism?" I asked as an opener.

"After fifteen years in the service?" he countered. "What do you think basic training and all that comes after it might be?"

I'd been looking at him, but now I did a sort of double take and really saw him for the first time.

"Well now," I grinned as broadly as he. "How have you managed to survive?"

He took my question at face value.

"One of the more or less valid facts about hypnotism is that you can't be hypnotized if you don't want to be. Of course that presupposes you know what is happening—as most don't. But I knew. And I also knew that the only way to survive that, or any other mass hypnotism framework, was to become so completely imitative that no one would realize I knew I was imitating."

"Well now," I said again. "You and I might be able to work together. We've had a series of stuffed pouter pigeons, and—"

"I know," he interrupted. "You've got yourself quite a reputation back at the Pentagon, Kennedy. For bringing an end to fine, promising careers, that is. We've got plenty of brave men who can stand up under bullets, or bombs, or even ridicule when it comes in from the outside. But when a man becomes ridiculous in his own eyes. . . . You've got quite a nasty faculty for that, Kennedy." He'd stopped grinning, but his eyes were still twinkling with real mirth. Yet a man who could consciously learn to be so imitative as to give the illusion he thought he was being creative could succeed in simulating almost anything. So I could only hope the mirth was real.

"That's why it was relatively easy for me to get assigned to this Company. General Sanfordwaithe was in a hole. He could order men to their death under fire without a twinge, because that's part of the hypnosis. But to order career suicide is something else. So I expect he was pretty relieved when I volunteered, or rather when I begged for the assignment."

He stopped and looked at me.

"Of course there's more," I said, and pushed a box of cigarettes across the desk to him. He took one, lit it, and so did I.

"Yes," he said. "There's more. Considerably more."

"Naturally."

"I'm interested in George," he said. "I've always known that sooner or later a George would come on the scene. That is, if I got the story straight. Would you mind. . . ."

I repeated the story of George for him. How these five young college grads came to me with the yarn that through mental identification, interplay and feedback, they had succeeded in creating a superentity, an incorporeal being for which they were merely body, hands and feet. Unlike the fleeting entity that comes into being in a mob, or other gathering of people with mental feedback and interplay, George was a permanent, an enduring—ah—personality? quality? being?—anyhow, whatever.

I told him how I had tried for months to find something that only a George could do, something that five unconnected guys couldn't do, something that required instant communication and coordination. I told him how I'd failed to think of anything because science and industry are both constructed to compensate for the lack of instant communication and coordination. I told him how George had gradually reached out and begun to take over the operation of the production planning functions of the plant; the furor caused by getting contracts out on time, for a change; the investigation and demonstration to the Pentagon officers of his reality as an entity. And the demonstration of his power.

"Demonstration of one of his powers," I amended. "What other powers he might have, or develop, I've . . . I've been a little too nervous to find out."

He nodded as if he understood and crushed out the butt of his cigarette in my ashtray.

"Pretty much as stated in the report," he conceded. "I was afraid it might have been—ah—interpreted. Strike you as peculiar that you couldn't think of anything for George to do?"

"Yes," I said emphatically. "There was a teasing, tantalizing feeling that there must be dozens, hundreds of things. Only I could never bring one right out into the foreground. Like a word or a name on the tip of our tongue that annoys because it will neither come clear nor go away."

"One of the interesting aspects of hypnotism," he said as if he were veering away from the subject, or maybe coming back to it. "The subject is partially conscious and knows things exist beyond his will's reach. But he can only think and act according to the compulsions given him, the things consistent with the framework of his commands. Ever occur to you that what you call 'frameworks' might be a kind of compulsion boundary you can't cross? You say industry and science is organized to compensate for the lack of instant communication and coordination because such things can't exist among people. Something for George to do would be outside your frame of compulsions."

"Look," I said. "Aren't you extending the definition of hypnotism a little far? After all, a word, too, has certain semantic boundaries."

"Who can draw the line," he asked, "between hypnotism and suggestion? Where does suggestion leave off and teaching begin? Where does propaganda leave off and belief begin? Where is the line between belief and compulsion? Where is the boundary between compulsion and hypnotism?"

"The music goes round and round," I said flippantly. But flippancy was a cover-up for some powerful mixed emotions I hadn't yet sorted out. More than the words, it was the semantic overtones back of them, such as the implications in substituting the word *teaching* and *propaganda*. By that, did he mean all teaching?

Personnel people, accustomed to twenty different versions a day of the only possible right way to think, become detached and are able to see these versions in perspective. But I felt something different from that—a glimpse of such far vision that I could look down on human beings, like two-dimensional creatures, forever imprisoned within the narrow walls of their compulsions, unable to break through the hypnotic suggestions of their frameworks. But only a glimpse.

For that comprehension was replaced by a reaction far less exalted. A deep disappointment. I'd run into his pattern before, on quite a few occasions. I had him pegged, classified. The mental exhibitionist. A fellow who dreams up startling things to say to gain attention and impress people. They don't need to mean anything, just sound as if they do. No doubt around the Pentagon, where the philosophical concepts must be at best on the primitive level—or the military framework couldn't exist at all—he'd made quite a splash with his semantic gymnastics. And, no doubt, he thought a display of his well-worn patter would push Kennedy over as easily.

After fifty thousand people or so, we never seem to get an original. Even in the first few dozens we start getting carbon copies, people who occupy a duplicate framework, and therefore duplicate all the same problems inherent in the framework. The hope that we may—perhaps even today!—encounter an original keeps us able to endure the deadly monotony of repetition where each person thinks himself to be . . . different. My hope that today I had discovered one died.

Oddly, his interest in me seemed to die simultaneously. Perhaps it was my flippant remark, yet if he had been truly perceptive he would have known. . . . Therefore his assumption that he hadn't impressed me, after all, was proof of the shallow level at which he operated. His eyes seemed to film over, grow remote. Outwardly he was still cordial, as was I. But rapport, for a few moments tantalizingly near, was gone. I understood him, and he was at least perceptive enough to realize it.

"Well," he said, after an appreciable pause, "I just dropped in to get acquainted. You understand, of course, that before discussing with you my real mission I must present it to your general manager, Mr. Grenoble."

"Of course," I agreed. "Never let it be forgotten that I'm just the Personnel Director here. I can't speak for the company except at that level."

We stood up simultaneously. He reached across the desk and we shook hands. His eyes looked at me as if he was perhaps a little sad at what they saw. And perhaps my eyes showed him the same. He was disappointed that he hadn't made an impression. I was disappointed that he had tried it on such an obvious level. He left.

The office seemed singularly empty and barren after he had gone. And that was odd, because if he hadn't made a deep impression, why should it? Had I been right in my first reaction, and not my second? Of course not. The man was an obvious poseur, transparently so. The pity of it was, he didn't need to be. Because there was something about him. . . .

Something, like a word or a name on the tip of the tongue, wouldn't go away. Some hypnotic compulsion shut me off from. . . . Nonsense!

II

The next day Old Stone Face and Colonel Logart left for Washington. The deal proposed by the Pentagon must have been a good one, interesting enough to cause the general manager to make the trip. Henry gave me no hint before he left of what it might involve. Usually I can surmise what's in the wind, even when he thinks he's playing it close to his chest, because he wants this or that kind of expert. This time there was no such clue.

There was a clue as to the magnitude of the deal, for Old Stone Face stayed in Washington more than a week. This meant he had to hang around while a little time could be found here and there in the calendars of the big boys. From the time involved, some of these boys were right up there on the first team.

Still there were a couple of straws in the wind. When Henry called me into his office for his going-away pep talk, which usually amounted to instructions to kind of keep an eye on the store while he was out to lunch, he betrayed at least one source of interest.

"How's George doing these days, Ralph?" he asked with what he considered to be a disinterested, friendly smile. On him it always looked like an earthquake splitting open the side of a granite mountain.

"Your production reports will tell you better than I can," I said. "He's practically taken over the running of production. I don't know about you, but it's cut my work in half. Grievances have dropped off to practically nothing."

"I can't complain about production quantity or quality," he conceded. Which, for him, was like saying that output was exceeding his wildest dreams.

"I'm borrowing trouble, I know," I said. "But somehow I'm a little uneasy."

I could see by the disappearance of the crack in the granite cliff that he was getting ready for the bad news. He didn't say anything.

"You know, Henry," I said hesitantly, "I get the feeling of a little boy absorbed with playing train. I sometimes wonder what's going to happen if he gets bored with the gadgets, and starts looking around to see what else might be interesting. Anyhow," I said idly, "Playing train belongs to an older generation. I get the feeling that George is still a very small boy, and today's small boys are interested in spaceships."

He flashed me a quick look from under his craggy brows to see if there was guile behind my words, thereby revealing the guile behind his.

"If the government made those boys a good offer, you think they'd leave us—and take George with them?"

"I'm not close to the boys," I said. "But I doubt it. Not if we had anything comparable. The government is killing the goose that lays the golden egg with its security attempts to make unusual people conform to mediocre standards. Scientists don't like to work for government, and wouldn't if they could get comparable deals in private industry. If we lose George it will be our own fault."

"Thank you, Ralph," he said absently, as if he had got the information he wanted.

"Have a good trip," I said as I went out the door. I doubt he heard me.

The other straw in the wind came from an unexpected direction. Sara set up an appointment for me to see Annie Malasek.

Annie Malasek, P–1 Assembler, had been with us a number of years now. She was the mother of Jennie Malasek, the little poltergeist girl who had first activated the Auerbach cylinders and made them into antigrav units. I'd cut my own feet out from under me by helping Jennie to get out of the psi framework and over into normalcy—thereby winning the undying gratitude of her mother, Annie. In turn, Annie had helped me to pull a stunt on the fake Swami, who had been claiming psi powers, which proved he really had them, even though he had thought he was faking.

A little to my surprise, when Sara ushered Annie into my office, the Swami came with her. There was that intangible something surrounding the two of them that told me their news before he had finished seating her and found his own chair.

"We wanted you to be the first to know, Mr. Kennedy," Annie said, and simpered. "We're going to get married, Swami and me."

I stood up and came around from behind my desk.

"One look at the pair of you and anybody would know," I said as I crossed the room. I took her hand in my left and his hand in my right, squeezed them, and brought their hands together. Swami was grinning like a foolish boy, and Annie began to cry like a foolish girl. I went back to my desk, opened a top drawer, fished out a clean handkerchief, and took it over to Annie. It wasn't the first time. Only this time her tears were not troubled. While Swami was wiping away her tears with tender care, I went back and sat down behind my desk.

I didn't know which to congratulate. By my standards the Swami was a pretty worthless catch, while Annie was a hard-working, faithful, loyal woman worth her weight in gold. Yet it wasn't my standards that had to be satisfied. Hers had been the drab, gray life of a poor factory worker, always struggling to make ends meet; and to her the Swami must have been all that was mysterious, romantic, wonderful. Perhaps his very worthlessness made him all the more precious. Certainly in the eyes of the various factory women who went in heavily for mysticism, she had walked off with the prize catch. Who was I to say that she should not have this triumph? Or that each of them should not have what was most needed—she to be folded in the physical arms of the mysterious infinite; he to have a woman who would joyfully work hard for him, keep him well fed.

I glanced at his white turban. Already she seemed to be doing his laundry. The customary dark grease mark around the edges had disappeared; and come to think of it I hadn't got that faint whiff of malodor from his heavy red-and-gold robe when I'd gone near him.

"Fine, fine," I said heartily, and meant it. "I can't think of anybody more suited to each other."

The faint look of wary apprehension behind the Swami's huge, liquid black eyes disappeared, and was replaced by real gratitude. Annie was melting all over. My approval had meant a great deal to them. But Annie was Annie, and her character shapelessness didn't last long.

"There was two things we had to see you about, Mr. Kennedy," she said. "The other was about Jennie."

"Oh?" I questioned. "I understood she was in grammar school and doing very well. Trouble?"

"No," she answered. "Not yet, anyhow. It's that new Colonel from Washington. He came to me about Jennie. He knew all about . . . about the trouble she used to have. He asked me if I'd let him see her, talk to her."

"Oh, he did?" I said. Apparently Colonel Logart was letting no grass grow under his feet. First those questions from Henry about George must have meant that Logart had talked to the five lads. Now Jennie.

"I don't want Jennie in trouble no more," Annie was saying. "She wasn't happy when she wasn't like other kids. Now she's like them and she's happy."

"Did Colonel Logart speak to you?" I turned to the Swami.

"Just casually," the Swami answered in his deep, sonorous tones. "But I agree with my little bride. I wouldn't want my daughter disturbed." It sounded very authoritative and firm. The term "little bride" didn't seem to sicken Annie the way it did me. She looked at him with adoration.

"Don't worry about it," I told the both of them. "If Colonel Logart brings up the subject again, send him to me."

"That's what I already did," Annie said, and stood up. Hastily the Swami jumped to his feet.

When they had gone, I picked up the phone and got young Jim Bellows in the Engineering Department.

"Did Colonel Logart approach you fellows about going to work for the government while he was here?" I asked.

"Yes, sir," he answered readily. "We told him to see you. We wouldn't make a move without letting you know—not after all you've done for us and George."

"Thanks," I said, and hung up. Thanks, too, for loyalty.

I sent off a wire to Henry's hotel in Washington:

> HAVE LEARNED LOGART TRIED TO SHANGHAI OUR SPECIAL EMPLOYEES, REPEAT SPECIAL EMPLOYEES, BEHIND MY BACK. POUR IT ON, HENRY.
> KENNEDY

His wire came back in a few hours.

> JUST WHAT I NEEDED TO BEAR DOWN HARD. THANKS, RALPH.
> OLD STONE FACE

I looked at the telegram for several minutes before I found what was disturbing me. I was so used to thinking in that term that it merely bothered me, but didn't strike me.

I picked up the phone and called the mail room.

"Check the telegraph company for the accuracy of the signature on that message I just received," I said.

"I already did, Mr. Kennedy," the girl answered. "They insist he signed it that way himself."

"Oh well," I sighed. "I suppose that sooner or later he had to learn what we call him."

Colonel Logart came in to see me as soon as he and Henry got back from Washington. He stood before my desk and I didn't ask him to sit down.

"I want you to know," he said through thinned lips, "that in talking to your special employees, I was merely following orders."

My lips were equally thin. The common practice of pirating valuable employees is one in which I will not indulge and which I do not appreciate when others try it with me.

"You militarists," I said coldly, "seem to think that following orders justifies anything from a mild indignity to an outright criminal action. Talk about hypnotic frameworks! We may have become a militarist nation, but we're not under martial law just yet."

He sat down on the edge of the crying chair, without invitation, and pursed his lips as if to hide the twitch of amusement. He made no effort to hide the twinkle in his eyes.

"Oh, I don't know," he said speculatively. "In the life of an individual don't you find he spends the most of his money on what he wants most? So take a look at our national budget."

"There are such things as necessities of life," I said, "that determine how a person or a nation spends income."

"Well, Mr. Kennedy," he argued, soberly now, "don't you find, particularly in those whose thought stream runs shallow, that what one person considers to be a dire necessity he couldn't live without is something another person doesn't want and feels no need of whatever?"

"Goes back to group mores," I said. "If everybody. . . ."

"Exactly," he agreed.

"I hardly think we can solve national policy, militaristic or otherwise," I said drily. "Not just between the two of us."

"No," he answered. "We can't. And that's something of enormous importance. Will you remember that, Mr. Kennedy? It will help you to understand, when. . . ."

He trailed the sentence off and was silent. God help us, I classified it as more attempts to say startling things, that puny pattern of trying to be something special.

"I believe we're off the subject," I reminded him. "We were discussing your action of coming out here and trying to steal away some special employees behind my back."

"It's all part of the same big picture," he said.

"I'm sure it is. Did you bring along your ordnance maps and your pretty little colored pins to demonstrate the big picture?"

He ignored my sarcasm.

"Working on a certain government project would have been a long step upward for Jennie's mother, for example," he said, without responsive anger. "She'd never have to work again. Meantime, with her consent, and with Jennie's willing consent, we could try to restore Jennie's ability to activate antigrav cylinders. Not the little toy things you have stored in your bolted-down vault here, but the real thing—big ones."

"Assuming you could do it," I qualified. I lit a cigarette and pushed the box across the desk toward him. He took it as an invitation to slide down into a more comfortable position in the chair. He lit a cigarette.

"As for George," he continued through a puff of smoke, "how long do you think he will be content to play factory operation? One thing you seem to have overlooked, Kennedy. Jennie, Swami, George—they're all just children. Oh sure, the lads that make up George are mature young men, and Swami won't see thirty again, but as far as their psi development is concerned they're children. Children need to grow, and to grow they must have the kind of food they need to grow on."

"Assuming you know what psi food is," I said.

"Working on this certain government project would have given those young men real stature, and George something to challenge his growing mentality. Because, Kennedy," he said quietly, "*we were* able to think of something that only a George could do."

My arm froze with my cigarette lifted half way to my lips. I stared at him for a full minute, then, without taking another puff, I crushed out my cigarette in the tray.

"It was the way you went about it," I said slowly. "I've never stood in the way of an employee's chance at a real opportunity in my life."

He lifted an eyebrow, because it was a rash statement for any industry man to make.

"I know," I said. "Most companies operate on the policy of keeping a man where he can do them the most good, without much thought for what is good for the man. I don't. I operate on the policy that I'd rather have an ambitious, intelligent man for a short while than a stupid one forever. I've built a reputation around that. That's why the brightest and best are eager to come to work for us, because they know I'll try to push them upward, either in or out of the company. If you had come to me, instead of going behind my back—"

"You'd have given me your special employees," he said. "I knew that. So I made a mistake in the way I went about carrying out my orders. The mistake came to light when you sent that wire to Grenoble. So we didn't bring the psi children under government control with all its spying on employees, informing, watching them through little peekholes in false walls the way we watch the scientists. You think psi talented people could stand up under that?"

"Or," I said slowly, "having failed in your objective, you've been given a new set of orders to put the best possible interpretation on your mistake."

He shrugged his shoulders and grinned.

"Whatever you prefer to think, Kennedy," he said easily. "The fact remains that Computer Research has the job which, heretofore, has been one of the most carefully guarded secrets under direct government operation."

"Because," I said, "George is necessary to it."

"George is necessary," he agreed. "Only a George could do it.

Ever see the inside of the control cabin in one of the big, modern flying superforts, Kennedy?"

I nodded.

"No human mind can see all those instruments simultaneously and take the necessary actions, so we try to divide up the work and responsibility among various members of the flight crew. It works all right as long as everything goes all right, but when it doesn't we read about it in the papers. Almost every day, in fact, we read about it in the papers. And that's just the simple little problem of flying along over the Earth's surface, where all the factors are known and precalculated."

I waited. I gave him the benefit of my assumption that he didn't mean to make an ordinary flight crew out of George.

"If the problems of coordination are becoming more and more insurmountable in just flying through the air," he said, "think what the problems would be in traveling through space to another body."

"Sure," he went on, "we've been making progress with guided missiles, putting in servomechanisms to handle specific and known factors, but what about unknown factors? Or even a complexity of known factors would require a huge hall full of servomechanisms. Marvelous though it may be, the guided missile is a one track mind, equipped to do one thing, equipped to make only one choice when a given condition arises. And even there, the accuracy leaves much to be desired."

I didn't say anything. I could see what was coming.

"In approaching the problem of traversing space, we haven't had any choice, ourselves. We've had to attack it from the angle of a guided missile because no ordinary group of human beings could work together with the necessary instantaneous speed and direction to control the ship from the inside, to analyze unknown factors as they arise and take original, creative action among a multiple of choices."

"But George could," I said.

"George would have a chance of doing it," he qualified. "We've got to make a break-through somewhere. Either we have to take an entirely new approach to cybernetic machines, so we can get them down to payload dimensions, or we have to learn how to synthetically create more Georges. We've always assumed it had to be the former, but George may change our minds. So now," he said, as he put his hands on his knees and began to stand up, "instead of taking George to the project, we're going to bring the project to

George. I haven't talked to the boys about it. I came first to you for your permission."

"Quite a project," I said. "There's a long time and a lot of steps between deciding to build an inner-controlled spaceship and taking it up for a test."

"We'd like George to be in on it from the beginning," he answered. "It would be essential that he know everything there is to be known about the ship itself. Because, in space, we can't know which bit of knowledge will be vital."

"Whenever you're ready, I'll talk to the boys," I agreed.

"I'm ready now," he said. "The government has already taken steps to condemn that whole section of area next to your plant. The clearing and new construction will go fast. In the meantime, the design engineering can be picked up from where it has already been carried by the Pentagon staff. The boys are engineering-trained, but they'll have to be checked out on the specifics of this one."

"I trust you're prepared to listen to their ideas, instead of making them adopt yours," I said.

"Of course," he answered.

"Where do Jennie and the Swami come into the picture?"

"We expect to power it with antigrav units," he said. "We couldn't get unlimited range, otherwise. To say nothing of maneuverability."

"I'll confirm with Henry," I said, and stood up also. "I'll talk with the boys. I'll talk with Jennie's mother and her new dad, the Swami. I'll talk with Jennie. It all depends on how willing they are."

I followed him to the door, and watched him go through Sara's office and on out of the department. I leaned up against the door jamb.

"I can't figure that fellow," I said to Sara. "First I thought he was the real McCoy. Then I thought he was a shallow blowhard. Now I don't know."

"Nice to see that everybody isn't just a pawn on your chessboard," Sara said with a sigh.

"It's pretty certain I'm a pawn on his," I said. "But I don't know what game he's playing."

"Does he have to be playing any special game?" she asked.

"I don't even know that," I answered.

"My," she said, and her teasing smile broke up the sharpness of her words. "First thing you know, you're going to be down on the level of all the rest of us blind, stoopid pawns."

"Maybe I've never been above that level," I answered seriously. "Maybe I'm just a hypnotized victim of a framework, with one of my commands being to think I control my thoughts and actions."

"You lost me back there somewhere, Boss," she answered flippantly, and dug into her work box for another sheaf of reports.

Henry confirmed that we were now in the spaceship business, as a sideline to our regular computer business, a not too improbable side line, since a spaceship without computer servomechanisms would be just a bulky hull. I would have my hands full, he warned me, in rounding up the necessary experts, even with all the help I could get from the government.

"The less help I get from the government, the better," I said drily. "Their ideas of merit are more concerned with a man's sex life, and what idle remark he may have made in an off moment twenty years ago, or whether he was ever arrested by some moronic cop. The more we get to be like Russia the less I like it. Have you ever noticed, Henry, that when a man takes on an enemy, he also takes on the characteristics of the enemy? Seems to work with nations, too."

"Very interesting," he commented impassively. "I thought we were talking about building a spaceship."

"There's a connection somewhere," I said. "Maybe it has to do with the fact that when you take on a framework you take on all the problems and defects inherent in it. Passing laws against those defects is like making it a criminal offense for blue-eyed parents to have a blue-eyed child: if they're going to have children at all they'll be blue-eyed, criminal offense or none. So I don't want to get involved with the government's having anything at all to say about the kind of men we hire. Only thing I'll care about is have they got brains and are they still able to use them in spite of everything we've done to prevent it."

"Just so you get them," he said. "Logart is going to head up the project."

"Here we go again," I groaned. "They'll have to satisfy him."

"He's no longer a Colonel," Henry said. "Starting tomorrow he's just plain Mister Logart, private citizen."

"Shedding the uniform and the badges doesn't make him shed the frame of thinking," I argued. "That's how we became a militarist nation: we got saturated."

"You're not in a very constructive mood today, Ralph," he complained with enough irritation to show me I'd griped my limit. "You work with him the way you do with the rest of the supervisors. All he's got to say is whether the man is technically capable. Same as any other project head."

"I don't know what's the matter with me, Henry," I said slowly. "I don't trust Logart, I guess. There's something I can't put my finger on."

"He knows his business," Henry said. "Maybe better than any man in the country. I checked into that carefully. Everybody says he's *the* man for the job. If you're gonna build a spaceship, you got to put a man in charge that knows at least what one ought to look like. I don't. Do you?"

"It surprises me that he's such an expert. Maybe that's the trouble. He's always surprising me. He doesn't seem to fit—anywhere."

"Why should he fit something?"

"You walk out into the factory stores, Henry. We have thousands of parts, but they all fit somewhere in the machines we make. By knowing the machines and looking at the parts, you can tell just about what every part is for and where it fits. Now suppose you ran across a part that didn't belong. Wouldn't it bother you?"

"You keep telling me people aren't machines, Ralph."

"But they fit," I said. "They fit into a recognizable framework, all except a George, or a Jennie, and sometimes a Swa—"

My voice trailed off and I stared at Henry.

"You think he might be another one of those?" Old Stone Face asked.

"If he is," I said slowly, "he's concealed it. Or has he? Not belittling your negotiating ability any, Henry, but hasn't it seemed to you that we got into the spaceship business mighty quick and easy?"

Old Stone Face didn't answer for a minute. Then he heaved a big sigh, as if he'd been holding his breath all along.

"We're in it now," he said at last. "The way they fell over themselves around the Pentagon, giving me everything I wanted, made me think I was getting real good at my trade. Better keep an eye on Logart, Ralph. No telling what he might be up to."

"What could I do about it?" I asked.

III

My talk with the five boys was a little like the time when I interviewed them for jobs. I knew their names well by now, and of course I'd spoken to each of them a few times on the job. In their several departments I never seemed to have any trouble keeping the names straight, but as the five of them filed through my office door and took chairs, I couldn't sort out which name belonged to which face. It didn't matter.

Very briefly I told them about the project, and the part we hoped George could play.

"We knew"
   "you could think of"
      "something,"
         "sir."

It was Numbers One, Two, Three and Four who had answered. Number Five nodded in agreement.

"Now I don't want to underestimate this," I warned. "It's new. You'll be the first to leave Earth in any kind of a ship. There'll be bugs, bound to be. A challenge to everything George has got."

"Yeah!" they breathed in ecstasy, their eyes shining.

"Physical danger," I said as impressively as I could. "All we've got is what we've surmised from the information that came back from the satellites. It seems like a lot. But on the other hand it isn't much, maybe not enough. Maybe we only think we can build the necessary mechanisms the first time. And, of course, we can only build to handle the known or suspected factors. There could be others."

Apparently they were communing with one another up on Cloud Nine, lost in such a roseate dream that, before I thought, I sniffed the air to see if there was any hint of a reefer's odor clinging to their clothes. Every now and then a young fellow came in who was really flying. But apparently they didn't need any help.

"You'll have a hand in designing the ship," I said, not sure whether I was talking to anybody or not. "You'll answer only to Mr. Logart, the head of the project. Naturally, your salaries will be raised commensurate with your new jobs."

Either that got through to them, or their silent conference was over.

"We've got some news for you, sir," Numbers Three and Five said simultaneously. "We're all going to be married."

"Not all to the same gi—" I said impulsively. "Of course not," I corrected myself hurriedly.

"Of course not," they agreed in chorus.

I wanted to ask them something, maybe to warn them, but in this area one man will rarely meddle with another man's intentions. I was alarmed about George. George's existence depended upon the five of them remaining in closest communion, but a young wife's first big project is to cut her new husband off from his past life and alienate all his old buddies. It's instinctive, and takes place even when neither the wife nor the husband wants it to happen. What would happen to George? Apparently they had thought of it, too.

"A year ago," they said, "when George was confined to just the five of us, it might have destroyed him. But not now. Anyhow, it's a pair of twins and a set of triplets, all sisters, so they know at least a little of what a George is like. It'll be all right, sir. You needn't worry. And . . . we do need wives, just like anybody else."

"Of course," I answered.

"They're very wonderful girls," Five said shyly.

"Of course," I said.

They looked at each other and their eyes sparkled with mischief.

"It's possible," Two said, "that in time there could be a Mrs. George."

I didn't say anything. They were in a framework I couldn't share.

"It must be spring," I finally gasped. "A regular epidemic."

"Yeah," they breathed, their eyes shining.

I went out into the factory and got a forelady's permission to talk to Annie Malasek on the job.

"Bother you, Annie, if I talk while you work?" I asked, when I came to a stop beside her workbench.

"Oh, no, sir," she said. "I can do this in my sleep."

Her fingers flying, pausing briefly, flying, pausing over a module, one of the more intricate parts of a computer, reminded me of butterflies hovering over a bed of flowers, darting in and out, pausing and tasting briefly. I caught the flush of pleasure on her face, and the sidelong look in her eyes when she checked to make sure it was duly noted in the department that I had come to see her instead of sending for her. Apparently that meant something.

"It's about Jennie," I said in a low voice just loud enough for her to hear me over the constant department hum. "Logart wants your permission to talk with her, and see if we can bring back any of her old—ah—abilities. It's very important now that we should try. If you're willing, and if she's willing."

Her eyes flashed to my face quickly, and clung there questioning, anxious. But her fingers didn't falter.

"I don't want her throwing things without touching them," she said with a trace of that old stubbornness which was a major characteristic of hers before she and I had got to know one another, trust one another. "I don't want her setting fires without no matches.

Them were old country ways, Slavonic mountain ways. We're Americans now, citizens. Jennie was lonesome and unhappy then. Now she's one of the most popular girls in her class and makes the best grades, even if I am her mother."

"She's older now," I said gently. "It's barely possible she would be able to move from one framework to the other at will."

Her eyes left my face and she looked down at the completed assembly. Expertly she whirled it beneath her hands, her sharp eyes inspecting every part. Satisfied, she lifted it from her stationary bench and put it on the moving belt line which ran beside the benches. She picked up the shell of another from the parts bin, and her fingers began darting in and out of smaller bins to pick up screws, bolts, wires. As if of their own volition, her fingers started putting the things into place. Her eyes came back to me.

"I don't understand about frameworks," she said.

"It's just a technical name for different conditions," I said. I very nearly used Einstein's phrase "coordinate system" and decided it would merely confuse things further. "For instance, when you were a girl in the Slav mountains where you came from, things were different from here. Things were true there that aren't true here."

"You can say that again," she agreed heartily.

"But you could go back there on a visit," I said. "Without losing your American citizenship. You could understand the old country ways because you grew up among them. At the same time, you would remember American ways, and when you came back you could pick up American ways again, without any trouble, because you understand those, too. It's what we mean by different frameworks."

"You think Jennie lived in a different. . . ." She hesitated over the new word, tasting it for meaning, ". . . framework?"

"I'm pretty sure of it," I said.

"And she could travel back and forth without hurting herself?"

"Possibly. We don't know for sure."

"My," she said. "Think of that. That's some daughter I've got, eh, Mr. Kennedy?"

"You can say that again," I agreed.

"That Logart fellow," she said. "He seems like a nice enough man. Awful young to be a full colonel. I guess it wouldn't do any harm for him to talk to Jennie—if you was there. You think it would do her any harm?"

"She wouldn't have to agree unless she wanted to," I said. "I'm not going to put any pressure on her. I made up my mind to that two, three years ago when I first got to know her."

"Then I'll tell her to come see you tomorrow when she gets out of school in the afternoon."

I started to leave, then turned back.

"How's Swami?" I asked.

Her face began to glow.

"He's the most wonderf—" She paused and then smiled teasingly. "But you wouldn't know anything about him in that framework."

I tried to picture Swami in the role of ardent lover. It wasn't too difficult. He probably would have made an art of it, a supplement to his art of fakery in reading palms, telling fortunes, gazing into the crystal ball. Perhaps it would be better if I didn't acknowledge that to Annie.

"No," I laughed. "I guess you're right. I wouldn't know anything about his abilities in that framework."

"Jennie's crazy about him," she said. "Sometimes I think those two understand each other better than I understand either one of them."

"Oh?" I said.

"They're two of a kind," she said. "They play games together." Then cryptically, she added, "But it's all right, because he's there to see that she don't come to no harm."

I felt my eyes widen a little. Perhaps we wouldn't have too much trouble in getting Jennie back into the old framework after all.

"They claim that together they can do things that neither one of them can do by themselves," she added.

"If they're that close," I said, "maybe Swami had better come with Jennie tomorrow afternoon."

Her face lit up and the last vestige of doubt left it.

"Then I know it will be all right," she said confidently.

I hoped so.

Sara kept Jennie and the Swami in the outer waiting room until Logart could be located. It wasn't difficult to find him. He'd left word with the switchboard that he'd be in conference with Old Stone Face and was to be notified immediately when I was ready. He left the conference at once, and I hoped Old Stone Face would realize that there really were times when a little girl and a fake swami might be more important than the general manager.

The three of them came in together and I introduced them as I gave them chairs.

"You're a bigger girl than I thought you'd be," Logart said to Jennie. "Prettier, too."

I caught a flash of dark jealousy in Swami's eyes. Jennie, still in the preteen age of a child at one moment and a young lady the next, suddenly became a very demure and shy young lady. Apparently Logart caught the look in Swami's face, too, for he addressed most of his remarks to the man, and gradually I could see him winning over the highly temperamental, unstable personality.

I had visualized myself as carrying the conversational ball, drawing them out, bringing them closer together, and finally with great subtlety introducing the psi subject. Logart picked up the ball immediately and I became no more than a nonparticipating spectator. In fact, I wasn't quite sure that I caught all the plays, or understood fully those I did see.

Whatever it was that happened, Jennie was completely captivated. Yet it was to the Swami that she turned and drew closer. Suddenly I realized that it was no longer to Jennie as separate from the Swami, but both of them as a team that Logart was appealing. Logart had somehow caught the implications of the games that Swami and Jennie played together where as a team they could do things that neither could do separately.

Had Logart still been in uniform I might have credited the way they turned to him, accepted his leadership, yes, domination over them as subservience to military command. But he had shed his uniform and badges, and had become an uncolorful, nondescript civilian. But not to them! They recognized something in him I could not see. They gave acquiescence long before it was asked. In fact, he never asked their agreement, he took it for granted. And they gave it in the same spirit.

I had to stop them at one point, they were going too fast toward their destination, whatever it might be.

"Whoa!" I exclaimed. "Wait a minute. You can't pull Jennie out of school and ensconce her over there in the laboratory building just because you want her. There are such things as school laws and child labor laws here in California."

"Isn't that your problem, Mr. Kennedy?" Logart asked, with an undercurrent of impatience in his voice.

"Yes," I said reasonably. "And it's quite a problem. It's true that we have special provision for, say, child actors. The State gives special permission when adequate and compensating educational facilities are provided. I can set up the educational facilities without any trouble. The problem is this. The State Board understands about child actors. But what am I going to give the State as an excuse for taking Jennie out of regular school and putting her to work in our factory?"

"It seems to me that the success or failure of Earth's first space ship is more important than some stupid motion picture," Logart said, with his impatience increasing.

"Ah," I said. "But now we're dealing with a framework of bureaucracy. Remember your military framework, *Mister* Logart. They're going to ask what has this little girl got so necessary to our success that the graduates of our finest technical universities don't have?"

"What is the procedure to deal with other unusual children?" he asked.

"There aren't supposed to be any unusual children," I said. "That's the whole point. There aren't supposed to be any unusual people of any kind, or any unusual circumstances. What did you do with those unusual young fellows you pulled into the services, *Colonel* Logart? You ground them down to complete conformity and mediocrity, or you destroyed them in trying. Now the disease is no longer confined to the military. Because nothing is done to reverse this process when the man has finished his term of service, it has saturated the whole culture."

All three of them were looking at me with different expressions. Jennie was politely waiting while an adult finished saying something she didn't understand. Swami was looking at me with eyebrows cocked in puzzled surprise. Logart was patient, with a little smile that seemed comprised of both amusement and pity playing around his lips. I couldn't interpret it then, I didn't understand it until months later, when the pattern he was now developing finished in its inevitable result.

I was puzzled, too. At myself. I had never been particularly concerned for the ultimate fate of our culture, of mankind. I conceded that I didn't have many illusions left, but mine had always been an attitude of "If you can't lick 'em, join 'em." Yet every time I came in contact with Logart, or even thought about him, I started getting up on a soapbox and philosophizing off into the blue yonder. And I was supposed to be the one who was skilled in keeping people on the subject until the matter in hand had been covered!

"What I'm saying," I supplemented a little lamely, because it wasn't what I'd been saying at all, "is that in dealing with a specific framework, you've got to make certain concessions to it, even though they prove a nuisance. Now I can see only one way to justify bringing Jennie here into the plant laboratory on a full-time basis, and that is in the role of a child actor. The State could understand that, because there's precedence. So we'll have to go through the process of making a motion picture record of the building of this spaceship. The State will understand if we interpret that record through a child's eyes, because the State is convinced that the people have the minds of small children.''

I started to swing into another diatribe about administrative attitudes of telling people only what the government thought the people ought to know, and keeping from them what they thought the people were too innocent to suspect—and resolutely closed my lips. Now that I had realized Logart's effect on me, I could at least be on guard. What effect did he have on others? Was he also arousing in them deep, latent concepts—abilities?

''As you say,'' he was conceding, ''a motion picture record will be an added nuisance. But if it takes that to get up off the surface of the Earth, we'll do it.'' There was a vibrant chord of deep yearning, longing, in his voice.

''There will be quite a few such nuisances,'' I said drily.

IV

There were quite a few nuisances.

Not the least of them was the sudden withdrawal of George from the production departments of the factory. George had largely dispensed with red tape in favor of his more immediate form of communication. When George withdrew to concentrate on spaceship plans, like a little boy who drops his tricycle and never gives it a backward glance when he sees daddy untying a real bike from the rear bumper of the car, this form of communication was suddenly cut off. Nobody knew what to do.

Red tape is not only communication, it is history. No one knew what to do, and from the few sparse records no one could tell what had been done.

The workers turned to their supervisors. Here were the machines, here was the blank stock. But what were they supposed to do with it? The supervisors turned to the production planning departments. Where are the work orders, the job tickets? Production Planning turned to Engineering. Where are the blueprints? Engineering turned to Plant Management. What are we supposed to be doing? Plant Management turned to General Management. Old Stone Face had nowhere to turn. It is one thing to build a huge organization one step at a time. It is something else to have five thousand idle employees turn at once and say, ''What am I supposed to do?''

In this hectic period of readjustment which loaded me down with quarrels, complaints, grievances, I noticed a peculiar state of mind creeping over me. Ordinarily there is a joy in the skill of being able to juggle dozens of problems without dropping any of them to smash, but there was no joy in this. I simply slugged through the days somehow. I put it down to overwork, overpressure, and the fact that I really wanted to be active in the preliminary stages of planning the spaceship. Compared with that, the job of getting the plant running smoothly again was sheer tedious drudgery.

All through the months I never really had any hand at all in the building of the spaceship. Peripheral nuisances kept me busy, a sort of picking up the pieces that Logart dropped as he pushed the project along. He never shoved me out of things. He just didn't need me at the central core, and there always seemed to be some emergency that prevented my real participation.

Such as the nuisance of getting a motion picture record started, the subterfuge that would give us Jennie without too many questions. This meant dealing with thirty-two more unions necessary to film a professional picture, to say nothing of State Boards, Local Boards, and Bureaucrats at every level. Anybody who still thinks we have free enterprise is living in a previous century. Simply making it possible for Jennie to get additional training from Logart kept me from sitting in on those sessions to see what was going on.

The nuisances piled up and as customary around Computer Research the buck passes from hand to hand until, somehow, it finally winds up on my desk. For instance there wasn't any reason why I should have got involved in the court actions that would condemn the adjoining property and give us more space. But I did.

One little old lady chose this particular time to decide that science had gone far enough. She picked up Asimov's famous sardonic jest made when the American satellite was first being publicly described: "If God had wanted basketballs to fly he'd have given them wings." She clung to it with literal sincerity, and talked about the Tower of Babel. Somehow the notion got fixed that if man left Earth, where he had been put to work out expiations for his sins, the whole plan of the universe would be destroyed. She had a lot of followers. The Press, treating it first as a joke, gradually began to concede she might have a point. And, although the court decreed against her, when she sat down in her little parlor with a shotgun across her lap and defied anybody to remove her bodily from her property—still hers no matter what a federal court judge said—our Public Relations Department somehow passed the buck to me. Rationalizing her into believing man was following out the predestined plan of the universe and science was proof that man was making progress in the expiation of his original sin took time. By the time I finished, her house was a little island in a sea of bulldozers.

Old Stone Face didn't help any.

"I thought I was pretty well adapted," he said to me one day, "to the government attitude that a fellow isn't any kind of business manager at all if he can't make a ten-thousand-dollar item cost the tax payers a half million, but Ralph, the costs of this project are ridiculous."

Arguments that the more money we wasted the more profit we made, as is accepted custom, didn't sway his attempts to cut costs. The amazing Logart had somehow managed to pry open the Federal till so that we could just reach in and help ourselves. Old Stone Face insisted it wasn't the money, it was the principle of the thing. The more he tried to cut costs the greater the clamor and the more problems that somehow got piled on top of me.

I saw the land cleared, the spaceship hangar and side buildings arise without any help from me. By now, I seemed to be past caring.

When Logart insisted he had to have a laboratory separate from everything else, where only he, Jennie, Swami, and George could enter, and pointed out a private residence on the north side of our property he thought would do, somehow I took it for granted it was my problem to get it for him. Somehow, working through our legal department, of course, I did. Somehow, I didn't ever get around to pointing out that the Personnel Director cannot be excluded from any company property; that the Personnel Director has the right to participate in any employee training program. After they moved into their new "laboratory" I never even got a peek inside it. The astonishing bit about that was that I couldn't seem to care.

I still thought it was because I was too busy!

The hull of the spaceship was well on its way to taking form before I realized that in the midst of all my headaches, there had *not* been the nuisance of trying to find a zillion experts. Now no matter how much of a genius a man may be, he can't know everything. A genius, perhaps more than anybody else, would want experts around if for no more than to check his work. It took me quite a while to realize that there was such a radical departure from all previous concepts of space flight that experts would simply be still more nuisance.

Well, George was the one who had to fly it. Let him plan it.

There was the nuisance also of trying to explain to our Public Relations Department, so they could explain to the Press, why the designs of a certain animated-cartoon manufacturer were not being followed in building our spaceship. No one else seemed to care whether Public Relations, and the Press, got an answer to this important question.

But how could I explain that maybe a cartoonist didn't really know everything there was to know about designing a real spaceship? The public would never accept that. They had already accepted the cartoon design, and that was what they expected to see. They were paying for it, weren't they?

How could I explain something I didn't understand myself? For it didn't look like a spaceship to me, either. If anything, it more closely resembled a small apartment building!

One entered what was obviously a basement. You mean to tell me that small space off to the side is going to be the entire control room?!! Yes, I can see these are storage bins and closets, but if this thing should work won't you want to take it to the Moon? Maybe Mars and Venus? Where are you going to store enough food, and oxygen, and water? To say nothing of the thousand other necessities? Or, I suppose this is only a test model?

None of the answers Logart gave me were satisfactory. All seemed to boil down to not worrying my pretty little head about it. As for power units, well, Jennie really didn't take up much room, did she? There was a twinkle in his eye as he asked it, so I knew he was kidding. I hoped.

There was a shaft running upward, through the center of the ceiling, but no elevator in it. A small flight of metal stairs wound around the open shaft, for ordinary people, like myself, to climb to the upper decks. On the first floor there were five apartments, small but as comfortably and completely equipped as a good house trailer. The second floor had an additional five apartments, and that was all.

This was a spaceship?

I preferred not to think about it. Of course I knew it wasn't going to be powered by any such thing as Jennie sitting over in a corner and psiing earnestly. Dr. Auerbach had already completed one large cylinder, about the size of a thirty-gallon water heater, and had delivered it to the laboratory building which Logart had demanded.

I didn't have to wonder very long whether Jennie and Swami, under Logart's specialized teaching, could make the cylinders work.

It was one mid-morning when I was on my way over from our regular plant to the section housing the space ship. Over to my right I saw the one-time residence, now Logart's laboratory, lift up off its foundations and float about a foot into the air. There was the rending sound of torn masonry, torn plumbing and sewer pipes, electrical wiring. Water started gushing out of the pipes, and as I ran toward the building, I remember being thankful there were no gas lines.

The house settled back down slowly, but not quite straight; on its foundations. I ran up to the front door and pounded frantically on the panel. After a moment, Logart came and opened the door a mere crack.

"Yes?" he asked, as if I were a house-to-house salesman.

"It floated up into the air," I gasped.

"Yes?" There was still a question in his voice. What did I want?

"It broke your water mains, sewer connections, electrical wiring," I said lamely.

"Oh, yes," he answered a little absently. "I suppose it did. Would you be good enough to get them fixed, Kennedy?" he asked. He closed the door.

More nuisance.

A little later that morning, I saw the lift truck go over to the laboratory, and pick up the cylinder which had now been shunted out on the porch. From the way it lifted, I knew the cylinder was now inert. I didn't ask how it got out on the porch. There were five husky young men, besides Swami and Logart, in that building. I was sure they could have managed to get it out on the porch . . . somehow.

The lift truck carried the cylinder over to the ship—I still kept thinking of it as a compact apartment building—and installed it in a rack on the north wall of the basement. There were similar racks on each of the other three walls, and Auerbach was completing, on order, three more such cylinders. I supposed there was some psientific reason for it. I had given up inquiring about it.

By now I was in a state of perpetual shock, partly from overwork and overworry about too many nuisances, partly because I understood just enough to understand that I didn't know anything at all. Such items, for example, as:

Logart had insisted on a special formula of metal alloy to be made up in bars about the size of bricks. The idea seemed to be to pack as many molecules in as small a space as possible. I ventured, one day, to ask what they were for.

"Jennie-Swami's powers are limited," Logart said, a little sadly I thought. "They need molecules of some kind; can't make food, water, other things, out of nothing."

"Of course not," I said. I vaguely wondered what the term "other things" might cover. But I was past normal curiosity about anything. I didn't bother to ask.

"Swami's prescience is irregular," he said. "Your idea of increasing psi powers through hypnotism has its limits."

In these hectic months I had completely forgotten my intent to attempt hypnotism on psi. Apparently Logart hadn't.

"We don't know what we may need before we come to matter again," he went on.

"Of course not," I agreed.

"So it's well to have plenty of molecules on hand," he said.

"Of course," I said. As if from forgotten childhood there came the memory of a fairy story about Little Three-Eyes, "Little table appear," she would say, and there would be a table laden with all the delicacies a hungry child can visualize. "Little table go away," she would say when she had eaten, and that took care of the automatic dishwasher problem. Three-Eyes? The third eye a psisense organ? The story founded on fact in some dim past? At the moment, it seemed to make their human needs all easy of fulfillment.

At the moment I didn't realize I was in a complete daze to the point that I would have readily agreed that when they grew hungry all they'd have to do is slice off a piece of the green-cheese moon.

The alloy bricks were completed and stacked in the "basement" until only corridors remained. The workmen doing it seemed never to have had any curiosity. Our Public Relations Department had failed completely with the Press, and the Press had settled in their own minds that the whole thing was a hoax. A congressional committee had promised to investigate the Pentagon's folly.

By now everyone had ceased to be curious. This was not unexpected on the part of the public. Conditioned by newspapers and television commentators to a new shock at least every three days, they responded by losing interest in anything after about three days. But it was surprising that those of us deeply involved should stop questioning.

I remember one curious conversation around this time. I didn't give it enough reflection at the time, possibly because it was with Swami, whose attitudes and opinions I respected least.

He came into my office with a sort of hang-dog look on his face and said he wanted to talk with me, to explain something to me.

"I don't—none of us want you to feel hurt," he said. "Afterwards."

"Afterwards what?" I asked.

"After this is all over."

"What am I not to feel hurt about?"

"Even explaining it is going to hurt you."

"Look, fellow," I said with a slight exasperation. "I've been at this game of dealing with human beings for a long time. I've been insulted in just about every way the mind of man can conceive. I've been lied to, cheated, double-crossed, lied about, and had the truth told about me. I've survived. I expect I can survive what you have to say."

"I suppose," he said slowly, "you've got a vocabulary of around twenty-five thousand words."

"More or less, perhaps," I conceded.

"And an equally large vocabulary of word combinations, and then another block of phrase combinations, so that all told you're probably capable of around a hundred thousand concepts. Say a hundred thousand for the sake of argument."

"For the sake of argument," I agreed.

"Suppose you found yourself living with a band of great apes who have a vocabulary of grunts, growls, roars, whistles, and chest beatings that number up to a hundred concepts. The ratio is a thousand to one, isn't it?"

I started to tell him he should have been a mathematician, but the look of sadness in his big black eyes stopped me.

"But for all your disproportionate ratio of concepts," he said, "you can still be hurt, get sick, feel a mosquito bite, get too cold, too hot, too hungry. You can only communicate to the limit of their hundred concepts. They judge you within these hundred concepts. They have no way of knowing or appreciating this vast number you can't communicate. To them you are a pretty worthless creature. You can't overpower them in a fight, you don't take an interest in their she-apes and fight over them, you don't try to become master of the herd because it wouldn't interest you, you don't appreciate the delicacies of the grubs to be found under the bark of rotting trees; you're puny, sickly, and obviously you are also cowardly by their standards."

"But I've got a hundred thousand concepts—which makes me superior to them," I said.

"No," he disagreed. "Not superior, because what standard are you going by? Theirs, or yours?"

"Different then," I said.

"Different," he answered. "That's the point. Now suppose you found a group of human beings, your equals. Suppose you found a way to escape from the tribe of apes, to set up a community of human beings, so that your hundred thousand concepts had value. More important, so that you could start using them, and all they mean. Wouldn't you do it?"

"We're talking about psi, of course," I said, "and I see the analogy. But suppose the apes recognized my difference, recognized that I could think in areas denied to them. Suppose, for example, they saw the relation of the rotting tree to a supply of grubs under its bark. Suppose they tried to use my extra concepts, asked me to figure out a way to make more trees fall so there could be more grubs?"

"Would you really care?" he asked. "All right, suppose they invented another grunt which was a recognition of your difference. So now they've got a vocabulary of a hundred and one concepts. As against your hundred thousand, would it make much difference to you?"

"Look, Swami," I said earnestly. "I've been trying to understand your psi talents. Not just to recognize them, but to understand them. All of them. I'm trying to find a way to bring them under scientific scrutiny, to work out an approach to the natural laws governing them, measure them, control them, predict them. They're real, they work—somewhere, in some way, they are a part of natural law. Man can understand natural law, if he tries. That's science."

He shook his head.

"A long time ago," he said, "we had a conversation along this line. I was offended then, and scared. I gave you some metaphysical mumbo jumbo. But my feelings, my psi feelings if you will, were sound. Maybe I can express it better this time. The flaw lies in what you call scientific method. Yes, psi is a part of natural law, but scientific method, as you conceive it, can't get hold of it. There has to be. . . . There has to be. . . ."

He paused. Obviously he was trying to find a grunt, whistle, or chest thump which was in my vocabulary.

"Let's go to another analogy," he said.

"Let's," I agreed.

"Suppose an ancient Greek philosopher met up with a modern solar scientist. Suppose this ancient Greek said to the solar scientist, 'Tell me about the sun.' The solar scientist starts sketching in his basic knowledge of the sun. 'No, no!' the ancient Greek objects. 'Don't give me all that vague and mystical mumbo jumbo. That doesn't mean anything to me. Tell me how many wheels Apollo's chariot has, how many horses draw it across the sky, what metal the chariot is made of, what its dimensions are, what figures are embossed on its doors. Be scientific, man!' What could the solar scientist say?"

"In short," I said, "our science, in trying to measure psi, get a description of it, is like trying to measure a chariot that doesn't exist, driven by a god who doesn't exist."

"Yes."

"But psi does exist."

"The sun exists," he said. "It is the framework of approach to knowledge, to measurement that is wrong. Man couldn't learn anything more about the sun until he quit thinking in terms of Apollo's chariot."

It was an impasse. I couldn't give up my scientific approach to knowledge—any more than the ancient Greek could give up his certainty that Apollo drove his chariot across the sky.

As I say, I remembered the conversation, but I didn't reflect on it enough. I interpreted it as just Swami wanting to talk to somebody, maybe build up his stock in my eyes since, obviously, I respected Jennie and George more than I did him. I didn't realize at the time that it was a kind of valedictory—from all of them.

I was much more concerned with the pressures of details that were weighing me down, and I fear my main reaction at the moment was irritation at the twenty minutes he'd taken up when other things were much more urgent.

Urgencies, for example, such as the details of their mass wedding. It didn't occur to me until much later that almost a year had passed since their announcement that they were going to get married—Annie and Swami, the boys and their girls. I'd not thought much about it, and if I did have a vague wonder now and then, I'd put the delay down to their being under white-hot pressures, too.

At any rate the multiple wedding finally did come off. Somehow the responsibility for that, too, got around to my office. But as usual, Sara was more capable of handling it than I would have been. I had only to officiate at the reception afterwards. The boys' parents were all there, the first time I'd met them; but somehow even they managed to pass the buck, and it was as if all these were my children.

After the reception, I had hardly enough energy left in me to stagger into my apartment. I was utterly exhausted and in a slight fever.

"Did anybody think to make arrangements for their honeymoons?" I heard myself mumbling as I lay down across the bed to gather enough energy to get up and undress.

I fell asleep patiently telling myself that Sara would take care of it.

I was awakened by the telephone on the stand beside my bed, and with that dim realization that it had been ringing for a long time. Through grainy eyelids I could see outside my window that it was a bleak gray dawn. I hadn't bothered to snap off my light, pull down my shade, and I was still dressed.

"Aw for . . . Why don't you look up the right number?" I grumbled into the phone when I finally managed to reach out and claw it off its stand.

"Ralph! Ralph! Don't hang up. This is Henry!"
Old Stone Face's granite voice blasted me a little more awake.

"Yes, Henry," I groaned without that brisk, glad alertness right-hand men are expected to feel on any occasion.

"The ship's gone," he said. "Just got a call from Plant Security. Meet you there."

There was a crash in my ear as he slammed down the phone. Well, at least I didn't have to dress. A slept-in tuxedo was just fine for going out to hunt a misplaced spaceship.

V

Henry and I pulled into the executives' parking section at the same time, and both of us spilled out of our cars and started running toward the spaceship hangar. A little knot of watchmen, security police, maintenance men had gathered at the doorway. They stepped back as we puffed our way up to the door and came to a halt. Yes, the spaceship was gone. The ceiling of the hangar was neatly folded back, as planned, to let the pink clouds and blue sky show through.

"Some honeymoon," I said to Henry.

"You think they'd have taken their wives?" he asked me.

"You think they'd have chosen this particular morning for a routine test run?" I asked him.

"You think they'd have risked their wives before they tested it?" he asked.

"You think they weren't absolutely sure of what they were doing all along?" I asked.

We weren't bothering to answer each other.

"We'd better check the laboratory. Logart's been sleeping there lately," Henry said. "Those kids could have taken it up as a lark, you know." He shook his head angrily. "This younger generation!" he grumbled.

The little knot of employees, who had been crowding the doorway behind us, stepped back again and let us get out. They looked at us curiously, to see what we would do now. Executives were supposed to be able to handle anything, even spaceships that disappear.

We walked over toward the laboratory building that never had been straightened on its foundations. Neither of us seemed to be in any great hurry now. We went up on the porch and knocked politely at the door. We waited. No one answered our knock. There was no sound of movement inside. I tried the latch, and the door swung open without any trouble.

We peered into the hallway, and the house looked just as I remembered it when we bought it from its previous residents. As we stepped inside, I saw an envelope on the hall table. I looked at the front and saw it was addressed to me. I picked it up and carried it with me as we searched the house. There were no occupants, of course.

As we went from room to room a most peculiar realization came to me. In spite of my weariness, my lethargy wes gone. I no longer felt numbly swept along in currents I could not understand or control. I was back to a state of mind I remembered, a state of being awake, and already the events of the last few months had the haze of a remembered dream.

"You feel unusually sharp this morning, Henry?" I asked as we left the service porch area. He looked at me quickly.

"First I thought I was losing my grip because I got so I didn't care what was happening in building the spaceship," he said. "Then I got so I didn't care that I didn't care."

"Me too," I said. "Now I feel awake again."

"Me too," he said. Then added cryptically, "That Logart!"

We came into the living room. The chairs and divan were as neatly placed as in any home—Annie's work, no doubt. I hadn't been admitted to the house, but Annie had!

"This envelope is addressed to me," I said.

"Well, open it," Henry said.

We sat down in chairs, and I slipped a page out of the unsealed envelope. It was all neatly typed out. I had expected it to start with some such cliché as "When you read this, we will be gone," but Logart, whose signature was at the bottom, hadn't wasted words on the trivially obvious. I started reading aloud for Henry's benefit.

"A man can grow only so tall," Logart began. *"After that, he can merely grow fat. As with a man, so with a culture of man. When a culture has more to lose than to gain in trying to realize a dream, it is the dream that dies. When a culture starts walking backward into the future, with its eyes fixed on the past, the culture dies.*

"A youth must leave his home and the parents who bore and cherished him or suffer the consequences of being never more than were his parents. History is full of the migrations

*of such youth groups. Youth groups with a dream that can
only be realized where there is room for a dream to grow.
"Sorry you couldn't go with us, Kennedy. You tried. We
tried. But what would life be like for you in a framework you
could never share, where all your dependable patterns are no
longer true, where all your wisdom of coping with people
avails you nothing? For all your sympathy, you never quite
believed that psi is an entirely different framework. You were
always trying to make it conform to your already fixed notions of what truth must be.*

*"All of us will remember you with deep gratitude, for you
brought together a critical psi mass. It needed only me to
'arrange' the parts into its dynamic potential. Jennie, Swami
and George were, in a sense, your psi children. Be glad you
gave them a good start.*

*"Somewhere, out among the stars, where there is room to
grow, we will form a colony, and then a culture based in psi.
Give us your blessing, and wish us luck.*

Logart."

I looked up at Old Stone Face. He looked back at me.

"Too bad, Ralph," he said. He had helped, too. It was a disappointment that Logart had not given him credit. That Logart!
"Well," he said finally, as if squaring his shoulders. "First thing is
to get some breakfast. Next thing is to get that sluggish Public Relations Department waked up and working on some handouts for the
Press, who, I guess, will sort of wake up now, too. Next thing is to
try to explain all this to the Pentagon, and how come we didn't stop
them from taking the spaceship. Then there's Congress to explain
to, why we used all that money they urged us to take. After all that's
boiled down, and reflected itself in the voting machines, we still got
computers to make."

"Why?" I asked.

"Now you look here, Ralphie, my boy," he said and shook his
finger at me. It shocked me into an upright position. He didn't seem
to notice, because his eyes were veiled as if he were looking into a
far distance. "That Logart didn't have a corner on new frameworks.
Maybe he's right about the old folks having grown too set in their
ways to change, but there'll be other wild and independent children
who want something different. You'll see."

"But first things first. Let's go get some breakfast."

We walked over to the plant cafeteria which does a brisk breakfast business in men whose wives are too lazy to get up and see them off to work properly. There was a hush over the room, so still that the inadvertent clink of a spoon against a coffeecup sounded like a gong. The story had spread.

The sight of Henry and me, at one end of a long and otherwise empty table, calmly eating our stacks of hotcakes seemed to restore some confidence. If we could eat, then things might not be so bad. Henry had calculated the effect; and I should have, because that's my job. The cafeteria noise picked up until it reached normal, and provided a mask for the sound of our voices.

"Look here," Henry pointed a spoon at me. "Don't you give up. You were on the right track. It still takes unusual people to do unusual things. Don't sit around and sulk just because your unusual people did something unusual. You better get used to that. Remember that."

I stared down into the remaining syrup in the bottom of my plate.

Yes, I would remember. There might be other unusual people sometime in the future, but I could never forget Jennie, Swami, George. Logart was right. Now in remembrance and reflection, they were like children of mine. Children who, in the perfectly normal course of growing up, had been attracted to a fascinating stranger—for Logart would always remain a stranger in my inability to comprehend him—to go out into the world, the universe, to make their own way apart from my protection, to build a new kind of life which I could never share.

But they had not taken everything. They'd left me something precious—remembrance, and reflection.

1/58

Hide! Hide! Witch!

with Alex Apostolides
From *Astounding Science Fiction*

Like "Crazy Joey," "Hide! Hide! Witch!" foreshadowed the novel, *They'd Rather Be Right* and was incorporated into the book; what is interesting is that Clifton used two separate collaborators for the same characters and theme. Riley did appear several times in *Worlds of If* on his own; Apostolides never appeared other than as Clifton's collaborator on a few stories and the role he (or Riley for that matter) played in collaboration with a writer who could obviously do quite well on his own is worth pondering, probably never to be resolved.

Hide! Hide! Witch!
The good folk come to burn thee!
Their keen enjoyment hid beneath
The gothic mask of duty.

Jonathan Billings, Dean of Psychosomatic Research at Hoxworth University, heard the knock on his study door, and looked up from his work at his desk. But before he could call out an invitation to enter, the door opened.

That would be Mr. Rogan, Resident Investigator. Anyone else would have waited.

Billings watched him without expression as he came through the door—a little man, a negative quantity, who wore heavy silver-rimmed glasses in the hope they would give character to a characterless face. The brief case he carried, too, was heavily decorated with silver, proclaiming its unusual importance. He needed these trappings, and more. He was the kind of man one forgot to introduce, and his whole bearing suggested his determination to command the attention he never quite received.

There was a portentous frown on his gray face, and without any preliminaries of greeting he bustled over and laid a new issue of the college paper on Billings' desk. Billings looked down at the open page, and a cartoon of himself looked slyly back.

That was the trouble of having an old, old face with a thousand wrinkles. Even seventy years had been unkind in putting so many wrinkles there. In a cartoon, and he was often the subject of them throughout the country, those wrinkles could be slanted to make him appear fine and noble, or sly and scheming. It would depend upon which faction of the public the cartoonist wanted to please.

This time, in the cartoon, he was sly; and had his finger held up toward his lips in a cautioning, secretive gesture. There was a caption in bold print beneath the cartoon.

"You were quite wrong, Albert, about the nature of the universe!"

Billings looked up from the cartoon with a slight smile and met the accusing expression in Rogan's washed blue eyes.

"This is highly irregular, doctor," Rogan said firmly, before Billings could comment. "I trust you have not been questioning indisputable facts! I trust you have not been planting disturbing doubts in the minds of our future citizens! I trust you know Congress approved those facts for school textbooks long ago! It would be most subversive, not to mention a waste of time and tax money, to question them now!"

Billings felt a flare of sudden irritation, an emotion he considered quite unworthy of the circumstances. He should be accustomed to this sort of thing by now. For the past thirty years there had been a Resident Investigator, some worse and some not any worse than Rogan; monitoring what the teachers said, the lines of thought they pursued. He remembered a long succession of them who had come through his door; some of them resentful that he was world famous and must be handled with especial care; others seeing in it a golden opportunity for personal publicity if they could catch him in some subversive remark.

Out of the montage of accusations and sly traps written in their collective expressions, one face stood out clearly from all the rest. What was the remark the man had made? Oh, yes, he remembered it now.

"I am completely impartial, Dr. Billings," the man had said. "I merely see to it that you teachers say nothing which might threaten our freedom of speech!"

The memory of that incredible twist of semantics, so characteristic of the early days, cleared the irritation from his mind, and he looked back into Rogan's face with equal firmness. His answering tones were just far enough away from Rogan's speech that he could not be accused of Contempt For An Investigator.

"I trust you know, Mr. Rogan, that my subject is psychosomatics. I trust you are aware that I have no knowledge of approved astronomy courses, and would not feel qualified to comment upon it."

Rogan slapped the cartoon on the desk with the back of his fingers imperatively. He had studied the old films assiduously in an attempt to impart authority into his own attitudes and gestures.

"How do you account for this cartoon, then, doctor?" he asked with the triumphant expression of having scored an irrefutable point. The characteristic puerility of it washed away the final residue of irritation on Billings' mind, and he smiled in genuine amusement.

"Why, I suspect young Tyler, its author, is just having a bit of fun," he said slowly. "He's quite a mischief maker."

Rogan's eyes lighted up with delight at the possibility of a new scent.

"A student, eh?" he asked quickly. "One of these subversive cults probably. Trying to undermine our faith in our institutions."

"The cartoonist is young Raymond Tyler, of Tyler Synthetics," Billings said quietly. "An only son of the family, I believe."

"Ah," Rogan's face smoothed of all suspicion instantly. "Just a boyhood prank then." He was obsequious at the very name of such a powerful industry. "Boys will be boys, eh, doctor?"

"This one in particular," Billings said with a heavy note of irony. "Was that all, Mr. Rogan?" There was a note of unmistakable dismissal in his voice. Even Rogan could not miss it. The little man flushed, and pointedly sat down in a chair as his answer.

"No, doctor, that was just a preliminary," he said. "I have a commission for you from Washington. You are to head up a new line of research."

"I haven't completed my old line of research, Mr. Rogan," Billings reminded him. "Inquiry into the reasons for Citizen Neurosis."

"That's canceled, doctor," Rogan said firmly. "Washington is no longer interested in Civilian Fatigue." He reached out for his ornate brief case, fondled it lovingly as he opened it, and drew from it a thick sheaf of papers in a blue binding.

Billings made an impatient gesture, as if to remonstrate that months of work should not be so easily discarded, and then realized the futility of it. He settled back into his chair again.

"Very well, Mr. Rogan," he said in a resigned voice. "What does Washington instruct me to work on now?"

Even after thirty years of it, he was not yet accustomed to universities being operated on sound businesslike principles, with orders coming from the front office telling the boys in the lab what they should be thinking about today.

Or even more than thirty years. It was impossible to draw a hard line on just when it had happened. Perhaps it was the outgrowth of the practice when he had been a research student and young instructor. The local industry would come to the university with a problem. The university was eager to show its cooperation, its practical place in the industrial life of the nation. They got into the habit of delaying their own lines of research and working on those immediate ones required by industry. The habit grew into a custom. A few universities saw the danger and rebelled. Overnight, custom became a law. To rebel against a law, even a bad one, was subversion.

But he must not let his mind wander into the past. That was the mark of senility, they said. And what was Rogan saying now? And why didn't the man just leave the folder with him? Why did the man have to read it to him, word for word?

The opening pages were filled with gobbledegook, replete with such phrases as "by order of," and "under penalty of." Why did these government agencies always feel they had to threaten citizens? He could not recall any government communication which did not carry a threat of what would happen to him if he failed to comply. Surely after seven thousand years of trying it, governments should have learned that threats and punishment were not the way to accomplish their aims.

His eyes wandered around the room, and scowled at the gray November sky outside the window. The cold light made the dark paneled wood of his walls seem dingy and grimed. The shabby, old-fashioned furniture seemed even more shabby as the little man's voice droned on and on through the phrases.

". . . As revised . . . authorized . . . official . . . top secret . . ." Rogan apparently liked the sound of the governmental jargon, and gave each phase a full measure of expression.

Gradually the sense of the order became dimly apparent through all the legal phrasing. As Billings had feared, it was an old problem, just now coming to light.

That was significant, even though only a few men might recognize it. Not one new principle had come out of the universities in the past thirty years. Not one problem had arisen which hadn't been foreseen then. It was as if something geared to tremendous momentum had had powerful brakes applied. The forward movement seemed to continue satisfactorily; yet it was apparent to anyone who cared to look that it was grinding to a halt.

Odd how the human mind, once it became conscious of the unyielding pressure of limits and restrictions, refused to think constructively. There was a lot of loose talk about the indestructibility of the human will, how it strove onward and upward, overcoming all obstacles. But that was just talk, of the most irresponsible kind. Actually the human will to progress was the most delicate mechanism imaginable, and refused to work at all if conditions were not precisely right.

In the half million years man had been on earth, there were only twenty occasions when he had been able to pull himself up beyond the primitive animal level. It was significant, too, that most of these generated their forward momentum in one spurt, and often within one lifetime. Momentum reached its point where rulers became satisfied and clamped down restrictions against any change of the *status quo*. Then began, over and over in each civilization, the slow retrogression and the long night.

In the typical fashion of governmental directives, the order said the same thing over and over, yet never succeeded in saying outright what it meant. Man's inventive techniques had outstripped his reaction time possibilities. A plane, hurtling into an unforeseen disaster, would strike it before the pilot could become aware of the danger and react to avert it.

To protect his own life, man had had to place a limit upon the speed of his vehicles. True, he tried to cope with the situation by inventing servomechanisms, but most of these merely registered their findings upon a dial. The cockpits of ships became a solid wall of dials. No human eye could read all their messages simultaneously and react as they directed.

And, too, the servomechanisms, intricate and marvelous though they might be, were blind and senseless things, capable of following only one design of action.

Only the human mind was sufficiently flexible to vary the patterns of behavior to meet the variation of possible circumstances. But the human mind was too slow, too inefficient, too easily distorted. It was—an understatement—undependable.

Billings watched the unfolding of the inexorable logic in the order with a growing dread which began to mount to the level of horror.

For it was clear to him where the logic must lead. Since we did have weapons, the order pursued its line of thinking, which could seek out a target, follow it, strike and destroy it; the work of Hoxworth University was quite simple, and should require little time or tax monies.

The university was simply required to reverse the known mechanical principle and see that a plane, or an automobile, or other moving vehicle, struck nothing!

The order ended with its usual propaganda. Thus the citizens could see that, once again, out of war came great benefits to peace.

Rogan closed the stiff back page of the order and looked up at Billings with an expression of satisfaction at having delivered the government's instructions concisely and completely.

"In other words," Billings said slowly, "they want a servomechanism designed which can foresee the future, and work out a pattern of mechanical operation which will cope with that future at the time it becomes present." He realized his voice showed his incredulity, and that it would displease Rogan. It did.

"I believe the order is quite clear, doctor," Rogan said decisively. "And there is certainly nothing difficult about it, now that Washington has shown you the way to solve it. What a target-finder missile does, you simply have to do in reverse."

"But why did Washington select me, Mr. Rogan?" Billings asked carefully. "I am not a mechanical technician or engineer. I work with the human mind and body, their interaction. I wouldn't know anything about this project at all."

He was sorry he mentioned it, for it could be construed as Unwillingness to Cooperate, a fellow traveler act if not actually subversive. And it was a foolish question to ask, too, since government did not usually take capability into consideration in making an appointment—no more than the people did in electing government. Still, his question did bring him unexpected results.

Rogan hesitated, pulled at his lip, decided not to make anything out of the doctor's slip.

"Washington does not usually have to explain to a citizen," he said, "but I am instructed to answer you. This project is not a new one. It has been assigned before—several times."

"You mean the mechanical engineers have refused it?" Billings asked.

"Those who did are serving their sentences, of course," Rogan said, and his voice implied that Dr. Billings could join them without loss to the world. "But there was one thread of agreement at their trials. They all said that this would be duplicating the work of the human brain, and we'd better go to an expert on the human brain if we wanted to know how that worked.

"So," he finished simply, "here we are."

Billings had thought he was beyond further astonishment, but he had underestimated his own capacity for it.

"Mr. Rogan," he said slowly, trying not to show that he was aghast at the vacuity of such logic. "I do not question Washington's wisdom. But for the sake of the record, I know only a few of the secondary effects of mental action; I do not know how the mind works; I do not know of any human being who does."

He stopped short, for there flashed into his mind the possibility of one who might. Joe Carter, a student—a telepath.

The house where Joe lived was nearly a century old, and did not need the aid of the fog and the dusk to give it an air of grimy neglect. The weather-stained sign which proclaimed light-housekeeping rooms for students seemed almost as old, but at least it did not misrepresent them as being cheery or bright or comfortable.

Billings hesitated briefly at the foot of the steps leading up to its front door, and mentally pictured with dread the two long flights of wooden stairs he must climb to reach Joe's room.

He could have summoned Joe to his office, of course, but tonight that would have been adding insult to injury. And, too, in his own room, the boy seemed to have a little less reserve than in the office or the classrooms.

He started the slow, careful climb up the steps, opened the front door which was never locked for it was obvious that no one here could have anything worth taking, walked across the short hall, and started up the first flight of stairs. He glanced farther down the hall, saw the landlady's door close abruptly, and smiled. It was the same, every time he came to see Joe.

He had known Joe Carter for twelve years. First there had been the letter from Martin at Steiffel University, telling him about an eight-year-old telepath whose parents thought him insane. He, himself, had gone to the small college town and talked with the boy. He had arrived at a bad time. The story, as he got it from others, was that the boy had picked up a stray dog. The boy's parents had turned the dog over to the pound, and it had been destroyed. Joe had become silent, uncommunicative, unresponsive to any of Billings' attempts to draw him out.

Twelve years. From the sidelines he had watched Joe get through primary and secondary schools. He had marveled at the continued, never-breaking concealment the boy practiced in covering his unique talent. But concealment breeds distrust. The boy grew up friendless and alone.

Every year Billings had reviewed the grades which Joe had made. They were uniformly, monotonously, equivalent of C. He was determined to be neither sharp nor dull; determined that he would do nothing to make anyone notice him for any reason. As if his life, itself, depended upon remaining unnoticed.

Both his high school associates and Joe's parents were astonished when Hoxworth University offered him a scholarship. It wasn't much of a scholarship, true, for Joe's parents had no influence and Joe was not an athlete. Since there would be neither prestige nor financial return to the University, it hadn't been easy, but Billings had managed it, and without revealing the reasons for it.

He paused and caught his breath in the hallway at the top of the first flight of stairs, and then resumed his upward climb. They could talk all they pleased about how hale and hearty he was at seventy, but two flights of stairs—

Twelve years. That would make Joe about twenty now. The last three years had been at Hoxworth. And Joe had been as colorless in college as in high school.

Billings had tried, many times, to draw him out, make him flare into life. He had shown infinite patience; he had strived to radiate sympathy and understanding. Joe Carter had remained polite, friendly, appreciative—and closed. Billings had tried to show community of spirit, transcending the fifty years gap in their ages—and Joe had remained respectful, considerate, and aware of the honor of personal friendship from such a famous man. If Joe had known who wheedled a scholarship for him, he had never shown the knowledge.

Tonight Billings would try a different method. Tonight he would sink to the common level of the mean in spirit. He would demand acknowledgment and some repayment for his benefaction.

He hesitated in front of the wooden paneled door, almost withdrew back down the stairs in preference to portraying himself in such a petty light; and then before he could make up his mind to give it up, he knocked.

The door opened, almost immediately, as if Joe had been waiting for the knock. The boy's face was withdrawn and expressionless, as usual. Yet Billings felt there was a greater wariness than usual.

"Come in, doctor," Joe said. "I heard you coming up the stairs. I've just made some coffee."

Two chairs were placed at the pitiful little table; two heavy china cups wreathed vapor. A battered coffeepot sat on a gas plate. The housekeeping was light, indeed.

The two of them sat down in chairs, straight hard chairs and picked up the mugs of coffee.

"I'm in trouble, Joe," Billings began. "I need your help." Somehow he felt that an immediate opening, without preliminary fencing, would be more appreciated. And on this basis, he proceeded into the story of the newest order he had just received that afternoon from Rogan. He made no effort, either, to draw Joe out, to get the boy to acknowledge his talent of telepathy. Billings took it for granted, and became aware as he progressed that Joe was making no effort to deny it.

That, at least, was hopeful. He switched suddenly to a frontal approach, although he knew that young men usually resented it when an older man, particularly a successful one, did it.

"Have you given any thought, Joe, to what you intend to do with your life? Any way you can turn your gift into constructive use?"

"A great deal, of course," Joe answered without hesitation. "In that, at least, I'm no different from the average fellow. You want me to work with you on this synthetic brain, don't you, doctor? You think I may have some understanding you lack? Is that it?"

"Yes, Joe."

"It could destroy the human race, you know," Joe said quietly.

Billings was brought up short. He felt a sudden chill, not entirely due to the bleak and heatless room in which they sat.

"You foresee that, Joe, definitely?" he asked. "Or are you merely speculating?"

"I'm an imperfect," Joe answered quietly. "I often see seconds or minutes ahead. Occasionally I see days or weeks but not accurately. The future isn't fixed. But I'm afraid of this thing. I'm afraid that if we make a machine which can think better than man, mankind wouldn't survive it."

"Do you think man is worth surviving, Joe? After the things he's done?"

Joe fell silent, looking down at the table. Seconds became minutes. The cheap clock on the dresser ticked away a quarter of an hour. The coffee in the cups grew cold. Billings shivered in the damp cold of the unheated room, contrasted it with the animal warren comfort of the dormitories, the luxury of the frat houses. He became suddenly afraid of Joe's answer. He had at least some conception of what it must be like to be alone, the only one of its kind, a man who could see in a world of totally blind without even a concept of sight. How much bitterness did Joe carry over from childhood?

"Do you believe that man has reached his evolutionary peak, doctor?" Joe asked at last, breaking the heavy silence.

"No–o," Billings answered slowly.

"Couldn't the whole psi area be something which is latent, just really beginning to develop as the photosensitive cells of primitive life in animals once did? I have the feeling," he paused, and changed his phrasing. "I know that everyone experiences psi phenomena on a subconscious level. Occasionally a freak comes along"—he used the term without bitterness—"who has no barrier to shut it out of the conscious. I . . . I think we're trending toward the psi and not away from it."

"You think man should be given the chance to go on farther, then?" Billings asked.

"Yes," Joe said.

"And you think that if he finds out what the true nature of thought is, at the level he uses it, it would destroy him?"

"It might."

"Why?"

"He's proud, vain, superficial, egotistical, superstitious," Joe said without any emphasis. "This machine, to do what Washington wants, would have to use judgment, determine right from wrong, good from bad. Man has kept a monopoly on that—or thinks he has."

"What do you mean—thinks he has?" Billings asked, and felt he was nearing some door which might open on a new vista.

"Suppose we say that white is good and black is bad," Joe said quietly. "Any photoelectric cell then can tell good from bad. Suppose we say a high number is right and a low number is wrong. Any self-respecting cybernetic machine then can tell right from wrong."

"But those are purely arbitrary values, Joe," Billings objected. "Set up for a specific expediency."

"You're something of a historian, doctor," Joe answered obliquely. "Aren't all of them?"

Billings started to argue along the lines of inherent human nature, instinct for good and right, basic moralities, the things man believed set him apart from the other animals. He realized that he would be talking to a telepath; that he had better stick to the facts.

"At least man has arbitrarily set his own values, Joe," he said. "The photoelectric cell or cybernetic machine can't do that." Yet he caught a glimpse of things beyond the opening door, and became suddenly silent.

"We must emphasize that fact, doctor," Joe said earnestly. "Man must go on, for a while, thinking that; in spite of the contrary evidence which this servomechanism will reveal. That shouldn't be too hard to maintain. Man generally believes what he prefers to believe. Most evidence can be twisted to filter through his screen mesh of prejudices and tensions, so that it confirms rather than confounds.

Billings felt a wave of apprehension. He almost wished that he had not come to Joe for help on this project. Yet he felt relief, too. Joe, by the plural pronoun, had indicated that he would work on the project. Relief, because he knew that he had no knowledge whereby the problem could be approached. And he believed Joe did.

The illusion of a door opening remained before his vision. There were dark stirrings beyond.

The work did not progress.

It was not due to lack of organization, or lack of cooperation. The scientists had long ago adapted to the appointment of most anyone as head of a project, and they saw nothing unusual in a specialist in psychosomatics being assigned to make up a new servomechanism.

The lack of progress stemmed from the fact that their objective was not clearly defined. Through the days that followed, Billings was bothered, more than he cared to admit, by Joe's warning that the semantics of their objective must be kept away from any concept of duplicating the work of the human brain. Yet that was what they were trying to do.

He was helped none, either, by the several incidents, in meetings, when one or the other of the scientists on the project tried to tell him that was what they were trying to do.

"If you want a servomechanism," Gunther, the photoelectric man, said, "which will make the same decisions and take the same actions as a human plane pilot, then you must duplicate that pilot's mental processes."

"If we are trying to duplicate the processes of human thought, why have no psychologists, other than yourself, been assigned to this project?" asked Hoskins, the cybernetic man.

These questions were not easy to parry. Both of these men were first-rate scientists, and in the figurative underground, among friends who could be trusted, they asked questions to which they expected answers. The line which Joe had insisted he adopt did not satisfy them.

"We must not permit ourselves to get confused with arguing the processes of human thought," Billings had replied. "We will bog down in that area and get nowhere. This is simply a machine and must be approached from the mechanical."

Yes, it was unsatisfactory, for it was precisely the same kind of thought control which had blanketed the country. You must solve the problem, but you are not permitted to explore this and this and this avenue in your search for the possible solution.

Joe, too, was a disappointment. Billings had succeeded in getting him appointed as project secretary. No one objected since the job required a great deal of paper work, carried little prestige, and the pay was not enticing. There would be other students assigned later to various phases of production. Billings made a mental note to assign young Tyler to something which sounded particularly impressive. The undercurrents of that cartoon could not go ignored. Joe's appointment, therefore, seemed natural enough, and brought him into the thick of activity.

But Joe did no more than the recording. Billings found himself in the frustrating position of having engineered the situation so that Joe would be there for question on how they should proceed, but Joe gave only vague and evasive answers. The progress reports, turned over to Rogan for forwarding on to Washington, contained a great deal of wordage and little else. That would keep Washington quiet for a while, since their tendency was to measure the worth of a report by its poundage; but it was also dangerous in case anybody felt he was slipping out of the public eye, and began to cast about for some juicy publicity.

One of Joe's typical answers brought typical results.

"We already know enough to build it," Joe had said firmly. "We've got all the basic principles. We can duplicate the action of the human brain, at its present level of thinking, any time we want to. Only if we realize that's what we're doing, we won't want to do it. So, on a mechanical level, we simply have to bring all the principles together and coordinate them."

That added up to nothing when Billings tried it. Suggestions from various departments, working piecemeal, ranged all the way from pinhead size transistors, to city block long banks of cybernetic machines. Even though they had the knowledge, if they did, to build a separate machine to take care of each possible pattern which might arise in the piloting of a plane, it would create an accumulation large enough to fill the old Empire State building.

In exasperation, Billings called Joe to account in his office. They were alone, and Billings minced no words about the way Joe was dragging his feet.

"Why do you want to build this machine, doctor?" Joe asked abruptly. "You're not afraid of the consequences if you fail?"

Billings had not expected this attack from Joe. As the weeks had passed, he had felt a growing urgency to succeed, but he had not tried to put his feelings into words. To answer Joe, he tried now.

"Every man, who thinks, wants there to be a meaning to his life," he said carefully, for he sensed that this was the critical point. "I've spent my life trying to know, to understand. Everything I've ever learned seems to come together in this one thing. Say I'm looking for a monument, that there should be an apex, a crowning achievement. Every man would like there to be something remaining after him, which says, 'This is the meaning of his life.' "

Joe was silent, and looked at him steadily. Billings realized he had expressed only a part of it, perhaps the most insignificant part. He picked up a cigarette, lit it, and took another approach.

"A civilization, too," he said. "Each one of them has produced some one great achievement, one specialty. There're not all the same and with the same goals. But each succeeding civilization seems to adopt what results it can use from past achievements. It synthesizes them into its own special achievement. Our specialty has been technological advance. Never mind that everything else is borrowed and doesn't fit us—we have achieved that. But what we have achieved could be meaningless to some future civilization unless we give it meaning now. Here, again, this thing would sum up and embody in one object the total of our technology.

"If man's advance is toward a broader intellect, it seems we should sum up his intellect to this point—if we can, and in our own language, that of technology. It's the only one we speak without an accent."

Still Joe sat in silence, and picked absently at a frayed thread in the drape which hung near his chair. Though he meant them to be constructive, Billings realized that to Joe such arguments were futile, hopeless, destructive. An old man may think with detachment about thousand-year periods of history, and view with little concern the infinitesimal part his own life plays out of all the trillions of people who may live. But a young man is impatient with such maundering. He wants the answers to his own life, the drive which will give purpose to his own acts. And the purpose was there, too, enough to satisfy even—a Joe.

"No man watches happily," Billings said, "while his civilization passes and sinks back into the Dark Ages. Every man has the tragic feeling that it need not happen; that if some eventual civilization is to endure, then why not his own? True, most civilizations had one spurt which made them shine for a while before they flickered out again. But some had several spurts. Some new thing entered the life of the people. They found the energy to meet the new challenge and solve its problem."

Joe's head came up at this, and he stopped pulling at the string on the curtain.

"According to you, Joe," Billings said in final argument, "this thing may destroy man. It may also bump him up to the next step of evolution."

"You'd be willing to face personal danger for that, doctor?" Joe asked suddenly.

The room grew very still. Billings did not answer lightly, for he suspected Joe saw farther beyond the door than he could.

"Yes," he said firmly. "Of course."

That was the turning point in Joe's attitude toward the project, but it had no effect upon the various scientists, of course. They still operated on the basis of a separate machine for every requirement, and the list of requirements was endless.

Superficially, to anyone who had not thought it through, the problem seemed not too difficult, as Washington had stated. A self-aiming gun, a self-guided missile which fastened upon a distant object, plotted its course to intersect the object, and changed its course to compensate for the change in the fleeing object's maneuvers—these should certainly show the way.

And back of that there had been pilotless radio-controlled planes. And back of that the catapult and the bow and arrow.

But whether it was a self-guided missile, or a spear, there was a human mind back of it which had already predicted, used judgment, set the forces in motion according to that judgment.

Human mind? What about the monkey who threw the coconut from the tree at its enemy? What about the skunk with its own version of the catapult? Well, mind of some kind.

Even the amoeba varied its actions to suit the circumstances. There couldn't be much of a brain in one cell. Yet it did react, within its limits, through variable patterns. Any psychosomaticist knows that every cell has a sort of mind of its own. But certainly a cybernetic machine has capacity for varied patterns, too, according to the circumstances. But preset, man, prechosen! But didn't blind and reasonless environment present and prechoose what an amoeba would do? Need it be a mind, as we think of mind?

Billings was not the only one whose thoughts went around and around in this vein, exploring the possible concepts; not the only one who found a yea for every nay. All the scientists, singly and in groups, inescapably followed the same train of reasoning; and came up against the same futility. In spite of Billings' instructions to keep their concepts mechanical, if they were to duplicate the results of judgment between the best courses of action among the many courses of action a plane or an automobile might take, then they had to think about the processes of judging; and the nature of choosing.

Unfortunately, each of them had had courses in psychology, absorbed its strange conclusions, allowed themselves to be influenced by its influence on man's thinking. They arrived nowhere in their analyses. They made the mistake of judging it by the other sciences, assumed it had its foundation based in fact; and felt it must be their own fault when its results gave them nothing.

Yet Billings remembered that Joe had told him they knew enough to build the machine. Still, what was the use of the finest watch if one had no concept of the measurement of time? One might build endless and complex speculation on the way its metal case flashed in the sun, or how it ticked with a life of its own against the ear, in the way that psychology and philosophy speculated endlessly and built complex structures of pointless word games about the nature of man.

Billings smiled with wry amusement at the position in which he found himself. He was like a student who has been given a knotty problem to solve, knows there must be a solution but can't find it. For he did not doubt the conviction of Joe's statement.

Like the bewildered student, he went to teacher. He was sincere enough and had sufficient stature that he could disregard the disparity of their ages, positions, experience, credentials. He was not too proud to accept knowledge, wherever he may find it.

"It's inability to communicate with each other," Joe answered his question. "It's like the spokes of a wheel, without any bridging rim connecting them. The hub is basic scientific knowledge. Specialized sciences radiate out from that, and in moving outward they build up their own special semantics."

"I've heard the analogy before," Billings objected. "It's not a good one; because, if you think about it, you'll see that none get very far out from the hub without the assistance of the others. The concepts of one must be incorporated into the other before any of them can progress very far."

"They use one another's products, doctor," Joe corrected without emphasis. "Whether those products be gadgets or ideas, they're still the result of another's specialized thinking. A mechanical engineer uses the product of the petroleum engineer without more than superficially knowing or caring about how its molecules were tailored. Say the product doesn't work. The mechanical engineer doesn't drop everything and spend a dozen years or so trying to find the proper lubricant. He goes back to the petroleum engineer, puts in his beef, describes the conditions which the lubricant must meet. The petroleum engineer goes away, polymerizes and catalyzes some more molecules, brings back a new sample, and now the mechanical engineer can go a little farther out on his spoke. But he doesn't communicate except at the product use level."

"Then how are we going to get these men to use each other's products, Joe?" Billings asked impatiently. "This thing is all out of hand. It isn't taking shape at any point. The more we think about it the less it resolves itself, the more chaotic it becomes."

He turned to Joe and spoke levelly, almost accusingly.

"You seem to know what needs to be done, but you don't do anything about it, Joe. I counted on you. Maybe I shouldn't have, but I did. It seemed to me that this thing was a solution for you as well as for me. You've never known how to put your talent to use constructively, and you must have wanted that. Well, here's your chance."

He saw Joe's face turn pale, and a mask of no expression settle over it. But his irritation and frustration made Billings plunge in where consideration had held him back before.

"Why can't you do that, Joe?"

"That would mean going into their minds," Joe said slowly, through stiff lips. "Taking over portions of their thinking, directing their actions. I haven't done that since I played around with it as a child, before I realized what I was doing. It isn't right for one human being—and I do think of myself as human—to control another human being."

Billings threw back his head and laughed with sudden relief.

"Joe!" he exclaimed. "You're the living example that special talent or knowledges does not bring with it special wisdom or common sense! Don't you realize that every time we ask somebody to pass the salt at the table, or honk our horn at someone on the street, or buy a pair of socks, or give a lecture, that we are controlling the thought and action of others?"

"It isn't the same," Joe insisted. "You normals are blind and fumbling and crude about it. You just bump into one another in your threshing about. And you can always refuse to obey one another."

"Not really, Joe," Billings said. "How long would a man last in his freedom if he refused to do the million things society required of him? I doubt if there's much essential difference in the kind of pressure you could bring, and the kind which the whole society brings upon a man. You say we fumble, while you could do it expertly. I think I'd rather have an expert work on me than a fumbler. What is the difference in your planting the thought of what these scientists should do, and my sending them a written order? Great Scott, boy, if you can get them to accomplish this thing, then you must go ahead."

"Whatever I think needs to be done to accomplish it, doctor?"

"Whatever the project requires to carry it to completion," Billings defined, "remembering that this thing can be the solution for mankind, push him up to the next evolutionary rung."

Joe was silent for a little while, and then spoke slowly.

"But they mustn't known. Outside of a man's own isolated field of knowledge, he's as superstitious as all the rest. They've got all kinds of the wildest ideas about how dangerous and evil a telepath might be. They mustn't known. You've got to remember that sanity in a person or a civilization is like a small boat on the surface of an ocean. If the subterranean depths get roiled up enough, the boat capsizes and there's nothing but the storming chaos of madness."

"Is that the way we appear to you, Joe?"

"That's the way man is," Joe said simply.

"Then if you can keep from rocking the boat when you direct their thinking on this project, you can depend on me to keep it secret, Joe." Billings said reassuringly.

"It's perfectly ethical, all right, for me to control their thinking on this project, then?"

"Perfectly all right, Joe," Billings said with emphasis. And he thought he meant it.

The door opened wider.

It was Hoskins, in charge of the cybernetic aspects, who put the general feeling into words a few days later.

"I've often observed," Hoskins said to no one in particular, as several of them sat around the general meeting room, "that you'll be faced with a problem which looks completely unsolvable—there's just no point at which you can grab hold of it—then suddenly, for no reason at all, the whole thing smooths out."

Billings darted a quick look at Joe, but that young man, busy at a small table over in the corner of the room, did not look up from his job of assembling various reports into order.

Another, perhaps even more significant piece of evidence became apparent, that the men were incorporating the problem into their thinking normally. The thing acquired a name—Bossy. Suddenly everyone was using it. The animal husbandry department had supplied it.

"Anybody who has ever handled cows knows they can be the most onery, cantankerous, stubborn critters you ever saw one minute, and completely gentle and obedient the next," one of the men from that department said.

And that about described their feelings toward Bossy at this time.

Billings had been trying for some time to find a descriptive name, using the familiar method of initials of descriptive words — sensory — apperceptor — indexer — appraiser — comparer — extrapolator — predictor — chooser — activator — He bogged down, not only in that the initials seemed to add up to nothing pronounceable, but the list of terms themselves merely added to the confusion. He, too, called it Bossy. Somehow that was best—for Bossy was, in spite of her contrariness, domesticated, inferior to man, controllable—and gave milk. Quite consciously, he was comforted by the semantics of the name.

Rogan, too, accepted the name. He was a little scandalized and as yet Washington hadn't give any reaction which would guide his attitude, but unless the meat or dairy industry objected, there seemed to be nothing subversive about it.

A third evidence, stronger than the other two, was that everyone began talking about sensory receptors. They reasoned that if a pilot sees and hears and feels the external world about him, even though instruments are measuring these things more accurately than he can determine them, then Bossy must also have the receptors to bring sight and sound and feeling.

First, as a joke, and then no longer kidding about it, they decided to give her taste and smell while they were about it. And then someone spoke out in the commons room and said they were pikers. They'd give her sight that a human pilot couldn't have, such as radar. They'd give her sensitivity such as no human being could feel—like the seismograph. They'd give her gyroscopic balance that would make the inner fluid of the human ear less than mentionable. They'd give her—

The talk of what they would give Bossy, all the delicate ways man has evolved to detect things beyond the range of his crude dull senses, went on far into the night.

Sensory receptors were not too difficult to manage. It was rather astonishing, when one assembled them all together, how widely man had already duplicated human sense receptors. For sight, in the human visual range, there was the electronic camera, the light sensitive film of the photographic plate, the selenium cell, and other. Beyond the normal eye range there was radar, and other infrared and violet-light detectors. There was a wealth of sound-sensitive instruments; and a plethora of touch and feel instruments used by industry in product inspection and analysis. The taste and scent instruments were not so well developed, but there were some, and, approaching it through chemical effect, there could be others.

It was common knowledge, too, that all these instruments converted the external senses to electrical impulse—not too far removed from the way the nerves carry the impact of the sense receptors to the brain.

No one seemed to be bothered about what they would do when they got that far; that an electronic camera could pick up light rays and convert them into electrical impulses until it fogged its lenses, but the picture would have no meaning until the human eye viewed it and gave it meaning.

They went about their job, instead, in the way a skilled artisan goes about his—knowing that problems may arise which he hasn't yet worked out, but also confident that he can handle them when they do arise.

Their work, at this point, was the reduction of size, greater sensitivity, combining the principles of many instruments into one. The human eye contains a hundred and thirty million light sensitive cells. It would be nice if they could get their camera orifices as tidy and sensitive.

Each of the departments put its best students to work on its own problem, until the entire university was coordinated into working on some aspect of the job. The singleness of purpose, the drive for accomplishment was as much as could be asked by any industrialist.

Rogan, too, was caught up in the enthusiasm, and surveyed the activity with a certain approval—for busy hands have no time for mischief. And he found himself with new duties, strange for a Resident Investigator. Hoxworth University did not have all the talent and equipment it needed for this project, not by any means. Rogan found himself assuming the role of a go-between with Washington, requesting, requisitioning, requiring services and specialists not only from other schools, but from industry itself.

Operation Bossy became a familiar term in the administrative offices of Washington, and throughout the industrial and educational life of the nation. As with most other top-secret projects, everybody knew about it and was talking about it. The stories grew with the telling, and Joe's insistence to Billings that it be kept in the mechanical language began to have reason behind it. It was merely another form of the guided missile. No one realized what was really happening, not even the men working at its central core—not even Billings.

Things were happening too fast for that. It was as if the pieces of a giant jigsaw puzzle, cast carelessly upon a table, began to assemble themselves at various places, without much regard for one another, or where each would fit into the whole once the picture was done.

Although no one had thought of synthetic textiles as being more than remotely connected with the project, it was that laboratory which came up with the impulse-storing ribbon. Yet they were the most logical to accomplish this. That field knows probably more than any other how to tailor and alter molecules to suit their purpose. Sound had long been stored on plastic tape; light, too, in photographic plastic.

Without a hitch, Hoskins of cybernetics, began working in the synthetic textiles department, finding in its ability to polymerize and catalyze molecules the ideal opportunity for memory storage units. Again, the elimination of grossness became a major concern, and from the apertures there began to spew a thread, all but invisible, not more than a few molecules in breadth and thickness, with each molecule tailored to pick up and store its own burden of electrical impulse.

Bossy began to take shape, and, oddly enough, the box took on a faint resemblance to a cow. Perhaps this was mainly due to the two eyestalks which sprouted out from near its upper surface, like horns topped with dragonfly eye lenses. None of this poor human vision for their Bossy. The diaphragm for picking up sound on the front of the box was vaguely like the blaze on an animal's face, the apertures for air entrance where scent and taste could be sampled where like nostrils.

It was as if there was an unconscious determination to see that the thing remained Bossy.

A stream of specialized molecules poured past each sense receptor, picked up the electronic vibration, combined to make a thread, in the way that a motion-picture film picks up light and sound, so that when played back they coincide, and stored itself at the bottom of the case.

They had not yet arrived at any point where a new basic principle needed to be found. Although, at this point, they had no more than a superior sense-recording machine. The thread could be played back, but that was all. And no one worried about it.

It was music, another unlikely department, who gave the clue to the next step. A note struck on one key of the piano will, through the principle of harmonics, vibrate the strings at octaves above so that they also give off sound. Shouldn't there be a vibronic code signal inherent in each sense stream, so that like things will activate harmonically with other like things? Wasn't that how recognition took place through harmonically awakened association with like experience in the past?

It was.

Outwardly, Bossy ceased to take shape. To codify every sound, every shape, every vibration translated into touch and feel and scent and taste, every degree of light and color density was a monumental task—in terms of detail work, although its organization was not difficult. To translate these into electrical code impulses was difficult. But here again, no new principle was needed. Here again, man had merely the task defining the world in terms of symbol—and symbol in terms of code impulse.

Nor was it too difficult to again tailor the molecules to carry electrical current, which, theoretically, would keep these code impulses vibrating in harmonics with those passing the sense receptor apertures.

And still it was no more than an impulse storage bank. Only in theory was a new impulse activating its counterpart in old impulses. They had no way of testing it in practice. And felt supremely confident that a way would be found.

No one who has not directed a large scale activity, coordinated the work of thousands of people and synthesized their results could fully comprehend the mass of work which fell upon Billings and his immediate staff. Many times he felt he had taken on more than he could handle, that the scope of activity had got out of hand. Yet inquiries and suggestions came from everywhere, and many of them were pertinent and valuable.

It was as if the whole academic life of the nation had been swept up in the same urgency which had compelled him; as if men had something to think about which, for the moment, was unimpeded with restrictions and investigations.

Yet, in spite of the weight of administrative detail, he had the feeling that he had full grasp of everything that was happening, and with a clarity of mind he had never experienced before he was able to see the relation of concepts one to the other.

Perhaps it was this clarity which made him call a halt to the coding as it was developing, scrap much of what had been done, and start over. For it should have been obvious all along that identical things receiving identical codes was not enough. This had been the stumbling block of all cybernetic machines in the past. A tabulating pattern combined only identicals. They could combine the symbols for two apples and six apples correctly into eight apples, but when it came across one apple, it broke this out into a separate category, for the latter symbol differed from the former in that the letter "s" was missing. The cybernetic machines in the past had no sense, were not keyed to vagaries of grammar, spelling mistakes, variations which a child of eight would know were not really variations.

A way must be found to duplicate the dull stupidity of the human mind which could not detect differences unless they were glaring, and yet retain the fine sensitivity of the cybernetic machine.

It became apparent that not only must there be a code impulse for each isolated aspect of the external world, there must also be an interlocking code for activation to bring back the total picture. Remembrances are by association, one thing leads to another.

A symbol of a square must not only activate any previous experience of the symbol of a square but also the circumstances in which that symbol was experienced. Yes, there must be a horizontal interlocking of codes, as well as vertical. For was not that the way decisions were made? In terms of how things, similar things, under similar circumstances, worked out in the past?

Much had been written that the patterns of life duplicate themselves again and again and again; that the intelligent man recognizes this duplication even though it may be in a different guise, while the unintelligent and the machine do not and must solve each thing as if it were new.

While they were setting up the new system of coding, the art department threw the worst curve of all. There was the matter of foreshortening. A square on a card looks square when faced head-on, but looks rectangular if the card is turned at an angle. The human mind learns to make adjustments for foreshortening, so shouldn't Bossy? They asked it blandly, and perhaps a little maliciously, for they had not been consulted up to this point.

Billings was dismayed at this obvious difficulty, and his spirits were not lifted either by the knowledge that it took over three thousand years of art painting for man to move from the side view of the foot, as portrayed by the Egyptians, to the front view, as discovered by the Greeks. And almost another five hundred years to move from the profile of the face to a front view.

It would be difficult to achieve this for Bossy. Still, there was no new principles involved, simply a coding method which would tell Bossy that one object was truly a rectangle seen head-on, and another which appeared to be the same was really a square seen at an angle. It was the same kind of lateral coding which would solve this.

The key to Bossy's first overt reaction to stimuli came from one of the younger assistant professors one night in the common room. He was ruefully telling how his new baby responded to his wife's hands with contentment and to his hands with fright. The baby was much too young to recognize the difference between mama and papa. It must be familiarity versus unfamiliarity in the manner of touch.

A few days later, safety guards were installed around Bossy. They had long since installed the yes-no principle to be found in other cybernetic machines. There was jubilation and something approaching awe when Bossy demonstrated it could learn—and learn with only one trial. The safety guards were keyed to the reject pattern, but when Hoskins, who installed the guards, depressed the accept key for his own hands, thereafter the machine threw up its guards when approached by alien hands, but left them down for Hoskins' hands. Perhaps it was mass, or shape codes. Perhaps it was color. Perhaps it was scent, for Hoskins had been working around the machine when scent codes were being fed into it. Still Hoskins had no code of his own scent as differeing from others. Scent was out, for the machine had no equipment whereby it might do its own coding.

They were not sure just what process had occurred which made Bossy distinguish safe hands from unsafe hands. She had the sense receptors to observe the outside world. She had the codes, a great many and more being added constantly, whereby through keyed harmonics she associated new perception with old. Some moves had been made to key her with similarities and differences. The mechanism was there to compare the new with the old and to determine the identities and the differences. And now she had demonstrated that she could distinguish through the sense perceptors and the established coding.

Further, she had demonstrated that she could take automatic action.

The men cautioned one another, again and again, that they must not fall into the habit of thinking the machine could do anything they hadn't keyed it to do. It had no sense. None at all. Really, this throwing up the bars to keep alien hands out was no more than any selenium cell would do—well, modified by coding.

Even without Joe's warning glance, Billings felt they were reassuring one another on this point perhaps a little too much. He noticed, too, that the gender changed overnight from it to she. But it was several days before he noticed that Gunther had begun to stammer the name to B-b-b-ossy, each time he said it, although the man never stammered on anything else. And Hoskins always hesitated with an audible "ah" before saying the name.

The shadows beyond the door began to stir and swell, and seemed to writhe around one another.

Spring came, and then it was June. Commencement exercises were no more than a reluctant interlude from the work. Billings watched Joe throw off his graduating cap and gown, and in almost the same movement start assembling the requests for student deferments from compulsory military service. A summer session extraordinary had been declared that no time be lost in the work on Bossy, and the entire university was humming on a factory schedule.

A new respect had been gained for a baby's mind. Ordinarily adults thought of the newborn baby as just lying there, inert mentally, accomplishing little learning beyond finding out that a cry would summon attention, a nipple placed between its lips would start the reflex of sucking. Now they realized the multitudes of unrelated sense impressions that mind must be storing, the repeated patterns which impressed themselves upon its brain—and prediction of the future.

"If I cry, there will be approaching footsteps. I stop my crying to listen for them. If I do not hear them, I cry again. Soon there will be comforting hands and I will be dry and warm again."

And any young mother knows this is accomplished in a few weeks. One by one the patterns are learned, the sensation relationships repeat themselves, a word is spoken in connection with an object or an action. Always the word and the object appear simultaneously—they are cojoined, one produces the other. Relationships become vaguely apparent. Cause and effect emerge as an expectancy.

If it were not that a baby was human, one might set up certain laws of procedure. An outside world datum makes an impact upon a sensory receptor. This is accompanied by other impacts of other data. There is a relationship of each to the other. And long before there is any concept of self, as an entity, there is a realization of self to the data. Not all the data appear each time and in the same order. But if enough data appear to strike up the harmonics of association with a previous experience—judgment is assumed. Through repetition of patterns of trial and error, some reflex and some calculated, action upon judgment takes place.

But the baby is human, and therefore mysterious, and we may not simplify the awful metaphysics of an awakening human mind into a set of mechanical steps. The human mind is set apart, the human mind could not contemplate itself as being no more than an operation of an understandable process.

But it was different with Bossy. Bossy was a machine, and therefore the processes which would substitute for thought must be approached mechanically. Bossy recognized solely through mechanical indexing—no different in principle from the old-fashioned punched card sorter. This and this and this is the same as that and that and that—therefore these two things have a relationship to one another. Comparison of new data with old data, a feedback process of numerous indexed impulses and these to the external sense receptors and their stream of new impulses—really it was quite trivial.

It was only coincidence that it seemed, here and there, to duplicate the results of an infant mind. Only coincidence that as new experience and new data were being constantly applied, new areas of experience exposed to Bossy, that she should seem to follow the process of the learning child.

Strictly coincidence, and one must not be fooled by coincidence.

As Billings watched Joe assemble the lists of deferments, he wondered about the young man. Since their conversation, when he had asked Joe to use his talents to further the project, they had talked no more than the work required. Billings was no closer to knowing Joe than he had ever been, and Joe volunteered nothing. He did not know what Joe had done to clear away the mental blocks which had prevented the scientists from grasping the problem, he had only the overt evidence that something had been done.

Really this project was all he had claimed it would be. Attempt to reduce it to simplicity though they may, it still remained that all of man's science up to the present had been required to produce it. Bossy's accomplishment was for all time the monument to the triumph of science, the refutation that science exists only through the indifferent tolerance of the average man, the refutation also that man has never used his intellect except to rationalize, justify and decorate with high-sounding phrases the primitive urges he intended to foster anyway. For it had taken intellect to produce Bossy, intellect of a high order, reaching up to—detachment.

"Oh, by the way, doctor," Joe looked up from his work at the desk and interrupted Billings' thinking, "have you been following the articles on witchcraft?"

"Why . . . why no, Joe," Billings answered. "I hadn't noticed. What about them?"

"There's a trend," Joe said. "At first the articles started out faintly deploring, and then explaining. Now there is the current theory that scientists and thinkers generally tend to get off the right track. That there is a mass wisdom for doing the right thing for mankind, embodied in the masses of people. That mankind has proved steadily and progressively he knows what is best for him; and therefore the so-called witchcraft suppression was simply man's way, an instinctive inherent rightness, to keep from being led into the wrong ways of thinking."

"That is a very common line of thinking," Billings said without much interest. "How are you coming along with that roster of deferments?"

He saw Joe throw him a quick, appraising look, and then turn back to his work again. Probably nothing significant about Joe's remarks. Young men tended to become much too horrified as they realized the terrible stupidity of mankind. As one grows older, one doesn't expect so much; loses some of the idealism of what man should be.

"It's pretty extensive, doctor," Joe said in a colorless voice. "When I think that a similar list is being prepared in every college throughout the country . . . well, the military isn't going to like not being able to harvest its new crop. There'll be an investigation."

Billings hardly heard him. His mind continued along the track of comparison of Bossy and a child. Every day new sensations fed into the child, new admonitions, corrections, approvals, patterns fed into stored accumulation of past sensations and conclusions. Sensations on the order of billions, perhaps trillions—no wonder that thought seemed complex, ungraspable. But as with so many problems the difficulty was size and bulk—and complexity was no more than superimposure of simple upon simple.

But human beings did not learn fast, most of them required many repetitions of a pattern before they grasped it. The man was rare, indeed, who could memorize a book in scanning it once. Really now, a very poor job had been done in tailoring the molecular structure of—

Bossy required only once. Perhaps Joe was right. Perhaps man was still evolving. Perhaps his brain was no more than a rudimentary light-sensitive cell as compared with the eye. Perhaps that was why his brain gave such a poor performance, it had not evolved into its potential.

Billings sat, gazing out of the window at the elm trees and the sky.

"Yes," he murmured, moments later to Joe's comment. "No doubt there will be an investigation." He wondered, vaguely, what there would be an investigation about—but no matter, there were always investigations.

Surely it would have nothing to do with Hoxworth University, or himself. For the assignment had succeeded beyond the wildest imaginings. Perhaps it was immodest, but surely the success of Bossy would be emblazoned across the pages of history for a thousand years—the greatest achievement of all time; and his name would be that of its author.

Man! Know thyself!

"We must not allow ourselves to become fascinated with the sensation mongering of these investigations, Joe," he said chidingly. "We are thinkers, and we have work to do."

Again he felt the quick, questioning look from Joe, but dismissed it and continued with his development of vision. Plainly, Joe still lacked wisdom.

Through the weeks that followed another tension began to assume proportions too great to be ignored. As long as there had been such a recognized thing as science, itself, here had been a controversy concerning one aspect of it. A thing is composed of numerous properties which a theory or an equation must take into account if a satisfactory solution is to be attained. Some of these properties are intangible, but none the less real, such as friction, or gravity. Some are still variable and unpredictable. Thus one of the real and inescapable properties of a thing is—human reaction to it. An automobile could not be called a satisfactory invention if no one would drive it; an electric light could not be called a solution to illuminating darkness if man smashed it in frenzied rage each time he saw it. Since man can know a thing only through the mind of man, then the mind of man is one of its inherent properties. So said a school of philosophy.

This pro school held that human reaction to a thing was as real as gravity or friction; that a scientist who ignored it was like a mechanical engineer who persisted in ignoring the effects of friction, a structural engineer who ignored gravity. On the con side, it was considered that the physical scientist had plenty to do in measuring physical forces and properties; that the force of human reaction, if it existed, belonged in someone else's problem basket.

The pro school held this was not true; that the pharmaceutical chemist did assume responsibility for the effect of his concoctions upon human mind and tissues, the structural engineer did assume some responsibility for the end use of his houses or bridges, the mechanical engineer did assume some responsibility for people using his motor; that no arbitrary line could be drawn separating responsibility from nonresponsibility.

The con school, in the vast majority because it is easier to evade responsibility than to assume it, still passed the buck.

And because this real property of things continued to be ignored, the gap between the scientist and the man in the street widened, and widened, and stretched out farther and farther. Any physical scientist knows that regardless of theory, there is a practical limit to the elasticity of a material. There is also a limit to the elasticity of human reaction to a science it can not understand, and therefore fears.

It became also apparent, in these weeks, that there was a serious leak of details on the progress of Bossy. No project as widespread as the work on Bossy could be kept entirely under security. Even where trained scientists possess only scraps and portions of the whole knowledge, misconceptions will occur. And multitudes of those working on some phase of Bossy were not yet trained scientists. They were students. Students, for all the grave respect they hold for the weight and importance of their knowledge, are notorious for misconceptions. There is a dividing line between effective scientist and student, but it has nothing to do with graduation exercises. Too many remain students, multiplying misconception upon misconception. An astonishing number of these, unable to make their way in the laboratory, turn to teaching for their living. The gap between science and superstition widens.

Beyond a serious central leak, which was becoming apparent, there were widespread rumors and bits of information leaking out. Each, in itself, was perhaps a harmless thing—if properly weighed and stripped of its exaggerations and misinterpretations. But human beings, generally, are not noted for their ability to weigh judiciously, discount exaggerations, and allow for possible misunderstanding. People like sensationalism, and in the telling add their bit to it.

Bossy, at first ignored as being the business of the scientists and having no relationship to bread and bed, suddenly became a topic of conversation everywhere. Everyone found he had an opinion. Ready-made opinions by the score poured through the news columns and over video. Bossy began to assume proportions of concern, dread, then outright fear.

When you stop to think of it, some of the more articulate would say, the most inefficient, unpredictable, costly and exasperating machine used in industry is the human being. The only advantage it has over other machines, the only reason an industrialist uses it, is its wide flexibility of adaptation to numerous conditions, the ease of replacement if it doesn't function properly.

But now there was Bossy.

It did not take long for the sensationalists to predict manless factories, manless shops and stores, manless utility and transportation services. Once the coals were breathed into flame, it did not take long for the fire to gather fuel and spread in white heat. And like a gasoline poured into the flames was the wholesale student deferment.

Some of this reaction trickled, much diffused, into the ivory towers. Billings tried to offset it. He made a personal appearance on a national hook-up, but he mistook fire for water and poured oil on the waves to quiet them.

"There is nothing to fear," he said. "The brain of Bossy is no more than a compound of synthetic proteins, colloids, enzymes, metallic salts, fatty acids—each molecule designed and shaped to do a specific task, picking up codified impulse charges to complete their structure, and then combining into a threadlike substance for storage and release."

If he had spoken in Hottentot, it would have been as comprehensible and less dangerous. For without conveying the slightest understanding, and even in his attempts to show this thing was not human, he heightened the dread.

Bossy was truly a machine, a synthetic thing, Its inventor, the famous Billings, had said so, himself. Had it been alive, man might have understood it better, even though alien and inimical it would have shared with him the mystery of life and thought.

As he droned on and on through his talk, as he described the lenses, the diaphragms, the metallic, glassite, plastic receptors, showing how they saw and felt and tasted and heard, he confirmed all the rumors. Bossy *was* capable of replacing man.

And Bossy had no soul.

Letters by the thousands, the hundreds of thousands, poured into Congress. Congress, far more receptive to the will of the people than is generally realized, tried to act. But it was the Administrative Department who had cut the orders for work on Bossy. The Administrative Department unfortunately chose this issue as a battle arena to show Congress it could no longer be shoved around so easily. The resultant conflict, the raw tempers which flared into print and over national hookups, served merely to heighten the tension throughout the country. There was something to it!

The quiet and doubtful words of the mollifiers, the advocates of let's wait and see, the admonishers of you're not hurt yet, their voices were lost in the angry outpourings of revolt against this manufacture of a soulless machine to replace man, this deferment of favored young men, these irresponsible scientists—science itself.

In damning the very idea of science, it never occurred to most that they were using the products of science to get their message into every corner of the land, into every mind.

The first overt move came from a small band of men who chose to have a parade of protest. It was national news. They fed upon the publicity. The parade regrouped and formed into a march—a march across two states toward Hoxworth University. The ranks of the marchers swelled. Other marchers started.

And in the village of Hoxworth, near the university, the residents decided they did not need to be reminded of their duty by people from other communities.

There sprang from the mind of a fanatic, and couched in the lyrical language so often used by the psychotic, a huge placard that was set up at the corner of the library park one night. In one corner of it, there was a copy of young Tyler's cartoon of Billings. And in bold lettering:

HIDE! HIDE! WITCH! THE GOOD FOLK COME TO BURN THEE!

All day there was a crowd around it. In the strange manner of disturbed people, some stood for hours just looking at it, letting its message seep into the bottom fibers of their beings—awakening ancestral memories.

But during the small hours of the night, some student, perhaps

equally psychotic in his bitterness against such medieval reaction, added another placard below with these scornful words:
THEIR KEEN ENJOYMENT HID BENEATH THE GOTHIC MASK OF DUTY!
It was a most unfortunate thing, for it struck deep into the roots of guilt, and even where some had hung back, now they raged and stormed with the rest when it was discovered the next morning.

A pall of quietness, inactivity, hung over Hoxworth University. A miasma of gloom, apprehension, like the somatics within a prison, filled the grounds and seeped through the halls. Classes were sparsely attended, and instructors found themselves straying away from the subject of their lectures. Most of the students had gone home in the weeks before.

All work on Bossy had ceased at the orders of the Board of Governors of the University. She had been dismantled and her parts stored away. The activated brain floes had been carefully lifted out of its case and folded into a thin aluminum box. No one was sure what damage even this handling might do, and no one had the urge to test and experiment to find out.

"I tried to warn you, Dr. Billings," Joe said once, in the dean's office.

"But if you knew this, Joe!" Billings exclaimed. "Why didn't you tell us?"

"Each time I tried, doctor," Joe said quietly, "you told me to mind my own business, that I lacked wisdom. I didn't know for sure what would happen, or I'd have forced you to listen. I knew only that men of science have failed to bring the people along with them, that human beings are capable of terrible things when they are terrified. You told me, many times, that scientists are not concerned with these things; that scientists don't want to hear about doom consequences; that scientists are quite certain everything will be all right if they're just permitted to do as they please."

"People have predicted doom at every single advance of science, Joe," Billings admonished him. "Look at all the doom written around the time of atomic discovery. It never happened."

"I know," Joe said. "It's case of 'Wolf, wolf' being cried too often, isn't it? Too bad. But your history should tell you, doctor, there always comes a time when the wolf really does come."

There wasn't any more conversation along this line. There wasn't anything more that either of them could say. Joe went back to his work at his desk in the corner of the room, trying to fill in the new batch of questionnaires Rogan had received from Washington. Rogan had taken them from his silver incrusted brief case, wordlessly, and laid them on Joe's desk. Rogan was as grim and apprehensive as all the rest. He had followed orders all the way, but it had gone wrong. Rogan could see only one thing; he would be blamed for it all—and yet he had merely followed orders.

Billings was a little glad when Joe finished his work and left the room. He realized he had been stupid. He had had an instrument at his hand, a delicately tuned instrument capable of picking up facts far beyond the range of his own senses, Joe, a telepath, and he had chosen to ignore the readings of the instrument, to depend upon his own crude and dull senses. The guilt of his stupidity weighed heavily upon him. He was glad that Joe did not like to look into the mind of a normal. He hoped Joe had not looked too deeply into his. The vague discomfort he felt when Joe was around was heightened now.

He sat behind his desk, alone, and reflected with profound disappointment upon scientists, collectively and individuallly, himself included. They could tear apart the atom and milk it of its strength, they could reconstruct the molecules of nature and improve upon them, they could design instruments far beyond the range of man's senses, solve the riddles of the universe, and, yes, reconstruct the very processes of thought.

Yet they were powerless against the most ignorant of men. Against the most primitive flares of superstition and dread of the unknown, they had no defense. Weakly, in such a situation, they would try to explain, to reason, to appeal to rationality and logic— against minds preset against all explanations, never having learned reason, alien to rationality and logic.

Was this intelligence? To use against one's most bitter foe a weapon which they knew, in advance, would not touch him?

And knowing that, knowing the potential of it which is always present, still they said with impatient superiority, "Spell us no evil consequences of our acts. We are tired of hearing about doom."

A fresh newspaper, a regular city daily, had been laid on his desk. He pulled it toward him, flipped open its pages, and looked at another cartoon of himself. Yes, it was signed by young Tyler—but a glance showed it had not been drawn by him.

And suddenly he knew where the central leak had been. Young Tyler had been in the thick of everything; but young Tyler was a violent and arrogant young man. He seemed to thrive on trouble, to generate it, to know that in mischief or crime itself his father would rescue him. Billings had been blind to that potential, too.

The central figure in the cartoon, himself, was drawn in massive impressiveness, almost Michelangelo in treatment, dressed in classical flowing robes, holding Bossy up in one hand, and surrounded by a glowing nimbus. The cartoon needed no title nor identification. Every expert line of it was innuendo—Billings' pretense at nobility, transcendency. Every expert line revealed the blasphemy. In it was the age-old message that it was forbidden to eat of the tree of knowledge, to reach for the stars. In it was the stern admonitions driven into the innermost fiber of almost every child's being.

"You're too young to know! Keep your hands off of that! Mother and Daddy know best! That's none of your business! That's over your head! Wait till you're older! That's too deep for you to understand!"

The message of defeat, weakness, dependency upon higher authority, driven in day by day and hour by hour into the child's basic structure of reaction. And to offset that solid bedrock, a few mumbling teachers said occasionally that the child should think for himself.

It was no wonder that there was a suppressed desire in most small boys' hearts to burn down the schoolhouse which tried to make them learn, when their whole world and all that was safe in it had been composed of not learning. When the very act of knowing, meant punishment. "You *know* better than to do a thing like that, young man!" And the obvious conclusion drawn by the child, "If I didn't know better, I wouldn't be punished."

What could be done when the very act of knowing brought penalty?

In anger, Billings crumbled the paper and threw it in the wastebasket. It occurred to him that, in like manner, he had just crumpled his whole life and thrown that, too, in the wastebasket. He leaned forward and flipped on his desk radio. He listened, almost without comprehension, to a trained and professional rabble-rouser shouting into a microphone, down in the village below.

". . . Torn stone from stone . . . so that we may wipe out this evil from our midst. . . . Let us not wait for others to show us our duty . . . let us march upon it . . . now. . . ."

"What a miserable string of worn-out clichés," Billings murmured in amusement. Then he realized, with a shock, they were talking about Hoxworth University.

He flipped off the switch, cupped his chin in his fingers, and stared at the wall.

Well, let them come, It didn't matter. Nothing mattered. He smiled in self-scorn when he realized he could say this because he was quite sure they would not come, that reason would prevail, always prevail.

How unrealistic can a man get? What guarantee was there that they would not come? Had man's basic nature changed since yesterday? What had happened before would happen again, in endless repetition. The cycle would repeat itself.

Primitive man, who knows no step taken beyond that of his father's—the bright and courageous dawn of reason—the rise to a comprehension beyond that of his father's—the brief hesitation at the height of the cycle when sanity and rationality soared—the beginning of the downward curve of revolt against sanity and rationality—the retrogression of comprehension—the final dying embers of reason—and, again, the primitive man who knows no step taken beyond that of his father's.

The circle was endless, enduring on and on for a million years now since dawn man emerged. It would endure on and on for—

How long?

Was there no solution? Was man doomed to follow in the circle endlessly, like a two-dimensional animal bounded by a carelessly thrown thread, unable to conceive of a third dimension whereby it might change direction and crawl *upward?*

Was Joe's idea the right one? That man was just biding his time, slowly evolving, that psionics would mark the next stage, that it was a spiral and not a circle? He must talk further with Joe about this. Now, for the first time, perhaps, he was prepared to listen to something he had not thought of himself. Had he been like the kind of scientist he scorned, refusing to listen to anything which did not fit in with his already formed conceptions?

Outside his windows, the elm trees rustled in the rising breeze of night. It had grown quite dark. Yet, there in the distance down the hill, was the glow of a light. It was a flickering, leaping, orange light, in the direction of the library park. The light grew brighter in the darkness—as if flames were mounting. Faintly, on the rising wind, there came the murmur of a crowd noise.

He wondered, idly, what the occasion was among the villagers, what they were celebrating, what was the reason for such a huge bonfire. For some strange reason, the placard lines leaped into his consciousness. He connected the lines, the bonfire, with the radio speech.

His head slumped forward on the desk.

He did not hear the door open, or see Joe's grin fade to quick concern. Quickly Joe darted across the room, felt Billings' pulse, put his ear to Billings' chest and heard the heart still beat.

"Just fainted," Joe said to Hoskins, who had come in behind him. "We'll have to carry him. We can't wait any longer."

"Fool thing to delay this long," Hoskins grumbled. "Don't know why you stalled, Joe."

"He had to grow up," Joe said cryptically, and began massaging the flesh at the back of Billing's neck.

Billings came out of his shock coma at the handling, and stiffened his head.

"That's better," Joe grinned. "Come on. Let's get him out of here. We've got work to do. Science isn't licked yet, not by any means." He turned to Hoskins. "You sure you've smuggled all of Bossy's parts out of here safely?"

"Sure, I'm sure," Hoskins grinned back at him. "You sure you've got a safe hiding place for us?"

"Sure, I'm sure," Joe said.

Billings stood up then, and suddenly he was quite strong.

"All right, Joe." Billings shook his head dazedly. "Making a mistake isn't too bad, I guess—if you live long enough to learn from it, and do something about it. Science has had a lot of knowledge, but mighty little understanding.

"Let's go find out what *that* is."

12/53

Clerical Error

From *Astounding Science Fiction*

"Clerical Error," Clifton's last story but two in his major market, is probably his best story and certainly his most provocative; up until its casual and hastily contrived ending (probably to meet the demands of the imperious John W. Campbell, Jr., *Astounding*'s editor) it is a low-key and highly upsetting investigation of the limits of a technocratically-controlled science. It can be reasonably assumed that Campbell either insisted on the ending or that Clifton tacked it on before submission as a kind of self-censorship to insure the sale of the story.

The case of David Storm came to the attention of Dr. K. Heidrich Kingston when Dr. Ernest Moss, psychiatrist in charge of the Q Security wing of the government workers' mental hospital, recommended lobotomy. The recommendation was on the lead-off sheet in Storm's medical history file. It was expressed more in the terms of a declaration of intention than a request for permission.

"I had a little trouble in getting his complete file, doctor," Miss Verity said, as she laid it on his desk. "The fact is Dr. Moss simply brought in the recommendation and asked me to put your initials on it so he could go ahead. I told him that I was still just your secretary, and hadn't replaced you yet as Division Administrator."

Kingston visualized her aloof, almost unfriendly eyes and the faint sarcasm of her clipped speech as she respectfully told off Dr. Moss in the way an old time nurse learns to put doctors in their place, unmistakable but not quite insubordinate. He knew Miss Verity well; she had been with him for twenty years; they understood one another. His lips twitched with a wry grin of appreciation. He looked up at her as she stood beside his desk, waiting for his reaction.

"I gather he's testing the strength of my order that I must personally approve all lobotomies," Kingston commented dryly.

"I'm quite certain the staff already knows your basic opposition to the principle of lobotomy, doctor," she answered him formally. "You made it quite clear in an article you wrote several years ago, May 1958, to be exact, wherein you stated—"

"Yes, yes, I know," he interrupted, and quoted himself from the article, " 'The human brain is more than a mere machine to be disconnected if the attending psychiatrist just doesn't happen to like the way it operates.' I still feel that way, Miss Verity."

"I'm not questioning your medical or moral judgment, doctor," she answered, with a note of faint reproof, "merely your tactical. At the time you alienated a very large block of the profession, and they haven't forgotten it. Psychiatrists are particularly touchy about any public question of their omnipotent right and rightness. In view of our climb to power, that was a tactical error. I also feel the issuance of this order, so soon after taking over the administration of this department, was a bit premature. Dr. Moss said he was not accustomed to being treated like an intern. He merely expressed what the whole staff is thinking, of course."

"So he's the patsy the staff is using to test my authority," Kingston mused. "He is in complete charge of the Q. S. wing. None of the rest of us, not even I, have the proper Security clearances to go into that wing, because we might hear the poor demented fellows mumbling secrets which are too important for us to know."

"You'll have to admit they've set a rather neat trap, doctor," Miss Verity said. A master of tactics, herself, she could admire an excellent stroke of the opposition. "Without a chance to see the patient and make a personal study, you can't very well override the recommendations of the psychiatrist in charge. You'd be the laughingstock of the entire profession if you tried it. You can't see the patient because I haven't been able to get Q. S. clearance for you, yet. And you can't ignore the Security program, because that's a sacred cow which no one dares question."

It was a clear summation, but Kingston knew she was also reproving him for having laid himself open to such a trap. She had advised against the order and he had insisted upon it anyway.

He pushed himself back from his desk and got to his feet. He was not a big man, but he gave the impression of solid strength as he walked over to the window of his office. He looked out through the window and down the avenue toward various governmental office buildings which lined the street as far as he could see. His features were strong and serene, and, with his shock of prematurely white hair, gave him the characteristic look of a governmental administrator.

"I've not been in this government job very long," he said, as much to the occupants of the buildings down the street as to her, "but I've learned one thing already. When you don't want to face up to the consequences of a bad decision, you just promise to make an investigation." He turned around and faced his secretary. "Tell Dr. Moss," he said, "that I'll make an investigation of the . . . who is it? . . . the David Storm case."

Miss Verity looked as if she wanted to say something more, then clamped her thin lips shut. But at the door, leading out to her own office, she changed her mind.

"Doctor," she said with a mixture of exasperation and curiosity, "suppose you do find a way to make effective intercession in the David Storm case? After all, he's nobody. He's just another case. Suppose you are able to get another psychiatrist assigned to the case. Suppose Dr. Moss is wrong about him being an incurable, and you really get a cure. What have you gained?"

"I've got to start somewhere, Miss Verity," Kingston said gently, without resentment. "Have you had a recent look at the sharply rising incident of disturbance among these young scientists in government work, Miss Verity? The curing of Storm, if that could happen, might be only incidental, true—but it would be a start. I've got some suspicions about what's causing this rising incident. The Storm case may help to resolve them, or dismiss them. It's considerably more than merely making my orders stick. I've got to start somewhere. It might as well be with Storm."

"Very well, doctor," she answered, barely opening her lips. Obviously this was not the way she would have handled it. Even a cursory glance through the Storm file had shown her he was a person of no consequence. Even if Dr. Kingston succeeded, there was no tactical or publicity value to be gained from it. If Storm were a big-name scientist, then the issue would be different. A cause célèbre could be made of it. But as it was, well, facing facts squarely, who would care? One way or the other?

The case history on David Storm was characteristic of Dr. Moss. It was the meticulous work of a thorough technician who had mastered the primary level of detachment. It recorded the various treatments and therapies which Dr. Moss had tried. It reported sundry rambling conversations, incoherent rantings and complaints of David Storm.

And it lacked comprehension.

Kingston, as he plowed through the dossier, felt the frustrated irritation, almost despair, of the creative administrator who must depend upon technicians who lack any basic feeling for the work they do. The work was all technically correct, but in the way a routine machinist would grind a piece of metal to the precise measurements of the specs.

"How does one go about criticizing a man for his total lack of any creative intuition?" Kingston mumbled angrily at the report. "He leaves no loopholes for technical criticism, and, in his frame of thinking, if you tried to go beyond that you'd merely be picking on vague generalities."

The work was all technically correct. There wasn't even a clerical error in it.

A vague idea, nothing more than a slight feeling of a hunch, stirred in Kingston's mind. In some of the arts you could say to a man, "Well, yes, you've mastered all the technicalities, but, man, you're just not an artist." But he couldn't tell Dr. Moss he wasn't a doctor, because Dr. Moss had a diploma which said he was. Men with minds of clerks could only understand error on a clerical level.

He tried to make the idea more vivid in his mind, but it refused to jell. It simply remained a commentary. The case history told a complete story, but David Storm never emerged from it as a human being. He remained nothing more than a case history. Kingston could get no feeling of the substance of the man. The report might as well have dealt with lengths of steel or gallons of chemical.

In a sort of self-defense, Kingston called in Miss Verity, away from her complex of administrative duties, and resorted to a practice they had established together, years before.

He had started his technique with simple gestalt exercises in empathy; such as the deliberate psychosomatic stimulation of pain in one's own arm to better understand the pain in some other person's broken arm. Through the years it had been possible to progress to the higher gestalt empathies of personality identification with a patient. Like other dark areas of the unknown in sciences, there had been many ludicrous mistakes, some danger, and discouragement amounting to despair. But in the long run he had found a technique for a significant increase in his effectiveness as a psychiatrist.

The expression on Miss Verity's face, when she sat down at the side of his desk with her notebook, was interesting. They were both big wheels now, he and she, and she resented taking time out from her control over hundreds of lesser wheels. Yet she was a part of the pattern of empathy. Her hard and unyielding core of practicality, realism, provided a background to contrast, in sharp relief, to the patterns of madness. Obscurely, she derived a pleasure from this contrast; and a nostalgic pleasure, also, from a return to the old days when he had been a young and struggling psychiatrist and she, his nurse, had believed in him enough to stick by him. Kingston wondered if Miss Verity really knew what she did want out of life. He pushed the speculation aside and began his dictation.

As a student, David Storm represented the all too common phenomenon of a young man who takes up the study of a science because it is the socially accepted thing to do, rather than because he had the basic instincts of the true scientist.

Kingston felt himself slipping away into the familiar sensation syndrome of true empathy with his subject. As always, he had to play a dual role. It was insufficient to enter into the other person's mind and senses, feel and see as he felt and saw. No, at the same time he must also reconstruct the individual's life pattern to show the conflicts inherent in that framework which would later lead him into such frustrations as to mature into psychosis.

In the Storm case this was particularly important. A great deal more than just an obscure patient was at stake. By building up a typical framework of conflict, using Storm as merely the focal point, he might be better able to understand this trend which was proving so dangerous to young men in science. And since our total culture had become irrevocably tied to progress in science, he might be better able to prevent a blight from destroying that culture.

His own office furniture faded away. He was there; Miss Verity was there; the precise and empty notes of Dr. Moss were there in front of him; but, to him, these things became shadows, and in the way a motion picture or television screen takes over the senses of reality, he went back to the college classrooms where David Storm had received instruction.

It was unfortunate that the real fire of science did not burn in any of his college instructors, either. Instead, they were also the all too common phenomenon of small souls who had grasped frantically at a few "proved" facts, and had clung to these with the desperate tenacity of drowning men in seas of chaos. "You cannot cheat science," these instructors were fond of saying with much didactic positiveness. "If you will follow the procedures we give you, exactly, your experiment will work. That is proof we are right!"

"If it works, it must be right" was so obviously true to

Storm that he simply could not have thought of any reason or way to doubt it. He graduated without ever having been handed the most necessary tool in all science, skepticism, much less instructed in its dangers and its wise uses. For there are true-believer fanatics to be found in science, also.

Under normal conditions, Storm would have found some mediocre and unimportant niche he deserved. For some young graduates in science the routine technician's job in a laboratory or shop is simply an opening wedge, a foot on the first rung of his ladder. For David Storm's kind, that same job is a haven, a lifetime of small but secure wage. Under such conditions the conflicts, leading to psychosis, would not have occurred.

But these are not normal times. We have science allied to big government, and controlled by individuals who have neither the instincts nor the knowledge of what science really is. This has given birth to a Security program which places more value upon a stainless past and an innocuous mind than upon real talent and ability. It was the socially acceptable and the secure thing for Storm to seek work in government-controlled research. With his record of complete and unquestioning conformity, it was as inevitable as sunrise that he should be favored.

It was as normal as gravity that his Security ratings should increase into the higher echelons of secrecy as he continued to prove complaisant, and, therefore, trustworthy. The young man with a true instinct for science is a doubter, a dissenter, and, therefore, a trouble maker. He, therefore, cannot be trusted with real importance. Under this condition, it was as natural as rain that when a time came for someone to head up a research section, Storm was the only man available.

It was after this promotion into the ranks of the Q. S. men that the falsity of the whole framework began to make itself felt. He had proved to be a good second man, who always did what he was told, who followed instructions faithfully and to the letter. But now he found himself in a position where there were no ready-made instructions for him to follow.

Kingston took up the Moss report and turned some pages to find the exact reference he wanted. Miss Verity remained passively poised, ready to speed into her shorthand notes again. Kingston found the sheet he wanted and resumed his dictation.

Storm got no satisfaction from his section administrator. "You're the expert," his boss told him. "You're supposed to *tell* us the answers, not *ask* us for them." His tentative questions of other research men got him no satisfaction. Either they were in the same boat as he, and as confused, or they weren't talking to his new breed who called himself a research scientist.

But one old fellow did talk, a little. He asked Storm, with disdain, if he expected the universe to furnish him with printed instructions on how it was put together. He commented, acidly, that in his opinion we were handing the fate of our civilization to a bunch of cookbook technicians.

Storm was furious, of course. He debated with himself as to whether he should, as a good loyal citizen, report the old fellow to the loyalty board. But he didn't. Something stopped him, something quite horrible—a thought all his own. This man was a world-famous scientist. He had once been a professor of science at a great university. Storm had been trained to believe what professors said. What if this one were right?

The doubts that our wise men have already found all the necessary right answers, which should have disturbed him by the time he was a sophomore in high school, began now to trouble him. The questions he should have begun to ask by the time he was a freshman in college began to seep through the tiny cracks that were opening in his tight little framework of inadequate certainties.

Kingston looked up from the report in his hands; thought for a moment; flipped a few pages of the dossier; failed to find what he wanted; turned back a couple of pages; and skimmed down the closely written record of Storm's demented ravings. "Oh yes, here it is," he said, when he found the reference.

It was about that time that Storm began to think about something else he would have preferred to forget. It had been one of those beer-drinking and pipe-smoking bull sessions which act as a sort of teething ring upon which college men exercise their gums in preparation for idea maturity. The guy who was dominating the talking already had a reputation for being a radical; and Storm had listened with the censor's self-assurance that it was all right for *him* to listen so he would be better able to protect others, with inferior minds and weaker wills, from such exposures.

"The great danger to our culture," this fellow was holding forth, "doesn't come from the nuclear bomb, the guided missile, germ warfare, or even internal subversion. Granted there's reason why our culture should endure, there's a much greater danger, and one, apparently, quite unexpected.

"Let's take our diplomatic attitudes and moves as a cross section of the best thinking our culture, as a whole, can produce. For surely here, at this critical level, the finest minds, skilled in the science of statecraft, are at work. And there is no question but that our best is no higher than a grammer-school level. A kid draws a line with his toe across the sidewalk and dares, double dares, his challenger to step across it. 'My father can lick your father' is not removed, in substance, from 'My air force can lick your air force.' What is our Security program but the childish chanting of 'I've got a secret! I've got a secret?' Add to that the tendency to assemble a gang so that one can feel safer when he talks tough, the tendency to indiscriminate name calling, the inability to think in other terms than 'good guys' and 'bad guys.' Here you have the classical picture of the grammar-school level of thinking—and an exact parallel with our diplomacy.

"Now, sure, it's true that one kid of grammar-school mental age can pretty well hold his own with another of his own kind and strength. But here's the real danger. He doesn't stand a chance if he comes up against a mature adult. What if our opponent, whoever he may be, should grow up before we do? There's the real danger!"

Storm had considered the diatribe ridiculous at the time, and agreed with some of the other fellows that the guy should be locked up, or at least kicked off the campus. But now he began to wonder about certain aspects which he had simply overlooked before. "Consider the evidence, gentlemen," one of his instructors had repeated, like a parrot, at each stage of some experiment. Only now it occurred to Storm that the old boy had invariably selected, with considerable care, the particular evidence he wanted them to consider.

With equal care our statecraft had presented us with the evidence that over there, in the enemy territory, science was forced to follow the party line or get itself purged. And the party line was totally false and wrong. Therefore their notions of science must be equally wrong. And you can't cheat science. If a thing is wrong it won't work. Yet the evidence also showed that they, too, had successful nuclear fission, guided missiles, and all the rest.

This led Storm into another cycle of questions. What parts of the evidence could a man elect to believe, and what interpretations of that evidence might he dispute and still remain a totally loyal citizen, still retain his right to highest Security confidence? This posed another problem, for he was still accustomed to turning to higher authority for instruction. But of whom could he ask such questions as these? Not his associates, for they were as wary of him as he of them. In such an atmosphere where it becomes habitual for a man to guard his tongue against any and all slips, there is an automatic complex of suspicions built up to freeze out all real exchange of ideas.

Every problem has a solution. He found the only solution open to him. He went on asking such questions of himself. But, as usual, the solution to one problem merely opened the door to a host of greater ones. The very act of admitting, openly acknowledging, such questions to himself, and knowing he dared not ask them of anyone else, filled him with an overpowering sense of furtive shame and guilt. It was an axiom of the Security famework that you were either totally loyal, or you were potentially a subversive. Had he any right to keep his Security ratings when these doubts were a turmoil in his mind?

Through the months, especially during the nights, as he lay in miserable sleeplessness, he pondered these obvious flaws in his own nature, turning them over and over like a squirrel in a cage. Then, one night, there came a whole series of questions that were even more terrifying.

What if it were not he, but the culture, which contained the basic flaw? Who, in or out of science, is so immutably right that he can pass judgment on what man is meant to know and what he may never question? If we are not to ask questions beyond accepted dogma, be it textbook or statecraft, from where is man's further knowledge and advancement to come? What if these questions which filled him with such maddening doubts were the very ones most necessary to answer? Indeed, what if our very survival depended upon just such questions and answers? Would he then be giving his utmost in loyalty if he did *not* ask them?

The walls of his too narrow framework of thinking had broken away, and he felt himself drowning in a flood of dilemmas he was unprepared to solve. When a man, in a dream, finds his life in deadly peril an automatic function takes over—the man wakes up. There is also an automatic function which takes over when the problems of reality become a deadly peril.

Storm withdrew from reality.

Kingston was silent for a moment, then his consciousness returned to the surroundings of his office, and the desk in front of him. He looked over at Miss Verity.

"Well, now," he said. "I think we begin to understand our young man a little better."

"But are you sure his conflict is typical?" Miss Verity asked.

"Consider the evidence," Kingston said with deliberate irony. "Science can progress, even exist, only where there is free exchange of ideas, and minds completely open to variant ideas. When by law, or social custom, we forbid this, we stop scientific development. Consider the evidence! he said again. "There is already a great deal of it to show that our science is beginning to go around in circles, developing the details of the frameworks already acceptable, but not reaching out to reveal new and totally unexpected frameworks."

"I'll type this up, in case you want to review it," Miss Verity answered dryly. She did not go along with him, at all, in these flights of fancy. Certainly she saw no tactical advantage to be gained from taking such attitudes. On the contrary, if he didn't learn to curb his tongue better, all she had worked so hard to gain for the both of them could be threatened.

Kingston watched her reactions with an inward smile. It apparently had never occurred to her that his ability in gestalt empathy could be directed toward her.

There might be quite a simple solution to the Storm matter. Too many government administrators and personnel had come to regard an act under general Security regulations to be a dictum straight from Heaven. It was possible that Storm's section had already written him off as a total loss in their minds, and no one had taken the trouble to get him declassified. Kingston felt he should explore that possibility first.

He made an appointment to see Logan Maxfield, Chief Administrator of the section where Storm had worked.

His first glance, when he walked into Maxfield's office, put a damper on his confidence. Here was a man who was more of a politician than a scientist, probably a capable enough administrator within his given boundaries, but the strained cautiousness of his greeting told Kingston he would not take any unusual risks to his own safety and reputation. He belonged to that large and ever growing class of job holders in government whose safety lies in preserving the status quo, who would desperately police and defend things as they are, for any change might be a threat.

It would take unusual tactics to jar him out of his secure rightness in attitude. Kingston was prepared to employ unusual tactics.

"Storm has been electrocuted," he said quietly, "with a charge just barely short of that used on murderers. Not once, of course, but again and again. Then, also, we've stunned him over and over with hypos jabbed down through his skull into his brain. We've sent him into numerous bone-crushing and muscle-tearing spasms with drugs. But," he sighed heavily, "he's obstinate. He refuses to be cured by these healing therapies."

Maxfield's face turned a shade whiter, and his eyes fixed uncertainly on his pudgy hands lying on top of his desk. He looked over toward his special water cooler, as if he longed for a drink, but he did not get out of his chair. A silence grew. It was obvious he felt called upon to make some comment. He tried to make it jocular, man to man.

"Of course I don't know anything about the science of psychiatry, doctor," he said at last, "but in the physical sciences we feel that methods which don't work may not be entirely scientific."

"Man," Kingston exploded with heavy irony, "you imply that psychiatry isn't an exact science? Of course it is a science! Why, man, we have all sorts of intricate laboratories, and arrays of nice shiny tools, and flashing lights on electronic screens, and mechanical pencils drawing jagged lines on revolving drums of paper, and charts and graphs, and statistics. And theory? Why, man, we've got more theory than you ever dreamed of in physical science! Of course it's a science. Any rational man has to agree that the psychiatrist is a scientist. We ought to know. We are the ones who define rationality!"

Maxfield could apparently find no answer to that bit of reasoning. Along with many others he saw no particular fallacy in defining a thing in terms of itself.

"What do you want me to do?" he asked finally.

"Here's the problem," Kingston answered, in the tone of one administrator to another. "It is unethical for one doctor to question the techniques of another doctor, so let's put it this way. Suppose you had a mathematician in your department who took up a sledge hammer and deliberately wrecked his calculating machines because they would not answer a question *he did not know how to ask.* Then failing to get the answer, suppose he recommended just disconnecting what was left of the machines and abandoning them. What would you do?"

"I think I'd get myself another mathematician," Maxfield said with a sickly attempt at lightness.

"Well, now that's a problem, too," Kingston answered easily. "I'm not questioning the methods of Dr. Moss, and obviously his attitudes are the right ones, because he's the only available psychiatrist who had been cleared to treat all these fellows you keep sending over to us under Q. S. secrecy. But there's a way out of that," he said with the attitude of a salesman on television who will now let you in on the panacea for all your troubles. "If you lifted the Security on Storm, then we could move him to another ward and try a different kind of therapy. We might even find a man who did know how to ask the question which would get the right answer."

"Absolutely impossible," Maxfield said with finality.

"Now look at it this way," Kingston said in a tone of reasonableness. "If Storm just chose to quit his job, you'd have to declassify him, wouldn't you?"

"That's different," Maxfield said. "There are proper procedures for that."

"I know" Kingston said, a little wearily. "The parting interview to impress him with the need for continued secrecy, the terrible weight of knowing that bolt number seventy-two in motor XYZ has a three eighths thread instead of a five eighths. So why can't you consider that Storm has left his job and declassify him in absentia. Then we could remove him to an ordinary ward and give him what may be a more effective treatment. I really don't think he can endure very much more of his present therapy."

Kingston leaned back in his chair and spoke in a tone of speculation.

"There's a theory that this treatment isn't really torture, Mr. Maxfield, because an insane person doesn't know what is happening to him. But I'm afraid that theory is fallacious. I believe the so-called insane person does know what is happening, and feels all the exqui-

site torture we use in trying to drive the devils out of his soul."
"Absolutely impossible," Maxfield repeated. "Although you are
not a Q. S. man"—this with a certain smugness—"I'll tell you this
much." He leaned forward and placed his fingertips together in his
most impressive air of administrative deliberation. "We have reason
to believe that David Storm was on the trail of something big. *Big,*
Dr. Kingston. So big, indeed, that perhaps the very survival of the
nation depends upon it!"

He hesitated a few seconds, to let the gravity of his statement sink
in. Then he unlocked a desk drawer and took out a file folder.

"I had this file sent in when you made the appointment to see
me," he explained. "As you no doubt know, we must have inspec-
tors who are constantly observing our scientists, although unseen,
themselves. Here is a sentence from one of our most trusted inspec-
tors. 'Subject repeats over and over, under great emotional stress, to
himself, aloud, that our very survival depends upon his finding the
answers to a series of questions!' There, Dr. Kingston, does that
sound like no more than the knowledge of a three eighths thread on a
bolt? No, doctor," he answered his own rhetoric, "this can only
mean something of monumental significance—with the fate of a
world, our world, hanging in the balance. Now you see why we
couldn't take chances with declassifying him!"

Kingston was on the verge of telling him what the pattern of
Storm's questions really was, then better judgment prevailed. First
the Security board would become more than a little alarmed that he,
a non-Q. S. man, had already learned what was on Storm's mind,
and pass some more silly rules trying to put a man's mind in solitary
confinement. Second, Maxfield was convinced these questions must
be concerned with some super gadget, and wouldn't believe his
revealment of their true nature. And anyway, what business does a
scientist have, asking such questions? Any sympathy he might have
gained for Storm would be lost. Serves the fellow right for not sticking strictly to his slide rules and Bunsen burners!

"Mr. Maxfield," Kingston said gravely, patiently. "It is our experience that a disturbed patient often considers something entirely
trivial to be of world-shaking importance. The momentous question
Storm feels he must solve may be no more than some nonsensical
conundrum—such as why does a chicken cross the road. It may
mean nothing whatever."

"And then again it may," Maxfield answered. "We can't take the
chance. You must remember, doctor, this statement was overheard
and recorded while Storm was still a sane man."

"Before he was committed, you mean," Kingston corrected softly.

"At any rate, it must have been something quite terrible to drive a man insane, just the thought of it," Maxfield argued.

"I'll not deny that possibility," Kingston agreed seriously. "The questions could have terrified him, and the rest of us, too, if we really stopped to think about them. Wouldn't it be worth the risk of say my own doubtful loyalty to make a genuine effort to find out what they were, and deal with them, instead of torturing him to drive them out of his mind?"

"I'm not sure I know what you mean," Maxfield faltered. This doctor seemed to have the most callous way of describing beneficial therapies!

"Mr. Maxfield," Kingston said with an air of candor, "I'll let you in on a trade secret. Up until now psychiatry has fitted all the descriptions applicable to a cult, and few indeed applicable to a science. We try to tailor the mind to fit the theory. But some of us, even in the field of psychiatry, are beginning to ask questions—the first dawn of any science. Do you know anything about psychosomatic medicine?"

"Very little, just an idea of what it means," Maxfield answered cautiously.

"Enough," Kingston conceded. "You know that the human body-mind may take on very real symptoms and pains of an illness as overt objection to an untenable environment. Now we are starting to ask the question: Can it be possible that our so-called cures, brought about through electro and drug shock, are a type of psychosomatic response to unendurable torture?

"I see a mind frantically darting from framework to framework, pursued inexorably by the vengeful psychiatrist with the implements of torture in his hands—the mind desperately trying to find a framework which the psychiatrist will approve and so slacken the torture. We have called that a return to sanity. But is it really anything more than a psychosomatic escape from an impossible situation? A compounded withdrawal from withdrawal?

"As I say, a few of us are beginning to ask ourselves these questions. But most continue to practice the cult rituals which can be duplicated point by point, item by item, with the rites of a savage witch doctor attempting to drive out devils from some poor unfortunate of the tribe."

From the stricken look on Maxfield's face, there was no doubt he had finally scored. The man stood up as if to indicate he could take no more. He was distressed by the problem, so distressed, in fact, that he obviously wished this psychiatrist would leave his office and just forget the whole thing.

"I . . . I want to be reasonable, doctor," he faltered through trembling lips. "I want to do the right thing." Then his face cleared. He saw a way out. "I'll tell you what I can do. I'll make another investigation of the matter!"

"Thank you, Mr. Maxfield," Kingston said gravely, without showing the bitterness of his defeat. "I thought that is what you might do."

When he got back to his office, Kingston learned that Dr. Moss had not been content merely to lay a neat little professional trap. His indignation over being thwarted in his intention to perform a lobotomy on Storm had apparently got the better of his judgment. In a rage, he had insisted upon a meeting with a loyalty board at top level. In the avid atmosphere of Government by Informers, they had shown themselves eager to hear what he might say against his superior.

But a private review of the Storm file reminded them of those mysterious and fearful questions in his deranged mind, questions which might forever be lost through lobotomy. So they advised Moss that Dr. Kingston's opposition was purely a medical matter, and did not necessarily constitute subversion.

In the report of this meeting which lay on his desk, some clerk along the way had underscored the word "necessarily" as if, gently, to remind him to watch his step in the future.

"God save our country from the clerical mind," he murmured. And then the solution to his problem began to unfold for him.

His first step in putting his plan into operation had all the appearances of being a very stupid move. It was the first of a series of equally obvious stupidities, which, in total, might add up to a solution. For stupid people are perpetually on guard against cleverness, but will fall in with and further a pattern of stupidity as if they had a natural affinity for it.

His first move was to send Dr. Moss out to the West Coast to make a survey of mental hospitals in that area.

"This memorandum certainly surprised me," Dr. Moss said curiously, as he came through Kingston's office door, waving the paper in his hand. He seated himself rather tentatively on the edge of a chair, and looked piercingly across the desk, to see if he could fathom the ulterior motives behind the move. "It is true that my section is in good order, and my patients can be adequately cared for by the attendants for a couple of weeks or so. But that you should ask me to make the survey of West Coast conditions for you—''

He let the statement trail off into the air, demanding an explanation.

"Why not you?" Kingston asked, as if surprised by the question.

"I . . . ah . . . feared our little differences in the . . . ah . . . Storm matter might prejudice you against me," Moss said, with the attitude of a man laying his cards on the table. Kingston surmised there were cards not laid out for inspection also. The move had two obvious implications. It could be a bribe, a sort of promotion, to regain Moss' good will. Or, more subtly, it could be a threat—"You see I can transfer you out of my way, any time I may want to."

"Oh, the Storm matter," Kingston said with some astonishment. "Frankly, doctor, I hadn't connected up the two. I've been most impressed with your attention to detail, and the fine points of organization. It seemed to me you were the most logical one on the staff to spot any operational flaws out there. The fact that you can confidently leave your section in the care of your attendants is proof of that."

Moss gave a slight smirk at this praise, and said nothing.

"Now I'd be a rather poor executive administrator if I let a minor difference of professional opinion stand in the way of the total efficient organization, wouldn't I?" Kingston asked, with an amiable smile.

"Dr. Kingston," Moss began, and hesitated. Then he decided to be frank. "I . . . ah . . . the staff has felt that your appointment to this position was purely political. I begin to see it might also have been because of your ability, and your capacity to rise above small differences of . . . ah . . . opinion."

Kingston let that pass. If he happened to rise a little in the estimation of his staff through these maneuvers, that would be simply a side benefit.

"Now you're sure I'm not interrupting a course of vital treatment of your patients, Dr. Moss?" he asked.

"Most of my patients are totally and completely incurable, doctor," Moss said with finality. "Not that I don't keep trying. I do try. I try everything known to the science of psychiatry to get them thinking rationally again. But let's face it. Most of them will progress—or regress—equally well with simple human care. I fear my orderlies, guards, nurses regard me as something of a tyrant," he said with obvious satisfaction. "And it isn't likely that in the space of a couple of weeks they'll let down during my absence. You needn't worry, I'll set up the proper measures."

Kingston breathed a small sigh of relief as the man left his office. That would get Dr. Moss off the scene for a while.

Equally important, but not so easily accomplished, he must get Miss Verity away at the same time. And Miss Verity was anything but stupid.

"Has it occurred to you, Miss Verity," he asked with the grin of a man who has a nice surprise up his sleeve, "that this month you will have been with me for twenty-five years?" It was probably a foolish question, Miss Verity would know the years, months, days, hours. Not for any special reason, except that she always kenw everything down to the last decimal. The stern lines of her martinet face did not relax, but her pale blue eyes showed a flicker of pleasure that he would remember.

"It has been my pleasure to serve you, doctor," she said formally. That formality between them had never been relaxed, and probably never would be since both of them wanted it. It was not an unusual relationship either in medicine or industry—as if the man should never become too apparent through the image of the executive, lest both parties lose confidence and falter.

"We've come a long way in a quarter of a century," he said reminiscently, "from that little two-room office in Seattle. And if it weren't for you, we might still be there." Rigidly he suppressed any tone which would betray any implication that he might have been happier remaining obscure.

"Oh no, doctor," she said instantly. "A man with your ability—"

"Ability is not enough," he cut in. "Ability has to be combined with ambition. I didn't have the ambition. I simply wanted to learn, to go on learning perpetually, I suppose. You know how it was before you came with me. Patients didn't pay me. I didn't check to see what their bank account or social position was before I took them on. I was getting the reputation for being a poor man's psychiatrist, before you took charge of my office and changed all that."

"That's true," she agreed candidly, with a small secret smile. "But I looked at it this way: You were . . . you are . . . a great man dedicated to the service of humanity. I felt it would do no harm for the Right People to know about it. You can cure a disturbed rich man as easily as you can cure a poor one. And as long as your job was to listen to secrets, they might as well be important secrets—those of industrialists, statesmen, people who really matter."

She looked about the well appointed office, and out of the window toward the great governmental buildings rising in view, as if to survey the concrete results of his policies in managing his affairs. Kingston wondered how much of her ambition had been for him, and how much for herself. In the strange hierarchy of castes among government workers, she was certainly not without stature.

That remark about secrets. He knew her ability to rationalize. He wondered how much of his phenomenal rise, and his position now, was due to polite and delicate pressures she had applied in the right places.

"So now I want to do something I've put off too long," he said, letting the grin come back on his face. "I want you to take a month's vacation, all expenses paid."

She half arose out of her chair, then settled back into it again. He had never seen her so perturbed.

"I couldn't do that," she said with a rising tone of incredulity. "There are too many things of importance. We've just barely got things organized since taking over this position. You . . . you . . . why a dozen times a day there are things coming up you wouldn't know how to handle. You . . . I don't mean to sound disrespectful, doctor, but . . . well . . . you make mistakes. A great man, such as you, well, you live in another world, and without somebody to shield you, constantly—"

She broke off and smiled at him placatingly. All at once she was a tyrant mother with an adored son who has made an independent decision; a wife with a well-broken husband who has unexpectedly asserted a remnant of the manhood he once had; a career secretary who believes her boss to be a fool—a woman whose Security depended upon her indispensability.

Then her face calmed. Her expression was easily readable. The accepted more of our culture is that men exist for the benefit of women. But they can be stubborn creatures at times. The often repeated lessons in the female magazines was that they can be driven where you want them to go only so long as they think they are leading the way there. She must go cautiously.

"Right now, particularly, I shouldn't leave," she said with more composure. "I'm trying, very hard, to get you cleared for a Q. S. As you know, the Justice Department has a rather complete file folder on anybody in the country of any consequence. They have gone back through your life. They have interviewed numerous patients you have treated. I am trying to convince the Loyalty Board that a psychiatrist must, at times, make statements to his patients which he may not necessarily believe. I am trying to convince them that the statements of neurotic and psychotic patients are not necessarily an indication of a man's loyalty to his country.

"Then, too," she continued with faint reproach, "you've made public statements questioning the basic foundations upon which modern psychology is built. You've questioned the value of considering everyone who doesn't blend in with the average norm as being aberrated."

"I still question that," he said firmly.

"I know, I know," she said impatiently. "But do you have to say such things—in public?"

"Well, now, Miss Verity," he said reasonably, "if a scientist must shape his opinions to suit the standards of the Loyalty Board or Justice Department before he is allowed to serve his country—"

"They don't say you are disloyal, doctor," she said impatiently. "They just say: Why take a chance? I'm campaigning to get the right Important People to vouch for you."

"I think the work of setting up organization has been a very great strain on you," he answered with the attitude of a doctor toward a patient. "And there's a great deal more to be done. I want to make many changes. I think you should have some rest before we undertake it."

There had been more, much more. But in the end he had won a partial victory. She consented to a week's vacation. He had to be satisfied with that. If Storm were really badly demented, he could certainly make little progress in that time. But on the other hand, he would have accomplished his main purpose. He would have seen Storm, talked with him, contaminated him through letting him talk to a non-Q. S. man.

Miss Verity departed for a week's vacation with her brothers and sisters and their families—all of whom she detested.

Kingston did not try to push his plan too fast. He had a certain document in mind, and nothing must be done to call any special attention to it.

It was the following day after the simultaneous departure of Dr. Moss and Miss Verity, in the early afternoon, that he sat at his desk and signed a stack of documents in front of him.

Because of Miss Verity's martinet tactics in gearing up the department to prompt handling of all matters, the paper which interested him above all others should be in this stack.

While he signed one routine authorization after another, he grew conscious that his mind had been going back over the maneuvers and interviews he had taken thus far in the Storm case. The emotional impatience at their blind slavery to proper and safe procedure rekindled in him, and he found himself signing at a furious rate. Deliberately he slowed himself down. In event someone should begin wondering at a series of coincidences at some later date, his signature must betray no unusual mood.

It was vital to the success of his plan that the document go through proper channels for execution as a completely routine matter. So vital that, even here, alone in the privacy of his office, he would not permit himself to riff down through the stack to see if the paper which really mattered had cleared the typing section.

He felt his hand shaking slightly at the thought he might have miscalculated the mentality of the typists, that someone might have noticed the wild discrepancy and pulled the work sheet he had written out for further question.

Just how far could a man bank on the pattern of stupidity? If the document were prematurely discovered, his only hope to escape serious consequences with the Loyalty Board was to claim a simple clerical error—the designation of the wrong form number at the top of the work sheet. He could probably win, before or after the event, because it would be obvious to anyone that a ridiculous clerical error was the only possible explanation.

A psychiatrist simply does not commit himself to be confined as an insane person.

He lay down his pen, to compose himself until all traces of any muscular waver would disappear from his signature. He tried to reassure himself that nothing could have gone wrong. The girls who filled in the spaces of the forms were only routine typists. They had the clerical mind. They checked the number on the form with the number on the work sheet. They dealt with dozens and hundreds of forms, numerically stored in supply cabinets. Probably they didn't even read the printed words on such forms—merely filled in blank spaces. If the numbered items on the work sheet corresponded with the numbered blanks on the forms, that was all they needed to go ahead.

That was also the frame of mind of those who would carry out the instructions on the documents. Make sure the proper signature authorizes the act, and do it. If the action is wrong it is the signer's neck, not theirs. They simply did what they were told. And it was doubtful that such a vast machine as government could function if it were otherwise, if every clerk took it upon himself to question the wisdom of each move of the higher echelons.

Of course, under normal procedures, someone did check the documents before they were placed on his desk to sign. There again, if the signer took the time to check the accuracy of how the spaces were filled in, government would never get done. There had to be a checker, and in the case of his department that was a job Miss Verity had kept for herself. Her eagle eye would have caught the error immediately, and in contempt with such incompetence she would have bounced into the typing pool with fire in her eye to find out who would do such a stupid thing as this.

He had his answer ready, of course, just in case anybody did discover the mistake. He had closed out his apartment, where he lived alone, and booked a suite in a hotel. The work sheet was an order to have his things transferred to his new room number. The scribbled information was the same, and, obviously, he had simply designated the wrong form number.

But Miss Verity was away on her vacation, and there wasn't anybody to catch the mistake.

He lifted his eyes from the signature space on the paper in front of him at the rapidly dwindling stack. The document was next on top.

There it was, neatly typed, bearing no special marks to segregate it from other routine matters, and thereby call attention to it. There were no typing errors, no erasures, nothing to indicate that the typist might have been startled at what she was typing. Nothing to indicate it had been anything more than a piece of paper for her to thread into her machine, fill in, and thread out again with assembly-line regularity.

He lifted the paper off the stack and placed it in front of himself, in position for signature. He sighed, a deep and gasping sigh, almost a groan. Then he grinned in self derision. Was he already regretting his wild action, an action not yet taken?

All right then, tear up the document. Forget about David Storm and his problem. Forget about trying to buck the system. Miss Verity was quite right. Storm was a nobody. As compared with the other events of the world, it didn't matter whether Storm got cured, or had his intellect disconnected through lobotomy, or just rotted there in his cell because he had asked some impertinent questions of the culture in which he lived.

Never mind that the trap into which Storm had fallen was symbolic of the trap which was miring down modern science in the same manner. By freeing the symbol, he would in no way be moving to free all science from its dilemma.

He pushed himself back, away from his desk, and got to his feet. He walked over to the window and looked down the avenue of government buildings. Skyscrapers of offices, as far as his eye could reach. How many of them held men whose state of mind matched his own? How many men quietly, desperately wanted to do a good job, but were already beaten by the pattern for frustration, the inability to take independent action?

There was one of the more curious of the psychological curiosities. In private an individual may confess to highly intelligent sympathies, but when he gets on a board or a panel or a committee, he has not the courage to stand up against what he thinks to be the mass temper or mores.

Courage, that was the element lacking. The courage to fight for progress, enlightenment, against the belief that one's neighbors may not think the same way. The courage to fight over the issue, for the sake of the issue, rather than for the votes one's action is calculated to win.

And in that sense David Storm was not unimportant. Kingston confessed to himself, standing there in front of the window, that he had begun this gambit in a sort of petty defiance—defiance of the efforts of Moss and the rest of his staff to thwart his instructions, defiance of Miss Verity's efforts to make him into an important figurehead, defiance of the whole ridiculous dilemma that the Loyalty program had become.

He wondered if he had ever really intended to go through with his plan. Hadn't he kept the reservation, in the back of his mind, that as long as he hadn't signed the order, as long as it wasn't released for implementation, he could withdraw? Why make such an issue over such a triviality as this Storm fellow?

Yet wasn't that the essence? Wasn't that the question every true scientist had to ask himself every day? To buck the accepted and the acceptable, or to swing along with it and rush with the tide of man toward oblivion?

In the popular books courage was always embodied in a well-muscled, handsome, well-intentioned, and rather stupid young man. But what about that wispy little unhandsome fellow, behind the thick glasses perhaps, who, against ridicule, calumny, misunder-standing, poverty, ignorance, kept on with his intent to find an aspect of truth?

Resolutely he walked over to his desk, picked up his pen again, and signed the document. There! He was insane! The document said so! And the document was signed by the Chief Administrator of Psychiatric Division, Bureau of Science Co-ordination. That should be enough authority for anybody!

He tossed it into the outgoing basket, where it would be picked up by the mail clerk and routed for further handling. Rapidly now, he continued signing other papers, tossing them into the same basket, covering the vital one so that it was down in the middle of the stack, unlikely to call special attention to itself.

They came for him at six o'clock the next morning. That was what the order had stipulated, that they make the pickup at this early hour. Two of them walked into his room, through the door which he had left unlocked, and immediately separated so that they could come at him from either side. Two burly young men who had a job to do, and who knew how to do that job. He couldn't remember having seen either of them before, and there was no look of recognition on their faces either.

"What is the meaning of this intrusion?" he said loudly, in alarm. His intonation sounded like something from a rather bad melodrama. "How dare you walk into my room!" He sat up in bed and pulled the covers up around his neck.

"There, there, Buster," one of them said soothingly. "Take it easy now. We're not going to hurt you." With a lithe grace they moved into position. One of them stood near the foot of his bed, the other came up to the head, and with a swirling motion, almost too quick to follow, slipped his hands under Kingston's armpits.

"Time to get up, Buster," the man said, and propelled him upward and outward. The covers fell away from him, and he found himself standing on his feet, without quite knowing how he got there. The second man was already eying his clothes, which he had hung over a chair the night before. They were beautifully trained, he'd have to give Moss that much credit. It spoke well for the routine administration of the Q. S. wing if all the attendants were as experienced in being firm, yet gentle. It wasn't that psychiatry was intentionally sadistic, just mistaken in its idea of treatment.

"What is the meaning of this?" he spluttered again. "Do you know who I am?" He tried to draw himself up proudly, but found it somewhat difficult with his head being slipped through a singlet undershirt.

"Sure, sure, your majesty," one of them said soothingly. "Sure we know."

"I am not 'your majesty,' " Kingston said bitingly. "I am Dr. K. Heidrich Kingston!"

"Oh, pardon me," the fellow said apologetically, and flipped

Kingston's feet into the air just long enough for his helper to slip trousers onto his legs. "I'm pleased to meet you."

"Kingston!" the other fellow said in an awed voice. "That's the big shot, the wheel, himself."

"Well," the first one said, as he slipped suspenders over the shoulders, "at least he's not Napoleon." From somewhere underneath his uniform jacket he suddenly whipped out a canvas garment, a shapeless thing Kingston might not have recognized as a strait jacket if he hadn't been experienced. "You gonna cooperate, Dr. Kingston, or will we have to put this on you?"

"Oh, he's not so bad," the other fellow said. "This must be his up cycle. You're not going to give us any trouble at all, are you Dr. Kingston? You're going to go over to the hospital with us nicely, aren't you?" It was a statement, a soothing persuasive statement, not a question. "They need you over at the hospital, Dr. Kingston. That's why we came for you."

He looked at them suspiciously, craftily. Then he smoothed his face into arrogant lines of overweening ego.

"Of course," he said firmly. "Let's go to the hospital. They'll soon tell you over there who I am!"

"Sure they will, Dr. Kingston," the first attendant said. "We don't doubt it for a minute."

"Let's go," the other one said.

They walked him out the door, in perfect timing. They seemed relaxed, but their fingertips on his arms where they held him were tense, ready for an expected explosion of insane violence. They'd been all through this before, many times, and their faces seemed to say that you can always expect the unexpected. Why, he might even surprise them and go all the way to his cell without trying to murder six people in the process. It just depended on how long his up cycle lasted, and what period of the phase he was in when they came for him. Probably that was the real reason why the real Dr. Kingston had specified this early hour; probably knew when this nut was in and out of his phases.

"Wonder what it's like to be such a big shot that some poor dope goes nuts thinking he's you?" one of them asked the other as they took him out of the apartment house door and down the steps to the ambulance waiting at the curb.

"I don't think I'd like to find out," the other answered.

"I tell you for the last time, I am Dr. Kingston!" Kingston insisted and allowed the right amount of exasperation to mingle with a note of fear.

"I hope it's the last time, doctor," the first one said. "It gets kinda tiresome telling you that we already know who you are. You don't have to keep telling us, you know. We believe you.''

The way they got him into the body of the ambulance couldn't exactly be called a pull and a push. At one instant they were standing on either side of him at the back door, and in the next instant one of them was in front of him and the other behind him—and there they were, all sitting in a row inside the ambulance. The driver didn't even look back at him.

He kept silent all the way over to the hospital buildings. He had made his point. He had offered the reactions of a normal man caught up in a mistake, but certain it would all get straightened out without making a fuss about it. They had responded to the reactions of an insane man, and they hoped they could get him all straightened out and nicely deposited in his cell before he began to kick up a fuss about it. It just depended on the framework from which you viewed it, and he neither wanted to overdo nor underplay his part to jar them out of their frame with discrepancies.

But the vital check point was yet to come. There was nothing in the commitment form about his being a Q. S. man, but he had assigned David Storm's cell number in the Q. S. wing. He'd had to check a half dozen hotels before he'd found one with an open room of the same number, so that the clerical error would stand up all the way down the line.

The guards of the Q. S. wing were pretty stuffy about keeping non-Q. S. men out. He might still fail in the first phase of his solution to the problem, to provide David Storm with a doctor, one who might be able to help him.

The attendants wasted no time with red tape. The document didn't call for preexaminations, or quarantine, or anything. It just said put him into room number 1782. So they went through a side door and by-passed all the usual routines. They were good boys who always did what the coach said. And the document, signed by the Chief Coach, himself, Dr. Kingston, said put the patient in cell 1782. They were doing what they were told.

Would the two guards at the entrance of the Q. S. wing be equally good boys?

"You're taking me to my office, I assume," he said as they were walking down the corridor toward the cell wing.

"Sure, doctor," one of them said. "Nice warm cozy office. Just for you."

They turned a corner, and the two guards got up from chairs where they had been sitting at a hallway desk. One of the attendants pulled out the document from his inner jacket pocket and handed it to the guard.

"Got another customer for you," he said laconically. "For *office* number 1782." He winked broadly.

"That cell's . . . er . . . office's already occupied," the guard said instantly. "Must be a mistake."

"Maybe they're starting to double them up, now," the attendant said. "You wanna go up to the Big Chief's office and tell him he's made a mistake? He signed it, you know."

"I don't know what you men are up to!" Kingston burst out. "This whole thing is a mistake. I tell you I am Dr. Kingston. I'll have all your jobs for this . . . this . . . this practical joke! You are not taking me any farther! I refuse to go any farther!"

He laid them out for five minutes, calling upon strings of profanity, heard again and again from the lips of uncontrolled minds, that would make an old time mariner blush for shame. The four of them looked at him at first with admiration, then with disgust.

"You'd better get him into his cell," one of the guards mumbled to the attendants. "Before he really blows his stack."

"Yeah," the attendant agreed. "Looks like he's going into phase two, and we have not as yet got phase one typed. No telling what phase three might be like."

The guards stepped back. The attendants took him on down the hall of the Q. S. wing.

All the way up the elevator, to the seventeenth floor, and down the hall to the doorway of Storm's cell, Kingston kept wondering if any of them had ever heard of the Uncle Remus story of Bre'r Rabbit and the Briar Patch. "Oh don't throw me in the briar patch, Bre'r Fox. Don't throw me in the briar patch!"

Stupid people resist clever moves but willingly carry out stupid patterns. These guards and attendants were keyed to keeping out anyone who tried to get in—but if someone tried to keep out, obviously he must be forced to go in.

There hadn't even been a question about a lack of Q. S. rating on the form. His vitriolic diatribe had driven it out of their minds for a moment, and if they happened to check it before they stamped the order completed, well, the damage would already have been done.

He would have talked with David Storm.

But Storm was not quite that cooperative. His eyes flared with wild resentment, suspicion, when the attendants ushered Kingston into the cell.

"You see, doctor," one of the attendants said with soothing

irony, and not too concealed humor, "we provide you with a patient and everything. We'll move in another couch, and you two can just lie back, relax, and just tell each other all about what's in your subconscious."

"Oh, no you don't," Storm said instantly, and backed into a corner of the cell with an attitude of exaggerated rejection. "That's an old trick. Pretending to be a cell mate so you can learn my secret. That's an old trick, an old, old, old, old, o-l-d—" His lips kept moving, but the sound of his voice trailed away.

"You needn't think you're going to make me listen to your troubles," Kingston snapped at him. "I've got troubles of my own."

Storm's lips ceased moving, and he stared at Kingston without blinking.

"You big-shot scientists try to get along with one another," one of the attendants said as they went out the door.

"Scientists just argue," the other attendant commented. "They never *do* anything."

But Kingston hardly heard them, and hardly noticed them when, a few minutes later, they brought in a cot for him and placed it on the opposite side of the cell from Storm's cot. He was busy analyzing Storm's first reactions. Yes, the pattern was disturbed, possibly demented, certainly regressive—and yet, it was not so much irrational as adolescent, the bitterness of the adolescent when he first begins to really realize that the merchandise of humanity is not living up to the advertising under which it has been sold to him.

Under the attendants' watchful eyes, Kingston changed into the shapeless garments of the inmates. He flared up at them once again, carrying out his pattern of indignation that they should do this to him, but he didn't put much heart into it. No point in overdoing the act.

"Looks like he might have passed his peak," one of the attendants muttered. "He's calming down again. Maybe he won't be too hard to handle." They went out the door again with the admonishment: "Now you fellows be quiet, and you'll get breakfast pretty soon. But if you get naughty—" With his fist and thumb he made an exaggerated motion of working a hypodermic syringe. Storm cowered back into his corner of the cell.

"I've given up trying to convince you numskulls," Kingston said with contempt. "I'll just wait now until my office hears about this."

"Yeah," the attendant said. "Yeah, you just sit tight and wait. Just keep waiting—and quiet!"

The sound of their steps receded down the hallway. Kingston lay back on his couch and said nothing. He knew Storm's eyes were on him, watching him, as nervous, excited, and wary as an animal. The cell was barren, containing only the cots covered with a tough plastic which defied tearing with the bare fingers, and a water closet. There wasn't a seat on the latter because that can be torn off and used as a weapon either against one's self or others. In the wards there would be books, magazines, games, implements of various skills and physical therapies, all under the eyes of watchful attendants; but in these cells there was nothing, because there weren't enough attendants to watch the occupants of each cell.

Kingston lay on his couch and waited. In a little while Storm came out of his corner and sat down on the edge of his own couch. His attitude was half wary, half belligerent.

"You needn't be afraid of me," Kingston said softly, and kept looking upward at the ceiling. "I really am Dr. Heidrich Kingston. I'm a psychiatrist. And I already know all about you and your secrets."

He heard a faint whimper, the rustling of garments on the plastic couch cover, as if Storm were shrinking back against the wall, as if he expected this to be the prelude to more punishment for having such secret thoughts. Then a form of reasoning seemed to prevail, and Kingston could feel the tension relaxing in the room.

"You're as crazy as I am," Storm said loudly. There was relief in his voice, and yet regret.

Kingston said nothing. There was no point in pushing it. If his luck held, he would have several days. Miss Verity could be counted on to cut her vacation short and come back ahead of time, but even with that, he should have at least three days. And while Storm was badly disoriented, he could be reached.

"And that's an old, old trick, too," Storm said in a bitter singsong. "Pretending you already know, so I'll talk. Well I'm not a commie! I'm not a traitor! I'm not any of those things. I just think—" He broke off abruptly. "Oh, no you don't!" he exclaimed. "You can't trick me into telling you what I think. That's an old, old, old, old—"

It was quite clear why the therapies used by Moss hadn't worked. Storm was obsessed with guilt. He had been working in the highest echelons of Loyalty and at the same time had been harboring secret doubts that the framework was right. The Moss therapies then were simply punishments for his guilt, punishments which he felt he deserved, punishments which confirmed his wrongdoing. And Moss would be so convinced that Storm's thoughts were entirely wrong, that he couldn't possibly use the technique of agreement to lead Storm out of his syndrome. That was why Moss' past was stainless, why the Security Board trusted him with a Q. S., he was as narrow in his estimate of right and wrong as they.

"Old, old, old, old—" Storm kept repeating. He was stuck in the adolescent groove of bitter cynicism, not yet progressed to the point of realizing that in spite of its faults and hypocrisies, there were some elements in humanity worth a man's respect and faith. Even a thinking man.

It was a full day later before Kingston attempted the first significant move in reaching through to Storm. The previous day had confirmed the pattern of the attendants: A breakfast of adequate but plain food. Moss would never get caught on the technicality so prevalent in many institutions where the inmates can't help themselves—chiseling on food and pocketing the difference. After breakfast a clean-up of the cells and their persons. Four hours alone. Lunch. Carefully supervised and highly limited exercise period. Back to the cell again for another four hours. Supper. And soon, lights out.

It varied, somewhat, from most mental hospital routine; but these were all Q. S. men, each bearing terrible secrets which had snapped their minds. They mustn't be allowed to talk to one another. It varied, too, from patient to patient. It varied mainly in that the cells were largely soundproof; they had little of the screaming, raging, cursing, strangling, choking bedlam common in many such institutions.

Moss was a good administrator. He had his wing under thorough control. It was as humane as his limited point of view could make it. There were too few attendants, but then that was always the case in mental hospitals. In this instance it worked in Kingston's favor. There would be little chance of interruption, except at the planned times. In going into another person's mind that was a hazard to be guarded against, as potentially disastrous as a disruption of a major operation.

No reverberation of alarm at his absence from his office reached this far, and Kingston doubted there would be much. Miss Verity was more efficient than Moss and the organization she had set up would run indefinitely during his absence and hers. Decisions, which only he could make, would pile up in the staff offices, but that was nothing unusual in government.

He didn't try to rush Storm. With a combination of the facts he had gleaned from the file and the empathy he possessed, he lay on his cot and talked quietly to the ceiling about Storm. His childhood, his days in school, his attitudes toward his parents, teachers, scout masters, all the carefully tailored and planned sociology surrounding growing youth in respectable circumstances of today. It was called planned youth development, but it could better be called youth suppression, for its object was to quell any divergent tendencies, make the youth docile and complaisant—a good boy, which meant no trouble to anybody.

He translated the standard pattern into specifics about Storm, for obviously, until his breakup. David had been the epitome of a model boy. There are several standard patterns of reaction to this procedure. Eager credulity, where the individual is looking for a concrete father image to carry his burdens; rejective skepticism, where the individual seizes upon the slightest discrepancy to prove the speaker cannot know; occasionally superstitious fear and awe; and even less occasionally a comprehension of how gestalt empathy works. But whatever the pattern of reaction, it is the rare person, indeed, who can keep from listening to an analysis of himself.

Storm lay on his side on his cot, facing Kingston—a good sign because the previous day he had faced the wall—and watched the older man talk quietly and easily at the ceiling. Kingston knew when he came close to dangerous areas from the catch in Storm's breathing, but there was no other sign. Deliberately he broke off in the middle of telling Storm what his reactions had been at the bull session where the radical had been talking.

There was about ten minutes of silence. Several times there was an indrawn breath, as if Storm were starting to say something. But he kept quiet. Kingston picked up the thread and continued on, as if no time had elapsed.

He got his reward during the exercise period. Storm kept close to him, manifestly preferred his company to that of the attendants. They were among the less self-destructive few who were allowed a little time at handball. The previous day Storm had swung on the ball, wildly, angrily, as if to work off some terrible rage by hitting the ball. There hadn't been even the excuse of a game. Storm, younger and quicker, much more intense, had kept the ball to himself. Today Storm seemed the opposite. The few times he did hit the ball he deliberately placed it where Kingston could get it easily. Then he lost interest and sat down in a corner of the court. The attendants hustled them out quickly, to make room for others.

Back in the cell, Kingston picked up the thread again. Genuine accomplishment in gestalt empathy allows one to enter directly into another man's mind; his whole life is laid open for reading. Specific events are often obscure, but the man's pattern of reactions to events, the psychological reality of it, is open to view. Kingston narrated, with neither implied criticism nor praise, until, midafternoon, he sprang a bombshell.

"But you were wrong about one thing, Storm," he said abruptly. He felt Storm's instant withdrawal, the return of hostility. "You thought you were alone. You thought you were the only one with this terrible flaw in your nature. But you were not alone, son. And you aren't alone now.

"You put your finger on the major dilemma facing science today."

Now, for the first time, he glanced over at Storm. The young man was up on his elbow, staring at Kingston with an expression of horror. As easily as that, his secret had come out. And he did not doubt that Kingston knew his thoughts. The rest of it had fitted, and this fitted, too. He began to weep, at first quietly, then with great, wracking sobs.

"Disgrace," he muttered. "Disgrace, disgrace, disgrace. My mother, my father—" He buried his face in his arms. His whole body shook. He turned his face to the wall.

"All over the world, the genuine men of science are fighting out these same problems, David," Kingston said. "You are not alone."

Storm started to put his hands over his ears—then took them away. Kingston appeared not to notice.

"Politicians, not only ours, but all over the world, have discovered that science is a tremendous weapon. As with any other weapon they have seized it and turned it to their use. But it would be a great mistake to cast the politician in the role of villain. He is not a villain. He simply operates in an entirely different framework from that of science.

"Science does not understand his framework. A man of science grows extremely cautious with his words. He makes no claims he cannot substantiate. He freely admits it when he does not know something. He would be horrified to recommend the imposition of a mere theory of conduct upon a culture. The politician is not bothered by any of this. He has no hesitancy in recommending what he believes be imposed upon a culture; whatever is necessary for him to get the votes he will say.

"The scientist states again and again that saying a thing is true will not make it true. In classical physics this may have been accurate, although there is doubt of its truth in relative physics, and it is manifestly untrue in the living sciences. For often the politician says a thing with such a positive strength of confidence that the people begin operating in a framework of its truth and so implement it that it does become true.

"The public follows the politician by preference. Most of us have never outgrown our emotional childhood, and when the silver cord, the apron strings are broken from our real parents, we set about trying to find parent substitutes to bear the responsibility for our lives. The scientist stands in uncertainty, without panaceas, without sure-fire solutions of how to have all we want and think we want. The politician admits to no such uncertainties. He becomes an excellent father substitute. He will take care of us, bear the brunt of responsibility for us.

"But this clash of frameworks goes much deeper than that. Just as the scientist cannot understand the politician, so the politician does not understand science. Like most people, to him the scientist is just a super trained mechanic. He's learned how to manipulate some laboratory equipment. He has memorized some vague and mysterious higher math formulae. But he's just a highly skilled mechanic, and, as such, is employed by the politician to do a given job. He is not expected to meddle in things which are none of his concern.

"But in science we know this is a false estimation. For science is far more than the development of a skill. It is a frame of thought, a philosophy, a way of life. That was the source of your conflict, son. You were trying to operate in the field of science under the politician's estimation of what it is.

"The scientist is human. He loves his home, his flag, his country. Like any other man he wishes to protect and preserve them. But the political rules under which he is expected to do this come in direct conflict with his basic philosophy and approach to enlightenment. We have one framework, then, forced to make itself subservient to another framework, and the points of difference between the two are so great, that tremendous inner conflicts are aroused.

"The problem is not insuperable. Science has dealt with such problems before. Without risk to home, flag and country, science will find a way to deal with this dilemma, also. You are not alone."

There was a long silence, and then Storm spoke, quite rationally, from his cot.

"That's all very nice," he said, "but there's one thing wrong with it. You're just as crazy as I am, or you wouldn't be here."

Kingston looked over at him and laughed.

"Now you're thinking like the politician, Storm," he said.

"You're taking the evidence and saying it can have only one possible interpretation." He was tempted to tell Storm the truth of why he was here, and to show him that science could find a way, without harm, to circumvent the too narrow restrictions placed upon it by the political mind. But that would be unwise. Better never to let anyone know how he had manipulated it so that a simple clerical error could account for the whole chain of events.

"I really am Dr. Heidrich Kingston," he said.

"Yeah," Storm agreed, too quickly. There was derision in his eyes, but there was also pity. That was a good sign, too. Storm was showing evidence that he could think of the plight of someone else, other than himself. "Yeah, sure you are," he added.

"You don't think so, now," Kingston laughed. "But tomorrow, or the next day, my secretary will come to the door, there, and get me out of here."

"Yeah, sure. Tomorrow—or the next day." Storm agreed. "You just go on thinking that, fellow. It helps, believe me, it helps."

"And shortly afterwards you'll be released, too. Because there's no point now in keeping you locked up, incommunicado. I know all about your secrets, you see."

"Yeah," Storm breathed softly. "Tomorrow or the next day, or the day after that, or the day after— Yeah, I think I'll believe it, too, fellow. Yeah, got to believe in something."

In a limited fashion the patterns of human conduct can be accurately predicted. Cause leads to effect in the lives of human beings, just as it does in the physical sciences. The old fellow who had once told Storm that the universe does not hand out printed instructions on how it is put together was only literally correct. Figuratively, he was in error, for the universe does bear the imprints of precisely how it is put together and operates. It is the business of science to learn to read those imprints and know their meanings. Life is a part of the universe, bearing imprints of how it operates, too. And we already read them, after a limited fashion. We couldn't have an organized society, at all, if this were not true.

Kingston had made some movement beyond generalized quantum theory, and could predict the given movements of certain individuals in the total motion of human affairs.

Faithful to the last drawn line on the charted pattern, it was the next morning that Miss Verity, with clenched jaws and pale face, stepped through the cell door, followed by a very worried and incredulous guard.

"Dr. Kingston," she said firmly, then faltered. She stood silent for an instant, fighting to subdue her relief, anger, exasperation, tears. She won. She did not break through the reserve she treasured.

She spoke then, quite in the secretarial manner, but she could not subdue a certain triumph in her eyes.

"Dr. Kingston," she repeated, "it seems that while I was on my vacation, you made a . . . ah . . . clerical error."

2/56

What Now, Little Man?

From *The Magazine of Fantasy and Science Fiction*

Clifton's next-to-last story appeared symbolically at the dark end of science fiction's most fruitful decade, which began in splendor and ended in almost total commercial failure; the interconnection between Clifton's career and the decade is disturbing and the thematic underlay of this story at decade's end of some real sadness. Clifton had come to see—or at least to suggest—that the improvability of the race was much in doubt.

The mystery of what made the goonie tick tormented me for twenty years.

Why, when that first party of big game hunters came to Libo, why didn't the goonies run away and hide, or fight back? Why did they instantly, immediately, almost seem to say, "You want us to die, Man? For you we will do it gladly!" Didn't they have any sense of survival at all? How could a species survive if it lacked that sense?

"Even when one of the hunters, furious at being denied the thrill of the chase, turned a machine gun on the drove of them," I said to Paul Tyler, "they just stood there and let him mow them down."

Paul started to say something in quick protest, then simply looked sick.

"Oh, yes," I assured him. "One of them did just that. There was a hassle over it. Somebody reminded him that the machine gun was designed just to kill human beings, that it wasn't sporting to turn it on game. The hassle sort of took the edge off their fun, so they piled into their space yacht and took off for some other place where they could count on a chase before the kill."

I felt his sharp stare, but I pretended to be engrossed in measuring the height of Libo's second sun above the mountain range in the west. Down below us, from where we sat and smoked on Sentinel

250

Rock, down in my valley and along the sides of the river, we could see the goonie herds gathering under their groves of pal trees before night fell.

Paul didn't take issue, or feed me that line about harvesting the game like crops, or this time even kid me about my contempt for Earthers. He was beginning to realize that all the older-timer Liboans felt as I did, and that there was reasonable justification for doing so. In fact, Paul was fast becoming Liboan himself. I probably wouldn't have told him the yarn about that first hunting party if I hadn't sensed it, seen the way he handled his own goonies, the affection he felt for them.

"Why were our animals ever called goonies, Jim?" he asked.

"They're . . . Well, you know the goonie."

I smiled to myself at his use of the possessive pronoun, but I didn't comment on it.

"That too," I said, and knocked the dottle out of my pipe. "That came out of the first hunting party." I stood up and stretched to get a kink out of my left leg, and looked back toward the house to see if my wife had sent a goonie to call us in to dinner. It was a little early, but I stood a moment to watch Paul's team of goonies up in the yard, still folding their harness beside his rickshaw. I'd sold them to him, as yearlings, a couple of years before, as soon as their second pelt showed they'd be a matched pair. Now they were mature young males, and as handsome a team as could be found anywhere on Libo.

I shook my head and marveled, oh, for maybe the thousandth time, at the impossibility of communicating the goonie to anyone who hadn't seen them. The ancient Greek sculptors didn't mind combining human and animal form, and somebody once said the goonie began where those sculptors left off. No human muscle cultist ever managed quite the perfect symmetry natural to the goonie—grace without calculation, beauty without artifice. Their pelts varied in color from the silver blond of this pair to a coal black, and their huge eyes from the palest topaz to an emerald green, and from emerald green to deep-hued amethyst. The tightly curled mane spread down the nape and flared out over the shoulders like a cape to blend with the short, fine pelt covering the body. Their faces were like Greek sculpture, too, yet not human. No, not human. Not even humanoid, because—well, because, that was a comparison never made on Libo. That comparison was one thing we couldn't tolerate. Definitely, then, neither human nor humanoid.

I turned from watching the team which, by now, had finished

folding their harness into neat little piles and had stretched out on the ground to rest beside the rickshaw. I sat back down and packed my pipe again with a Libo weed we called tobacco.

"Why do we call them goonies?" I repeated Paul's question. "There's a big bird on Earth. Inhabits some of the South Sea islands, millions of them crowd together to nest. Most stupid creature on Earth, seems like, the way they behave on their nesting grounds. A man can hardly walk among them; they don't seem to know enough to move out of the way, and don't try to protect themselves or their nests. Some reason I don't know, it's called the Goonie Bird. Guess the way these animals on Libo behaved when that hunting party came and shot them down, didn't run away, hide, or fight, reminded somebody of that bird, The name stuck."

Paul didn't say anything for a while. Then he surprised me.

"It's called the Goonie Bird when it's on the ground," he said slowly. "But in the air it's the most magnificent flying creature known to man. In the air, it's called the albatross."

I felt a chill. I knew the legend, of course, the old-time sailor superstition. Kill an albatross and bad luck will haunt you, dog you all the rest of your days. But either Paul didn't know *The Rime of the Ancient Mariner* or was too tactful a young man to make it plainer. I supplied the Libo colony with its fresh meat. The only edible animal on the planet was the goonie.

Carson's Hill comes into the yarn I have to tell—in a way is responsible. Sooner or later almost every young tenderfoot finds it, and in his mind it is linked with anguish, bitterness, emotional violence, suppressed fury.

It is a knoll, the highest point in the low range of hills that separates my valley from the smaller cup which shelters Libo City. Hal Carson, a buddy of mine in the charter colony, discovered it. Flat on top, it is a kind of granite table surrounded by giant trees, which make of it a natural amphitheater, almost like a cathedral in feeling. A young man can climb up there and be alone to have it out with his soul.

At one time or another, most do. *"Go out to the stars, young man, and grow up with the universe!"* the posters say all over Earth. It has its appeal for the strongest, the brightest, the best. Only the dull-eyed breeders are content to stay at home.

In the Company recruiting offices they didn't take just anybody, no matter what his attitude was—no indeed. Anybody, for example, who started asking questions about how and when he might get back home—with the fortune he would make—was coldly told that if he was already worrying about getting back he shouldn't be going.

Somehow, the young man was never quite sure how, it became a challenge to his bravery, his daring, his resourcefulness. It was a bait which a young fellow, anxious to prove his masculinity, the most important issue of his life, couldn't resist. The burden of proof shifted from the Company to the applicant, so that where he had started out cautiously inquiring to see if this offer might suit him, he wound up anxiously trying to prove he was the one they wanted.

Some wag in the barracks scuttlebutt once said, "They make you so afraid they won't take you, it never occurs to you that you'd be better off if they didn't."

"A fine mess," somebody else exclaimed, and let a little of his secret despair show through. "To prove you are a man, you lose the reason for being one."

That was the rub, of course.

Back when man was first learning how to misuse atomic power, everybody got all excited about the effects of radiation on germ plasm. Yet nobody seemed much concerned over the effects of unshielded radiation in space on that germ plasm—out from under the protecting blanket of Earth's atmosphere, away from the natural conditions where man had evolved.

There could be no normal colony of man here on Libo—no children. Yet the goonies, so unspeakably resembling man, could breed and bear. It gave the tenderfoot a smoldering resentment against the goonie which a psychologist could have explained; that wild, unreasoning fury man must feel when frustration is tied in with prime sex—submerged and festering because simple reason told the tenderfoot that the goonie was not to blame.

The tide of bitterness would swell up to choke the young tenderfoot there alone on Carson's Hill. No point to thinking of home, now. No point to dreaming of his triumphant return—space-burnt, strong, virile, remote with the vastness of space in his eyes—ever.

Unfair to the girl he had left behind that he should hold her with promises of loyalty, the girl, with ignorance equal to his own, who had urged him on. Better to let her think he had changed, grown cold, lost his love of her—so that she could fulfill her function, turn to someone else, some damned Company reject—but a reject who could still father children.

Let them. Let them strain themselves to populate the universe!

At this point the angry bitterness would often spill over into unmanly tears (somebody in the barracks had once said that Carson's

Hill should be renamed Crying Hill, or Tenderfoot's Lament). And the tortured boy, despising himself, would gaze out over my valley and long for home, long for the impossible undoing of what had been done to him.

Yes, if there hadn't been a Carson's Hill there wouldn't be a yarn to tell. But then, almost every place has a Carson's Hill, in one form or another, and Earthers remain Earthers for quite a while. They can go out to the stars in a few days or weeks, but it takes a little longer before they begin to grow up with the universe.

Quite a little longer, I was to find. Still ahead of me, I was to have my own bitter session there again, alone—an irony because I'd thought I'd come to terms with myself up there some twenty years ago.

It is the young man who is assumed to be in conflict with his society, who questions its moral and ethical structures, and yet I wonder. Or did I come of age late, very late? Still, when I look back, it was the normal thing to accept things as we found them, to be so concerned with things in their relationship to us that we had no time for wonder about relationships not connected with us. Only later, as man matures, has time to reflect—has something left over from the effort to survive. . . .

When I first came to Libo, I accepted the goonie as an animal, a mere source of food. It was Company policy not to attempt a colony where there was no chance for self-support. Space shipping-rates made it impossible to supply a colony with food for more than a short time while it was being established. Those same shipping-rates make it uneconomical to ship much in the way of machinery, to say nothing of luxuries. A colony has to have an indigenous source of food and materials, and if any of that can also be turned into labor, all the better, I knew that. I accepted it as a matter of course.

And even as I learned about my own dead seed, I learned that the same genetic principles applied to other Earth life, that neither animal nor plant could be expected to propagate away from Earth. No, the local ecology had to be favorable to man's survival, else no colony. I accepted that, it was reasonable.

The colony of Libo was completely dependent on the goonie as the main source of its food. The goonie was an animal to be used for food, as is the chicken, the cow, the rabbit, on Earth. The goonie is beautiful, but so is the gazelle, which is delicious. The goonie is vaguely shaped like a human, but so is the monkey which was once the prime source of protein food for a big part of Earth's population. I accepted all that, without question.

Perhaps it was easy for me, I was raised on a farm, where slaughtering of animals for food was commonplace. I had the average farm boy's contempt for the dainty young lady in the fashionable city restaurant who, without thought, lifts a bite of rare steak, dripping with blood, to her pearly teeth; but who would turn pale and retch at the very thought of killing an animal. Where did she think that steak came from?

At first we killed the goonies around our encampment which was to become Libo City; went out and shot them as we needed them, precisely as hunters do on Earth. In time we had to go farther and farther in our search for them, so I began to study them, in hope I could domesticate them. I learned one of their peculiarities—they were completely dependent upon the fruit of the pal tree, an everbearing tree. Each goonie had its own pal tree, and we learned by experiment that they would starve before they would eat the fruit from any other pal tree.

There was another peculiarity which we don't yet understand, and yet we see it in rudimentary form on Earth where game breeds heartily during seasons of plentiful food, and sparsely in bad years. Here, the goonie did not bear young unless there were unclaimed pal trees available, and did bear young up to a limit of such trees.

My future was clear, then. Obtain the land and plant the pal trees to insure a constant supply of meat for the colony. It was the farm boy coming out in me, no doubt, but no different from any farm boy who grows up and wants to own his own farm, his own cattle ranch.

I was a young man trying to build a secure future for himself. There was no thought of the goonie except as a meat supply. I accepted that as a matter of course. And as Libo City grew, I continued to increase my planting of pal trees in my valley, and my herds of goonies.

It was only later, much later, that I found the goonie could also be trained for work of various kinds. I accepted this, too, in the same spirit we trained colts on the farm to ride, to pull the plow, to work.

Perhaps it was this training, only for the crudest tasks at first, then later, calling for more and more skill, that proved my undoing. On the farm we separated our pet animals from the rest; we gave our pets names, but we never gave names to those destined for slaughter, nor formed any affection for them. This was taboo. I found myself carrying out the same procedures here. I separated those goonies I trained from the meat herds. Then I separated the common labor goonies from the skilled labor.

I should have stopped there—at least there. But when man's curiosity is aroused. . . . Can we say to the research scientist, "You may ask this question, but you are forbidden to ask that one. You may take this step, but you must not take a second, to see what lies beyond." Can we say that to the human mind? I did not say it to myself.

I taught certain goonies to speak, to read, to write.

The goonies accepted this training in the same joyful exuberance they accepted everything else from man. I never understood it, not until now. Their whole behavior, their whole being seemed the same as greeted the first hunting party. "You want us to die, man? For you, we will do it gladly."

Whatever man wanted, the goonie gave, to the limit of his capacity. And I had not found that limit.

I took one step too many. I know that now.

And yet, should I not have taken that last step—teaching them to speak, to read, to write? The capacity was in them for learning it all the time. Was it finding it out that made the difference? But what kind of moral and ethic structure is it that depends on ignorance for its support?

Miriam Wellman comes into the yarn, too. She was the catalyst. My destruction was not her fault. It would have come about anyway. She merely hastened it. She had a job to do, she did it well. It worked out as she planned, a cauterizing kind of thing, burning out a sore that was beginning to fester on Libo—to leave us hurting a little, but clean.

Important though she was, she still remains a little hazy to me, a little unreal. Perhaps I was already so deep into my quandary, without knowing it, that both people and things were a little hazy, and the problem deep within me my only reality.

I was in Libo City the day she landed from the tender that serviced the planets from the mother ship orbiting out in space. I saw her briefly from the barbershop across the street when she came out of the warehouse and walked down our short main street to the Company Administration Building. She was a dark-haired little thing, sharp-eyed, neither young nor old—a crisp, efficient career gal, she seemed to me. I didn't see any of the men on the street make a pass at her. She had the looks, all right, but not the look.

There weren't more than a dozen women on the whole planet, childless women who had forgone having children, who had raked up the exorbitant space fare and come on out to join their man anyhow; and the men should have been falling all over Miriam Wellman—but they weren't. They just looked, and then looked at each other. Nobody whistled.

I got a little more of what had happened from the head warehouseman, who was a friend of mine. He smelled something wrong, he said, the minute the tender cut its blasts and settled down. Usually there's joshing, not always friendly, between the tender crew and the warehouse crew—the contempt of the spaceman for the landbound; the scorn of the landbound for the glamor-boy spacemen who think their sweat is wine.

Not today. The pilot didn't come out of his cabin at all to stretch his legs; he sat there looking straight ahead, and the ship's crew started hustling the dock loaders almost before the hatches opened for unloading a few supplies and loading our packages of libolines— the jewel stone which is our excuse for being.

She came down the gangplank, he said, gave a crisp, careless flick of her hand toward the pilot, who must have caught it out of the corner of his eye for he nodded briefly, formally, and froze. Later we learned he was not supposed to tell us who she really was, but he did his best. Only we didn't catch it.

She came across the yard with all the human warehousemen staring, but not stepping toward her. Only the goonies seemed unaware. In their fashion, laughing and playing, and still turning out more work than humans could, they were already cleaning out the holds and trucking the supplies over to the loading dock.

She came up the little flight of stairs at the end of the dock and approached Hall, the head warehouseman, who, he said, was by that time bug-eyed.

"Do you always let those creatures go around stark naked?" she asked in a low, curious voice. She waved toward the gangs of goonies.

He managed to get his jaw unhinged enough to stammer.

"Why, ma'am," he says he said, "they're only animals."

Nowadays, when he tells it, he claims he saw a twinkle of laughter in her eyes. I don't believe it. She was too skilled in the part she was playing.

She looked at him, she looked back at the goonies, and she looked at him again. By then he said he was blushing all over, and sweating as if the dry air of Libo was a steam room. It wasn't any trick to see how she was comparing, what she was thinking. And every stranger was warned, before he landed, that the one thing the easy-going Liboan wouldn't tolerate was comparison of goonie with man. Beside them we looked raw, unfinished, poorly done by an amateur. There was only one way we could bear it—there could be no comparison.

He says he knows he turned purple, but before he could think of anything else to say, she swept on past him, through the main aisle of the warehouse, and out the front door. All he could do was stand there and try to think of some excuse for living, he said.

She had that effect on people—she cut them down to bedrock with a word, a glance. She did it deliberately. Yes, she came as a Mass Psychology Therapist, a branch of pseudoscience currently epidemic on Earth which believed in the value of emotional purges whipped up into frenzies. She came as a prime trouble-maker, as far as we could see at the time. She came to see that the dear, fresh boys who were swarming out to conquer the universe didn't fall into the evil temptations of space.

She came at the critical time. Libo City had always been a small frontier spaceport, a lot like the old frontier towns of primitive Earth—a street of warehouses, commissaries, an Administration building, couple of saloons, a meeting hall, the barracks, a handful of cottages for the men with wives, a few more cottages built by pairs of young men who wanted to shake free of barracks life for a while, but usually went back to it. Maybe there should have been another kind of House, also, but Earth was having another of its periodic moral spasms, and the old women of the male sex who comprised the Company's Board of Directors threw up their hands in hypocrit-ical horror at the idea of sex where there was no profit to be made from the sale of diapers and cribs and pap!

Now it was all changing. Libo City was mushrooming. The Com-pany had made it into a shipping terminal to serve the network of planets still out beyond as the Company extended its areas of exploi-tation. More barracks and more executive cottages were going up as fast as goonie labor could build them. Hundreds of tenderfoot Earthers were being shipped in to handle the clerical work of the terminal. Hundreds of Earthers, all at once, to bring with them their tensions, their callousness, swaggering, boasting, cruelties and sadisms which were natural products of life on Earth—and all out of place here where we'd been able to assimilate a couple or so at a time, when there hadn't been enough to clique up among them-selves; they'd had to learn a life of calmness and reason if they wanted to stay.

Perhaps Miriam Wellman was a necessity. The dear, fresh boys filled the meeting hall, overflowed it, moved the nightly meetings to the open ground of the landing field. She used every emotional trick of the rabble-rouser to whip them up into frenzies, made them drunk on emotion, created a scene of back-pounding, shouting, jittering maniacs. It was a good lesson for anybody who might believe in the progress of the human race toward reason, intelligence.

I had my doubts about the value of what she was doing, but for what it was, she was good. She knew her business.

Paul Tyler put the next part of the pattern into motion. I hadn't seen him since our talk about the first hunting party, but when we settled down in our living-room chairs with our pipes and our tall cool glasses, it was apparent he'd been doing some thinking. He started off obliquely.

"About three years ago," he said, as he set his glass back down on the table, "just before I came out here from Earth, I read a book by an Australian hunter of kangaroos."

The tone of his voice made it more than idle comment. I waited.

"This fellow *told* the reader, every page or so, how stupid the kangaroo is. But everything he said *showed* how intelligent it is, how perfectly it adapts to its natural environment, takes every advantage. Even a kind of rough tribal organization in the herds, a recognized tribal ownership of lands, battles between tribes or individuals that try to poach, an organized initiation of a stray before it can be adopted into a tribe."

"Then how did he justify calling it stupid?" I asked.

"Maybe the real question is 'Why?' "

"You answer it," I said.

"The economy of Australia is based on sheep," he said. "And sheep, unaided, can't compete with kangaroos. The kangaroo's teeth are wedge-shaped to bite clumps, and they can grow fat on new growth while sheep are still down into the heart of grass unable to get anything to eat. The kangaroo's jump takes him from clump to sparse clump where the sheep will walk himself to death trying to stave off starvation. So the kangaroo has to go, because it interferes with man's desires."

"Does that answer 'Why?' " I asked.

"Doesn't it?" he countered. "They have to keep it killed off, if man is to prosper. So they have to deprecate it, to keep their conscience clear. If we granted the goonie equal intelligence with man, could we use it for food? Enslave it for labor?"

I was quick with a denial.

"The goonie was tested for intelligence," I said sharply. "Only a few months after the colony was founded. The Department of Extraterrestrial Psychology sent out a team of testers. Their work was exhaustive, and their findings unequivocal."

"This was before you trained goonies for work?" he asked.

"Well, yes," I conceded. "But as I understood it, their findings ran deeper than just breaking an animal to do some work patterns. It had to do with super-ego, conscience. You know, we've never seen any evidence of tribal organization, any of the customs of the primitive man, no sense of awe, fear, worship. Even their mating seems to be casual, without sense of pairing, permanence. Hardly even herd instinct, except that they grouped where pal trees clustered. But on their own, undirected, nobody ever saw them plant the pal tree. The psychologists were thorough. They just didn't find evidence to justify calling the goonie intelligent."

"That was twenty years ago," he said. "Now they understand our language, complicated instruction. You've taught them to speak, read, and write."

I raised my brows. I didn't think anyone knew about that except Ruth, my wife.

"Ruth let the cat out of the bag," he said with a smile. "But I already knew about the speaking. As you say, the goonie has no fear, no conscience, no sense of concealment. They speak around anybody. You can't keep it concealed, Jim."

"I suppose not," I said.

"Which brings me to the point. Have you gone a step farther? Have you trained any to do clerical work?"

"Matter of fact," I admitted, "I have. The Company has sharp pencils. If I didn't keep up my records, they'd take the fillings out of my teeth before I knew what was happening. I didn't have humans, so I trained goonies to do the job. Under detailed instruction, of course," I added.

"I need such a clerk, myself," he said. "There's a new office manager, fellow by the name of Carl Hest. A—well, maybe you know the kind. He's taken a particular dislike to me for some reason—well, all right, I know the reason. I caught him abusing his rickshaw goonie, and told him off before I knew who he was. Now he's getting back at me through my reports. I spend more time making corrected reports, trying to please him, than I do in mining libolines. It's rough. I've got to do something, or he'll accumulate enough evidence to get me shipped back to Earth. My reports didn't matter before, so long as I brought in my quota of libolines—the clerks in Libo City fixed up my reports for me. But now I've got to do both, with every T crossed and I dotted. It's driving me nuts."

"I had a super like that when I was a Company man," I said, with sympathy. "It's part of the nature of the breed."

"You train goonies and sell them for all other kinds of work," he said, at last. "I couldn't afford to buy an animal trained that far, but could you rent me one? At least while I get over this hump?"

I was reluctant, but then, why not? As Paul said, I trained goonies for all other kinds of work, why not make a profit on my clerks? What was the difference? And, it wouldn't be too hard to replace a clerk. They may have no intelligence, as the psychologists defined it, but they learned fast, needed to be shown only once.

"About those kangaroos," I said curiously. "How did that author justify calling them stupid?"

Paul looked at me with a little frown.

"Oh," he said, "various ways. For example, a rancher puts up a fence, and a chased kangaroo will beat himself to death trying to jump over it or go through it. Doesn't seem to get the idea of going around it. Things like that."

"Does seem pretty stupid," I commented.

"An artificial, man-made barrier," he said. "Not a part of its natural environment, so it can't cope with it."

"Isn't that the essence of intelligence?" I asked. "To analyze new situations, and master them?"

"Looking at it from man's definition of intelligence, I guess," he admitted.

"What other definition do we have?" I asked. . . .

I went back to the rental of the goonie, then, and we came to a mutually satisfactory figure. I was still a little reluctant, but I couldn't have explained why. There was something about the speaking, reading, writing, clerical work—I was reluctant to let it get out of my own hands, but reason kept asking me why. Pulling a rickshaw, or cooking, or serving the table, or building a house, or writing figures into a ledger and adding them up—what difference?

In the days that followed, I couldn't seem to get Paul's conversation out of my mind. It wasn't only that I'd rented him a clerk against my feelings of reluctance. It was something he'd said, something about the kangaroos. I went back over the conversation, reconstructed it sentence by sentence, until I pinned it down.

"Looking at it from man's definition of intelligence," he had said.

"What other definition do we have?" I had asked.

"What about the goonie's definition? That was a silly question. As far as I knew, goonies never defined anything. They seemed to live only for the moment. Perhaps the unfailing supply of fruit from their pal tree, the lack of any natural enemy, had never taught them a sense of want, or fear. And therefore, of conscience? There was no violence in their nature, no resistance to anything. How, then, could man ever hope to understand the goonie? All right, perhaps a resemblance in physical shape, but a mental life so totally alien. . . .

Part of the answer came to me then.

Animal psychology tests, I reasoned, to some degree *must* be based on how man, himself, would react in a given situation. The animal's intelligence is measured largely in terms of how close it comes to the behavior of man. A man would discover, after a few tries, that he must go around the fence; but the kangaroo couldn't figure that out—it was too far removed from anything in a past experience which included no fences, no barriers.

Alien beings are not man, and do not, cannot, react in the same way as man. Man's tests, therefore, based solely on his own standards, will never prove any other intelligence in the universe equal to man's own!

The tests were as rigged as a crooked slot machine.

But the goonie did learn to go around the fence. On his own? No, I couldn't say that. He had the capacity for doing what was shown him, and repeating it when told. But he never did anything on his own, never initiated anything, never created anything. He followed complicated instructions by rote, but only by rote. Never as if he understood the meanings, the abstract meanings. He made sense when he did speak, did not just jabber like a parrot, but he spoke only in direct monosyllables—the words, themselves, a part of the mechanical pattern. I gave it up. Perhaps the psychologists were right, after all.

A couple of weeks went by before the next part of the pattern fell into place. Paul brought back the goonie clerk.

"What happened?" I asked, when we were settled in the living room with drinks and pipes. "Couldn't he do the work?"

"Nothing wrong with the goonie," he said, a little sullenly. "I don't deserve a smart goonie. I don't deserve to associate with grown men. I'm still a kid with no sense."

"Well, now," I said with a grin. "Far be it from me to disagree with a man's own opinion of himself. What happened?"

"I told you about this Carl Hest? The office manager?"

I nodded.

"This morning my monthly reports were due, I took them into Libo City with my libolines. I wasn't content just to leave them with the receiving clerk, as usual. Oh, no! I took them right on in to Mr. High-and-mighty Hest, himself. I slapped them down on his desk and I said, 'All right, bud, see what you can find wrong with them this time.' "

Paul began scraping the dottle out of his pipe and looked at me out of the corner of his eyes.

I grinned more broadly.

"I can understand," I said. "I was a Company man once, myself."

"This guy Hest," Paul continued, "raised his eyebrows, picked up the reports as if they'd dirty his hands, flicked through them to find my dozens of mistakes, at a glance. Then he went back over them—slowly. Finally, after about ten minutes, he laid them down on his desk. 'Well, Mr. Tyler,' he said in that nasty voice of his. 'What happened to you? Come down with an attack of intelligence?'

"I should have quit when my cup was full," Paul said, after I'd had my laugh. "But oh, no. I had to keep pouring and mess up the works—I wasn't thinking about anything but wiping that sneer off his face. 'Those reports you think are so intelligent,' I said, 'were done by a goonie.' Then I said, real loud because the whole office was dead silent, 'How does it feel to know that a goonie can do this work as well as your own suck-up goons—as well as you could, probably, and maybe better?'

"I walked out while his mouth was still hanging open. You know how the tenderfeet are. They pick up the attitude that the goonie is an inferior animal, and they ride it for all it's worth; they take easily to having something they can push around. You know, Jim, you can call a man a dirty name with a smile, and he'll sort of take it; maybe not quite happy about it but he'll take it because you said it right. But here on Libo you don't compare a man with a goonie—not anytime, no how, no matter how you say it."

"So then what happened?" I'd lost my grin suddenly.

"It all happened in front of his office staff. He's got a lot of those suck-ups that enjoy his humor when he tongueskins us stupid bastards from out in the field. Their ears were all flapping. They heard the works. I went on about my business around town, and it wasn't more than an hour before I knew I was an untouchable. The word had spread. It grew with the telling. Maybe an outsider wouldn't get the full force of it, but here in Libo, well, you know what it would mean to tell a man he could be replaced by a goonie."

"I know," I said around the stem of my pipe, while I watched his face. Something had grabbed my tailbone and was twisting it with that tingling feeling we get in the face of danger. I wondered if Paul even yet, had fully realized what he'd done.

"Hell! All right, Jim, goddamn it!" he exploded. "Suppose a goonie could do their work better? That's not going to throw them out of a job. There's plenty of work, plenty of planets besides this one—even if the Company heard about it and put in goonies at the desks."

"It's not just that," I said slowly. "No matter how low down a man is, he's got to have something he thinks is still lower before he can be happy. The more inferior he is, the more he needs it. Take it away from him and you've started something."

"I guess," Paul agreed, but I could see he had his reserve of doubt. Well, he was young, and he'd been fed that scout-master line about how noble mankind is. He'd learn.

"Anyhow," he said. "Friend of mine, better friend than most, I've found out, tipped me off. Said I'd better get rid of that goonie clerk, and quick, if I knew which side was up. I'm still a Company man, Jim. I'm like the rest of these poor bastards out here, still indentured for my space fare, and wouldn't know how to keep alive if the Company kicked me out and left me stranded. That's what could happen. Those guys can cut my feet out from under me every step I take. You know it. What can I do but knuckle under? So—I brought the goonie back."

I nodded.

"Too bad you didn't keep it under your hat, the way I have," I said. "But it's done now."

I sat and thought about it. I wasn't worried about my part in it—I had a part because everybody would know I'd trained the goonie, that Paul had got him from me. It wasn't likely a little two-bit office manager could hurt me with the Company. They needed me too much. I could raise and train, or butcher, goonies and deliver them cheaper than they could do it themselves. As long as you don't step on their personal egos, the big boys in business don't mind slapping down their underlings and telling them to behave themselves, if there's a buck to be made out of it.

Besides, I was damn good advertising, a real shill for their recruiting offices. "See?" they'd say. "Look at Jim MacPherson. Just twenty years ago he signed up with the Company to go out to the stars. Today he's a rich man, independent, free enterprise. What he did, you can do." Or they'd make it seem that way. And they were right. I could go on being an independent operator so long as I kept off the toes of the big boys.

But Paul was a different matter.

"Look," I said. "You go back to Libo City and tell it around that it was just a training experiment I was trying. That it was a failure. That you exaggerated, even lied, to jolt Hest. Maybe that'll get you out from under. Maybe we won't hear any more about it."

He looked at me, his face stricken. But he could still try to joke about it, after a fashion.

"You said everybody finds something inferior to himself," he said. "I can't think of anything lower than I am. I just can't."

I laughed.

"Fine," I said with more heartiness than I really felt. "At one time or another most of us have to get clear down to rock bottom before we can begin to grow up."

I didn't know then that there was a depth beyond rock bottom, a hole one could get into, with no way out. But I was to learn.

I was wrong in telling Paul we wouldn't hear anything more about it. I heard, the very next day. I was down in the south valley, taking care of the last planting in the new orchard, when I saw a caller coming down the dirt lane between the groves of pal trees. His rickshaw was being pulled by a single goonie, and even at a distance I could see the animal was abused with overwork, if not worse.

Yes, worse, because as they came nearer I could see whip welts across the pelt covering the goonie's back and shoulders. I began a slow boil inside at the needless cruelty, needless because anybody knows the goonie will kill himself with overwork if the master simply asks for it. So my caller was one of the new Earthers, one of the petty little squirts who had to demonstrate his power over the inferior animal.

Apparently Ruth had had the same opinion for instead of treating the caller as an honored guest and sending a goonie to fetch me, as was Libo custom, she'd sent him on down to the orchard. I wondered if he had enough sense to know he'd been insulted. I hoped he did.

Even if I hadn't been scorched to a simmering rage by the time the goonie halted at the edge of the orchard—and sank down to the ground without even unbuckling his harness—I wouldn't have liked the caller. The important way he climbed down out of the rickshaw, the pompous stride he affected as he strode toward me, marked him as some petty Company official.

I wondered how he had managed to get past Personnel. Usually they picked the fine, upstanding, cleancut hero type—a little short on brains, maybe, but full of noble derring-do, and so anxious to be admired they never made any trouble. It must have been Personnel's off day when this one got through—or maybe he had an uncle.

"Afternoon," I greeted him, without friendliness, as he came up.

"I see you're busy," he said briskly. 'I am, too. My time is valuable, so I'll come right to the point. My name is Mr. Hest. I'm an executive. You're MacPherson?"

"Mister MacPherson," I answered dryly.

He ignored it.

"I hear you've got a goonie trained to bookkeeping. You leased it to Tyler on a thousand-dollar evaluation. And outrageous price, but I'll buy it. I hear Tyler turned it back."

I didn't like what I saw in his eyes, or his loose, fat-lipped mouth. Not at all.

"The goonie is unsatisfactory," I said. "The experiment didn't work, and he's not for sale."

"You can't kid me, MacPherson," he said. "Tyler never made up those reports. He hasn't the capacity. I'm an accountant. If you can train a goonie that far, I can train him on into real accounting. The Company could save millions if goonies could take the place of humans in office work."

I knew there were guys who'd sell their own mothers into a two-bit dive if they thought it would impress the boss, but I didn't believe this one had that motive. There was something else, something in the way his avid little eyes looked me over, the way he licked his lips, the way he came out with an explanation that a smart man would have kept to himself.

"Maybe you're a pretty smart accountant," I said in my best hayseed drawl, "but you don't know anything at all about training goonies." I gestured with my head. "How come you're overworking your animal that way, beating him to make him run up those steep hills on those rough roads? Can't you afford a team?"

"He's my property," he said.

"You're not fit to own him," I said, as abruptly. "I wouldn't sell you a goonie of any kind, for any price."

Either the man had the hide of a rhinoceros, or he was driven by a passion I couldn't understand.

"Fifteen hundred," he bid. "Not a penny more."

"Not at any price. Good day, Mr. Hest."

He looked at me sharply, as if he couldn't believe I'd refuse such a profit, as if it were a new experience for him to find a man without a price. He started to say something, then shut his mouth with a snap. He turned abruptly and strode back to his rickshaw. Before he reached it, he was shouting angrily to his goonie to get up out of that dirt and look alive.

I took an angry step toward them and changed my mind. Whatever I did, Hest would later take it out on the goonie. He was that kind of man. I was stopped, too, by the old Liboan custom of never meddling in another man's affairs. There weren't any laws about handling goonies. We hadn't needed them. Disapproval had been enough to bring tenderfeet into line, before. And I hated to see laws like that come to Libo, morals-meddling laws—because it was men like Hest who had the compulsion to get in control of making and enforcing them, who hid behind the badge so they could get their kicks without fear of reprisal.

I didn't know what to do. I went back to planting the orchard and worked until the first sun had set and the second was close behind. Then I knocked off, sent the goonies to their pal groves, and went on up to the house.

Ruth's first question, when I came through the kitchen door, flared my rage up again.

"Jim," she said curiously, and a little angry, "why did you sell that clerk to a man like Hest?"

"But I didn't," I said.

"Here's the thousand, cash, he left with me," she said and pointed to the corner of the kitchen table. "He said it was the price you agreed on. He had me make out a bill of sale. I thought it peculiar because you always take care of business, but he said you wanted to go on working."

"He pulled a fast one, Ruth," I said, my anger rising.

"What are you going to do?" she asked.

"Right after supper I'm going into Libo City. Bill of sale, or not, I'm going to get that goonie back."

"Jim," she said, "be careful." There was worry in her eyes. "You're not a violent man—and you're not as young as you used to be."

That was something a man would rather not be reminded of, not even by his wife—especially not by his wife.

Inquiry in Libo City led me to Hest's private cottage, but it was dark. I couldn't arouse any response, not even a goonie. I tried the men's dormitories to get a line on him. Most of the young Earthers seemed to think it was a lark, and their idea of good sportsmanship kept them from telling me where to find him. From some of them I sensed a deeper, more turgid undercurrent where good, clean fun might not be either so good or so clean.

In one of the crowded saloons there was a booth of older men, men who'd been here longer, and kept a disdainful distance away from the new Earthers.

"There's something going on, Jim," one of them said. "I don't know just what. Try that hell-raisin', snortin' female. Hest's always hanging around her."

I looked around the booth. They were all grinning a little. So the story of how Hest had outfoxed me had spread, and they could enjoy that part of it. I didn't blame them. But I could tell they didn't sense there was anything more to it than that. They told me where to locate Miriam Wellman's cottage, and added as I started to leave, "You need any help, Jim, you know where to look." Part of it was to say that in a showdown again the Earthers they were on my side, but most of it was a bid to get in one a little fun, break the monotony.

I found the woman's cottage without trouble, and she answered the door in person. I told her who I was, and she invited me in without any coy implications about what the neighbors might think. The cottage was standard, furnished with goonie-made furniture of native materials.

"I'll come right to the point, Miss Wellman," I said.

"Good," she answered crisply. "The boys will be gathering for their meeting, and I like to be prompt."

I started to tell her what I thought of her meetings, how much damage she was doing, how far she was setting Libo back. I decided there wouldn't be any use. People who do that kind of thing, her kind of thing, get their kicks out of the ego-bloating effect of their power over audiences and don't give a good goddamn about how much damage they do.

"I'm looking for Carl Hest," I said. "I understand he's one of your apple-polishers."

She was wearing standard coverall fatigues, but she made a gesture as if she were gathering up folds of a voluminous skirt to show me there was nothing behind them. "I am not hiding Carl Hest," she said scornfully.

"Then you know he is hiding." I paused, and added, "And you probably know he conned my wife out of a valuable goonie. You probably know what he's got in mind to do."

"I do, Mr. MacPherson," she said crisply. "I know very well."

I looked at her, and felt a deep discouragement. I couldn't see any way to get past that shell of hers, that armor of self-righteousness—No, that wasn't it. She wasn't quoting fanatic, meaningless phrases at me, clouding the issue with junk. She was a crisp business woman who had a situation well in hand.

"Then you know more than I do," I said. "But I can guess some things. I don't like what I can guess. I trained that goonie, I'm responsible. I'm not going to have it—well, whatever they plan to do with it—just because I trained it to a work that Hest and his toadies don't approve."

"Very commendable sentiments, Mr. MacPherson," she said

dryly. "But suppose you keep out of an affair that's none of your business. I understood that was Liboan custom, not to meddle in other people's doings."

"That *was* the custom," I said.

She stood up suddenly and walked with quick, short strides across the room to a closet door. She turned around and looked at me, as if she had made up her mind to something.

"It's still a good custom," she said. "Believe it or not, I'm trying to preserve it."

I looked at her dumfounded.

"By letting things happen, whatever's going to happen to that goonie?" I asked incredulously. "By coming out here and whipping up the emotions of these boys, stirring up who knows what in them?"

She opened the door of the closet and I could see she was taking out a robe, an iridescent, shimmering thing.

"I know precisely what I'm stirring up," she said. "That's my business. That's what I'm here for."

I couldn't believe it. To whip up the emotions of a mob just for the kicks of being able to do it was one thing. But to do it deliberately, knowing the effect of arousing primitive savagery. . . .

She turned around and began slipping into the garment. She zipped up the front of it with a crisp motion, and it transformed her. In darkness, under the proper spotlights, the ethereal softness completely masked her calculating efficiency.

"Why?" I demanded. "If you know, if you really do know, why?"

"My work here is about finished," she said, as she came over to her chair and sat down again. "It will do no harm to tell you why. You're not a Company man, and your reputation is one of discretion. . . . The point is, in mass hiring for jobs in such places as Libo, we make mistakes in Personnel. Our tests are not perfect."

"We?" I asked.

"I'm a trouble-shooter for Company Personnel," she said.

"All this mumbo-jumbo," I said. "Getting out there and whipping these boys up into frenzies. . . ."

"You know about medical inoculation, vaccination," she said. "Under proper controls, it can be psychologically applied. A little virus, a little fever, and from there on, most people are immune. Some aren't. With some, it goes into a full-stage disease. We don't know which is which without test. We have to test. Those who can't pass the test, Mr. MacPherson, are shipped back to Earth. This way we find out quickly, instead of letting some Typhoid Marys gradually infect a whole colony.''

"Hest," I said.

"Hest is valuable," she said. "He thinks he is transferred often because we need him to set up procedures and routines. Actually it's because he is a natural focal point for the wrong ones to gather round. Birds of a feather. Sending him out a couple months in advance of a trouble-shooter saves us a lot of time. We already know where to look when we get there."

"He doesn't catch on?" I asked.

"People get blinded by their own self-importance," she said. "He can't see beyond himself. And," she added, "we vary our techniques."

I sat there and thought about it for a few minutes. I could see the sense in it, and I could see, in the long run, how Libo would be a better, saner place for the inoculation that would make the better-balanced Earthers so sick of this kind of thing they'd never want any more of it. But it was damned cold-blooded. These scientists! And it was aside from the issue of my goonie clerk.

"All right," I said. "I guess you know what you're doing. But it happens I'm more interested in that goonie clerk."

"That goonie clerk is another focal point," she said. "I've been waiting for some such incident."

"You might have waited a long time," I said.

"Oh, no," she answered. "There's always an incident. We wait for a particularly effective one."

I stood up.

"You'd sacrifice the goonie to the job you're doing," I said.

"Yes," she said shortly, "If it were necessary," she added.

"You can find some other incident, then," I said. "I don't intend to see that goonie mistreated, maybe worse, just to get a result for you."

She stood up quickly, a flash of shimmering light.

"You will keep your hands entirely off it, Mr. MacPherson," she said crisply. "I do not intend to have my work spoiled by amateur meddling. I'm a professional. This kind of thing is my business. I know how to handle it. Keep off, Mr. MacPherson. You don't realize how much damage you could do at this point."

"I'm not a Company man, Miss Wellman," I said hotly. "You can't order me."

I turned around and stalked out of her door and went back to the main street of town. It was nearly deserted now. Only a few of the older hands were sitting around in the saloons, a few so disgusted with the frenetic meetings they wouldn't go even to break the monotony.

I went over to the main warehouse and through the gate to the landing field. The crowd was there, sitting around, standing around, moving around, waiting for the show to start. At the far end there was a platform, all lighted up with floods. It was bare except for a simple lectern at the center. Very effective. Miss Wellman hadn't arrived.

Maybe I could spot Hest somewhere up near the platform.

I threaded my way through the crowd, through knots of young Earthers who were shooting the breeze about happenings of the day, the usual endless gossip over trivialities. For a while I couldn't pin it down, the something that was lacking. Then I realized that the rapt, trancelike hypnotism I expected to see just wasn't there. The magic was wearing off. It was at this stage of the game that a smart rabble-rouser would move on, would sense the satiation and leave while he was still ahead, before everybody began to realize how temporary, pointless and empty the whole emotional binge had been. As Miss Wellman had said, her work here was about finished.

But I didn't spot Hest anywhere. I moved on up near the platform. There was a group of five at one corner of the platform.

"Where could I find Mr. Hest?" I asked them casually.

They gave me the big eye, the innocent face, the don't-know shake of the head. They didn't know. I turned away and heard a snicker. I whirled back around and saw only wooden faces, the sudden poker face an amateur puts on when he gets a good hand— later he wonders why everybody dropped out of the pot.

I wandered around some more. I stood on the outside of little knots of men and eavesdropped. I didn't hear anything of value for a while.

It wasn't until there was a buzz in the crowd, and a spotlight swept over to the gate to highlight Miss Wellman's entrance that I heard a snatch of phrase. Maybe it was the excitement that raised that voice just enough for me to hear.

". . . Carson's Hill tonight . . ."

"Shut up, you fool!"

There was a deep silence as the crowd watched Miss Wellman in her shimmering robe; she swept down the path that opened in front of her as if she were floating. But I had the feeling it was an appreciation of good showmanship they felt. I wondered what it had been like a couple of weeks back.

But I wasn't waiting here for anything more. I'd got my answer. Carson's Hill, of course! If Hest and his gang were staging another kind of show, a private one for their own enjoyment, Carson's Hill would be the place. It fitted—the gang of juvenile delinquents who are compelled to burn down the school, desecrate the chapel, stab to death the mother image in some innocent old woman who just happened to walk by at the wrong moment—wild destruction of a place or symbol that represented inner travail.

I was moving quickly through the crowd, the silent crowd. There was only a low grumble as I pushed somebody aside so I could get through. Near the edge I heard her voice come through the speakers, low and thrilling, dulcet sweet.

"My children," she began, "tonight's meeting must be brief. This is farewell, and I must not burden you with my grief at leaving you. . . ."

I made the yard gate and ran down the street to where my goonie team still waited beside the rickshaw.

"Let's get out to Carson's Hill as fast as we can," I said to the team. In the darkness I caught the answering flash of their eyes, and heard the soft sound of harness being slipped over pelt. By the time I was seated, they were away in a smart mile-covering trot.

Miriam Wellman had been damned sure of herself, burning her bridges behind her while Hest and his rowdies were still on the loose, probably up there in Carson's Hill, torturing that goonie for their own amusement. I wondered how in hell she thought that was taking care of anything.

The road that led toward home was smooth enough for a while, but it got rough as soon as the goonies took the trail that branched off toward Carson's Hill. It was a balmy night, warm and sweet with the frangrance of pal tree blossoms. The sky was full of stars, still close, not yet faded in the light of the first moon that was now rising in the East. It was a world of beauty, and the only flaw in it was Man.

In the starlight, and now the increasing moonlight, Carson's Hill began to stand forth, blocking off the stars to the west. In the blackness of that silhouette, near its crest, I seemed to catch a hint of reddish glow—a fire had been built in the amphitheater.

Farther along, where the steep climb began, I spoke softly to the team, had them pull off the path into a small grove of pal trees. From here on the path wound around and took forever to get to the top. I could make better time with a stiff climb on foot. Avoid sentries, too—assuming they'd had enough sense to post any.

The team seemed uneasy, as if they sensed my tenseness, or knew what was happening up there on top. We understood them so little, how could we know what the goonie sensed? But as always they were obedient, anxious to please man, only to please him, whatever he wanted. I told them to conceal themselves and wait for me. They would.

I left the path and struck off in a straight line toward the top. The going wasn't too bad at first. Wide patches of no trees, no undergrowth, open to the moonlight. I worried about it a little. To anyone watching from above I would be a dark spot moving against the light-colored grass. But I gambled they would be too intent with their pleasures, or would be watching only the path, which entered the grove from the other side of the hill.

Now I was high enough to look off to the southeast where Libo City lay. I saw the lights of the main street, tiny as a relief map. I did not see the bright spot of the platform on the landing field. Too far away to distinguish, something blocking my view at that point . . . or was the meeting already over and the landing field dark?

I plunged into a thicket of vines and brush. The advantage of concealment was offset by slower climbing. But I had no fear of losing my way so long as I climbed. The glow of light was my beacon, but not a friendly one. It grew stronger as I climbed, and once there was a shower of sparks wafting upward as though somebody had disturbed the fire. Disturbed it, in what way?

I realized I was almost running up the hill and gasping for breath. The sound of my feet was a loud rustle of leaves, and I tried to go more slowly, more quietly as I neared the top.

At my first sight of flickering raw flame through the trunks of trees, I stopped.

I had no plan in mind. I wasn't fool enough to think I could plow in there and fight a whole gang of crazed sadists. A fictional hero would do it, of course—and win without mussing his pretty hair. I was no such hero, and nobody knew it better than I.

What would I do then? Try it anyway? At my age? Already panting for breath from my climb, from excitement? Maybe from a fear that I wouldn't admit? Or would I simply watch, horror-stricken, as witnesses on Earth had watched crazed mobs from time immemorial? Surely man could have found some way to leave his barbarisms back on Earth, where they were normal.

I didn't know, I felt compelled to steal closer, to see what was happening. Was this, too, a part of the human pattern? The horror-stricken witness, powerless to turn away, powerless to intervene, appalled at seeing the human being in the raw? To carry the scar of it in his mind all the rest of his days?

Was this, too, a form of participation? And from it a kind of inverse satisfaction of superiority to the mob?

What the hell. I pushed my way on through the last thickets, on toward the flames. I didn't know I was sobbing deep, wracking coughs, until I choked on a hiccup. Careful MacPherson! You're just asking for it. How would you like to join the goonie?

As it was, I almost missed the climax. Five minutes more and I would have found only an empty glade, a fire starting to burn lower for lack of wood, trampled grass between the crevices of flat granite stones.

Now from where I hid I saw human silhouettes limned against the flames, moving in random patterns. I drew closer and closer, dodging from tree to tree. Softly and carefully I crept closer, until the blackness of silhouette gave way to the color-tones of firelight on flesh. I could hear the hoarseness of their passion-drunk voices, and crept still closer until I could distinguish words.

Yet in this, as in the equally barbaric meeting I'd left, something was missing. There wasn't an experienced lyncher among them. At least Personnel had had the foresight to refuse the applications from areas where lynching was an endemic pleasure. The right words, at the right time, would have jelled thought and action into ultimate sadism, but as it was, the men here milled about uncertainly—driven by the desire, the urge, but not knowing quite how to go about it . . . the adolescent in his first sex attempt.

"Well, let's do something," one voice came clearly. "If hanging's too good for a goonie that tries to be a man, how about burning?"

"Let skin him alive and auction off the pelt. Teach these goonies a lesson."

I saw the goonie then, spreadeagled on the ground. He did not struggle. He had not fought, nor tried to run away. Naturally; he was a goonie. I felt a wave of relief, so strong it was a sickness. That, too. If he had fought or tried to run away, they wouldn't have needed an experienced lyncher to tell them what to do. The opposition would have been enough to turn them into a raving mob, all acting in one accord.

And then I knew. I knew the answer to the puzzle that had tortured me for twenty years.

But I was not to think about it further then, for the incredible happened. She must have left only moments after I did, and I must have been hesitating there, hiding longer than I'd realized. In any event, Miriam Wellman, in her shimmering robe, walking as calmly as if she were out for an evening stroll, now came into the circle of firelight.

"Boys! Boys!" she said commandingly, chiding, sorrowfully, and without the slightest tremor of uncertainty in her voice. "Aren't you ashamed of yourselves? Teasing that poor animal that way? Cutting up the minute my back is turned? And I trusted you, too!"

I gasped at the complete inadequacy, the unbelievable stupidity of the woman, unprotected, walking into the middle of it and speaking as if to a roomful of kindergarten kids. But these were not kids! They were grown human males in a frenzy of lust for killing. Neither fire hoses, nor tear gas, nor machine-gun bullets had stopped such mobs on Earth.

But she had stopped them. I realized they were standing there, shock still, agape with consternation. For a tense ten seconds they stood there frozen in tableau, while Miss Wellman clucked her tongue and looked about with exasperation. Slowly the tableau began to melt, almost imperceptibly at first—the droop of a shoulder, the eyes that stared at the ground, one sheepish, foolish grin, a toe that made little circles on the rock. One, on the outskirts, tried to melt back into the darkness.

"Oh, no, you don't, Peter Blackburn!" Miss Wellman snapped at him, as if he were four years old. "You come right back here and untie this poor goonie. Shame on you, You, too, Carl Hest. The very idea!"

One by one she called them by name, whipped them with phrases used on small children—but never on grown men.

She was a professional, she knew what she was doing. And she had been right in what she had told me—if I'd butted in, there might have been incalculable damage done.

Force would not have stopped them. It would have egged them on, increased the passion. They would have gloried in resisting it. It would have given meaning to a meaningless thing. The resistance would have been a part, a needed part, and given them the triumph of rape instead of the frustration of encountering motionless, indifferent acceptance.

But she had shocked them out of it, by not recognizing their grown maleness, their lustful dangerousness. She saw them as no more than naughty children—and they became that, in their own eyes.

I watched them in a kind of daze, while, in their own daze, they untied the goonie, lifted him carefully as if to be sure they didn't hurt him. The goonie looked at them from his great glowing green eyes without fear, without wonder. He seemed only to say that whatever man needed of him, man could have.

With complete casualness, Miss Wellman stepped forward and took the goonie's hand. She led it to her own rickshaw at the edge of the grove. She spoke to her team, and without a backward look she drove away.

Even in this she had shown her complete mastery of technique. With no show of hurry, she had driven away before they had time to remember they were determined, angry men.

They stared after her into the darkness. Then meekly, tamely, without looking at one another, gradually even as if repelled by the presence of one another, they moved out of the grove toward their own rickshaws on the other side of the grove near the path.

The party was over.

For those who find violent action a sufficient end in itself, the yarn is over. The goonie was rescued and would be returned to me. The emotional Typhoid Marys had been isolated and would be shipped back to Earth where the disease was endemic and would not be noticed. Paul Tyler would be acceptable again in the company of men. Miriam Wellman would soon be on her way to her next assignment of trouble-shooting, a different situation calling for techniques which would be different but equally effective. The Company was saved some trouble that could have become unprofitable. Libo would return to sanity and reason, the tenderfeet would gradually become Liboans, insured against the spread of disease by their inoculation. . . . The mob unrest and disorders were finished.

But the yarn was not over for me. What purpose to action if, beyond giving some release to the manic-depressive, it has no meaning? In the middle of it all, the answer to the goonie puzzle had hit me. But the answer solved nothing; it served only to raise much larger questions.

At home that night I slept badly, so fitfully that Ruth grew worried and asked if there was anything she could do.

"The goonie," I blurted out as I lay and stared into the darkness. "That first hunting party. If the goonie had run away, they would have given those hunters, man, the chase he needed for sport. After a satisfactory chase, man would have caught and killed the goonie down to the last one. If it had hid, it would have furnished another kind of chase, the challenge of finding it, until one by one all would have been found out, and killed. If it had fought, it would have given man his thrill of battle, and the end would have been the goonie's death.''

Ruth lay there beside me, saying nothing, but I knew she was not asleep.

"I've always thought the goonie had no sense of survival," I said. "But it took the only possible means of surviving. Only by the most complete compliance with man's wishes could it survive. Only by giving no resistance in any form. How did it know, Ruth? How did it know? First contact, no experience with man, Yet it knew. Not just some old wise ones knew, but all knew instantly, down to the tiniest cub. What kind of intelligence—?"

"Try to sleep, dear," Ruth said tenderly. "Try to sleep now. We'll talk about it tomorrow. You need your rest. . . ."

We did not talk about it the next day. The bigger questions it opened up for me had begun to take form. I couldn't talk about them. I went about my work in a daze, and in the later afternoon, compelled, drawn irresistibly, I asked the goonie team to take me again to Carson's Hill. I knew that there I would be alone.

The glade was empty, the grasses were already lifting themselves upright again. The fire had left a patch of ashes and blackened rock. It would be a long time before that scar was gone, but it would go eventually. The afternoon suns sent shafts of light down through the trees, and I found the spot that had been my favorite twenty years ago when I had looked out over a valley and resolved somehow to own it.

I sat down and looked out over my valley and should have felt a sense of achievement, of satisfaction that I had managed to do well. But my valley was like the ashes of the burned-out fire. For what had I really achieved?

Survival? What had I proved, except that I could do it? In going out to the stars, in conquering the universe, what was man proving, except that he could do it? What was he proving that the primitive tribesman on Earth hadn't already proved when he conquered the jungle enough to eat without being eaten?

Was survival the end, and all? What about all these noble aspirations of man? How quickly he discarded them when his survival was threatened. What were they then but luxuries of a self-adulation which he practiced only when he could safely afford it?

How was man superior to the goonie? Because he conquered it? Had he conquered it? Through my ranching, there were many more goonies on Libo now than when man had first arrived. The goonie did our work, we slaughtered it for our meat. But it multiplied and throve.

The satisfactions of pushing other life-forms around? We could do it. But wasn't it a pretty childish sort of satisfaction? Nobody knew where the goonie came from, there was no evolutionary chain to account for him here on Libo; and the pal tree on which he depended was unlike any other kind of tree on Libo. Those were important reasons for thinking I was right. Had the goonie once conquered the universe, too? Had it, too, found it good to push other life-forms around? Had it grown up with the universe, out of its childish satisfactions, and run up against the basic question: Is there really anything beyond survival, itself, and if so, what? Had it found an answer, an answer so magnificent that it simply didn't matter that man worked it, slaughtered it, as long as he multiplied it?

And would man, someday, too, submit willingly to a new, arrogant, brash young life-form—in the knowledge that it really didn't matter? But what was the end result of knowing nothing mattered except static survival?

To hell with the problems of man, let him solve them. What about yourself, MacPherson? What are you trying to avoid? What won't you face?

To the rest of man the goonie is an unintelligent animal, fit only for labor and food. But not to me. If I am right, the rest of man is wrong—and I must believe I am right. I *know*.

And tomorrow is slaughtering day.

I can forgive the psychologist his estimation of the goonie. He's trapped in his own rigged slot machine. I can forgive the Institute, for it is, must be, dedicated to the survival, the superiority, of man. I can forgive the Company—it must show a profit to its stockholders or go out of business. All survival, all survival. I can forgive man, because there's nothing wrong with wanting to survive, to prove that you can do it.

And it would be a long time before man had solved enough of his whole survival problem to look beyond it.

But I had looked beyond it. Had the goonie, the alien goonie, looked beyond it? And seen what? What had it seen that made anything we did to it not matter?

We could, in clear conscience, continue to use it for food only so long as we judged it my man's own definitions, and thereby found it unintelligent. But I knew now that there was something beyond man's definition.

All right. I've made my little pile. I can retire, go away. Would that solve anything? Soneone else would simply take my place. Would I become anything more than the dainty young thing who lifts a bloody dripping bite of steak to her lips, but shudders at the thought of killing anything? Suppose I started all over, on some other planet, forgot the goonie, wiped it out of my mind, as humans do when they find reality unpleasant. Would that solve anything? If there are definitions of intelligence beyond man's own, would I not merely be starting all over with new scenes, new creatures, to reach the same end?

Suppose I deadened my thought to reality, as man is wont to do? Could that be done? Could the question once asked, and never answered, be forgotten? Surely other men have asked the question? What is the purpose of survival if there is no purpose beyond survival?

Have any of the philosophies ever answered it? Yes, we've speculated on the survival of the ego after the flesh, that ego so overpoweringly precious to us that we cannot contemplate its end—but survival of ego to what purpose?

Was this the fence across our path? The fence so alien that we tore ourselves to pieces trying to get over it, go through it?

Had the goonies found a way around it, an answer so alien to our kind of mind that what we did to them, how we used them, didn't matter—so long as we did not destroy them all? I had said they did not initiate, did not create, had no conscience—not by *man's* standards. But by their own? How could I know? How could I know?

Go out to the stars, young man, and grow up with the universe!

All right! We're out there!

What now, little man?

12/59

Hang Head, Vandal!

From *Amazing Stories*

Clifton's final statement is both prognosticative of the moon landings at the end of the decade and retrospective upon his own career in science fiction. Read on either level—or both—it is one of the saddest stories to ever come from the genre and it was published in a bottom-line magazine presumably because none of his other markets would touch it.

Only reprinted once (by Judith Merril in the 8th *Annual Edition, The Year's Best S–F,* 1963), this powerful story, although weak in its science content, remains one of the most important indictments of our species to be found in all of science fiction.

On our abandoned Martian landing field there hangs a man's discarded spacesuit, suspended from the desensitized prongs of a Come-to-me tower. It is stuffed with straw that was filched, no doubt, from packing cases which brought out so many more delicate, sensitive, precision instruments than we will take back.

None knows which of our departing crew hanged the spacesuit there, nor exactly what he meant in the act. A scarecrow to frighten all others away?

More likely a mere Kilroy-was-here symbol: defacing initials irresistibly carved in a priceless, ancient work of art, saying, "I am too shoddy a specimen to create anything of worth, but I can deface. And this proves I, too, have been."

Or was it symbolic suicide: an expression of guilt so overpowering that man hanged himself in effigy upon the scene of his crime?

Captain Leyton saw it there on the morning of final departure. He saw it, and felt a sudden flush of his usual stern discipline surge within him; and he all but formed the harsh command to take that thing down at once. Find the one who hanged it there: Bring him to me!

The anger—the command. Died together. Unspoken.

Something in the pose of the stuffed effigy hanging there must have got down through to the diminishing person inside the ever-thickening rind of a commander. The forlorn sadness, the dejection; and yes, he too must have felt the shame, the guilt, that overwhelmed us all.

Whether the helmet had fallen forward of its own weight because the vandal had been careless in stuffing it with too little straw to hold its head erect—vandals being characteristically futile even in their vandalism—or whether, instead of the supposed vandal, this was the talent of a consummate artist molding steel and rubber, plastic and straw into an expression of how we all felt—no matter, the result was there.

The Captain did not command the effigy be taken down. No one offered and no one asked if that might be his wish—not even the ubiquitous Ensign perpetually bucking for approval.

So on an abandoned Martian landing field there hangs a discarded spacesuit—the image of man stuffed with straw; with straw where heart, and mind, and soul ought to be.

At the time it seemed a most logical solution to an almost impossible problem.

Dr. VanDam summed it up in his memorable speech before the United Nations. If he were visually conscious of the vault of face blurs in the hushed assembly, this lesser sight did not obscure his stronger vision of the great vaulted mass of shining stars in the black of space.

He may not even have been conscious of political realities, which ever obscure man's dreams. What he said would be weighed by each delegate in terms of personal advantage to be gained for his own status. Second, his words would be weighed again in terms of national interest. Third, what advantage could be squeezed out for the racial-religious-color blocs? At the fourth level of consideration, what advantage to the small nation bloc over the large; or how would his plan enhance the special privileges of the large over the small? Down at the fifth level, could it preserve the status quo, changing nothing so that those in power could remain in power, while, at the same time, giving the illusion of progress to confound the ever-clamoring liberals? At the deep sixth level, if one ever got down that far, one might give a small fleeting thought to what might be good for mankind.

If Dr. VanDam even knew that such political realities must ever take precedence over the dreams of science, he gave no sign of it. It was as if all his thought was upon the glory of the stars and the dream of man reaching out to them. It was the goal of reaching the stars that inspired his speech.

"We must sum up the problem," he was saying. "It is simply this. There is a limit to how far we can theorize in science without testing those theories to see if they will work. Sooner or later the theorist must submit to the engineer whose acid test of worth is simply this: 'Does it work?'

"We have always known that the Roman candles we are using for our timid little space flights can take us only to the nearest planets, for there is that inexorable ratio of time to initial thrust. Unless thrust continues and continues, the Mayfly lifetime of man will expire many times over before we can reach the nearest star. Nor will our limited resources fuel ion engines. We must learn how to replenish with space dust gathered along the way.

"To have continuous velocity we must have continuous nuclear power. To have continuous nuclear power, we must have more nuclear tests. Now we believe we know how to take not special ores but ordinary matter, of any kind, and convert it into nuclear power. We believe we can control this. We have this in theory. But the engineer has not tested it with his question, 'Does it work?'

"We cannot make these tests on Earth. For what if it does not work? We dare not use the Moon. Its lighter gravity makes it too valuable a piece of real estate in terms of future star journeys. It will be our busy landing stage; we dare not contaminate it nor risk destroying it.

"We have reached stalemate. On Earth and Moon we can go on no further without testing. On Earth and Moon we dare not test. Some other testing area must be found.

"Our explorers have brought us conclusive proof that Mars is a dead world. A useless world in terms of life. Useless, too, as a source of minerals, for our little Roman candles can carry no commercial pay load. A useless world for colonization, with air too tenuous for human lungs and water too scarce for growing food. Humans must be housed in sealed chambers, or wear spacesuits constantly. From all practical points of view, a worthless world.

"But invaluable to science. For there, without destroying anything of value to man, we can put our theories to test. We believe we can start a nuclear reaction in ordinary rock and dirt, and keep it under control to produce a continuous flow of power. We believe we can keep it from running wild out of control.

"If the innumerable tests we must run *do* contaminate the planet, or even destroy it slowly, our gain in knowledge will be greater than the loss of this worthless real estate."

There was a stir in the Assembly: something between a gasp of horror and a murmur of admiration at the audacity of man's sacrificing a whole planet to his knowledge. They had not known we were so far along the way.

And then, on second thought, a settling back in satisfaction. It seemed a simple solution to an impossible problem. To take not only VanDam's tests away from Earth, but nuclear testing of every kind! To quell the fears and still the clamoring of the humanists who would rather see man stagnate in ignorance than risk the future to learn. At every level of political reality this might turn to advantage. If there were any who still thought in such terms, it might even be good for mankind generally!

"I am not mystic minded," VanDam continued, when the rustle and murmur had diminished, "but the convenience of this particular planet, located precisely where it is, far enough away that we must have made great progress in science to reach it, and close enough to be ready when we need it for further progress—this seems almost mystical in its coincidence."

(That for the ones who would have to go through the usual motions of obtaining Higher Power approval for doing what they fully intended doing all along.)

"My question: Shall the nations of Earth agree upon our use of this so convenient and otherwise worthless stage placed right where we need it—waiting for us down through all the ages until we should be ready to make use of it?"

There ultimate response was favorable.

Dr. VanDam did not mention, and the members being only politicians unable to see beyond the next vote or appointment, did not say:

"True, we do have a theory of how to start and continue the slow-burn nuclear conversion of ordinary rock and dirt to energy. What we do not have, as yet, is a way to stop it.

"We *think* that eventually future man will probably find a way to stop the process. We *think* slow burn will not speed up and run out of control to consume an entire planet before we have found a way to stop it. We *think* that future science may even find a way to decontaminate the planet. We *hope* these things.

"But we *know* that the science of nucleonics will be stillborn and stunted to grow no further unless we go on testing. We convince ourselves that even if an entire planet is consumed, it is a worthless planet anyway, and will be worth it.''

Yet there was the usual small minority who questioned our right to destroy one of the planets of the solar system. There is always such a minority, and as always, the rest of the world, intent on turning what it intended to do anyway into the Right-Thing-To-Do, was able to shout them down.

Anyway, the consequences were for future man to face. Or so we thought.

I say we, because I was one of the members of Project Slow-Burn. Not that I'm the hero. There wasn't any hero. Mistaken or not, as it was conceived this wasn't one of those television spectaculars cooked up to convert science into public emotionalism. There was no country-wide search for special photogenic hero-types to front the project.

The reporters, true to their writing tradition of trying to reduce even the most profound scientific achievement to the lowest common denominator of sloppy sentimentalism or avid sensationalism, tried to heroize Dr. VanDam as head of the science side of the project. But he wasn't having any.

"Don't you think, gentlemen," he answered them with acid scorn, "it is about time the public grew up enough to support the search for knowledge because we need it, rather than because they'd like to go to bed with some handsome, brainless kook you've built up into a hero?"

This response was not likely to further the cause of journalism.

They tried to lionize Captain Leyton, as head of the transport side of it; but his remarks were even more unprintable.

They never got down far enough through the echelons of status to reach me. I was Chief of Communications, which is just another way of saying I was a television repairman with headaches. Not that it would have done them any good.

There isn't one thing about me that fits the sentimental notions of what a hero should be. I'm not even a colorful character. If I'm expert in my job it's only because I learned early what any lazy man with an ounce of brains also learns—that life goes easier for the expert than for the ignorant. Which is not exactly the hero attitude the public likes to hear, but true all the same.

I did have an advantage which qualifies me to tell this tale.

Supervision nowadays sits on its duff in an office, surrounded by television monitors showing them every phase of their responsibilities, and punches buttons when some guy tries to goof off or starts lousing up the operation.

Somebody has to maintain the system and check the same monitors. I saw everything of importance that happened. That's the only way I come into the yarn at all. I didn't start out a hero type. I didn't turn into one. I just watched what happened; and I got sick at my stomach along with everybody else. And now I slink away, sick and ashamed, and not understanding even that, along with the rest. Not heroes—no, none of us.

From the first this was intended and conducted as a genuine scientific project, a group effort, with each man's ego subdued to serve the needs of the whole. No special heroes emerging to show up the rest of the dopes. None of the usual stuff of romantic fiction was supposed to happen—those unusual dangers, horrible accidents, sudden frightful emergencies so dear to the little sadistic hearts of readers and viewers.

So far as I know, nobody beat up anybody with his fists, nor gunned anyone down, which is the usual, almost the only, fictional way yet found by the humanists for coping with life problems.

We assembled the mastership on the Moon base from parts which were Roman candled up, a few pieces at a time, from too heavily gravitied Earth.

The yelps of pain from taxpayers reached almost as high. It was one thing to wash the hands of the vexing problem of nuclear testing by wanting it shifted out to Mars. It was something else to pay for the project.

Against the Moon's lighter gravity we eventually were spaceborne with no more than the usual fight between power thrust and inertia, both physical and psychological.

Without touching that precious reserve of fuel which we hoped would bring us back again, we were able to build up so much speed that it took us only a month to reach Mars. No point in showing, because nobody would care, how the two dozen of us were cramped in the tiny spaces left by the equipment and instruments we had to carry.

Construction and maintenance had done their job properly, and, for once, inspection had actually done its job, too. We were able to reverse properly at the right time, and soft-cushion powered our way down into a Martian plain eastward of a low range of hills.

Surely everybody has watched the documentaries long enough to have some idea about the incredibly hostile surface of Mars: the too thin air, which lets some stars shine through even in daytime; the

waterless desert; the extremes of temperature; the desolation. . . .
Ah, the desolation! The terrifying desolation!

Moon surface is bad enough; but at least there is the great ball of
Earth, seeming so near in that airless world that one has the illusion
of being able to reach out and almost touch it, touch home, know
home is still there, imagine he can almost see it.

"See that little tip of land there on the east coast of the North
American continent? That's where I live!"

"Yeah," somebody answers. "And who is that guy walking
through your front door without knocking while you're away?"

Sometimes it seems that close.

On Mars, Earth is just another bright spot in the black night sky;
so far away that the first reaction is one of terrible despair, the
overpowering conviction that in all that vast hostility a man will
nevermore see home; nor know again the balmy twilight of soft,
moist summer; nor feel the arms of love.

Explorers had not lied. Nothing, anywhere, could be more worthless to man than the planet Mars. Worthless, except for the unique
purpose which brought us here.

We dug in beneath the surface.

Now surely, again, everyone has seen so many of the documentaries that it is unnecessary to show us digging out our living
quarters and laboratories beneath that merciless plain. We used the
displaced powdered rock to form a crude cement, not long lasting
but adequate for the time we would be there. With it, we surfaced
over our living area. This was not so much to provide a landing field,
since most of our journeying would be in individual jet-powered
spacesuits, but to help insure against any leakage of air if our inner
seals cracked.

To help seal out the killing radiation we intended to let loose—
that, too.

We erected Come-to-me towers at each elevator which would
lower space-suited men to lower levels where they could go through
locks to reach their quarters. One Come-to-me tower for each half
dozen men, tuned to the power source of their suits, to bring each
man safely back, as truly as a homing pigeon, to guarantee against
their becoming lost on that hostile planet; and, in emergency, should
one arise, to see that no panic mob ganged up at one lock and died
waiting there for entrance to safety while other locks remained
idle—the human way of doing things under stress.

We had to finish all that in the first few weeks before any nuclear
tests could be started. Anybody whose notions of science are de-

rived from white-frocked actors in television commercials hasn't the vaguest idea of how much back-breaking physical work at the common labor level a genuine scientist has to do.

There was some emotional relief once we had dug in and sealed out the awful desolation of an uncaring universe. (This is the hardest part of reconciling oneself to the science attitude. More comforting to believe even that the universe is hostile than to admit that it simply doesn't care about man, one way or another.) In our sealed quarters we might briefly imagine ourselves working in an air-conditioned laboratory back home.

It helped. It certainly helped.

Not that I seemed to find time for more than exhausted sleeping there. To see what would be going on at the various field sites where tests were to be run meant the cameras had to be installed at those spots. In spite of the purported rigid tests for expedition personnel, my two assistants must have been somebody's nephews. Somehow each installation seemed to require that I be there.

I was there and usually without some little piece of equipment which would have helped so much, but which had been deleted from the lists we submitted by clerks who were more concerned with making a big showing of how much weight they could eliminate than in helping us.

Somehow we managed.

But I have made a little list of guys I'm going to ferret out and poke in the nose once I get back to Earth. Maybe those Hollywood producers who think the only way to solve a problem is to beat up somebody or gun him down have something, after all. Right on top of that list, in big bold letters, is the spacesuit designer who thinks a man can handle the incredibly fine parts of miniaturized electronic equipment with those crude instruments they give us to screw into the arm ends of spacesuits.

Somehow we managed. Somehow, out of chaos, order came. Somehow tests got made. Sometimes the theories worked; sometimes, more often, there was only the human sigh, the gulp, the shrug, and back to the drawing board.

Big surprise at the end of the first three months. A supply ship landed. Mostly food and some champagne, yet! Stuff the folks back home thought they'd like to have if they were out here. Even some pin-up pictures, as if we weren't already having enough trouble without being reminded. But none of the equipment we'd radioed for in case the taxpayers could forego a drink and a cigarette apiece to raise money for sending it. The public couldn't understand our need for equipment, so they didn't send any. Miracles aren't supposed to need any equipment or effort; they just come into being because people want them.

The packages of home-baked cookies were welcome enough after our diet of hydroponic algae, but I'd still rather have had a handful of miniature transistors.

Some of the guys said they'd have been willing to substitute their cookies for an equal weight of big, buxom blonde; but that's something the cookie bakers probably preferred not to think about.

The little three-man crew of the supply ship promised, as they were taking off for their return journey, they'd tell 'em what we really wanted when they got back, but I doubt the message ever got broadcast over the home and family television sets. Anyway, scientists are supposed to be cold, unfeeling, inhuman creatures who wander around looking noble, wise, and above it all.

In the beginning I'd thought that once I got the heavy work of installation completed, I could do a little wandering around myself, looking wise and noble. No such luck. I'd no more than get set up to show one experiment than it was over; and I'd have to dismantle, move, and set up for another. We'd thought the lighter gravity of Mars, 38 percent, would make the labor easy. But somehow there was still lifting, tugging, pulling, hauling, cursing.

But then, nobody wants to hear how the scientist has to work to get his miracle. The whole essence is the illusion that miracles can be had without work, that all one needs is to wish.

All right. So we'll get to the miracle.

Now we were finally ready to get down to the real test, the main reason for our coming out to Mars—Project Slow-Burn.

VanDam chose a little pocket at the center of that little cluster of hills to our West—that little cluster of hills everybody has seen in the pictures radioed back to Earth.

We didn't know it at the time, but that little cluster of hills was causing quite an uproar among archeologists back home. No archeologists had been included in the expedition, and now they were beating their breasts because from the pictures those hills looked mighty artificial to them. There was too much of a hint that the hills might once have been pyramids, they said, incredibly ancient, perhaps weathered down eons ago when the planet was younger, before it had lost so much of its atmosphere, but maybe still containing something beneath them.

We didn't hear the uproar, of course. Administration deemed it unnecessary for us to bother our pretty little heads about such nonsense. In fact the uproar never got outside the academic cloister to reach the public at all. Administration should have listened. But then, when does man listen to what might interfere with his plans and spoil something?

We got all set to go in that little pocket at the center of the hills. The spot was ideal for us because the hill elevations gave us an opportunity to place our cameras on their tops to focus down into the crater we hoped would appear.

A whole ring of cameras was demanded. The physicists seemed to share too much of the public's attitude that all I needed to produce enough equipment was to wish for it. But by stripping the stuff from virtually every other project, I managed to balance the demands of the Slow-Burn crew against the outraged screams of the side-issue scientists.

VanDam's theories worked.

At first it took the instruments to detect that there was any activity; but gradually, even crude human eyes could see there was a hole beginning to appear, deepen and spread—progressively.

It was out of my line, but the general idea seemed to be that only one molecular layer at a time was affected, and that it, in turn, activated the next beneath and to the side while its own electrons and protons gave up their final energy.

The experiment did not work perfectly. The process should have been complete. There should have been no by-product of smoke and fire, no sign to human eyes of anything happening except a slowly deepening and spreading hole in the ground.

Instead there was some waste of improperly consumed molecules, resulting in an increasingly heavy, fire-laced smoke which arose sluggishly in the thin air, borne aloft only by its heat, funneling briefly while it gave up that heat. Then it settled down and contaminated everything it touched. To compound my troubles, of course.

The physicists were griping their guts out because I didn't have the proper infra-red equipment to penetrate the smoke; and somehow I wasn't smart enough to snap my fingers and—abracadabra—produce. Those damned cookie packages instead of equipment! Those damned clerks who had decided what we wouldn't need. My little list was getting longer.

Still, I guess I was able to get a feeble little snap from my fingers. I did manage to convert some stuff, never intended for that purpose, into infra-red penetration. We managed to see down into that smoke-and fire-filled crater.

To see enough.

It was the middle of a morning (somebody who still cared claimed it would be a Tuesday back home) some three basic weeks after the beginning of the experiment. The hole was now some thirty feet across and equally deep, growing faster than VanDam's figures predicted it should, but still not running wild and out of control. Even if it had been, we couldn't have stopped it. We didn't know how.

I was trying to work out a little cleaner fix on the south wall of the crater when that wall disappeared like the side of a soap bubble. My focus was sharp enough to see.

To see down and into that huge, vaulted room. To see the living Martians in that room shrivel, blacken, writhe and die. To see some priceless, alien works of art writhe and blacken and curl; some burst into flame; some shatter unto dust.

That was when the scientists, sitting there watching their monitors with horror-stricken eyes, felt jubilation replaced with terrible guilt.

I, too. For naturally I was watching the master monitors to see that the equipment kept working. I saw it all.

I saw those miniature people, yes people, whole and beautiful, in one brief instant blacken, writhe and die.

Out of the billions of gross people on Earth, once in a generation a tiny midget is born and matures to such perfection in proportion and surpassing beauty that the huge, coarse, normal person can only stare and marvel—and remember the delicate perfection of that miniature being with nostalgic yearning for the rest of his life.

From such, perhaps, come the legends common to all peoples in all ages, of the fairies. Or, eons ago, was there traffic between Earth and Mars? Or even original colonization from Mars to Earth, finally mutating into giants? They were people, miniatures of ourselves.

I saw them there. Perhaps not more than a dozen in that room. But in other rooms? Perhaps in a lacework of underground rooms? A whole civilization which, like ourselves on Mars, had gone underground, sealed themselves in against the thinning atmosphere, the dying planet?

And we had begun the atomic destruction of their planet. We had begun it. We could not stop it. The corrosion keeps growing, spreading.

I saw them die. Somehow I felt their pain.

But I did not die of it.

I carry it with me. I shall always carry it with me.

That's all there is.

In years to come people on Earth, people who did not see what we saw, did not feel the pain and guilt we felt, will wonder at our behavior following that.

Oh there is much to wonder. If there is a civilization, where does their food come from? If they are able to convert rock to food, why are they not able to stop the atomic destruction of their planet we have started? If they are able to fill us with such grief that we can think of nothing but to slink away, like whipped curs caught in vandalism, why didn't they do this before we started the fire we cannot stop?

Oh, there is so much unanswered. People will wonder at the fact that we simply abandoned most of our equipment, the very project itself; that for a sick hour we watched, then, with one accord, without anybody making the decision, we began to withdraw and start for home.

Like small boys, thinking only to vandalize a schoolhouse in their savage glee, discovering it is a shrine.

Or, perhaps in time, we can rationalize it all away. Perhaps so soon as during that long, journey back.

It wasn't our fault, we shall begin to say. They were as much to blame as we. Sure they were!

More to blame! They were more to blame than we!

Why didn't they come out of their holes and fight us? With their fists if they didn't have any guns? *Any* red-bloodied—er, red-blooded—Amuri—well, whatever they are—ought to have enough guts to come out and fight, to defend home, flag and mother!

We'll probably get around to that. It's the normal attitude to take after vandalism. It's the human way.

But as of now, our only thought is to slink away.

On our abandoned Martian landing field there hangs a man's discarded spacesuit, suspended from the desensitized prongs of a Come-to-me tower. It is stuffed with straw filched, no doubt, from packing cases which brought out so many more delicate, sensitive, precision instruments than we take back.

Although we have not been entirely irresponsible in our head-long flight back home.

We do bring back some of what we took out: the more valuable of the instruments. We have been most selective in this.

The only coarse, insensitive, unfinished instrument we bring back—is man.

4/62

Afterword

by
Barry N. Malzberg

Mark Clifton retired from twenty years as a practicing industrial psychologist (mostly personnel entrance and exit interviews) in the early 1950s, partly because of precarious health induced by a heart attack and partly out of a genuine desire to make an individual statement as a writer. Between July 1952 and his death in early 1963 Clifton published three novels and at least twenty stories and novelettes in the science fiction magazines of his time. Nearly a third of his stories were written in collaboration with Alex Apostolides and Frank Riley.

The first of his novels, *They'd Rather Be Right* in collaboration with Frank Riley, originally appeared in *Astounding Science Fiction* in late 1954 and subsequently won the second science fiction Hugo award for best novel of the year. The others, written alone, were not nearly as successful, and none of them had mass market editions during Clifton's lifetime.

During his last six years, Clifton published only four or five of his short stories and the last two novels: *When They Came From Space* (parts of which were published as "Pawn of the Black Fleet" in *Amazing Stories*) and *Eight Keys to Eden*. Well before his death Clifton had ceased to be a major figure in science fiction, pushed to the background and out of print. Although his first cluster of short stories, appearing in *Astounding Science Fiction* between 1952 and 1955, attracted vast attention and created the impression of enormous prolificacy, the fact is that Clifton's output, compared with other science fiction writers of his decade, was only moderate. During the last half of his career, public attention steadily waned.

Clifton, long divorced and lacking either visible relatives or a literary agent, died intestate. Because of this, publishers and anthologists found his works extremely difficult to procure, and consequently, he fell totally out of print almost immediately after his death. Some of his early stories reappeared during the 1970s in compilations from *Astounding Science Fiction,* but this book marks the first English language collection of his work. Regrettably he has become so obscure in modern science fiction circles that when I discussed him with science fiction editors in their twenties and thirties, several not only had never read any of his stories, but did not know who he was.

This is unfortunate but more common than it should be for the writer who works within the context of the commercial genre, "popular" fiction; I could easily reel off a list of twenty science fiction writers just as prominent as Clifton in the 1950s who are similarly unknown today. The subsequent course of his career would not have surprised Clifton, however, but probably would have granted him wry amusement. He was a deeply pained and sophisticated man with (toward the end) no illusions regarding the destiny of the science fiction writer or of the lasting nature of his accomplishments.

What makes Clifton's topple from the center to the outer regions of science fiction most unfortunate is that he was a writer of genuine importance who did significant work within the form. He changed the field irrevocably, proving to be one of the twelve most influential writers of science fiction during its fifty-four-year commercial publishing history. This book serves not only to make available once more some of Clifton's out-of-print stories, but also to show the interacting range and subtlety of his prose.

Clifton, like virtually every other science fiction writer of his generation, was a better short story writer than novelist. His novels, in a sense, were afterthoughts; he expanded his stories, puffing up what had originally been conceived as a story-length idea and making it fit a longer form. The novels grew awkwardly. Or sometimes he spliced bits and pieces of his stories together, thus achieving the length, but not really the form, of the novel. It was a procrustean-bed approach not likely to produce lasting literature. But the stories in this book represent Clifton's best efforts, and it is through them that Clifton's reputation will survive.

Clifton was an innovator in the early 1950s and such an impressive innovator that since then his approach has become standard among science fiction writers. He used the common themes of science fiction—alien invasion, expanding technology, revolution against political theocracy, and space colonization—but unlike any writer before him, he imposed upon these standard themes the full range of sophisticated psychological insight. His obsession was to show truthfully how a cross-section of humanity would react to a future alternately mindless and stunning. His view, never particularly optimistic, became steadily blacker as the decade progressed and by "Hang Head, Vandal!"—his last story—his concept of life had grown almost appallingly stark. He did not hold the general run of humanity in higher esteem than did Samuel Clemens in his last bleak years. (But it must be noted that his first published story, "What Have I Done?," stated at the outset of his career the belief that humanity was inalterably vile.)

For a variety of reasons, partly despair, partly editorial hostility, Clifton wrote very little toward the end of his career. It is possible to envision him dying an embittered man, destroyed by the perception that science fiction could not be taken seriously because its very audience, largely juvenile, could not assimilate seriousness. But Clifton did not attempt to write in another genre: he either could not or chose not to write anything other than science fiction.

This was a bad time not only for Clifton, but for science fiction generally, however. The market collapse in the late 1950s, the vanishing of 75 percent of the magazine market, the dwindling audience and public apathy toward science fiction could not have encouraged a writer like Clifton. Nor was Clifton helped by the knowledge that he, the most controversial writer of 1953 and winner of the 1955 best novel award, was to end his life obscure not only to the American reading public but to the tiny, hothouse world of science fiction.

Clifton decidedly was interested in presenting his message, but he also worked throughout his career at improving his craft. His invention and perception remained at a high level throughout, and his characterization, narrative voice, and story structure began to assume real stature toward the end of his productive years. One of Clifton's problems undoubtedly was that *as* he improved, he wrote himself to the borders of the commercial science fiction markets; his work became too sophisticated and individual to find easy access to the magazines and like many other science fiction writers—the late Cyril M. Kornbluth being the best example—Clifton simply took himself out of the markets as a concommitant to his artistic growth. As evidence, consider the fact that Mark Clifton—a major writer of his time, innovator who made a lasting impression on his field, winner of a major award—earned for the totality of his science fiction something considerably less than twenty thousand dollars.

Mark Clifton Bibliography

Novels

They'd Rather Be Right (with Frank Riley). New York: Gnome Press, 1957.
  Serialized in *Astounding Science Fiction*, August through November,
  1954.
Eight Keys To Eden. New York: Doubleday and Company, 1960.
When They Came From Space. New York: Doubleday and Company, 1962.
  Portions published as "Pawn of the Black Fleet," *Amazing Stories*, Janu-
  ary and February, 1962.

Short Fiction

"What Have I Done?" *Astounding Science Fiction* (May 1952).
"The Conqueror," *Astounding Science Fiction* (August 1952).
"Star, Bright," *Galaxy Science Fiction* (July 1952).
"The Kenzie Report," *Worlds of If* (May 1953).
"Bow Down to Them," *Worlds of If* (June 1953).
"Progress Report," *Worlds of If* (July 1953). With Alex Apostolides.
"Solution Delayed," *Astounding Science Fiction* (July 1953). With Alex
  Apostolides.
"We're Civilized," *Galaxy Science Fiction* (August 1953). With Alex Apos-
  tolides.
"What Thin Partitions," *Astounding Science Fiction* (September 1953).
  With Alex Apostolides.
"Crazy Joey," *Astounding Science Fiction* (August 1953). With Alex Apos-
  tolides.
"Reward for Valor," *Universe Science Fiction* (September 1953).
"Hide! Hide! Witch!" *Astounding Science Fiction* (December 1953). With
  Alex Apostolides.
"Sense From Thought Divide," *Astounding Science Fiction* (March 1955).
"A Woman's Place, *Galaxy Science Fiction* (May 1955).
"Clerical Error," *Astounding Science Fiction* (February 1956).
"How Allied," *Astounding Science Fiction* (March 1957).
"Remembrance and Reflection," *Magazine of Fantasy and Science Fiction*
  (January 1958).

"The Dread Tomato Addiction," *Astounding Science Fiction* (February 1958).
"Do Unto Others," *Worlds of If* (June 1958).
"What Now, Little Man?" *Magazine of Fantasy and Science Fiction* (December 1959).
"Hang Head, Vandal!" *Amazing Stories* (April 1962).